C
L
B

By the Same Author

Jerusalem Ablaze: Stories of Love and Other Obsessions

The Death
of Baseball

—⠶—

Orlando Ortega-Medina

—⚬—

The Death
of Baseball

—⚬—

A Novel

CLOUD LODGE BOOKS

LONDON

First published in paperback and eBook in 2019
by Cloud Lodge Books (CLB)

A CIP catalogue record for this book is available from the British Library.

PB ISBN 978-1-9995873-5-2
eBook ISBN 978-1-9995873-6-9

1 3 5 7 9 10 8 6 4 2

Printed and bound by CPI Group (UK) Ltd, Croydon, CR0 4YY

Cloud Lodge Books Ltd (CLB)
51 Holland Street, London W8 7JB
cloudlodgebooks.com

Dedicated to my father, for whom baseball never died.

Then Mara the Evil One, wishing to provoke fear, horror, and terror in Sister Cala, approached her and said, "What is it you don't approve of, Sister?"

"I don't approve of birth, friend."

"Why don't you approve of birth? One who is born enjoys a life of sensual pleasures. Who therefore has persuaded you: 'Sister, don't approve of birth'?"

Sister Cala replied, "One who is born suffers a life of bondage, flagellation, and unceasing agony. And one who is born *must die*. That is why I do not approve of birth."

—Cala Sutta (Saṃyutta Nikāya 5.6)

Contents

—⟐—

—w—

Norma Jean
Redux

1962

—w—

I left this world in the early hours of August 5, 1962, having given up on my mad life. The universe immediately recycled me back into the body of a baby boy, just as he shot out of his mother's womb in a rush of blood and mucus into a hospital birthing room in Pasadena—a mere twenty miles from the Brentwood home where my nude, lifeless body lay sprawled boobs-up on my bed, empty bottles of Nembutal and chloral hydrate strewn on the floor. I was not to be let off so easily.

All things are recycled.

My unusual [re]birth was not lost on the attending midwife, who let out a tympanum-splitting scream and—dangling me by my little ankles at arm's length—begged her supervising nurse to finish the job. When later questioned about her strange behaviour, the tremulous midwife reported that I'd stared at her "with open, knowing eyes" and that this had scared the living shit out of her. I understand from my momma that she stopped by our house at some point to apologise for her rudeness, but was never able to look at me directly.

I swear to you, I remember that midwife's crazy scream, like the shriek of a banshee, heralding the death of a Caomhánach. It's one of my earliest *new memories*. I also remember the glare of the fluorescent light glinting off the corner of the supervising nurse's cat-eye glasses as she sponged me clean in a stainless steel bassinet, her bloodshot blue eyes magnified to the size of golf balls by her refractor-like lenses.

Another distinct early new memory is of a mobile composed of little red sponge cherries rotating above my head as I lay in the hospital's nursery crib.

But the single most important memory I carry from the day of my rebirth is sensory—a black and overwhelming sadness followed by a sudden, disorienting cacophony of sound and colour, as I boomeranged from death back into life.

Clyde

1973

Chapter 1

Koneko jumps on my bed and wakes me. Silly kitty. I pull her close and kiss her furry white head.

"Hello, Kiki, you big snowball," I whisper, hugging her warm body against my chest. "I have a baseball game in the morning and need to sleep, remember?" I bury my nose in her fur and kiss her again.

I love my Kiki so much, and she loves me. She used to be my brother Hiro's kitty before he went crazy and died. But then she became mine, which is just as well since I take way better care of her than Hiro ever did.

Now that I'm wide awake, I hear the TV in the living room. I snatch up my alarm clock. It's almost midnight, nearly my birthday! *What are they still doing awake at this time?*

Koneko hops off the bed, coaxes open the door with her paw, and creeps out of the room. I pull the big fluffy pillow over my head, and then the blanket. But I can *still* hear the TV. And it's driving me crazy.

After forever, I pull on my fuzzy blue slippers and pad down the long hallway to the living room, illuminated by the glow of the TV. I peek inside. Nobody is in there. Just the people on the

TV—a pretty blonde lady in a white summer dress and an old cowboy-hatted man with a pointy moustache.

The lady's dress looks like it's covered in big polka dots. I inch-worm up to the TV to get a better look just as the lady bends over. Her bum takes up the whole screen for a second, shaking from side to side. That's when I realise the polka dots are actually little black-and-white cherries, stems and all, and I laugh out loud.

"What are you doing, Ku-rai-do?" my momma asks from the doorway in Japanese. In my head, I hear her say: *"What are you doing, Clyde?"* She does her best, my poor momma. It's not that she's stupid. She's just never learned how to speak English very well. The important thing is we understand each other a hundred per cent. She scoots up next to me and takes me in her arms. "It's so late. You should be in bed." She kisses me on the head and pulls aside a lock of hair that has fallen across my face.

"Who's that lady, Momma?" I ask in English, wriggling out of her embrace and moving closer to the TV. I watch as the blonde lady pushes Mr Moustachio to the ground and bounces away from him.

"That's Marilyn," she says, struggling with the pronunciation of the name. "She was a famous movie star back when I first came to this country."

"Marilyn..." I savour each beautiful syllable. "She's so pretty, Momma."

Momma opens her eyes wide. "Prettier than your momma?"

"No way! You're the prettiest momma in the whole wide world!" I say, because that's the truth.

Momma laughs and covers me in big, wet kisses while I sneak another peek at the blonde lady. All the men on the TV are smiling at her, buying her drinks, and trying to get her to pay attention to them.

"Marilyn," I say again, so I won't forget her name. I'm stupid about remembering things sometimes.

"Her real name was Norma Jean Baker," Momma says after a bit. "But she changed her name to Marilyn Monroe when she became famous."

Momma switches off the TV, picks me up, and sits me on our threadbare sofa. Koneko comes from out of nowhere and crawls into my lap, nudging her head against my belly.

"I want to meet her," I say, rubbing Koneko behind her ear.

"You can't."

"Why not?"

"You just can't." Momma looks really sad when she says that, like whenever she talks about Hiro. So I promise myself I won't ask her about Marilyn anymore.

"Now you go back to your room before your father gets home and sees you in here at this God-awful hour."

"But I'm not sleepy anymore, Momma. Besides,"—I look at the grandfather clock, which says it's past midnight—"it's already my birthday! I'm eleven now. Aren't you going to sing 'Happy Birthday' to me?"

Momma blinks at me for a moment and checks her watch, then she smiles and pats my leg.

"Wait here, baby," she says. "I'll be right back."

She runs out of the living room, and Koneko hops off my lap and follows her.

I switch the TV back on, and I'm surprised to see Marilyn holding a rope with a bucking horse on the other end. And the men that were with her in the bar are jumping up and down yelling at the horse and trying to take the rope away from her.

Just as I scoot closer to the TV, I hear Momma clearing her throat behind me. I whip around and see her coming into the room carrying a pink-and-white birthday cake with a bunch of lit candles on it.

"Surprise, baby. I was going to wait until tomorrow for this. But since you're up and it's already your birthday…"

She nods at the sofa, and I sit on it. Then she kneels in front of me still holding the birthday cake and starts to sing all breathy like:

"Happy birthday to you, happy birthday to you, happy birthday, Mister Birthday Boy ... Happy birthday to you!"

My heart does a bunch of cartwheels, and I say, "Thank you, Momma."

"Make a wish and blow out the candles, baby. Then you can have some cake and milk before you go back to bed."

I take a deep breath and blow out the candles while wishing for something I know will never happen: that my father will stop drinking and that he'll love Momma again like he used to before I was born.

Momma watches me eat some of my birthday cake, running her fingers through my hair every once in a while. Then we watch the rest of the Marilyn movie together all snuggled up on the sofa. It gets a little boring toward the end, and we doze off asleep.

Suddenly there's a loud pounding at the front door. Momma's head snaps up, and her face goes all tight and funny.

"Open up this fucking door, Tomoko," I hear my father yell. "I can't find my keys."

Momma runs to the sash window, pulls it open, and sticks out her head. "Be quiet, Yoshi! I'll be right there."

She runs across the room and tries to pick me up, but I'm too heavy for her.

"Please, baby," she says right into my ear, almost making me deaf. "You need to go to your room now. Do it for Momma."

"Tomoko, you goddamn slut," my father screams. "Open this door now, or I'll break it down."

He kicks the front door super hard, and the house shakes; Momma puts her hands up to her face and starts to cry, and that's when I get proper scared.

As I rush out of the room, I plough straight into Koneko, who is running away from the door-kicking noise, and step hard on her back. She screeches, and I fall flat in the dark hallway just as my father kicks open the door and staggers into the foyer, stinking of whiskey. He hasn't seen me yet. But there's no way I'll be able to make it back to my bedroom without him noticing. So I roll back to the living room and hurry to my hiding place behind the sofa. Momma is crying in a corner and my poor baby Koneko is dragging herself around the room, whimpering and leaving a trail of bloody cat poop.

After what seems like a million years, my father's face appears in the doorway.

"What's going on here?" He looks at my crying momma and then at broken Koneko, who isn't moving anymore.

"There was an accident, Yoshi," Momma says through her tears. "The *neko* got hurt. That's why I couldn't come to the door right away."

My father squints at Koneko until his eyes are just a pair of slits, and he snatches her by the tail. "This cat's dead!"

He stares like an idiot at the poopy mess Koneko made and at Koneko, dangling upside down in his hand. Then he sways like he's about to fall over. "This was Hiro's cat, Tomoko."

"It was an accident, Yoshi," Momma mumbles, bubbles of snot coming out her nose. "Please, put him down."

"I can't believe this," he croaks, tears streaming down his face. "You kill everything you touch."

I jump out from behind the sofa. "Stop saying those horrible things to Momma!"

"What the hell?" He blinks at me and wipes his face on the sleeve of his dirty work shirt. "What are you doing in here?"

"It's *your* fault! You scared Koneko with your kicking and screaming, and then I accidentally crashed into her. It's *your* big fat fault, like everything else. I wish you were dead! I wish you were *dead*!"

He drops Koneko and grabs me by the hair, dragging me to the mirror. "Look at yourself, you pathetic little bastard. You've wet yourself."

I shut my eyes because I don't want to see that I peed my jammies. I don't even remember when it happened. But now I can feel it, all cold and clammy against my legs.

"Look at yourself!" he screams.

I close my eyes even more tightly and struggle to get away from him. But he's holding my hair really hard.

"Stop it, Yoshi!" Momma lunges forward and tries to pull him off me, but my father pushes her away with his free hand, and she falls against the cabinet where my Little League trophies are displayed, knocking them to the floor.

For an instant, his grip on me loosens enough for me to squirm away. I run to help Momma, who's picking up my trophies, and she pulls me behind her.

My father shakes his head, blinks like a thousand times, and stares at us. Tears are pouring out of his eyes. But not like when someone's crying. More like when you get soap in your eye. He sways again, almost falling over, and steadies himself against the bookcase. "You're pathetic," he says with a croaky voice. "You weren't supposed to be here."

Momma holds out her hand at him the way crossing guards do when they want cars to stop. "He was having trouble sleeping, Yoshi. But he's going to bed now."

"He has a game tomorrow, for Christ's sake," he says, wiping his face with his sleeve. "It's almost one in the morning."

"Don't worry about the game," I say, stepping out from behind Momma. "I'm the best hitter they've got."

"That's thanks to me," he says. "If I hadn't signed you up you'd still be playing with Barbie dolls."

"Go to bed, baby," Momma whispers.

"But, Momma … Koneko—" I try to look at my little Kiki, but I can't. My body gets all shaky and I start to cry.

"Don't worry about the neko, baby. Push it out of your mind. I'll take care of everything. Just go, please."

My father collapses against the doorjamb and waves a hand in our direction. "Yeah, you do that. Go to bed. Go to fucking bed. I'm going to bed, too."

"It's my birthday," I scream, as I move to the door. "I'm eleven years old today!"

"Don't remind me," he says. "Biggest mistake of my life, apart from marrying little Miss Too-Good there."

He staggers to the sofa and drops into it. His head smacks against the wooden armrest, and he blacks out. (Between you and me, I love the sound of his fat head going smack against that armrest, the louder, the better. I hope he cracks it open one day, like Humpty Dumpty, so nobody can ever put him back together again.)

I run out of the room as fast as my feet can take me, change into clean jammies, and jump into bed before any more bad stuff can happen, pushing it all out of my mind the way Momma said to do.

Chapter 2

The next thing I know the sun is streaming through the holes in my tattered drapes and stabbing me in the eyes. It reminds me of my crazy brother, who hurt himself with a piece of glass before I was born. And *that* makes my stomach hurt really bad, especially since I'm sleeping in his old room. So I shove that out of my mind and grab the alarm clock, which didn't go off. It's already eight in the morning! I need to get moving since our game starts at ten.

I slide out of bed and listen at the door. The house is quiet, which I'm not sure is a good thing or a bad thing. So I crack open the door slowly, tip-toe down the hallway to the living room, and peek inside. Everything's tidy like nothing bad ever happened— no trophies on the floor, no poopy mess, no broken neko, and nobody on the sofa.

Padding back down the hallway, I listen at the door to Momma's bedroom and recognise the hiccupy-snory sounds my father makes when he's totally passed out. Then I hear the sound of our old juicer screeching.

I find Momma in our bright yellow kitchen, juicing oranges and making blueberry-banana pancakes. Her back is turned to me, so I watch her for a bit. She's wearing the light blue strapless summer dress that I like, with a nice string of pearls her rich parents sent her from Japan for her birthday. Her long black hair is pulled into a ponytail with a pretty blue ribbon that matches her dress.

"Hi, Momma."

Momma turns and flashes a lovely smile that shows all her teeth. I love Momma to bits. Best of all, she's prettier and way more stylish than all the other moms.

"Happy birthday, baby!"

"Thank you, Momma. Are those pancakes for me?" (Of course, I know they're for me. It just gives me a warm feeling to ask.)

"They're for my special birthday boy. I made the ones you like and filled them with plenty of fresh blueberries." She puts the plate on the table and sets a glass of fresh-squeezed orange juice next to it. "Come sit with Momma."

"Aren't you going to eat anything?" I ask after a while.

"I already ate," she says, with a funny smile that tells me she's fibbing.

"What did you eat?"

"I had a bit of rice and some fish cake earlier this morning."

"Did you sleep?" I ask. I figure it must have taken her a long time to fix everything and to get the pig into their bedroom. Just thinking about it makes me start to feel sad again.

"I slept," she says quickly.

"Momma…"

"Don't worry, baby. Everything is fine."

"I feel terrible about Koneko. I can't believe I killed her."

"It was an accident, baby. Accidents happen. We'll buy you a new neko."

"But I don't want a new one," I say. "I want my old neko."

"You can't have your old neko, baby. It's impossible."

"That's not what the monk said."

15

"What monk?"

"That old, wrinkly monk from the Buddhist temple in J-Town that talked to Father about Hiro. He said people and animals get to come back after they're dead."

"The monk is wrong," Momma whispers. She gets up from the table and stares out the window at our backyard. "Once someone is gone, they're gone forever."

"Never mind, Momma. It's OK." I gulp the last bite of pancake and rinse it down with what's left of the orange juice. "I've got to get dressed for my game now."

"Did I ever tell you about the beautiful house I lived in back in Japan?" Momma asks as I scrub the plate in the sink.

"Yes, Momma, only about a zillion times."

"We lived on a rambling country estate a few miles outside Kagoshima," she starts. "You couldn't see it from the road; there were lots of trees hiding the main house, even as you got close to it." She stares all shiny-eyed at the crabgrass growing in our backyard, but I think she's really seeing her parents' house in Japan instead.

"Yes, Momma, I know. It was a big, traditional house, not like the mansions they have in Beverly Hills." I stand next to her at the back window and stare out at the weeds.

"I had my own outbuilding all to myself," she says, "And the parties we would throw. It was a wonderful life. But once something's gone…"

"Don't worry, Momma." I take her by the hand and lead her away from the window. "One of these days you'll get to live in a nice house again. I'll make sure of that. My teacher, Mrs Worthington, says that I'm a manifestor; I make things happen. When I grow up, I'll make everything change for us, and you'll be happy again, just like before. So don't worry, OK? And thank you for the wonderful birthday breakfast, and for singing the birthday song to me last night. Everything's perfect."

Chapter 3

Momma drives me to the baseball field in Altadena, where my summer Little League team practices. My father's supposed to follow in his truck whenever he gets up from his drunken sleep, but I hope he doesn't.

As we drive up the hill toward the field, a big brown jackrabbit dashes across the road and Momma has to slam on the brakes to keep from hitting him. I hold my breath as he disappears into the bushes and then I start to cry.

"It's all right, baby," Momma says, hugging me tight against her boobies. "The bunny's safe. Momma stopped in time."

"It's not that, Momma." I pull away from her and wipe my face on my sleeve. "I'm still sad about Koneko. I feel like a murderer."

"Stop that!" Momma frowns at me. "It was an accident, pure and simple. You can't be guilty when it's an accident."

I stare out the window at the other kids on my team as Momma pulls into the parking lot, and I curl up on the front seat.

"Go join your teammates, baby. They're waiting for you."

I pop up and stare hard at Momma, who jumps a little and brings her hand to her mouth. "I don't care if it was an accident, and I *never* want another neko!"

Momma's eyes fill with tears. She pulls my head toward hers and whispers, "Let me tell you a little secret, baby. It's OK to be sad about something you've lost, but not for too long. If your sadness doesn't go away by itself, you'll need to take steps to make yourself feel better."

"What kind of steps?"

"Whenever you're sad, try putting the thing you're sad about into a box in your mind, bury it deep inside, and then pretend real hard that it never existed. Do you think you can do that, baby?"

Tears spill out of Momma's eyes and down her cheeks. I wipe them away with my fingers and kiss her.

"Yes, Momma. I can do that."

"Say it, baby: There never was a Koneko."

"There never was a Koneko."

"Say it again."

"There never was a Koneko."

Momma hugs me tight, then reaches across me and opens the passenger door.

I race across the parking lot to join my teammates, putting what Momma just said into a big black box like this one ➔ ▓▓▓.

Our team is called the Braves, which is sort of funny, because none of us is all that brave, except maybe my super handsome *hapa* cousin, Kevin, the son of my father's older sister, Doreen, and her rich English husband, Alistair. Kevin's not afraid of anything. Today, we're playing a team from Glendale called the Pirates. I'm the catcher, and I'm really good at it. I can also hit the ball real far, sometimes over the fence. Nobody else on our team can do that, which is why I've won so many trophies. But the truth is, I *hate* playing baseball. The only reason I play is because my father forces me to. He says playing baseball is what boys my age are supposed to do. (Momma secretly told me he used to force Hiro to play baseball, too.)

"Hey, Koba," the coach yells from the dugout, "get in here."

Momma waves from the bleachers with a big lipsticky smile. She's wearing a fuzzy red cardigan draped over her shoulders. The red of the cardigan looks pretty against her dress and the pearls.

My father hasn't arrived yet, and I'm hoping he doesn't make it because he always embarrasses Momma and me, yelling like a maniac from the sideline. Also, he hates it when Momma dresses too stylish, like today, because he imagines the other dads pay too much attention to her (which they sort of do). And that drives him crazy.

"Come on, Slugger," my cousin Kevin calls out. "You're making us all wait!"

I scamper into the dugout and squeeze in between Kevin and a tall, skinny kid we call Skunk. Kevin pulls off my cap and rubs my head. He says he rubs my head for luck. But I think he just likes rubbing my head. I like it, too.

"I have something to show you after the game," he says, with a big grin, "for your birthday." I nod and lean against him, taking in the smell of his freshly washed crisp white uniform, and bite him on the titty.

"Hey, watch that!" He gently pushes my face away. "These puppies are sensitive."

Kevin's one year older than me. I get to play on the same team as him because I'm bigger than other boys my age. The only reason I don't complain too much about coming to play baseball is because I get to spend time with him.

"Look sharp, Koba." Skunk jabs an elbow into my ribs. "Game's about to start."

I sit upright with a giggle. What's the use of baseball if you can't have a bit of fun, right?

The coach jumps into the dugout and gives us a quick pep talk, some purple-haired lady in an electric wheelchair with like a thousand earrings in each ear belts out *The Star Spangled Banner*, and the game starts. In the end, I bat in four home runs, and we win the game ten to three. Afterwards, a Mexican man with

Coke-bottle glasses and huge lips comes up to me and tells me I'm a little Joe DiMaggio.

"Thanks," I say, shrugging my shoulders. "Who's that?"

"Only the best baseball player that ever lived," Kevin whispers in my ear.

"That's right," Mr Coke Bottle says, "He had a fifty-six-game hitting streak, and nobody's ever broken his record. They called him Joltin' Joe."

"Joltin' Joe!" Kevin says, "I like that."

"I don't," I say. "It sounds weird."

"Sounds better than Clyde," Kevin says, winking at me. *Clyde* is the American name my father stuck me with so people wouldn't look down on me for being Japanese—my real name being Kimitake, after my momma's brother, who accidentally crashed his Zero plane into the ocean before it could reach Hawaii. But he should have thought of a better name than Clyde, seeing that kids are always making fun of me because it's old-fashioned and dorky.

Momma walks up and tells me that we have to get home, but Kevin jumps in and says I'm invited for lunch at his new house for my birthday and that his parents will get me home in time for dinner. I'm surprised by his invitation, especially since he hadn't mentioned it during the game. Then I remember he wants to show me something.

"I don't know," Momma says to Kevin. "Your Uncle Yoshi will probably be waiting for us at home since he wasn't able to make it to the game."

Kevin pushes out his lower lip. "Please, Auntie, I promise I'll take good care of him." He winks at me. "I'm sure Uncle won't mind. My mom already said it was OK with her, especially as it's Clyde's birthday." Kevin cups his hand around his mouth and pretend-whispers to Momma: "We have presents."

Momma nods, and looks in the direction of the parking lot, pursing and unpursing her lips. After a few moments, she turns back and lays a hand on my shoulder. "Clyde, do *you* want to go to your cousin's for lunch?"

"Yes, Momma, I do."

"But what about your clothes?" She points at my uniform.

"No worries, Auntie," Kevin says. I have plenty of clothes in my closet for him to choose from. We're practically the same size."

Momma half-smiles and kisses the top of my head. She makes Kevin promise *again* to get me home in time for dinner by five o'clock sharp, then she takes off.

Chapter 4

Kevin and I cross the baseball field in the direction of the old Cobb Estate, a big wooded area we have to hike through before we come out on the other side into his fancy neighbourhood. We hop the fence and slog through the dense underbrush between huge pine trees. I've never been on the grounds of the Cobb Estate before, but I've heard all about it from friends who've secretly camped here. Some people call it 'the enchanted forest' because they think it's haunted, which I think is totally dumb. There are little creeks here and there, a crumbling old mansion that used to belong to the Marx Brothers, and a few wild animals, but nothing dangerous that I'm aware of. I've never seen any place so beautiful.

As we make our way across the estate, Kevin rattles on and on about girls until I start to get dizzy.

"Don't *you* ever think about girls?" he asks as we get to the middle of the forest. "About doing it with them?"

Kevin starts to walk faster; he jumps and skips over tree roots and rocks and things.

"Wait up!" I sprint after him.

He stops and spins around with a grin on his face and catches me in his arms as I slam into him.

"I can't wait to have sex!" he says. "I think I'd really like it. I just need to find the right girl."

I pretend I know what he's talking about, but I don't. The first time he mentioned *sex* to me, I was completely confused. I'd never heard the word before. So I asked Momma to explain it to me, and she told me *sex* meant *the difference between boys and girls*.

"If someone asks 'what sex are you,'" she said, "your answer should be 'I'm a boy'. And if someone asks *me* that question, my answer would be 'I'm a girl.'"

But Momma's explanation doesn't make any sense. What does *the difference between boys and girls* have anything to do with *having sex*, like what Kevin is talking about?

Kevin finally shuts up about girls (thank God!) and gets all quiet.

We walk on a little farther and get to a part of the forest where there are more trees. It's cooler and darker, so I figure we're getting deeper into it. I slow down and look back. Kevin notices this, takes my hand, and gently pulls me along the trail. "Don't let go," he says. "There are ghosts."

"Don't worry; I won't."

I love the way his hand feels. It's big and warm and soft, with little rough patches where his fingers meet his palms from lifting weights in his dad's garage. I slow down a little so as to feel the pull of his arm.

As we reach a small clearing, Kevin stops and smiles, flashing his beautiful white teeth.

"What is it?" I say.

"I want to show you something." He leads me to a corner of the clearing.

We sit on the soft, mossy ground beside a little stand of birch trees. He pulls off my baseball cap and rubs my head again. Then he moves in and kisses me on the lips, like in the movies. And I close my eyes and let him. His lips are soft and moist and taste so sweet. I've never felt so good in all my life. I open my eyes and stare into his face as if for the very first time. He's the most hand-some boy I've ever seen. His hair is long and brown and wavy and beautiful, and it tickles my face each time he kisses me. He pulls me closer and holds me against his chest. His body is strong and soft at the same time, like a big firm pillow. It reminds me of how good he is at sports. But he's never mean like those other sporty guys who make fun of me all the time.

"I'm just practising," he says after a while.

"What do you mean?"

"Like for when I finally get together with a girl for real." He sits up and straightens his shirt. "I want to be ready."

"Oh," I say. Then it slowly dawns on me. "Was that sex?"

"Was what sex?"

"What we were just doing."

Kevin hops to his feet and chuckles. "No, silly! That was just kissing." He pulls me off the ground and brushes the leaves from the back of my uniform. "You mean you don't know what sex is yet?"

I shake my head, my face reddening a bit. "Nobody's ever explained it to me, sorry."

"Let's go," he says. "I'll explain all about it when we get to my place. I have a picture book you can look at."

We come out on the other side of the Cobb Estate and hike up the hill to Kevin's new neighbourhood, which is way nicer than our ugly one in Pasadena. The houses are bigger and there's lots of land between each of them, which I like. They're also different from each other, being that they're custom-made. In our neighbourhood, the houses are all exactly the same, squatty-looking one-stories pushed up against each other. Momma says they're like that because it's a cheaper way to build houses for poor people like us.

"You guys are lucky to live here," I say to Kevin.

"Ha!" Kevin says as we turn the corner to his street at the top of the hill. "Luck has nothing to do with it. It's not like we won the lottery or something like that."

"No, I don't mean that. I mean, I wish we lived up here, too."

"You mean like *with* us?"

"Never mind."

"No, really," Kevin says, with a big smile. "Maybe you can come live with us for a while. We have plenty of room. I can ask my mom."

"Nah," I say. "I wouldn't want to leave Momma all alone with my crazy father."

"Oh, yeah. No kidding. Your dad's twisted. Poor Auntie." My stomach hurts when he says that.

We finally reach the gates of Kevin's new house, which is super beautiful, almost like a movie star's mansion. It's a hundred-year-old three-story brick house with a green slate roof, a circular driveway in front, and a separate four-car garage, where Uncle Alistair has more space for his collection of antique British sports cars than at their old place in Glendale. Kevin tells me it has, like, six bedrooms, two kitchens, a library, and a basement where people in the old days used to keep wine.

Kevin punches his secret code into a little pad, and the gate swings open. As we cross his front lawn and approach the front door, he fishes deep into his pockets, looking for his keys.

"Ah, shoot." He takes a quick peek under the doormat. "Wait here. I'm gonna see if my mom left the back door open."

"I thought your parents were home."

"Don't worry. Just wait here. I'll be right back." Kevin disappears around the corner and leaves me standing like a dumb-dumb on the front porch.

After a few minutes, the front door to Kevin's house swings open, kind of creepy like, and I step into the foyer, but I don't see Kevin anywhere. I move a little farther inside and peek around the corner into the big, empty living room.

"Hello?" My voice echoes off the walls.

"Come upstairs," I hear Kevin say. "*All* the way up."

I bound up the big staircase, two steps at a time. When I finally get to the top floor, I climb the ladder that leads to Kevin's attic room.

As soon as my head pokes through the opening into his bedroom, I'm surprised to see a massive wall-to-wall, black-and-white poster of a cowboy above his waterbed. I climb the rest of the way into his room and stare at it. The cowboy is stretched out in an open-top truck, his cowboy-hat-covered head on one side of the poster, his stretched-out body across the middle, and his boots at the other end. And in between the cowboy's head and his boots, there's this old-fashioned Western-looking mansion far away in the background. I move closer until my knees are touching the side of Kevin's bed, and I peer at the cowboy's face, which is really handsome, even handsomer than Kevin's.

"You like it?" Kevin's voice comes from behind me.

"It's amazing!" I can't stop looking at the cowboy, and I suddenly get this hollow feeling high in my stomach that almost touches my heart.

"Don't forget to breathe, little cuz."

"Who is that?" I turn around and notice Kevin has already changed into a pair of kinda too-tight red gym shorts with a gold stripe down each side and a white tank top with the number 69 stencilled on it in red. He's smiling and pumping his eyebrows.

"That's James Dean. He's my idol."

"Is he a real person?"

"He was an actor." Kevin jumps up on the bed and runs a finger along the length of the cowboy's leg with a funny smile. "This poster's from a movie he made in the fifties called *Giant*."

"Where'd you get it?"

"From Ryo Murakawa, that kid from your class."

Ryo Murakawa is an *A-number-one* bully, and it surprises me to hear Kevin mention his stupid name. "How do you know Ryo?"

"He goes to our church."

"Ryo goes to church?" I can't believe a little jerk like Ryo would ever step foot in a church.

"Yeah, he does. But, more importantly, his dad owns a shop on Hollywood Boulevard, where they sell these kinds of things. He sold it to me for a really good price."

Kevin stretches out on the bed, right below the cowboy, and lifts his leg up and down against the poster, which makes me laugh. It looks like he's rubbing his foot against the cowboy's leg.

"He's dead now," he says.

"Who is?"

"James Dean! He died in a car crash ages ago. He was only twenty-four." Kevin jumps off the bed, skips to his desk, and snatches up a book. "But, still, I love his movies, and I love his style. Here, look." He hands me the book. "This is his life story. It's got lots of cool pictures of him from before he was famous, like when he lived in Indiana as a kid, and also from his movies. Everyone was crazy about him."

I flip through the pages for a few seconds, then hand it back to him and look at the poster again. I could look at it all day.

"I have other things, too. Check this out." He leads me by the hand to the bulletin board above his desk. It's covered in trading cards and pictures cut out from magazines and things, all of James Dean.

"How long have you been collecting this stuff?"

"It's not stuff. It's memorabilia. Look, this one's signed." He hands me a shiny black-and-white of James Dean wearing a black turtleneck sweater pulled up over his nose and mouth. It's signed in the corner, but I can't make out what it says, just a big curly J with a squiggly line after it.

"Is this for real?" I ask.

"Of course it's for real. Ryo scored it for me from his dad's private collection."

"You mean he stole it."

"No, he didn't steal it. I bought it."

"For how much?"

"Jeez!" Kevin grabs the photo out of my hand. "What's with the third degree? I paid him ten bucks."

"That's all? Something signed is worth way more than that, isn't it? Does his dad know he sold it to you—something from a private collection?"

"Of course, he knows!"

"Cause it's not nice if Ryo stole it."

"Like I said ..." Kevin stuffs the picture into his pencil drawer and pushes it shut super quick. "I'm not some lowlife thief if that's what you're implying."

"I didn't mean you. I'm talking about Ryo. He's a stuck-up big mouth. And I wouldn't put it past him if he stole it from his dad and sold it to you for a lousy ten bucks."

"Buying something stolen is the same as stealing it, Clyde." Kevin frowns and shakes his head at me, and I realise then I shouldn't have said anything because I really like him, and I don't want him to be mad at me.

I look back at the bulletin board and pretend I'm interested in the pictures. That's when I spot a black-and-white of James Dean and a blonde lady, both of them smoking cigarettes on a balcony. The focus of the picture is totally on James Dean. His face is all scowly and squinty, and he's gripping a cigarette between his teeth, almost like he wants to bite off the end. The blonde lady, who's wearing a tight white dress, is more in the background, not really paying attention to him. She's in her own world, bending over the edge of the balcony and sucking hard on her cigarette so that her cheeks are pulled in. You can see a bunch of tall New Yorky-looking buildings behind them, and some tiny spots down below that I guess are cars. I lean forward to take a closer look.

"Is that Marilyn?" I ask, pointing at the picture.

"Huh? Oh, yeah, Marilyn Monroe." He unpins the picture from the bulletin board and hands it to me. "It's a fake, I think. I'm not sure they ever met each other."

"I think she's the prettiest lady I've ever seen in my whole life. I love her blonde hair, the stylish way she dresses, and I really like her friendly face. She's perfect!"

"You can have it if you want, for your birthday."

"Really?" I sit on the bed and stare at the picture. "Thank you, Kev!"

Kevin sits next to me and looks at the picture again. "What I like is the cool way Dean's clenching the cigarette between his teeth. I hardly notice *her*." He lays back on the bed and stares at the ceiling.

"I saw her on TV last night," I say, after a moment. "I told Momma I want to meet her someday, but she told me that I can't."

"It's because she's dead," he says, still staring at the ceiling.

"She is…?" I glance at the ceiling to see what he's looking at and notice there's a big mirror up there where you can see yourself if you're lying flat on your back.

"Yeah, my mom says she took too many sleeping pills and died. Some people think she did it on purpose; other people think the CIA killed her because she was having sex with the president." Kevin sits up and grins. "But you don't know what sex is yet, do you?"

I shake my head and set aside the picture of Marilyn, feeling a little sad to know she's dead.

"So, as I promised, I'm going to show you!" He jumps up and rubs his hands together fast, the way you rub two sticks together when you want to make a fire. "But first, let's get you out of your dirty uniform."

"You're so lucky to be able to decorate your room the way you like," I say, taking off my cap and stripping off my uniform shirt and the T-shirt underneath.

"Mom doesn't like it," Kevin says. "But my dad says she should let me because it's good for me to develop my personality."

"That's probably because he's from England."

"Maybe so," Kevin says with a little shrug. "They argue about it sometimes. But, so far, so good."

Kevin takes my shirt and folds it into a perfect square just like they do in department stores, then he helps undo my belt, which has a tricky buckle I can't open very easily, and helps me wriggle out of my baseball pants and stockings.

"*My* father won't let me touch my room," I say.

"Have you asked him?"

"No way. It's Hiro's old room. He doesn't want me to touch anything."

"Hiro's been gone a long time. It's *your* room now. You should be able to decorate it however you want. Start with that picture I gave you. Pin it up on your wall."

Kevin puts my uniform on a chair and looks at me, standing there in my underpants. He points at the red patch on my left thigh. "Is that the thing?" he asks.

I nod, not wanting to think about it.

Kevin leans forward and kisses the patch. He keeps his lips against my leg for a few seconds, and it makes me feel better. Auntie Doreen says Kevin has healing powers, and I believe it, even though Uncle Alistair says it's a bunch of rubbish.

"I heard my parents talking about it one night," I say. "The doctor told them it's some kind of cancer. But my father said it's a curse for what happened before, with Hiro."

"Your dad's fricking nuts. Don't pay any attention to him." Kevin passes the tips of his fingers over my thigh. "My mom told me it's just some kind of rash that won't cause you any problems, at least not for a long time. Maybe never. So don't worry about it."

"How would she know?"

"I have no idea." Kevin gently rubs his fingers over the patch in a little circle. "She just knows."

"Make it better, Kev, please."

Kevin lays his hand flat against the patch. It feels warm and tingly. I close my eyes and imagine his healing energy flowing into my body. After a little while, his fingers move around to the back of my leg. They stop right under my bum and lift my underpants.

"What's this?" he asks.

"What's what?" I open my eyes and crane my neck to look at him.

"This scar." He rubs his fingers against my skin, right where my leg meets my bum cheek. "It's, like, two inches long."

"I don't know."

"How can you not know?" he says. "It looks like it was a deep cut."

"I mean, I don't remember."

"Haven't you ever seen it?" He leads me to a full-size mirror on his closet door. "Here, look." He points out a thick, reddish scar on the back of my leg in the shape of a crescent moon.

"I don't feel well, Kev."

"Sorry, little cuz." He leads me to the bed. "Sit here for a second."

He runs to his bathroom and comes back a few seconds later with a glass of water. I take a sip and draw a few deep breaths, the way Momma showed me to do whenever I feel nervous or scared.

"Maybe it happened when you were little," Kevin says, still frowning. "Maybe that's why you don't remember."

"Maybe."

"Anyway, it's not good to forget things. Especially things like that. You should ask your mom about it."

"OK, I'll ask her," I say, even though I know I'm not going to because Momma doesn't handle things very well. I take another sip of water.

"I'm serious, Clyde. Promise you'll ask her."

I nod and smile at him.

Kevin kisses me on the cheek again. "OK, cool." He takes the glass out of my hand and sets it on his nightstand. "Ready for the lesson I promised you?"

"What lesson?"

"The one about sex."

"Oh, yeah. But, shouldn't I get dressed first?"

"Not yet!"

He disappears into his big closet. I can hear him digging around in it for a couple of minutes. Then he reappears with a big book. He jumps on the bed and holds it up to me, showing me the front cover with a cartoon of a man and a lady smiling at a baby in a crib.

"What's this?"

"It's a book from Denmark that explains everything about sex. And it has lots of cool pictures." Kevin flips open the book to a cartoon of a naked man with a beard, whose arms are wrapped around a chubby naked lady with weird pigtails.

"Does your momma know you have this?" I ask, being that his parents are religious and kind of strict, especially Auntie Doreen.

"No way! And don't you tell them. My mom would kill me."

I take the book out of his hand and look more closely at the cartoon, which is really dorky-looking. I mean, it doesn't look like a real artist drew it. The man's *chinchin* looks like a tiny fish sausage, and I'm not sure what that white space is between the lady's legs. "Where did you get this?"

"Doesn't matter." Kevin takes it back. "The point is, I'm going to explain all about sex to you."

"OK..."

"So, first, you see how the man has hair around his chinchin?"

"Yeah, I guess..."

"OK, what that means is before you can have sex, you need to have hair around your chinchin. Like this." He pulls down his shorts a little and shows me some dark brown hair growing below his belly button. He reaches over and pulls down my underpants a little in the front, too. "You don't have any, so you're not ready yet."

"What if I never grow any hair there?"

"Don't worry," he says, with a short laugh. "You will. All guys do. Give it a year or two, and you'll grow hair. I guarantee it. Maybe it'll start growing on your *kintama* first. But, eventually, it'll grow right there." He rubs the space below my belly button.

His fingers feel cool against my skin. "Anyway, you see here in the picture how the lady has this long hole between her legs, and it's surrounded by hair?"

"Yeah..."

"That's her *omeko*. Girls need hair around their omekos before they can have sex, just like guys need it around their chinchins." He flips a couple of pages and shows me a picture of the same bearded cartoon man lying on top of the pigtailed lady. They're holding on to each other, and their lips are touching, sort of like they're kissing each other. "See that?"

"What am I supposed to be seeing now?"

"Right there!" He draws an invisible circle with his finger around their leg area. "The artist drew the picture so you can see inside their bodies."

I lean forward and squint my eyes.

"You can see the man's chinchin is pushed deep into the lady's omeko." He pokes his finger at the book.

"Oh, yeah..." I look up at Kevin and see he's raising his eyebrows up and down again with a big grin on his face. "That's kind of weird."

"It's not weird," he says. "It's sex. *Everyone* does it when they get older. And this," he says, raising his voice like a TV announcer as he flips the page, "is what happens afterwards." He points at the book, and I see a picture of the pigtailed lady with what looks like a big-eyed worm inside her belly. Kevin pokes at the picture again. "That's a baby growing inside the lady."

"It doesn't look like a baby."

"It's what a baby looks like before it grows into this." He flips the page again and shows me another picture of the pigtailed lady with something that looks more like a baby inside her belly, only all scrunched, almost into a ball.

"And finally," he says, flipping the page again and pushing the book up to my face, "the baby pops out of the lady's omeko."

I grab the book and hold it away from my face and see this crazy picture of the pigtailed lady lying flat on a table with her legs spread wide apart and a baby's head poking out of her omeko with a goofy smile on its face. The bearded man is standing on one side of the table, and a doctor is standing on the other, and neither of them is paying any attention to her, because, like, who would! I slam the book closed and hand it to Kevin.

"What's wrong?" he says. "I told you I was going to explain to you about sex. And that's what it is."

"Babies come out of omekos?"

"We *all* came out of our mothers' omekos!"

"That's gross!" I try hard not to picture Momma's omeko with me shooting out of it, or Kevin flying out of Auntie Doreen's.

"It's not gross! It's how babies are made."

"Whatever! And that's what you can't wait to do? Make babies?"

"No!"

"You *said* you can't wait to have sex!" I jump off the bed. "That's exactly what you told me back there on the Cobb Estate, didn't you? And then you told me you were practising for sex when you kissed me."

"Calm down! I'm not done explaining."

"Explaining what?"

"About sex! It's not *just* about making babies. Come on, sit back on the bed."

"No," I say, backing away from him. "I can hear you from here. Tell me what you meant, if it's not about making babies."

Kevin holds up his hands and says, "Fine. I'll explain from here. But stop being sore about it, because I didn't mean anything bad, OK?"

I nod and wait.

"So, the thing is, even though sex is *mainly* about making babies, you can do the part about sticking your chinchin inside a girl's omeko just for fun."

"What's fun about that? That's where her pee comes from."

"It's fun because it feels good. And it's not *just* about putting it in a girl's omeko either. It's more about rubbing your chinchin against something soft. The more you rub it, the better it feels."

I'm totally confused by what Kevin is saying and almost feel like running away. But he's been so nice to me, and I want to feel his arms around me again. So I shuffle a little closer to him.

"Come on, slugger." Kevin pats the bed. "We can practise kissing a little more."

I sit next to Kevin, and we kiss again. Then we stretch out on the waterbed to kiss some more, and I close my eyes and imagine I'm melting into his body.

Over the sound of his breathing, I hear a loud grinding noise in the background. It sounds like it's coming from outside of the house.

"Kev!"

"Don't stop," he says.

I point at the window. "I think your *parents* are home!"

"Oh, shit!" He sprints to the front window and pokes out his head. "Mom's just coming into the house now." Grabbing his hairbrush off the dresser, he passes it through his hair a few times. "Hurry up and get dressed, Clyde! Grab anything out of there." He waves the hairbrush at the closet. "Meet me downstairs in the kitchen."

He runs to the hole in his floor, stops for a second, then comes back and kisses me on the cheek. "Don't say anything, OK? This is our secret."

"I promise."

Kevin smiles the handsomest smile I've ever seen and kisses me again, this time on the mouth. "To be continued," he says, looking deep into my eyes, right before he disappears down the hole.

Chapter 5

Once Kevin's gone, the room gets super quiet and I feel completely alone like I'm the only person left in the whole world. I sit on the bed and think about everything that just happened, which makes my heart race. So I lay back and close my eyes, taking a few deep breaths to relax myself. When I finally open them, I find I'm looking up at the mirror on Kevin's ceiling, which is weird and a little scary at first. So I shut my eyes again and keep them that way for a while and think about how nice Kevin is to me, about how handsome he is. The bed bobs around from the water sloshing inside. It's warm and relaxing.

After a bit, I open my eyes and look up again. I look so strange, so far away up there on that high ceiling, almost like I'm another person—just a boy on a bed in his underpants.

Why would anyone put a mirror on the ceiling above their bed? I mean, it's not like you're going to be able to see anything when you're asleep. And people don't usually look so great in the morning either. And who's going to get dressed and lay on their bed to look at themselves, since clothes don't look right when you're flat on your back. So, I reckon the mirror must be there so you can look at yourself when you're relaxing or when you're thinking, like what I'm doing now.

I think it's strange that the boy on the bed, who's supposed to be me, doesn't look like either of my parents. I mean, Momma is classic city Japanese, with silky straight, black hair, black eyes, light creamy skin, and a delicate oval face with a high nose. Auntie Doreen says Momma's blessed because she's slender and shapely, with big boobies, but not too tall, which is supposed to be good for a lady.

My father's not very good-looking, poor thing. He's short and stocky with wiry, black hair and beady eyes that are set wide apart. He has one thick eyebrow with no break in the middle that sits above his eyes like a fuzzy caterpillar. His nose is flat, his chin juts out, and his skin is reddish and splotchy. I've seen lots of pictures of Hiro, and he looked almost exactly like my father, except his nose wasn't as flat, and he had better skin. But his hair was black and wiry like my father's, and he was short and a bit fat.

But the boy on the bed looks like someone else's kid.

I reach up and run my fingers through his hair. It's not black; it's brown. It's not straight; it's wavy. It's not hard; it's soft. The boy on the bed isn't short; he's tall. His lips aren't thin and dark; they're full and red like a ripe strawberry, like a girl's. Almost like Marilyn's.

Running my hands along his body, I pull down the boy's underpants and see that he has hips, almost like a girl's, which gives me an idea. I tuck the boy's chinchin between his legs so that it looks like he has an omeko. Then I roll over a bit to one side and see the big bum the kids at school are always pinching and slapping. The more I look at him, the more the boy on the bed looks like a girl to me.

It's no wonder my father is always saying I'm someone else's kid. It's true; I'm nothing like him. But I'm not like Momma either. I'm more like Kevin, who must be wondering what's taking me so long.

I jump off the bed, pull out a pair of dark blue bikini undies from Kevin's dresser, and quickly change out of my dirty white ones. Then I go deep inside his closet and pick out a nice light blue button shirt with a red strawberry pattern, a pair of tight white bell-bottoms, and some dark blue leather platform shoes and put them on.

I look at myself in the dresser mirror and notice my hair looks flat and not very stylish. So I try to feather it back with the brush the way Kevin does. But his hair is cut and layered that way. Mine is just a stupid bowl cut because my father doesn't think boys should spend so much money on their hair. After working with it a while, I step back and look at myself. My hair looks a lot better, but something's still not right about the overall look.

I open Kevin's dresser and rummage around in it looking for something else to wear. But it's just full of underclothes and socks and jammies. Then I look inside his pencil drawer, where he put the picture of James Dean before. I lift the picture and find a cool-looking pukka shell necklace underneath that I think would look great with my outfit. I pull out the necklace, and something else in the drawer catches my eye—the corner of another picture. Pulling out the drawer a bit farther, I slide out the other picture and am surprised to see it's a naked one of David Cassidy, only you can't see his chinchin, just the black hair above it like Kevin has. I stare at it for a second wondering why Kevin has a picture of a naked guy, then set it aside and dig around a little more inside Kevin's pencil drawer. At the bottom of the drawer, I find a few more pictures of naked guys, except the guys in these pictures are *completely* naked with moustaches and beards and hair all over their bodies. That's when I realise that Kevin likes guys, not girls like he's been saying.

Chapter 6

I poke my head into the kitchen and see Auntie Doreen, Kevin, and my cousin Maggie, who's the same age as me. They're all working on preparing lunch, chopping, and sprinkling, and pouring, with Auntie Doreen barking orders and Kevin and Maggie obeying like little soldiers. The rice maker is bubbling away on the counter, and there are pans and pots on every burner of the hob filling the house with the aroma of something delicious. It smells like something yummy is baking in the oven, too. Auntie Doreen holds up a red onion to the light, inspecting it for I don't know what.

"Hi, Auntie," I say, trying hard not to picture Kevin coming out of her hairy omeko.

Auntie swings around, onion and chopping knife in hand, and smiles at me as I walk into the kitchen. "Well, hello there, young man! Don't you look handsome."

Auntie Doreen looks a lot like my father, short and a little stocky. And her hair is black and wiry, not smooth and silky like Momma's. But since she has enough money to go to the hairdresser twice a week, it's always stylish. Today it's cut into a mullet the way the mom from *The Brady Bunch* wears hers.

Kevin sidles up to me. "What took you?" he says under his breath.

I shrug and mumble something about not being able to make up my mind about what to wear, then lift the pukka shell necklace and wink at him.

Auntie taps her cheek with the onion. "Come, give your Auntie a kiss, and take a seat there while your cousins and I finish preparing lunch." She points her chopping knife at the island in the middle of the room.

Maggie runs up, throws her arms around me, and squeezes me as hard as she can until I can barely breathe. "Happy birthday to my *favourite* cousin in all the world!" she says.

"I'm your *only* cousin," I say, trying to wriggle out of her bear hug.

"*And* my favourite!" She finally lets go of me and steps back with a giggle. She's tall for her age, like me. And her hair is wavy and brown like mine, which she wears in a short bob. She could almost be my twin sister, I think, except her eyes are dark brown instead of blue like mine.

"We're not finished, kids." Auntie points at the bubbling pots. "Keep an eye on those."

Kevin and Maggie run back to the hob, and I take a seat at the island and look around at their fantastic kitchen. It's comfy and warm, painted mustard yellow, and has a humongous picture window in front of the sink that looks at their backyard and their garage. It feels so special to be there with them, and I try to imagine what it would be like to be part of their family instead of mine.

A few minutes later, Uncle Alistair roars into the driveway in his red Austin-Healey Roadster and pulls to a stop at the garage door. Everyone looks up at the same time, and Maggie jumps around and claps her hands. Uncle Alistair pops out of the roadster with a bunch of shopping bags, glides across the driveway to the sliding glass door on his long spider-monkey legs, and lowers his head as he steps through the doorway into the kitchen carrying a few grocery bags in one arm and a transistor radio in his free hand blaring out the news. Maggie's fat Persian neko, Daidaiiro, follows him inside, creeps up to me, and rubs his orange face against my leg, and I bend down and scratch his ear.

"Alistair, *please* turn that off," Auntie says, waving her hand. "It's giving me a migraine." She bows her head toward me. "Kimi's here, remember?"

"Yes, of course!" he says, switching off the radio. "Happy birthday, young man. Don't you look smashing!" He puts the bags on the counter and squeezes my hand. "I understand you're eleven years old today."

"Yes, Uncle, thank you. But Auntie shouldn't call me Kimi. Father says everyone's supposed to call me Clyde now."

"Oh, pish," Auntie Doreen says, digging around inside the shopping bags.

Daidaiiro nudges my leg with his head and starts to make cute mewy sounds. So I bend down and pick him up and rub my nose against his head.

"Hey!" Maggie pulls Daidaiiro out of my hands and drops him back on the floor. "Don't do that! He's an outside cat. He's not clean." She opens the door and lets him out.

"I was just saying hello. Besides, he came up to *me*."

"He probably smells ███ on you," Auntie says.

As soon as she says that, the sound goes away...

... And then the sound comes back on.

"Clyde, honey," Auntie Doreen is saying. "Are you all right?"

"Young man?" Uncle Alistair says, his forehead furrowing into deep lines. "Are you still with us?"

I can see Kevin and Maggie standing far away in the background like I'm seeing them from the wrong side of a pair of binoculars.

"Earth to Clyde! Earth to Clyde!" Maggie is saying, waving her hand from side to side.

"Everything's fine, sorry," I say. I jump off the chair and force a smile at them. "This place is great, Uncle Alistair! I can't wait for Momma to see it. She used to live in a big house, too."

Auntie Doreen and Uncle Alistair look at each other, and back at me. Auntie Doreen draws in a slow breath and moves back to the kitchen counter. "That was something entirely different, dear." She cuts a piece of paper towel and dabs her face. "Your mother's parents were multimillionaires and lived on a vast estate. Your Uncle Alistair's just an accountant."

"Just?" Uncle Alistair's mouth turns down at the corners.

"You know what I mean, Ali." Auntie Doreen tosses the crumpled paper towel into the rubbish bin and goes back to digging around in the grocery bags.

"I'm no industrialist, but I've done quite well for myself if I do say so myself."

"OK, OK," Kevin says, throwing his arms around his father and giving him a big hug. "Let's not argue. Clyde and I are starving." He winks at me. "We're *well* spent after that game. Right, Slugger?"

I nod.

"How was the game, Clyde?" Maggie asks. "How many home runs did you bat in *this* time?"

"Game was OK," I say.

"OK? Oh, my God, give me a break. You practically won it for us single-handedly." Kevin turns to his parents and announces: "Clyde batted in four home runs!"

"Really?" Maggie says. "That's way cool." She skips around the kitchen like a little bronco, her hair bouncing all around. "Cool, so cool, that's way coolio! Did you hear, Mommy? Clyde won the game for Kevin's team!"

"Congratulations, Kimi," Auntie says. "Your grandparents would have been very proud of you."

"We're all very proud," Uncle Alistair says. "You can tell us all about it over lunch. Now move along into the dining room, Maggie, boys. Mother and I will be serving in a moment."

Kevin gives me a gentle push from behind and walks me out of the kitchen and into the dining room. We sit around the table, me at the end, Kevin to my left, and Maggie on my right. It's a big room with a chandelier over the table and a glass door with another view of the back garden.

"Hungry?" Kevin asks.

Starving!" I say. "I can't wait to see what your mom made."

"She didn't make anything," Maggie says, nervously kicking my chair. "We made it! She's just putting it all into serving dishes and bringing it in here."

Auntie Doreen marches into the room followed by Uncle Alistair, and they put a few bowls and some dishes on the table. After they've brought out all the food, Auntie lights a couple of long white dinner candles, and Uncle Alistair stands at the head of the table holding out his arms in our direction.

"Please join me over here," he says to us, "I'd like to say a special blessing over my children. You too, Clyde."

We all go to the head of the table and Uncle Alistair puts his hand on top of Maggie's head, which makes her go all quiet and peaceful, and he chants something religious. Then he turns to Kevin and me and puts his hands on top of our heads, and Kevin slips an arm around my waist. Auntie joins us and pulls the three of us into a huddle, and both she and Uncle Alistair say a prayer over the three of us and get all teary-eyed. They kiss each of us on the top of our heads and invite us to serve ourselves.

I don't remember ever feeling as happy as I do now. Auntie and Uncle Alistair are so kind to me even though I'm not their kid. And Kevin and Maggie smile at me and nod their heads whenever I say anything. I think about how lucky they are, and my throat starts to go tight. Auntie and Uncle Alistair ask me about the game, and about school, and they say how smart I am, and they tell me I'm welcome anytime I want to come over; then they bring out an ice cream cake from Baskin-Robbins with eleven burning candles just for me, and they sing happy birthday, and give me presents, and, and, and...

"Kimi!" Auntie says, "Kimi, what is it?"

Kevin hurries to my side and hands me a napkin. "Are you OK, little cuz?"

"Look, Daddy," Maggie says, jumping up from her chair. "He's crying."

"Young man, what's wrong?" Uncle Alistair says. He walks over to me and puts his hand on my shoulder.

I scoot away from the table and wipe my face with my hands. They're all looking at me again, which makes me feel self-conscious and stupid. So I run out of the dining room, through the kitchen, across the foyer, and hide behind a sofa in the living room.

Auntie Doreen follows me, and so do the rest of them. But she orders them back to the dining room and tells them to wait there. Auntie Doreen marches to the sofa I'm hiding behind, drops onto it, and pats the cushion next to her. "Come, join me here, Kimi."

I come out from behind the sofa and climb into it, then I rest my head on her lap the way I used to when I was little, and I start to cry again.

"There, there, Kimi." She rubs my back a little, which calms me. "What's this all about? Have we upset you?"

"No, Auntie. You've all been really nice to me." I sit up and hug her. "Thank you for the cake and the presents."

"Then what is it? What's got you so upset?"

"It's my father," I say. "He's so mean to me and to Momma. He hates me!"

"Don't say that, Kimi. Your father loves you."

"No, he doesn't! He hates me! He says I was a mistake."

"When did he say that?"

"Last night! He came home drunk again and screamed at Momma and me, and said I was a mistake. And it's not the first time he said it either. He says it every time he gets drunk. And he says other things, too."

"What other things?"

"He thinks Hiro's bad parts are inside me."

"Oh, my Lord."

"And he calls me names, too, like bastard. Why does he call me that?"

"Kimi, sweetie..."

"Stop calling me Kimi, Auntie, please."

"But it's your name!"

"Please, don't," I say. "Nobody calls me that, not even Momma."

"You should be proud of your name, sweetie. It's your heritage."

"I don't want a heritage name. I have my own American name, just like Kevin has."

"Please, Kimi, sit down." She pats the cushion next to her once more.

I sit down again, feeling kind of sore at her because she keeps calling me Kimi even though I've asked her a zillion times not to.

"Sometimes I wonder if they're even my parents, Auntie."

"Yoshi and Tomo?" Auntie cuts her eyes at me. "How can you think that? You're the spitting image of your mother. And you have something of *our* family too in your solid build."

"No! I don't look anything like them, Auntie. They have straight, black hair, and I have wavy, brown hair; they have black eyes, and I have blue eyes! And they're short, and I'm tall."

Auntie jumps up from the sofa and looks at me, her eyes widening.

"What's wrong?" I ask her.

"Oh, honey..." she says, taking me by the arm and leading me to a mirror. "Look at yourself, Kimi. Your hair is black, just like your mother's. And your eyes are dark brown, almost black, not blue."

I blink at myself a couple of times trying to see what Auntie is seeing.

"You *do* see that, don't you?"

I shrug and pull away from her. Auntie follows me back to the sofa.

"I'm afraid we're going to have to speak with your mother and father, honey."

"About what?"

"About this silly belief you have that they're not your parents when they clearly are."

"But how can you be sure?"

"Because I was in the hospital the night you were born."

"You were?" I whip around and face her.

"Yes, I was. Your father couldn't be there, so I was with your mother, holding her hand, in fact, when you arrived. You caused quite a stir; I can tell you that. Especially with the midwife."

"Maybe someone switched me."

"Nobody switched you, dear. I can assure you of that."

"But if I'm my father's kid, it doesn't make sense that he hates me so much and is so mean to me and Momma. He makes her cry all the time."

"That's another matter entirely. Your father has a serious problem; there's no denying that. Your uncle and I are trying to convince him to get some help. But he wasn't always this way. He used to be a hardworking, sober young man. He was actually able to buy his own house when he was only eighteen years old with the money he earned from repairing cars. But what happened with your brother Hiro broke him. He loved your brother so much that when he became ill, your father almost lost his mind. And after Hiro's accident, well, you know, he was so angry at your mother."

"That wasn't an accident, and it wasn't her fault!"

"Your father didn't see it that way. And neither did I, frankly. Your brother was a sick boy and shouldn't have been left alone. By the time you arrived, poor Yoshi was lost and broken. And then our parents died the same year. Your poor father's never been the same since."

"That doesn't change anything for me, does it?" I sit up and wipe my face on the sleeve of Kevin's shirt. "Or for Momma."

Auntie pulls back my hair and kisses my forehead. "If things get too bad at home, just let me know. You can always come stay with us for a while, yes?"

"You promise?"

"Yes, I promise, Sweetie. *Anytime.*" Auntie hugs me tight.

"Momma, too?"

Auntie stands up and fixes her hair in one of the mirrors. "Come back to the dining room, shall we? You should have some cake and ice cream."

After lunch, Uncle Alistair takes Kevin outside to talk about something private, and Auntie leaves Maggie and me to clear the dining table and rinse the dishes before loading them into the dishwasher. It's already four o'clock, and I start to get a stomach ache because I don't want to get home later than five like Kevin promised Momma.

"Don't just stand there!" Maggie snaps her fingers at me. "Hand me the dishes. I want to finish putting them away."

"Sorry." I grab a dish out of the sink and hand it to her. "I was just thinking that I need to go home soon."

"Well, then, let's hurry it up," she says. "Mommy! Clyde needs to go home!"

"Where did they all go?"

Maggie shrugs and holds out her hand. "Next dish, *please.*"

I hand her a few more dishes and some water glasses, and she stuffs them into the dishwasher all crooked-like because it's getting full.

"Why were you crying earlier?" she asks, her face inside the dishwasher pretending to look for more space.

"I had a stomach ache."

She straightens up and opens her eyes really wide at me. "No, you didn't."

47

"OK, then I got something in my eye."

"Yeah, right! Stop lying."

"I'm not lying. I just don't want to talk about it."

"Then just say so. Don't keep making things up, or no one will believe anything you say."

I grab the rice bowl and pour the leftovers into a Tupperware container Auntie left us, and give it a good rinse before holding it out to her. She looks at it for a second and slowly takes it out of my hand.

"Is it because of Kevin?" she asks.

"What about Kevin?"

Maggie sucks in her lower lip and turns back to the dish-washer, trying a few times to squeeze the rice bowl in between the other dishes.

"When are you starting school again?" she asks.

"In September, same as you. What about Kevin?"

"What day in September?"

"The fourth of September, Maggie. Just like you! What were you going to say about Kevin?"

"We'll be starting *after* we get back from our trip."

"What trip?"

"Our trip to England."

"What trip to England?"

"Mommy wants us to go to England to visit our nan and to maybe look for a school for Kevin. So we might not get back here until, like, a week or two after school starts."

I put the soapy serving plate back into the sink. "A school for Kevin?"

"Yeah, Mommy's scared they'll send him to Viet Nam, so she wants to get him away from here so he'll be safe. I thought maybe you'd heard about that from Kevin."

Just then Uncle Ali, Kevin, and my father step into the kitchen, and I feel all out of breath and dizzy like I'm going to pass out unless I sit down.

"Look who I found outside the gate waiting in his truck!" Uncle Alistair says.

"Uncle!" Maggie says. She runs to my father and throws her arms around him. "Do you like our new place? Do you?"

My father picks her up and swings her around before putting her back on the ground. "You're so grown up now. And so pretty, too."

"I'm not pretty! I'm clever."

My father laughs. "You're definitely that."

"Hello, son," he says, flashing the fake smile he always puts on in front of other people. "Ready to come home?"

"Auntie and Uncle Alistair invited me to lunch and bought me a cake for my birthday. I'm helping to wash up. Where's Momma?"

"Clyde batted in four home runs, Uncle," Kevin says. "He won the game for us."

Auntie Doreen comes into the kitchen and stops short when she sees my father. "Yoshi!" she says.

My father spins around and looks at her.

"We weren't expecting you."

"Hi, Sis," he says. "Nice place you got here. I just came by to pick up the kid. Hope it's OK."

"Of course, it's OK." Auntie Doreen comes the rest of the way into the kitchen and kisses my father on the cheek. "We just didn't know you were coming."

"Is it true you're sending Kevin to England, Auntie?" I turn to Kevin. "Is it true?"

Kevin shrugs. "She's scared I'll get drafted."

"Drafted?" my father says, looking first at Auntie and then at Uncle Alistair. "The draft's over."

"That's what they say now," Auntie Doreen says. "But there are still American troops there, and the fighting hasn't stopped. They could bring it back."

"But he ain't old enough for that anyway," my father says.

"Not now," Auntie Doreen says. "But eventually. We just want to be prepared. So we're taking an exploratory trip at the end of the month."

"You're tying yourself in a knot for nothing, Sono," my father says to Auntie. "Leave the kid alone. He's doing fine here. Ain't that right, Nephew?"

Kevin nods his head real fast, with a big goofy grin on his face.

"I don't want Kevin to go," I say.

Uncle Alistair clears his throat. "Can I interest you in the grand tour, Yoshi? I think you'd quite like what we've done with the garage."

"Some other time, thanks. We've got to get back. Tomoko will be waiting with dinner. Clyde, take off that silly apron and change back into your own clothes."

"It's OK, Uncle," Kevin says. "Clyde can keep them."

"No need for that. Clyde, go change."

"But, Father …"

My father's hand shoots out and takes hold of my wrist. "Don't talk back. I want you in your own clothes and outside in ten minutes."

Auntie Doreen steps forward and put her hand on my father's arm. "Yoshi, please."

My father lets go of my wrist and holds up his hands like he's surrendering. "OK, fine. He can wear them home. But we'll set them aside for you to pick up next time you stop by." He moves to the front door. "I'll be waiting in the truck, son."

Chapter 7

My father doesn't say anything for most of the ride home. He just stares ahead and doesn't look at me. After a couple of miles, I switch on the radio and hum along to *Goodbye to Love* by The Carpenters. Just when it's getting to the good part with the guitar, my father lurches forward and snaps off the radio, practically breaking off the knob, and we ride the rest of the way in total silence.

As soon as we pull into the driveway, I jump out of the truck and run into the house and find Momma waiting on the other side of the door. I give her a quick hug and then run into my room and shut the door, pulling out the picture of Marilyn that Kevin gave me and smoothening it out on top of my dresser since it had gotten a bit crushed in my pocket.

Momma comes into my room without knocking and sits on my bed. She looks like she's about to say something, but instead, she folds her hands and puts them on top of her pink housedress.

"Auntie Doreen and Uncle Alistair bought me a cake," I say, after a moment. "They sang happy birthday to me." Digging in my pocket, I pull out the pukka shell necklace and start to put it back on. Momma cuts her eyes when she sees it and shoots a quick glance at the doorway.

"Put that away, baby," she says real quiet-like.

I shake my head, tears filling my eyes, and finish putting it on. "They were *all* really nice to me, Momma ... especially Kevin." I wipe my face. "Auntie and Uncle Alistair gave me presents, too. But I accidentally left them at Auntie's."

"Your Auntie called a few minutes ago. She said they'll come by and bring you your presents and your uniform later in the week. Kevin, too. But *please*, baby," she says, "take that off before your father sees it."

Just then I hear my father's boots clomping down the hall, and, remembering the Marilyn picture on my dresser, I speed across the room and snatch it up.

"What is that?" he asks, stepping into my room and pointing at the picture.

I quickly put it behind my back. "Kevin gave it to me. It's a present."

My father holds out his hand and snaps his fingers. "Give it here."

"It's a present from Kevin," I repeat. "It's mine."

He pushes me to one side, and I fall against my bed, and he snatches up the picture, which has slipped to the floor.

"Yoshi!" Momma screams.

I scramble up and try to grab it out of his hands, but he holds it out of my reach.

"What is this?" he asks, waving it at me.

"It's a picture of James Dean smoking a cigarette! Kevin gave it to me."

"James Dean smoking a cigarette, eh?" He looks at the picture for a second, then glares at me like he wants to kill me and holds it higher. "What business do *you* have with a picture of a stinking *hakujin*? Or is it that you like boys?"

"There's a lady in the picture, too!" I say, straining to grab the picture out of his hands.

"Give it back to him, Yoshi!" Momma says.

He throws the picture at me, and it hits me in the face, which makes me real mad. "Look at you!" he says, as I snatch it off the floor and put it in my back pocket. "You look like a goddam sissy, dressed like that, with that necklace and them high heels."

"*These*"—I point at my feet—"are platform shoes, not high heels! *All* famous people wear them now." I take off the choker and hold it up to him. "And *this* is a pukka shell necklace. Open any magazine, and you'll see that *boys* are wearing them, not girls."

"Sissies are wearing them!"

"These are Kevin's clothes!" I scream. "And he's not a sissy."

"Don't raise your voice at your father," Momma says.

"I don't care whose clothes they are," he says. "I want you out of them, and I want you in the backyard in a half hour. We're gonna have a ceremony for ██████ and then *you're* going to bury her under the guava tree."

I look at Momma when he talks about the guava tree, and she nods at me for some reason I can't figure out. Then I look at my father and see his mouth moving, but I can't hear what he's saying anymore. Everything is quiet and confused at the same time, and I feel like I'm going to black out. So I take a few deep breaths to calm myself down.

Out of the corner of my eye, I catch my reflection in the cracked mirror perched above my dresser, cross the room, and stare into it. I see Momma and my father behind me, staring first at me, then at each other, as I slide open the top drawer, pull out the roll of scotch tape Momma keeps in there to wrap presents and cut a big piece. Then I reach into my back pocket and pull out the Marilyn picture and flatten it out against the top left corner of the mirror.

"What ... the ... *fuck* ... are you doing?" my father says.

"Yoshi ..." Momma says.

"I'm decorating my room."

"This is Hiro's room," my father says, his voice dropping to a whisper.

"Yoshi," Momma says, "come outside." She takes him by the hand, but he shakes her off.

"This was the last place we saw him before they took him away," he says, scrunching up his face at her. She reaches out a hand to him. Before I can blink, he whirls around and snatches the picture off the mirror. "You're not going to change Hiro's room."

"Stop talking about Hiro!" I scream, covering my ears with both hands. "It's not my fault he went crazy; it's not my fault the two of you left him alone that night, and it's definitely not my fault he hurt himself with a piece of broken glass"—I uncover my ears and point at my father—"from a bottle of *your* cheap whiskey."

My father brings his open hand across my face with a loud crack.

"How dare you?" Momma says, taking hold of my arm. "Your father and I are still mourning. You have no right to disrespect us or your brother's memory."

"Screw him!" I say, breaking away from her and turning on my father. "Give me back my picture!"

My father grabs me by the hair, drags me through the house, and shoves me into our stuffy laundry room. "That's it," he says. "You're punished. Don't you move!" He comes back after a few minutes and orders me to strip off Kevin's trousers. "I'm gonna fix you, dammit!" he says. "Now, I'm *finally* gonna fix you." He whips out a couple of uncooked soybeans from his shirt pocket and makes me kneel on them, which is a punishment he learned at Manzanar, that camp in the mountains where Americans stored Japanese people during the war. He and Auntie Doreen spent time there when they were kids.

Momma screams in the background, something like: "Please, Yoshi, he's just a little boy." And my father screams right back at her, something super naughty in Japanese that I am not going to repeat here. I hear some loud banging, and then it gets quiet. I imagine he probably locked her away somewhere in the house. But I don't care, because I'm really angry at Momma for siding with him, and I'm furious he took away the Marilyn picture Kevin gave me for my birthday.

Every once in a while, my father sticks his head into the laundry room to make sure I'm still kneeling on those crazy beans, and each time he shouts, "I'm gonna fix you" until I think I'm going to lose my mind between his shouting and the pain.

"I'm not going through this again, no fucking way," he says the next time he shows up.

"They're hurting bad," I whimper, tears stinging my eyes. "I'm afraid they're boring holes in my knees."

"Good," he says. "Now it's time for part two. Get on your feet."

He pulls me outside and makes me stand in the middle of the backyard in my underpants. The sun's going down and shines straight into my eyes. So I raise my hand to shield them from the glare while he goes to the garage and comes back outside carrying two buckets of water.

"Arms out to your sides," he barks.

He looks really scary in that moment, his face all twisted and red and his nostrils flared out to here. Almost like someone I've never seen before.

I stick out my arms, and he puts a bucket in each of my hands. They're crazy heavy, and I have no idea *how* I'm going to be able to hold them up for very long. But I do my best because I'm so tired of his yelling. I figure, the sooner this is over, the better. And so I hold the buckets.

As the sun goes down, I can see him digging a huge hole under the guava tree; when he's done he goes back into the garage and carries out a big wooden box; then he puts the box in the hole, covers it with dirt and chants some Buddhist stuff, lights incense, and disappears into the garage again. It keeps getting darker and darker. It gets so dark I have to squint to see the house. I have this terrible burning, tired feeling in my arms from holding those buckets. But worst of all, my stomach is rumbling and achy because I haven't eaten since lunch at Kevin's.

Just when I think I'm going to drop to the ground from exhaustion, buckets and all, *he* comes out of the garage, drags me back into the house, pushes me into my bedroom, and locks me inside. Thank God it's over, for now.

I climb into bed, pull the covers over my head and cry until my eyes feel like they're going to bleed. I cry from the burning pain in my arms that I think will never go away; I cry because I'm so fricking hungry, and I cry from how much I hate him, and Momma, too. And I swear that one day, when I'm a little older, I'll kill him.

I finally fall asleep to the image of me busting into his garage with a submachine gun and riddling him with bullets until he's a bloody, pulpy mess, and stomping on what's left of his face with Kevin's platform shoes until it looks like mashed potatoes covered in ketchup.

And then I dream.

I dream of a cowboy stretched out in an open-top truck, like the cowboy in the poster on Kevin's wall. Only, in my dream, it's not James Dean. It's Kevin. Music plays over the scene like in a movie, except instead of singing, I hear sobbing, and over the sobbing, I hear a lady screaming in the distance.

The cowboy wakes up, stretches his arms and legs, and lets out a big yawn. Then he sits up and takes off his hat and fans himself. Little streams of sweat trickle down the sides of his handsome face. He hops out of the truck and swaggers in the direction of a big poop-brown house in the distance, his spurs leaving blood-filled ruts in the dirt as he walks. The closer the cowboy gets to the house, the louder the sobbing gets.

I follow close behind as the cowboy climbs the creaky wooden steps to the front porch and pushes open the front door. Inside the foyer, gliding away from the open door is a woman with long black hair that reaches the middle of her back. She's wearing a tight, white ankle-length dress, with a rose-coloured sash wrapped around her waist. From where I'm standing the woman looks like Momma, only taller and shapelier, especially her bum. She glances over her shoulder at the cowboy and blows him a kiss, signalling for him to follow her with her middle finger, its red lacquered fingernail contrasting sharply against her pale skin. He steps into the house and pushes shut the door against my body, hard and steady against my chest, against my stomach, against my chinchin—especially against my chinchin. I hear Kevin's voice in my head saying: *The more you rub it, the better it feels.*

Somehow I can see through the door, and I watch as the cowboy reaches the woman. She holds him off with one hand while grabbing hold of her hair with the other, right where her forehead meets her hairline, and slowly peels it back. It's then I realise she's wearing a wig. Yanking it off, she kicks the wig into a corner and shakes out her blonde, shoulder-length hair, just as her face morphs from Momma's into Marilyn's, exactly as she looks in the picture Kevin gave me.

The woman grabs the cowboy and kisses him hard on the mouth. He wraps his arms around her waist and draws her against his chest; she pulls his shirt out of his jeans; he pushes back and rips it open, buttons flying everywhere, and flings it on the floor. Then they grab each other again and kiss some more.

The music gets louder, and so does the crying. It gets so loud that the cowboy and the woman stop their kissing and stare at the front door, at me and past me, wide-eyed and open-mouthed. I turn to see what they're looking at and find myself inside a darkened cinema crammed full of people watching a movie playing on a massive screen behind me. My parents are sitting in the back row of the cinema, my father leaning forward in his seat, and Momma snoring away next to him. Somehow I know they're watching *Rio Bravo*, a John Wayne movie about a drunk sheriff, a crippled boy, and a gunfighter who save their town from a bunch of criminals.

When the movie ends and the house lights come up, I follow my parents outside as they walk along Broadway. The Edison tower clock on Bunker Hill says it's already eleven o'clock at night. They're arguing about something all the way from the cinema to the two-dollar lot at the corner of Broadway and Third. Momma's face is all tight and scrunched, and she shakes her head as my father opens the passenger door and she clambers into her seat.

They speed home on the 110, and a CHP motorcycle cop pulls them over just as they're about to exit at Marengo. Momma buckles over and sobs into her hands as they wait for the *chippie* to write the ticket. My father reaches over and strokes her hair, but she pushes him away and beats on the dashboard with her fists. Finally, the chippie hands them the ticket and lets them go.

As they speed around the corner to come up our street, I see three Pasadena Police squad cars and an ambulance parked in front of our house, their red-and-blue flashing lights splitting the night. Momma screams when she sees them and launches herself from the truck, racing past our neighbours to the front door, just as the paramedics wheel a struggling young boy out of the house, strapped down on a gurney, blood streaming from the gashes he carved into his face.

Momma crumples to the ground.

And then I wake up.

Chapter 8

My pyjama bottoms are all wet, and I'm afraid I peed myself again. But it feels different this time, less cold and more sticky. So I reach down to touch my pyjama bottoms and bring my hand to my nose. It smells funny, like chlorine. I throw off the covers, switch on the light on my nightstand, peel down my pyjama bottoms, and find a bunch of sticky goo inside my underpants. And then I get scared. It came out of my chinchin, and some of the stuff is still oozing out. It's the cancer! It's here. The doctor was right!

I grab a white towel from my drawer and try to clean myself. But the stuff keeps oozing and oozing. And I feel like I'm going to pass out. I have to tell Momma so they can take me to the hospital before I die! I run to the door and try to open it, but it's still locked.

"Momma," I scream, pounding on the door. "Help, Momma! Help me, please!"

The room feels like it's spinning all around me, so I sit on the floor and keep pounding. After a while, I hear the door to Momma's bedroom open. My father is screaming something in the background, and then I hear their bedroom door close, and I can't hear him anymore. The sound of Momma's slippers padding down the hall toward my room calms me a little. Then the handle jiggles as she unlocks my door and pushes it open.

"What's this all about?" she asks, staring down at me. "Where are your pyjamas?"

"Momma, I don't know what happened … but my chinchin … something came out of my chinchin."

"Go clean yourself off and put on some fresh pyjamas."

"I tried cleaning it already. It won't stop."

"Clean it again … it'll stop."

"I'm scared, Momma. Am I going to die? Is it the cancer?"

"You'll be fine." She pulls me off the floor and leads me to my bed. "You can talk to your father about it in the morning."

"I don't want to talk to him!"

Momma takes a pair of clean underpants and pyjama bottoms from my dresser and drops them on my bed. Then she puts her hand on the top of my head, angles it over, and hisses into my ear. "No more commotion tonight, OK? We've had quite enough of you this weekend. Your father and I need to sleep now. It's a workday tomorrow."

"But, Momma!"

She walks out without answering and locks the door behind her. I check myself and see that the oozing stopped. So I put on the clean bedclothes, feeling relieved I'm not dying, and switch off the light.

I spend the rest of the night staring into the dark thinking about everything that's been happening to me. Everything is so confused in my head. My father hates me, that's for sure. He wishes Hiro were here instead of me.

Momma used to tell me I was a *gift child* for her after Hiro died. But she's not acting like that now. And my father definitely doesn't think of me that way. I once heard him tell the old, wrinkly monk from the Buddhist temple in J-Town that he thinks I have a bad spirit inside me, the same crazy spirit that made Hiro do what he did to himself. Maybe he's right; maybe I *do* have a spirit inside me. But it's not a bad one. The spirit inside me is sad sometimes, sometimes a bit angry, but mostly it likes to be hugged. And it likes nice music, bright colours, and stylish clothes. Every once in a while, the spirit inside me feels a little happy. But it's never bad, and it would *never* do what Hiro did.

At around five o'clock, the dawn light pushes into my bedroom, above, below, and between the moth-eaten *Sound of Music* drapes that've been hanging in here forever. I roll on my side and look around. It's so ugly in here. Why did my parents give me Hiro's bedroom? What were they thinking? That was their first mistake when they brought me home from the hospital. Every time they pass it, I'm sure they must feel like it's Hiro in here instead of me, which must make them sad and a little afraid. And why won't my father let me change it? I could make it look so much better, which might help them forget about the bad days with Hiro.

I sit up and imagine how my room would look if they let me redecorate it. The first thing I'd do is change out those vomit-green drapes for nice wooden blinds like in Kevin's room. Then I'd repaint the boring brown walls, maybe eggshell blue with cute little cherry appliques, and I'd hang a dancing mobile above my bed with sponge cherries to match the appliques. And that scratched up wooden floor! It has to go. I think maybe deep blue wall-to-wall shag carpet would look perfect with my new light blue walls and would feel soft under my bare feet. I'd want stylish furniture, too. Maybe a Frenchie-looking dresser with a round mirror over it and a comfy cushioned chair to sit in to look at myself. And on the mirror, I'd tape the picture of Marilyn and James Dean that Kevin gave me for my birthday.

Outside I hear the sound of the garage door creaking open. I peek through the curtains and watch as my father rolls two garbage bins from the garage to the kerb for the Monday morning collection. I wonder if my Marilyn picture is inside one of them. Somehow I have to get to them before the garbage truck arrives.

On a normal day, my father and I sit together in our kitchen and have a Momma-cooked breakfast of bacon, eggs, toast, and fresh-squeezed orange juice before he leaves for work at the car repair shop he owns with his friend Sam Higashi, and afterwards Momma and I spend time talking about stuff while we wash the dishes. Then we drive to the tuxedo rental and wedding dress shop we inherited from my father's parents, singing along to the music on the radio. But today is different.

At around six thirty in the morning, I hear the roar of my father's truck as he guns the engine in the garage. I look through the curtains and watch as he rumbles down the road on his way to work. Almost right away, I hear Momma's slippers shuffling down the hall toward my room and see the door handle jiggle as she turns the key on the other side. Then she pads away.

After my shower, I poke my head into the kitchen and see a box of cornflakes and an empty cereal bowl on the table. Momma is staring out the window at the backyard in a yellow housedress, which is not my favourite thing for her to wear, as it's not the right colour for her.

"Hello, Momma."

Momma turns and points at the refrigerator. I shrug and pull out the milk bottle and pour myself some cereal. Momma watches me from across the room without saying a word as I gulp down my breakfast and rinse the bowl.

"We're starting our Summer Clearance today," she says. "So, I'll need for you to be ready to concentrate."

"I don't feel well, Momma."

"You'll feel better once you get busy."

"I mean I feel sick."

Momma feels my forehead and looks inside my mouth. "You're not running a fever. But your throat does look a little red."

"Can I stay home today, Momma? Please!"

"Yes, that's fine. But I want you to rest and get better. I'll need your help with the Fall inventory before you start school again."

I wave goodbye to Momma from the front porch as she drives away in her station wagon, but she doesn't look at me. As soon as she turns the corner, I run to the garbage cans and rummage through them. The first one is full of smelly food scraps, empty tins, and dead leaves my father raked up last week. The second one is full of cardboard, and waste paper, and bottles, and plastic bags. I dig around in it for a while and hold my nose because it smells so bad.

As I get near the bottom of the can, just this close to retching from the stink, I spy a folded piece of paper caught under a section of thick rope wrapped tight around a black plastic bag. Grabbing the rope, I lift out the bag, and fall back on the driveway, taking in big gulps of fresh air. After a few seconds, I turn to the plastic bag and slide the piece of paper out from under the rope and unfold it. It's the Marilyn picture! I'm so excited to have found it that I bring it up to my mouth to kiss it. That's when I notice it stinks *really* bad, just like the stink inside the garbage can. And it's not just the picture. The plastic bag stinks, too, if not worse. Holding it as far away from myself as I can, I work to untie the rope. I struggle with it for a few minutes, pulling here and pulling there, when it suddenly comes free, sending the bag rolling down the driveway to the gutter.

In the distance, the garbage truck is rumbling down the street. So, I run to the gutter, which is running with water and dead leaves, and fish out the bag. I open it up, and the smell that comes out is so bad I have to turn my head away and blink a few times before looking back at it. Inside, stuffed between a bunch of bloodied paper towels, I find the stiffened body of a dead neko. Before I know it, my stomach explodes into my mouth, and I heave sour milk and cornflakes on the lawn, the driveway, and into the gutter. I try to stand, feeling really *really* sick, and heave again and again until nothing else comes out except something clear and slimy. Then I shove everything back into the garbage cans, finishing up just as the skinny Mexican garbage man, who's wearing denim overalls that are way too big for him, pulls up to the kerb in front of our house. He hops out of his truck, pats me on the head with his dirty glove, and dumps the stuff in the garbage cans into the back of his truck. Then he jumps back inside, lights up a cigar, tosses the still-burning match into the gutter, and winks at me as he drives to the next house.

As I roll the garbage cans up the driveway and into the garage, I think it doesn't make sense there should be a dead neko in the garbage can being that I *thought* I saw my father bury ███ under the guava tree, and we only had one neko. So once I'm inside the garage with the door closed, I dig around in my father's messy tool cupboards until I find a shovel, a crowbar, and a hammer and nails.

It takes me more than a half hour to dig the wooden box out of the dirt under the guava tree. It's still not even noon, so I have plenty of time to pry open the box and look inside, and to get it back into the ground and buried before my father gets home. Hopefully, he won't detect anything different.

To make sure nobody sees me, I drag the box into the bushes behind the guava tree and carefully pry it open with the crowbar so as not to break the wood. Once the top part is loose, I take a deep breath, lift off the cover, and look inside.

The first thing I find is a layer of old newspapers. I pull out the first few and glance through them. They're mainly about sports, especially baseball and Pasadena Little League. One of them has a section that looks like it was shaded in with a yellow highlighter, and I look closer at it. It's a little article about Hiro, about what a great shortstop he is, and about how he might be good enough for the high school team. There's even a picture of him in his uniform. And I wonder why my father would have buried it instead of keeping it to remember the good stuff about Hiro because not everything was bad. I put aside the paper and look through the others. They're all the same, highlighted or underlined bits here and there about games and scores and awards, all having to do with Hiro.

I reach into the box to pull out the rest of the newspapers and freeze when I see what's underneath them. It's an old, beat-up baseball mitt. Turning it over, I realise right away it's Hiro's old mitt, being that it's left-handed like Hiro was. I look inside the glove and find *This is Hiro Koba's mitt!* written under the heel pad with a blue marker in scribbly handwriting. My eyes get all teary. I don't know why. I didn't even know Hiro. But I feel sad, really sad, as sad as I've ever felt in my life, and I bring the mitt to my mouth and kiss Hiro's inscription.

I sit on the dirt and cry—for Hiro, for Momma, and for my father who loved Hiro so much. I cry for myself too, because I feel sure my life would be a lot happier if Hiro hadn't hurt himself and died. It makes me sad and mad at the same time. So, I look up at the sky, which is really pretty today—deep blue with white puffy clouds—wipe my face and nose, and try to think about something else.

A low-flying TWA aeroplane crosses the sky right above my head, coming in for a landing at LAX, the airport that's not too far from our house. I can hear its engine—it's *that* close—and I think about how I've never been on an aeroplane before. I promise myself that one day, when I have some money, I'll buy a ticket and fly somewhere, maybe to England with Kevin. We'll visit the London Bridge and the castle where the Queen of England lives, and we'll go see Big Ben, that big clock on top of the fancy building by the London river. Maybe Kevin will take me to the big country mansion his great-grandfather used to own before the family sold it because they ran out of money. I think it's a museum now. We might even stay long enough to start speaking with an English accent, the way Uncle Alistair and the Beatles do.

Finally, when I feel calm again, I turn back to the box and find more old newspapers inside. And under the newspapers, I see some brown paper bags. I pull out one of the bags. Inside it, I find a magazine with pictures of naked people. But not like the ones I found in Kevin's pencil drawer, which are just pictures of naked guys posing by themselves. These are pictures of men and ladies doing all kinds of dangerous-looking things to each other with ropes and whips and chains. There are lots and lots of these bags inside the box, and they all have the same kind of magazines inside. What are Hiro's things doing mixed up with these crazy magazines?

Reaching into the box, I pull out the rest of the bags and toss them aside. It's then that I find, at the very bottom of the box, *not* a dead neko. Instead, I find an old, dust-caked greyish flannel washcloth, all flat and stiff from being pressed under all those paper bags. I blink a few times and stare at it for a bit. Then I reach deep into the box, pull out the washcloth, shake it out, and see it's stained with dark brown splotches. In that instant, my mouth goes totally spitless; hot, dry air streams up my nose like a current of electricity and pierces my brain, and everything around me turns red, like blood.

And then I remember everything he did.

"I like to watch you bleed."

I remember my father leaning over me while I'm sitting in the bath, tears streaming down his dirt-covered face; I remember him pushing down on my head and holding me under; I remember struggling and splashing and holding my breath, trying really hard not to drown; I remember him yanking me back up and how I managed to squirm away; I remember running down the hallway screaming, naked and soaking wet, and slamming into Momma, who dropped the grocery bags on the floor when she saw me; and I remember us finding him in the bathroom, sitting on the floor, his back against the tub, his head slumped to one side, and blood all over the place from his wrists, which he'd slashed open with a shaving blade. And then...

I remember the paring knife he used on me. And the scar on the back of my leg.

And I PUSH it back. And everything goes ➜ ███ .

It's dark and warm and really quiet. I'm not really sure where I am. I'm not even sure *who* I am. I just know that I am. But I'm *not afraid*. The only thing I know is that it's dark and warm and quiet—and clammy on one side of my face.

After what seems like a zillion years, I hear a sound far away in the distance. At first, I can't make out what it is, being that it's so far away. I have to pay close attention. It sounds like whimpering, a bit like when a puppy is crying, but different. It's a sad sound, but the sadness doesn't touch me. It's there, and I hear it, the way you hear a sad song on the radio, but it's someone else's sadness, not mine.

The whimpering gets louder, almost like it's moving closer, and that's when I realise it's not a whimpering puppy at all. It's the sound of a little boy crying, like in my dream. But it's not me. It will never be me. Still, somehow I *know* the adults who were supposed to take care of the little boy have locked him in a room, have tied his arms to a bed, have turned off all the lights, and have left him in total darkness. And I know he's scared and sad because nobody loves him anymore. I know all this, but I won't let it touch me. I'll *never* let it touch me again. And then the crying stops.

I open my eyes and find myself laying on my side in the dirt, surrounded by newspapers, magazines, and paper bags. I turn my head and see the wooden box, with Hiro's mitt and the other thing next to it. I sit up and rub my eyes and look at the sky. The sun is a lot lower now, so I figure I must have been passed out for a while.

In the distance, I hear our kitchen telephone ringing and ringing. So I sprint to the house and answer it. It's Momma. She tells me she's been calling the house every hour for the past three hours, trying to get hold of me, and was almost ready to call the police. I lie to her and tell her I went for a walk. I don't think she believes me because I never go for walks by myself. But at least she's relieved to hear I'm OK.

Once she hangs up, I run to the backyard and pile everything into the wooden box, everything except Hiro's mitt and *the other thing*, which I'm going to keep somewhere safe. I nail the box shut and drag it back to the hole and drop it inside. Then I spend the next hour making sure I cover it up like it was before.

I take a few steps back and look at the spot from halfway across the yard, the shovel still in my hand. It definitely doesn't look the same as before I dug up the box. So I go back and do some more work. But, no matter how much I try raking the dirt this way and that, I can't make it look exactly the same as before. Also, I left some ruts in the dirt from when I dragged the box behind the bushes, which I can't completely erase.

After several more tries, I throw down the shovel. *Screw it* if it's not perfect. If my father notices something, he's more likely to get scared than to get mad. And thinking that way makes me feel stronger. So I pick up the tools and put them away in the garage. Then I come back and grab Hiro's mitt and *the thing*, pop back into the house and hide them in the bottom of my book bag. Then I jump in the shower to wash off the dirt.

That afternoon when my father gets home, he goes straight from the garage to the backyard, like I knew he would. I watch from the kitchen window as he moves across the weeds to where the box is buried and stands there for a while, staring down at the dirt. My heart pounds really hard inside my chest, and I breathe deep to calm it down. My father sways a bit, and, for a moment, it looks like he's going to fall over. But then he reaches out a hand and steadies himself against the guava tree. After a bit, he pulls a long, blue-and-red box out of his back pocket that I recognise as a box of temple incense. He taps it against the palm of his hand, slides out a couple of incense sticks, fires up his Zippo, and lights both of them at the same time. Then he kneels in the dirt, pushes them into the ground, and hangs his head over the bluish smoke wafting heavenward from the sticks.

Almost from out of nowhere, Momma glides up to my father's side to join him in front of the incense sticks. He looks up at her as she gently strokes his head, then stands and holds her hand. The two of them bow in the direction of the smoking incense sticks and bob around a bit, chanting something Buddhist, I figure. Finally, as the sun dips, they turn around and slowly walk back to the house, holding hands.

Poor Momma, I think, as I run to my room and close the door behind me. *Poor all of us: Momma, Hiro, and Me.* I sit on my bed, pulling up my legs and crossing them Indian-style. Everyone knows my father is a big drunk. But nobody, except me, knows how bad he really is. But they will.

I stretch out on my bed, look up at the ceiling, and smile. Like Mrs Worthington said, I'm a manifestor. I make things happen. And that's exactly what I'm going to do.

Chapter 9

I decide to keep out of my father's way the rest of the summer before I go back to school, now that I know he's bad. I tell Momma this, but not the real reason why. She agrees keeping out of his way is the best plan for making things peaceful at home. So I don't eat breakfast with the two of them anymore. And I have my dinner before he gets home. And after dinner, I go to my room and read boring magazines and plan how I'm going to get him out of our lives forever. Even though I hear him clomping up and down the hall, I don't see him, and he doesn't come to see me. Best of all, he hasn't come home drunk lately.

Most of the rest of August, I work with Momma at the dress shop helping her with the tux rentals and stuff. Weekends I spend at Auntie Doreen's with Kevin and Maggie.

At first, Kevin and I think I'm going to get to sleep in his bedroom, being that he has a huge bed and lots of space in his closet. Perfect, right? But Auntie won't let me! Instead, she makes up a room for me right next to hers.

"It's better for Kimi to sleep in his own bed," she says to Kevin and nods her head at me, "like he does at home."

But I'm wondering if maybe she suspects something. Like, the other day, when Kevin and I were talking on the phone, I was right in the middle of telling him about the night the white goo came out of my chinchin (Kevin says it's called *aieki*) when suddenly I heard a click on the line. I asked Kevin if he'd heard anything, and he said no. But now I wonder if Auntie Doreen might have picked up the phone and listened to what we were saying. Anyway, aside from separating us at night, I don't notice anything different about the way Auntie treats me, and she lets Kevin and me hang around together as much as we want to in the daytime. So maybe I'm wrong.

On Saturdays, I go with them to their church on Lincoln Avenue, which is called Seventh-day Adventist. I mostly like it, except we see Ryo Murakawa there, who I can't stand. He wants to sit with us because Kevin and him are friends now on account of the James Dean stuff Kevin buys from him. Kevin wants me to be friends with Ryo, too, because we're in the same class. But I don't really want to because even though he's nicer to me than he used to be, I think he's a mean person deep inside. Still, to make Kevin happy, I pretend I like him. I even promise to go to his birthday party in September.

Since Auntie Doreen and Uncle Alistair are home most of the time on the weekend, Kevin and I have to be super careful when we're up in his room, because we never know when his parents or Maggie might suddenly show up. So, we mostly listen to albums and read books, and we sneak a kiss whenever we can.

The one thing I notice is that Kevin doesn't talk so much about girls anymore, which reminds me about the pictures I found in his pencil drawer. And I wonder if I'm right about what I thought—that Kevin likes guys. So one afternoon after we get back from church, I decide to ask him about it, hoping he won't get mad.

"Kevin," I say, as we're sitting on the floor of his room leafing through the latest copies of *Tiger Beat* with our backs against his waterbed and our feet stretched out in front of us. "When I was here on my birthday—"

He sets aside his magazine and looks at me.

"Remember when you left me alone up here?"

Kevin sits up on his knees. "Of course, I remember. What about it?"

"I found something"—I point at his desk—"in there."

Kevin stands, stretches his legs, and walks over to his desk. "Besides the pukka shell necklace, you mean?" He pulls out the drawer, not taking his eyes from me.

"Yeah, besides that."

He reaches inside and pulls out the picture of David Cassidy and holds it out to me. The lower part is scissored off so you can't tell it was a naked picture before.

"Not just that one," I say.

He pushes the drawer closed and sits next to me again, handing me the picture. I take it out of his hand and lay it upside down on the carpet.

"I got rid of the others," he says. "Stuck them in a cave on the Cobb Estate. I was afraid my mom would find them."

"You're not mad I saw them?"

Kevin shakes his head. "It's OK."

We sit quietly for a while, both of us staring straight ahead like we're waiting for something to happen. Finally, Kevin lets out a long breath, then turns his head and flashes a half-grin.

"I thought you liked girls," I say.

Kevin shrugs.

"You like guys?"

"Maybe." He reaches up and pulls his hair away from his face, then he digs in his pocket and brings out a black velvet scrunchie, which he uses to make a ponytail. "We'll see."

I lay my head on his lap, and he reaches down and strokes my hair. I want to tell him I love him. But I don't want to sound stupid. So I keep it to myself and hope he loves me too.

The Sunday before he's supposed to leave for England, I sit on Kevin's bed and watch him pick out the clothes he's going to take with him. Even though he's there in front of me, it feels like he's slipping away, and there's nothing I can do about it. Just as he pulls out his suitcase from his closet and opens it up, a really sad song called *Angie* comes on the radio. Something about the singing makes me pay close attention to the words. They make me feel like I have a big hole in my stomach, and I start to cry. I try to hold back the tears so Kevin doesn't notice, but he does. He closes the suitcase and sits next to me, putting his arm around my shoulder and letting me rest my head against his chest.

"Don't worry, little cuz," he says. "We're only going for a visit to please my mom. There's no draft anymore. So there's no reason for me to stay there."

"I'm afraid I won't see you anymore, Kev."

"That's not going to happen. I promise." He kisses me on the mouth, the same way he did in the Enchanted Forest. And I kiss him back. Then he holds me while I cry some more. I feel so close to Kevin, closer and more loved than I've ever felt to anyone before and safer than I've ever felt in my whole life.

Afterwards, he gives me a ring with a blue turquoise stone he got in New Mexico. He tells me he loves me and swears on his life he'll come back. And I believe him. But I'm *not* going to tell him I love him until he comes back from England.

I wake up with a start and see it's still dark outside. Kevin's snoring softly, face down on the bed. It's cold, so I pull the blanket over him. Then I look at the glowing clock radio on the nightstand. I'm surprised to see it's already four in the morning. I have to hurry and get back to my room before the rest of them wake up. So I snuggle up to Kevin and kiss him on his forehead and on his mouth, then I hurry downstairs.

I slide down the ladder, sprint toward the landing that leads to the floors below, and come *this close* to slamming into Auntie

Doreen, who's standing in the shadows at the top of the stairs. She steps into the soft light coming from the utility room that illuminates the hall, and I notice her face is all red. I try to run around her, but she reaches out, catches me by the scruff of my neck, and pulls me into the utility room.

"I'm sorry, Auntie," I blurt out before she can say anything. "I lost track of time and fell asleep."

Auntie Doreen glares at me and opens her mouth like she's about to scream when suddenly everything goes frozen like in those movies where time stops, and people who were walking down the sidewalk suddenly halt in mid-stride, and aeroplanes hang motionless in the sky.

I move out of the utility room, stepping away from Auntie Doreen, with her wide-open eyes and gaping mouth, and away from myself, crouching in a corner staring up at her with my hands over my ears. And I wonder how long she was standing in the hallway before I came downstairs. I mean, was she there the whole time? Or was she just coming up when I ran into her? Either way, I figure I'm in big trouble.

The next thing I know, I'm back inside the utility room with Auntie Doreen, who's slumped in a chair, her head resting against the wall. "Go to your room, Kimi," she's saying in a soft voice. She looks like she's about to cry, which is scary because Auntie Doreen never gets sad.

I move closer to her and whisper: "I'm sorry, Auntie. We weren't doing anything bad, I promise."

Auntie Doreen looks away from me and stares at the wall for a few seconds, then closes her eyes. "Just go, please," she whispers.

The next morning, Momma shows up really early and whispers in a corner with Auntie Doreen while I eat a cold breakfast on the island in the kitchen. Neither Kevin nor Maggie comes downstairs. I can see Uncle Alistair through the window, washing one of his sports cars. He said hello to me before he went outside, but he wasn't smiling like he usually does. So I know something's wrong.

When I get into Momma's station wagon, I look up at Kevin's room and see him looking down at me from his window. I wave at him, and he lifts his hand and rests it against the window. He's mouthing something to me, but I can't make out what he wants to say.

"Turn around in your seat and face straight ahead," Momma says, and I obey her. I steal a quick glance back up at the window as Momma drives away, but Kevin's not there anymore.

On the way home, I keep expecting Momma to say something. But she doesn't. Instead, she rolls down the window, turns on the radio, and starts to sing along to a stupid Carpenters song, smiling and waving at people as we drive by, almost like she's in some other story. By the time the song is over, I realise she's just going to pretend nothing happened, the way she always does.

Chapter 10

My sixth-grade teacher, Miss Johnson, likes for me to sit in the front row of the classroom. She tells me in private that I'm her pet student because I'm so smart. But I don't believe she's being totally honest, because I'm not all that smart. I think maybe she wants me to sit close to her so she can gawk at me since I look different from my classmates, who are all white, except for Ryo, who sits behind me. But who cares about him anyway!

This year I have a better desk than all the other years before. It's one of those where you can swivel open the part you write on and store things inside. And it has a little lock so you can keep all your stuff private. Inside my desk, I keep my English book and my maths book, a writing pad, some number 2 pencils, a couple of leaky pens, an orange plastic ruler and matching protractor, and a calendar from our dress shop. I've circled Sunday, September 16, 1973, which is the day Kevin's coming back from England, and I'm putting little "x"s in the date boxes as each day passes. Underneath all that are the ring and the picture of Marilyn that Kevin gave me.

One of the first assignments Miss Johnson gives us is to write a report about someone famous, like Abraham Lincoln, or Martin

Luther King, or Jesus. We're supposed to go to the library and find books about whomever we're writing about and write a summary of their life. Not their *whole* life, because that would take forever. But some interesting part most people might not know about. We're meant to fill five pages, which Miss Johnson says is around a thousand, five hundred words, and we're also supposed to give a speech about our famous person to share with the rest of the class. I'm going to write my report about Marilyn, about how she became famous, or maybe about how she was having sex with the president, or maybe about how the CIA killed her—if that's even true.

There's nothing in the school library about Marilyn, and the librarian recommends I go to the Pasadena Central Public Library on East Walnut Street, right across from the courthouse. She does me a favour and calls her librarian friend there, who sets aside a couple of books and some magazines and newspapers for me. I'll have Momma take me there after school because it's too far for me to walk from here, and way too far from home.

"Why are you writing about *her*?" Momma asks all surprised-like when I explain the assignment. "Why not write about someone important like President Kennedy or General MacArthur?"

"She's important to *me*," I say. "Miss Johnson told us we should write about someone we already like because we'll do our best work that way. Susie Meier's writing about Bonny and Clyde, and Spencer Shapiro's writing about Sandy Koufax, and Jill Spivens is writing about David Bowie, and Ryo Murakawa is writing about Charles Manson. So, I'm going to write about Marilyn."

Momma parks her station wagon across the street from the Central Library, which is in a beautiful building that reminds me of the Spanish Mission our fifth-grade class visited in San Juan Capistrano. I grab my book bag out of the back seat, and Momma takes my hand as we cross the street as if I were some kind of baby. She's going to stay in the library reading a magazine in the corner while I do my research because she thinks I'm too young to be alone.

The research librarian hands me a stack of books and magazines and points me in the direction of a cubicle. The first thing I find is a book about Marilyn's life that's supposedly written in her own words. It has a really cool picture of her on the cover, sitting all flirty-like on a wooden stool, wearing a tight black skirt that ends right above her knees, and an open green blouse with her boobies practically falling out of a lacy white bra thing, and a pair of black pumps. She's leaning forward over her bare legs, her hands balled up like fists on either side of her knees, with her head raised up kind of proud. Her eyes are half-closed, which gives her a funny Asian look, and I laugh at the thought of a Japanese Marilyn. The more I stare at that picture, the more I'm convinced how perfect she is.

I flip through all the great pictures—there are *so* many—and wish I owned the book so I could cut them all out and pin them on my wall, especially the ones where she's blonde, not the ones where she has dark hair, like before she dyed it. But, of course, I can't do that while my father's still around. So, instead, until I can get rid of him, I'll just borrow the book from the library and keep it in my desk at school so I can look at the pictures anytime I want. And, I think, maybe when I go to Ryo's house for his birthday, I can score my very own signed glossy of Marilyn for ten bucks, like Kevin did of James Dean.

I turn back to the front of the book and start to read a little, about how Marilyn was born in Los Angeles (same as me), and how her mother was a dancer who went crazy and couldn't take care of her, and how poor Marilyn was raised in other people's houses because of her crazy mother, and about how she got married a couple of times before she became famous. Boring!!! The pictures are way better than the story.

So I put aside the book and pick up a newspaper with Marilyn's face completely covering the front page and the words 'Marilyn

Dead' at the top in big letters. The newspaper is dated August 5, 1962. I blink a couple times and look at the date again. That's what it really says. August 5, 1962! That's my birthday! Something inside me goes tight, and I jump out of the chair, knocking it backwards, and I bend over and draw a few deep breaths because I feel like I'm going to pass out.

"Young man, are you all right?" an old blue-haired lady with a cane asks me. She leans her cane against the cubicle and rubs my back.

Another couple of people come running up to me. Don't ask me what they look like, because I'm not paying much attention at this point. What I *do* notice is that one of them picks up the chair and scoots it back into the cubicle, and the other one leads me to a comfy sofa next to the window. The research librarian runs up and hands me a cup of water, which I gulp down in one go.

"I'm OK," I say, waving them all away. "Sorry. I just…"

"Where's your mother?" the librarian asks.

"Over there by the magazines. But don't call her, please. I'm OK, I promise. I only felt a little dizzy for a second." I point at the cubicle. "I need to get back to my research." I stand and move to the cubicle.

The librarian stares at me and nods, then marches in the direction of the magazine section, which means he's going to get Momma. I grab the newspaper and read really fast about how Marilyn died: Her maid called Marilyn's doctor at three in the morning because she thought something was wrong with her. The doctor went there right away and found Marilyn dead on her bed, totally naked with empty bottles of sleeping pills on the floor. They figure she died just after midnight and had been lying boobs-up in bed for a couple of hours.

I push aside the newspaper and close my eyes. I feel so bad for poor Marilyn. Some people think it was an accident. But I *know* it wasn't. She was just sad, really sad. Even though she was famous, and lots of people loved her, nobody knew how sad she really was, and that she just wanted it all to be over. But I know.

"What time was I born, Momma?" I ask, clutching my book bag against my chest as she speeds home.

Momma looks at me out of the corner of her eye. "Why on earth did you *do* that back there, baby?" She swerves to avoid hitting a boy on a scooter and guns it down Marengo. "You nearly scared me to death!"

"I didn't do it on purpose! It just *happened*." I kick the glove box a couple of times.

"Stop that!" Momma slaps my arm really hard, and I pull back my foot.

"What *time* was I born?"

"I don't remember." Momma glares at me really mean-like and quickly looks back at the road as she reaches the traffic signal, which is turning red.

"Was it in the morning?"

Momma pulls her big Jackie O sunglasses out of her purse, slips them on, and looks away from me.

"It's night-time, Momma. Take those off."

The light changes back to green and Momma speeds down the road, still wearing her stupid sunglasses. Tears roll down her cheeks.

"Fine! I'll ask Auntie Doreen."

Momma swerves to the right, pulls to the side of the road, and yanks up the parking brake. "Ask her what exactly?"

"What time I was born. She was there, wasn't she?"

"Who told you that?"

"She did! She told me she was in the delivery room with you when I was born because Father wasn't there. And she told me the midwife screamed when she saw me."

Momma yanks off her sunglasses, shoves them back in her purse, and lowers her forehead to the steering wheel.

"Is it true, Momma?"

Momma lifts her head from the steering wheel and nods.

"Why did the midwife scream?"

Momma sits up and clears her throat. "She apologised for that." She turns her head and looks straight at me. "She came by the house a few days later and apologised. She said you'd stared at her with knowing eyes, not the eyes of a newborn baby, and that scared her. But she said she was sorry."

"I remember that, Momma."

Momma squints at me, and her mouth turns down at the sides. "You remember what?"

"I remember someone screaming, a lady, real loud. I hear her all the time, especially when I dream."

"That's nonsense. Nobody remembers anything from when they were born."

"What *time* was I born, Momma?"

"Early in the morning." Momma shakes her head. "I don't remember exactly. But it was very early. Why?"

"Was it before three in the morning?"

"I was admitted around midnight, and you came almost right away. So, yes, before three. What's this all about?"

I reach into my book bag and pull out the newspaper from the library and hand it to her. She switches on the reading light and looks at the front page and at the big letters above the picture of Marilyn that say *Marilyn Dead*.

"Look at the date."

She peers at the date under the words *Daily News*.

"It says Sunday, August 5, 1962," I say.

Momma nods.

"That's the day I was born, isn't it?"

Momma nods again.

I take the newspaper out of her hands and turn over the page to the main story and point to where it says they think Marilyn died after midnight, and that they found her dead body at three in the morning. "See that?"

Momma pulls the newspaper closer to her face, because the letters are small, and reads for a couple of minutes. Then she hands it back to me.

"It's not Hiro whose spirit is inside me, Momma."

Momma's head snaps in my direction when I say Hiro's name.

"It's not Hiro." I stick the newspaper back into my book bag. "It's Marilyn."

Chapter 11

All of us clap when Spencer finishes his speech about Sandy Koufax, a handsome baseball hero who used to pitch for the Dodgers. Sandy Koufax is Jewish and left-handed like Spencer, which are a couple of the reasons Spencer picked him. Spencer's a great speaker and a super good actor too, and everyone loves that he played out bits of Sandy Koufax's life.

As Spencer makes his way back to his desk, slapping our hands as he Gumbies down the aisle, Miss Johnson calls me to the front of the classroom to make my presentation. At the last minute, I decide to give my speech as if it's Marilyn who's talking, the way Spencer sort of did with Sandy Koufax, which I think will make it a lot more interesting.

I skip to the front of the room and plop my book bag down on a table. Then I pull out the newspaper and walk from one side of the classroom to the other, all swishy like, holding it up so everyone can see Marilyn's face on the front page. After that, I crawl up on the stool next to the table, put aside the newspaper, grab my notes, and cross my legs the way Marilyn does on the cover of the book about her life. A few of the kids giggle, and Ryo blows a raspberry, which makes Miss Johnson snap her fingers in the air and say, "Now everyone, please quiet down," or something adulty like that.

"Good afternoon, ladies and gentlemen," I say with as breathy a voice I can make, trying to sound the way Marilyn does in her movies.

"Good afternoon!" Ryo blurts out like a dumbhead. Miss Johnson claps her hands at him, and he sits up straight in his chair and salutes her as if she were an army sergeant. "Sorry, chief," he says with a quick shrug.

"*Anyway...*" I say, "you all know me as Marilyn Monroe, the movie star. But my real name, the name my crazy Momma gave me when I was born, is Norma Jean Mortenson. Mortenson was my Momma's second husband's last name. He dumped her before she got preggie with me. But she stuck me with *his* name anyway and just *pretended* that Mortenson was my father. I think she did that because she didn't want people to know who my real father was. The truth is, I don't think Momma had any idea who my real father was."

A few kids giggle, but less than before.

"Before I was born, and *before* she married Mortenson, Momma was married to *another* man whose last name was Baker. She had two kids with him. But he ended up dumping her, too, and took their two kids with him back to Kentucky, which was where he was from.

"It would have been nice to know I had a half-brother and half-sister, but Momma never told me about them. She just kept all that stuff secret from me, and I had to find out about it after I grew up. One day, out of the clear blue sky, Momma announced she wanted people to start calling me Norma Jean Baker instead of Norma Jean Mortenson, which was totally confusing, being that I didn't know who Baker was at the time. But that's the name that eventually stuck for a while."

I glance up from my notes. Most of my classmates are leaning forward now and listening to me, which makes me feel a little less self-conscious. Even Ryo is leaning forward, squeezing his eyebrows together and making his eyes small, which I guess means he's interested, too.

"Anyway, Momma eventually went completely bonkers, and I was taken away from her by, um, the police, I guess. They locked her in the big nuthouse in Norwalk, the same place they put away Clyde's brother, Hiro. And they stuck *me* in an orphanage, which made me feel super sad, like nobody wanted me. After a while, they decided to send me to a bunch of different foster homes all around Los Angeles. Most of them were awful, and I cried all the time because I didn't have a real family like regular kids.

"The worst foster home they sent me to was one where the foster dad was a total perv and did naughty stuff to me, which I hated. He said I'd get in trouble if I told the police, so I didn't. Instead, I asked the social worker to move me to a different foster home, which took a while for her to arrange. But it eventually happened, and that's how I got away from the perv. Finally, as soon as I turned sixteen, I married a twenty-one-year-old guy named Jimmy who lived next door, just to get away from all the bouncing around from home to home.

"A year after we got married, they shipped Jimmy off to fight in the war, and he dumped me on his parents, which I didn't like. It was like being in foster care again, only worse. So I ran away from them and decided to support myself by modelling since I was pretty. At first, nobody paid much attention to me. Then a girlfriend of mine convinced me to straighten my hair and dye it blonde, which looked a lot better than the curly dark brown hair I was born with. And that's when *everybody* started noticing me.

"My name changed a few more times before I became famous, but finally, some boss from the movie studio told me I had to stick with one name because it was better for my career. So he picked the name *Marilyn Monroe* for me because it sounded nice and, according to him, was way easier to remember than *Norma*

Jean, being that both the first name and last name started with the same letter. Once that was agreed, the studio bosses didn't let me change my name anymore. Even though I married, like, a gazillion guys, including the baseball hero Joe DiMaggio, the studio bosses wouldn't allow me to take their last names the way most American ladies get to, and this made my husbands mad and eventually leave me.

"So, fast forwarding to the important bit, I made a bunch of Hollywood movies and became super famous because I was the prettiest and most perfect lady in the whole world. People invited me to eat in the best restaurants, and I got to travel to the best cities like London and Paris and Miami for free, and famous designers like Chanel and Gucci and Yves Saint Laurent sent their latest outfits for me to wear whenever I went out (even though I preferred to throw on cut-off blue jeans and boy's shirts at home), and *everyone* loved me. Even President Kennedy's movie star brother-in-law Peter, uh"—I glance at my notes—"—Lawford, he loved me for a while when I was between husbands. After he was finished loving me, he introduced me to President Kennedy's brother, Bobby, who also loved me for a while. Finally, Bobby introduced me to his big brother, President Kennedy himself, who I really *really* loved because he was, like, totally handsome and more famous than me.

"President Kennedy and I became secret friends. Not even his wife, Jackie, knew about us, being that President Kennedy was good at keeping secrets and had a few best friends who helped cover up for him so Jackie wouldn't find out. Everything was going so nicely between us that after a while I imagined maybe he would leave Jackie and marry me instead so I could become First Lady. But some bad people found out about our secret friendship and were really mad about that, especially the spies in the CIA, the same spies who were trying to kill Fidel Castro in Cuba. They forced President Kennedy to stop being my secret friend, which made me *super* sad, as if all the sadness I ever felt in my whole life were suddenly bundled all together in one place and just exploded in my heart, like the A-bombs that wasted Hiroshima and Nagasaki and everyone who lived there, only worse. *I just couldn't take it.*

"So"—I hop off the stool and grab the newspaper from the table—"on August fifth, nineteen sixty-two, at around midnight, I washed down a bunch of sleeping pills with a bottle of whiskey to *try* and kill myself." I hold the newspaper high in one hand.

"What do you mean she *tried* to kill herself?" Susie Meier yells out from the back of the room. "She *did* kill herself, didn't she?"

Melissa Anderson, who is sitting in the front row, points at the newspaper and says, "She definitely did! It says *Marilyn Dead* right there."

Tony Lopez raises his hand and blurts out, "My dad told me the CIA killed her."

I bring my forefinger in front of my mouth, bend toward them, and make a *shhh* sound, and they all quiet down.

"*All things are recycled,*" I say. "That's what the monk from the temple in J-Town says."

I reach into my book bag, pull out an official-looking blue document, and hold it high. "I *tried* to kill myself. But karma didn't let me go." I move from one side of the classroom to the other, shaking the document at them. "*This* is the proof."

"What is it?" Spencer asks.

"It's a birth certificate for somebody who was born on the *same day*, at the *same time*, as the day and time I supposedly died."

"Whose birth certificate?" Miss Johnson asks.

"Yeah, whose is it?" Ryo calls out.

"*This*"—I shake the blue certificate at them again—"is Clyde Koba's birth certificate." I bring the newspaper and the birth certificate together and hold them up in one hand. "Like I said, I *tried* to kill myself. But as my spirit was leaving my body, karma recycled it into Clyde's body, right as he was being born. And that's how I got here today."

When I finish, the room goes quiet for what feels like a million years. Some of the kids look at each other and throw little glances my way, others whisper, and others stare at me like I'm some kind of weird space alien, all of which makes me hot and sweaty, the way I feel when Momma catches me doing something wrong. Then Spencer stands up and starts to clap and say *yes yes yes*, and the rest of them follow along. Some of them even whistle and cheer. Miss Johnson smiles too, nodding her head, and writing down something in her notebook while saying, "Excellent, Clyde, excellent!"

So I flutter my eyelashes and curtsy like a girl, which makes the kids laugh, and I take a bow like a boy, shove all my stuff back in my bag, and sashay to my desk blowing kisses at everyone.

Ryo slaps my back as I lock my book bag in my desk. "That was great, dude. Really good," he whispers.

"Thanks, Ryo." I can't stand it when Ryo touches me. But since he's been less of a jerk to me lately, and since Kevin wants us to be friends, I let him. But it's not easy. Whenever I feel his hand dancing on my shoulder, it makes me want to jump right out of my chair.

"You're still coming over for my birthday party on Sunday, right?"

"What, *this* Sunday?"

"Yeah, remember? You told me you'd come."

"Um, I don't know. That's the same day Kevin's coming back. Plus, I haven't asked my Momma yet."

"Boys, please pipe down," Miss Johnson says. "It's Marianne's turn."

I look up and see Marianne Leatherall standing at the front of the classroom dressed in a potato sack and holding a guitar. I have no idea who she's going to talk about, but it doesn't look very interesting, so I plaster on a fake smile and pretend to listen to her so she doesn't feel bad. But Ryo keeps nattering on behind me in a loud, annoying whisper.

"Dude, you *have* to come. It'll be fun."

"Maybe," I say out of the corner of my mouth.

"Now that I know you're into Marilyn Monroe, I have a bunch of stuff to show you. Collectables from my dad's shop."

I whip around in my seat. "Do you have a signed picture?"

Chapter 12

Momma stays quiet when she drives me to Ryo's place for his birthday party on Sunday. She doesn't turn on the radio to sing along to the music the way she usually does, she drives slowly on side streets instead of on the main roads, and she doesn't say a word. It's not like she's mad at me, or anything like that. When she's *mad* at me, she gets this deep crease between her eyebrows and presses her lips together until they turn white, and she looks away from me. Oh, and she also plays the radio blaringly loud, which is her way of yelling at me. But today she's just quiet and sighing a lot.

"What's wrong, Momma?"

Momma looks at me and shakes her head. I think back to earlier that morning to try and figure out why she's acting this way. I guess she was a little quiet at breakfast, too, but not as much as now. The only thing I remember is the telephone rang late last night as I was dozing off, and I heard Momma talking to someone for a while, even though I couldn't make out what she was saying.

"Who called last night, Momma?"

Momma pulls up in front of Ryo's house, leans over, and kisses me. "Don't worry about anything, baby. Momma's fine. Everything will be fine."

Now I'm *sure* Momma is hiding something. But I figure I can find out about it later. Right now, Ryo is waving at me from his front porch. "Pick me up at three, Momma." I grab Ryo's birthday present and jump out of the car without waiting for her to answer.

Even though I'm keen to see Ryo's dad's collection of Marilyn stuff, I'm way more excited about Kevin coming home later today. I've been missing him so much for the past few weeks. When he first went away, it was like someone ripped my heart from my body, especially since Auntie Doreen wouldn't let us talk to each other after she caught me coming out of his room that last night. At first, I cried a lot and wasn't sleeping very well. Then I had nightmares about my father and about Hiro and about the screaming lady. The only thing that saved me from going mad was my Marilyn project. Once I figured out that her spirit is inside me, and once I found out she tried to kill herself because of how sad she got from missing President Kennedy (the way I was missing Kevin), I decided I had to be strong for both of us—for Marilyn *and* for me—so that the same thing wouldn't happen to her again.

Ryo leads me through his house, which is a little bigger than ours, but in a nicer neighbourhood, and takes me into the kitchen. His mom is finishing putting two fat candles on his birthday cake, one in the shape of a number *one* and the other in the shape of a number *two*. The cake is brown with yellow frosting, and Ryo's name is spelt out on top in Japanese.

"Hi, Mrs Murakama," I say. Ryo's mom turns around and wipes her hands on her apron, and I bow to her. Even though Mrs Murakama's English is way worse than Momma's, she wears more modern American-style clothes, like stretch pants and halter-tops, being that she's about ten years younger than Momma. And she does up her hair in an afro, which I think looks ridiculous.

"Welcome, Koba-san." She points out the window to their backyard, where Ryo's dad is barbecuing something next to a wooden picnic table covered in a red-and-white chequered plastic tablecloth. "We'll be having lunch in twenty minutes."

Ryo takes me to his room and sits on his bed, which is covered by a comforter and pillows with the same pattern as the Partridge Family bus, a bunch of red, yellow, and blue squares of different sizes, connected by black lines on a white background. I glance around the room and notice lots of Partridge Family stuff, posters, album covers, and even a Partridge Family wall clock. I try hard not to roll my eyes, and I hand Ryo his birthday present.

"Thanks, Clyde!" He rips off the wrapping paper and uncovers the cardboard box.

"Where are the other kids?" I ask as he holds the box to his ear and shakes it a few times.

"What other kids?" Ryo tears open one end of the box and peers inside.

"For your birthday party."

"You're the only one." He slides out the red-and-blue clip-on necktie Momma bought for him and stares at it for a second. "Is this for real?" he asks, the tie dangling from his fingers.

"Matches your bedspread," I say with a shrug.

"Thanks." Ryo stuffs the tie back in the box and throws it behind his bed in a typical Ryo jerk-like way.

"I thought you invited me to a party. One person isn't a party."

"Don't worry, we'll have fun, just like Kevin does whenever he comes over. Plus, I have that Marilyn stuff to show you after lunch."

We spend the next hour with Ryo's parents at the picnic table in their backyard, eating stuff like barbecued fish, steamed rice, pickled vegetables, and 7 Up. They do their best to make it seem as much of a party as possible for Ryo, passing out pointy birthday hats and playing the Japanese birthday song *Otanjoubi Omedetou* over and over on an eight-track player until I think I'm going to lose my mind.

After a while, the wind kicks up and blows the paper plates off the table. So Mrs Murakawa moves us inside to sing

American Happy Birthday to Ryo in the kitchen, and we have some melty vanilla ice cream and some not-so-good chocolate cake. Then Ryo's dad, whom I never met before today and who is *way* too jolly for my taste, makes each of us sing karaoke songs. He belts out a tired one from the 1950s called *My Way*, Mrs Murakawa slaughters *I Wanna Hold Your Hand* by the Beatles, I sing *Puppy Love* by Donny Osmond, and Ryo wraps up the whole crazy thing with *I Think I Love You* by the Partridge Family.

As Mrs Murakawa puts everything away, Ryo's dad calls me into the family room and shows me all the amazing Marilyn Monroe stuff he has there: vintage magazines in plastic protectors, a real spicy signed picture of Marilyn wearing a fuzzy white sweater hanging off her shoulder, and a couple of framed posters from a movie called *Bus Stop*. He tells me there's a lot more at his shop on Hollywood Boulevard and that I'm welcome to visit anytime. I'm so amazed by everything he's showing me, and I wish I had enough money to buy it all. But then I remember that even if I had a trillion dollars my father would *never* let me put up any of it, which makes me mad and more determined to get rid of him.

"You can have the signed picture if you want it," Ryo says after his father leaves us alone in the family room. He slides the picture out of its paper frame and holds it out to me, flashing a big grin.

I look at the picture and at him. "It's not yours."

Ryo shakes it at me. "Just take it. My dad won't mind."

"He didn't offer it to me when he was here."

"It's OK. He knows I sometimes give stuff to my friends. Like the one of James Dean I gave to Kevin."

"Kevin paid you for that."

"No, he didn't."

"He told me he paid you ten dollars for the James Dean picture, the one where he has a black turtleneck sweater pulled up over his mouth."

Ryo pulls back the picture of Marilyn, which I *do* want, but not if it's stolen from Ryo's father.

"Forget it," he says. "Let's go play in the field behind the house."

"What are we gonna do there?"

"Explore and stuff. Your mom won't be here for another hour, and I don't want to be cooped up all afternoon."

Ryo leads me out a side gate to a big wooded field that all the houses in his neighbourhood are built against. According to Ryo, nobody ever goes back there, so it's a perfect place to explore and to get away from his parents whenever he gets in trouble.

We walk to the very edge of the field, where there's a cliff overlooking a long shaded gully with a running creek down below. Ryo points out a switchback trail to our left leading down to the gully, but I tell him I don't want to go down there because my shoes will get all muddy, and because, well, I don't want to have to climb all the way back up the hill in the hot sun. So he says *OK* and shows me another part of the field with lots of rabbits jumping around. After beaning a few of them with rocks, he leads me into a flat, shaded area between a stand of pine trees, clears away some stones and sits on the ground Indian-style.

He squints an eye at me. "Sit down for a sec."

So I sit down, stretch out my legs and lean back on my hands. It feels nice and relaxed in the shade, especially with the wind blowing through the trees. I close my eyes and imagine I'm back in the Enchanted Forest with Kevin.

"That was a cool speech you gave the other day," Ryo says after a bit.

"Thanks." I keep my eyes closed and hum a little tune to myself to try and block him out.

"I was surprised you picked Marilyn Monroe. I thought you'd pick someone more to do with baseball since you're into that."

I shrug my shoulders and think about how funny it is that people assume I'm into baseball just because I'm good at it. The truth is that the people who are the most into baseball are the ones who *aren't* any good at it, like my father. But I just keep quiet and let them think whatever they want because it's none of their business anyway.

"Spencer's a good actor. But you were way better than him, the way you swished around and talked in that girly voice. For a second you had me believing you really were a girl."

I open my eyes and sit up. Ryo winks at me and wiggles his eyebrows the way Kevin does.

"I wasn't acting."

"Yeah, right!" He stands and pats the dust off his trousers. "Hey, I've got to pee real bad."

"Me too." I stand and hop up and down a few times to get the circulation in my legs going again.

We move closer to the trees so the wind won't be able to blow the pee on us, take down our trousers and go for it. Since we're standing next to each other, I turn away for, like, some privacy. But Ryo edges closer and tells me to let him see my chinchin, which is OK with me as long as he lets me look at his. He laughs and sprays his pee all around, which makes me laugh, and I do the same thing.

"Let's see whose is bigger," he says, moving right up next to me.

"No, thanks," I say, pulling up my trousers. "You win."

"No, wait!" He grabs my hand hard, leads me back to where we were sitting before, and pulls me down.

"Hey! Watch that!" I say.

"Come on." He pulls his trousers to his ankles. "Let's jerk off."

I try to stand, but he yanks me back down, which makes me mad.

"Dude! It's my birthday. Do it with me just this once."

So, being that all I got him was the stupid necktie, and being that nobody else came to his birthday party, I decide it's OK this one time, just to get it over with. Right when we're in the middle of it, Ryo grabs my hand, but I pull it back.

"Do me," he says.

"Do yourself!"

"At least sit closer so I can feel you against me," he says.

I don't see the harm of that, so I scoot closer to Ryo until our legs are pressed up against each other, and I can feel the vibration of his body. Then, right when I think he's about to splatter, he grabs my neck and pulls my head down toward him, and says, "Suck it."

I pull away from him, but he grabs my neck again. "Suck it like Kevin does," he says.

The moment he says Kevin's name, I pry his hand off my neck and push him back hard against the tree.

"You liar!" I say, glaring at him as he sits back up.

"I'm not lying! Kevin sucks me off *every time* he comes over. Why do you think I gave him such a good deal on the James Dean shit?"

"You're a fricking liar! I'm going to tell Kevin what you said when he gets back tonight, and he'll *never* speak to you again." I pull up my underpants and my trousers. I'm so angry I could easily kick in Ryo's face.

"Kevin's not coming back, you stupid bumpkin. His mother put him in boarding school in England."

Everything in my stomach gushes into my chest when I hear those words, like when a roller coaster reaches the highest point in the ride and suddenly drops, and everything goes spackled and grey because I know Ryo is telling the truth. That's what the telephone call last night was about; that's why Momma was so quiet this morning. I try my best to hold back my tears, but this just makes me feel weak and I accidentally fall against Ryo's shoulder.

"Pastor Tanaka told my mom yesterday at church," he yells. "I wasn't supposed to say anything to you. But since you're being such a jerk about it"—he grabs my neck again and pulls my head toward him—"now, suck it!"

What happens next is a blur. All I remember is some paramedics are loading Ryo into an ambulance, and a bunch of adults are screaming at me. Seems I cracked open Ryo's head with a rock. I'm too embarrassed to explain what happened, and when he finally wakes up in the hospital a week later, Ryo can't even remember his own name.

Chapter 13

I'm lucky the police release me to my parents because most kids who crack open other people's heads usually get put into juvenile hall and don't get out for a long time. But since I've never been in trouble before, they think it's better for me to go home, as long as my parents promise to take me to court on Monday, which they do.

Nobody understands why I would've done such a thing to a school friend. I don't even know myself; it all happened so fast. And now my parents are afraid that what happened with Hiro is happening to me too. So between them, the social worker, the lawyers, and the Juvenile Court judge, they agree to put my case on hold until a psychiatrist can examine me and report back to the court, which gives me an idea about how I can finally use *the thing* from the box, which is still in my book bag.

On Wednesday, right after breakfast, I grab my book bag and run to Momma's station wagon. My father's in the driver's seat drumming on the steering wheel, and Momma is waiting for me by the passenger door, wearing big sunglasses so I can't see her eyes. She points at my book bag and says, "You won't need that."

"I don't want to fall behind in my schoolwork, Momma." I lift the flap and pull out my maths book. "It's just for *if* I have time while we're waiting to see the doctor."

Momma nods, pulls open the door, and I pop inside.

My father doesn't say anything as he drives. He hasn't really said anything to me for weeks. Earlier that morning, I heard him arguing with Momma, telling her that he didn't understand why he had to go to the psychiatrist's office since he wasn't the one being examined. Momma told him the psychiatrist might want to talk to them as part of his work. So he finally agreed. But he's still not happy about it. In fact, he looks totally nervous, which he should be.

The psychiatrist's office is in Beverly Hills, in a fancy, tall glass building next to Rodeo Drive. His secretary tells us we're fifteen minutes early and asks us to wait while Doctor Menner (that's the psychiatrist's name) finishes up with another patient.

Momma and I sit on a black leather sofa facing the door to Doctor Menner's office. Momma's still wearing her sunglasses, with her head turned away from me, her arms wrapped tightly around her purse. My father's squirming on a chair next to the front door and reading a magazine upside down. We're the only people in the waiting area. It's super quiet, the only sounds being father's raspy breathing, Momma's grumbly stomach, and the clack-clack-clack of the secretary's typewriter. After a bit, I pull my maths book out of my book bag, and quickly check underneath it to make sure *the thing* is still there. My heart does a somersault when I see it at the bottom of the bag, folded neatly in a plastic sandwich baggie. Momma swivels her head in my direction. I show her my teeth and close the flap slowly so it doesn't look suspicious, then I set the bag on the sofa next to me and open my book. Momma looks away again.

Just then, the door to Doctor Menner's office opens, and a tall man steps out. He's dressed in a dark grey suit and tie and wears a little black felt beanie on top of his head. The man has a short, black beard, dark blue eyes, and a kind face. I set aside my book and sit up on the sofa, and my father peers at him over the top of his magazine. The man is followed by a handsome boy, who's probably a couple years older than Kevin, with a big, shiny camera hanging from a strap around his neck, and carrying a black canvas book bag that looks a lot like mine. The boy is wearing tight blue jeans, a tight-fitting, black snap-button shirt with black braces, big black boots, and a black hat with a rounded top. A lock of his hair is sticking out from under the hat, completely covering one of his eyes. I'm surprised to see that under his *other* eye, which is dark blue like the man's, he's wearing a fake eyelash. More surprisingly, his fingernails are painted black.

The handsome boy moves past the man in the suit, who I reckon is his father, and stands next to the secretary's desk while Doctor Menner and the boy's father speak quietly. The boy takes off his hat and rakes his fingers through his hair. He lets out a loud sigh, then pivots around and glances into the waiting room. He catches my eye, smiles, and winks. Momma lifts her sunglasses, leans forward, and looks at him, then looks at me and frowns.

"Thank you very much for everything, Doctor," the boy's father says. "We appreciate all you've done."

Doctor Menner nods and pulls a fake smile, then goes back into his office and shuts the door kind of hard.

"Yeah, thank you for everything," the handsome boy calls out to the closed door with a smirk.

The man in the suit shakes his head at the boy, who shrugs and lifts his book bag, putting his arms through the shoulder straps and adjusting it on his back.

"All the best, Vivien," the man in the suit says to the secretary as he walks past her desk.

"Thank you, Mr Dweck. Goodbye, Raphael," she says to the handsome boy, who is already halfway across the waiting room. He lifts his hand goodbye without turning around.

As he passes the sofa, he flashes me a wicked smile and pumps his eyebrows the same way Kevin does and snaps a picture of me with his camera before gliding out the door. Momma lets out a surprised yelp and makes like she wants to get up and go after him. But she changes her mind, I guess, and sits back, and my father mumbles something rude about the boy's father being Jewish.

Ten minutes later, Doctor Menner calls me into his office. Momma stands and calls out to my father, whose face is buried deeper in the upside-down magazine. But Doctor Menner tells them not to worry; he needs to see me alone first since it's a court-ordered evaluation.

Doctor Menner has a thin brown moustache and stringy hair pulled over to one side like it's falling out or something. He's wearing a wrinkled short-sleeve white shirt, the kind you buy from Sears, and a crooked clip-on bow tie. He takes hold of my book bag and takes it around the back of his desk. "Sit there." He points at a long, brown leather sofa in the middle of the room with funny pyramid-shaped chrome feet.

He flips open a manila folder and reads something to himself while still standing. I plop down on the sofa and wait. The office feels stuffy, and smells funny, almost a little like aieki. I look around and see bunches of books—on shelves, stacked in little piles on the floor, and on his big wooden desk. On the wall behind me is a spacey-looking digital wall clock set in a white plastic case, and right next to it hangs a huge Frenchie-looking mirror that doesn't exactly go with the other decorations in the room.

"It's hot in here." I point at the window.

Doctor Menner looks up from the folder and squints at me. Big marbles of sweat quiver above his eyebrows, ready to stream down his face. He pulls a handkerchief out of his back pocket and mops his forehead, then pours himself a glass of water from a white plastic jug on his desk. His hand shakes a little, which makes me nervous.

"I said it's hot in here. Can you open the window or something?"

Doctor Menner looks over his half-glasses at me for a second. Then he picks up the telephone and asks his secretary to turn on the air conditioning. Finally, he grabs a pen out of a little box on his desk, sits down in the chair across from me, and flips open a steno pad.

"I'm Doctor Seth Menner." He arches one eyebrow at me the way Mr Spock does on *Star Trek*. "Do you know why you're here today, young man?"

"Because I cracked open Ryo's head."

Doctor Menner nods and writes something in his notepad, then looks up at me.

"Why did you do that? I understand from the police report that Ryo's a school friend of yours."

"If I tell you *why* I did it, will it stay private?"

"Normally, yes." He takes another sip of water and clears his throat.

"You mean it's *not* private."

"Not completely, no." He sits up in his chair. "But I do have discretion in these matters. So I'd urge you to be as honest with me as you can, and I promise to be selective with the information, revealing only what's relevant to the case."

Even though Doctor Menner is weird and nervous, and doesn't know how to dress or how to decorate his office, somehow I feel I can trust him. So I spend the rest of the session explaining how Ryo has always been mean to me, and about how he tried to force me to suck his chinchin. When I get to the sucking part, Doctor Menner's breathing changes and he starts to sweat again. He holds up a hand, pulls out his handkerchief one more time, and passes it over his forehead. Then he asks me if I think I'd do the same thing if I found myself in the same situation with someone else, and I tell him that I don't know. I really *don't* know, especially since I can't even remember hitting Ryo. It was just an automatic reaction.

Doctor Menner nods and writes some more in his steno pad. Then he sets it aside, takes off his glasses, and polishes them with a shiny cloth he pulls out of his shirt pocket. He sits quietly for a while and flashes a sad smile at me like he's about to cry. Then he slips back on his glasses and clears his throat.

"How did you feel when Ryo tried to force you to do that?"

"I don't know. I guess I hated him."

"Why do you think that is?"

"Because he wanted to make me do something I didn't want to do."

"But you don't hate everyone that makes you do something you don't want to do, correct?"

"What do you mean?"

"Well, for example, I'm sure your parents, or perhaps your teachers, from time to time, make you do things you don't want to do. You don't hate *them*, do you?"

I think about that for a moment. "No, I guess I don't. But Ryo was forcing me to do something stupid."

"Was it stupid? Or was it something you might have wanted to do if it hadn't been Ryo?"

"What do you mean?" The same hot feeling I felt out in the wooded field when I was with Ryo is spreading again from my stomach into my chest.

"Is there anyone in your life who you feel particularly close to besides your parents," he asks. "For example, another boy?"

"I feel close to my cousin Kevin." My throat goes a little tight, and my eyes start to sting.

Doctor Menner scribbles something in his notepad and looks up at me. "How old is your cousin Kevin?"

"Thirteen."

"What if your cousin Kevin tried to make you do what Ryo was demanding of you? Would you have the same reaction?"

I sit straight up on the sofa. "I don't want to talk about my cousin Kevin."

Doctor Menner flips closed his steno pad and sets it aside. "Why not?"

"His parents took him away to England. And it's all my fault."

"I see." Doctor Menner grabs a Kleenex box from his desk and holds it out to me. I pull out a few tissues and blow my nose. "Take your time, young man."

When I finish wiping my face, he pulls out a plastic-lined trash bucket from under his desk so I can drop the dirty tissues into it. I notice a bunch of other dirty tissues inside, and also something that looks like a flat balloon stuck to the side of the bucket. He quickly pulls back the bucket and shoves it under his desk.

"As difficult as you may find it to talk about Kevin," he says after a moment, "I think it's important for us to explore this a bit, as it may be relevant to your case."

I stare at Doctor Menner.

"Would that be OK?"

I nod.

"Good, let's try this: Lie back on the sofa and make yourself comfortable, and just answer my questions. Don't overthink your answers. Simply respond with the first thing that comes to your mind."

I swing my feet onto the sofa, put one of the cushions under my head, and stare at the ceiling, waiting for Doctor Menner's questions.

"Why do you believe it's your fault that Kevin's parents took him to England?"

"Because Auntie Doreen *thought* she caught us doing it."

"Doing it?"

"Yeah, the night before they went away on vacation. I was supposed to be sleeping in my own room, but I snuck into Kevin's in the middle of the night. Then Auntie Doreen woke up and found me."

"How long have you and Kevin been … doing it?"

I turn my head and look at Doctor Menner. He points his pencil up, and I look back at the ceiling.

"How long?" he asks again.

"We've *never* done it. We were just *kissing*. We've been kissing since my birthday. But that time when Auntie Doreen caught me was the first time I slept in his room."

"Why were you sleeping at Kevin's house? Why weren't you at your own house?"

"Auntie said I could stay there."

"Why?"

"Because of my father."

The room goes totally quiet except for Doctor Menner's breathing, the hum of his digital clock, and the faraway sound of traffic. After a bit, I turn my head and find him staring at me over the top of his half-glasses. He points up again, and I look back at the ceiling.

"What about your father?" he finally asks.

"I'm afraid of him."

Doctor Menner doesn't ask his next question for a while. But I'm ready for it when it comes.

"Why are you afraid of your father?"

"Are we finished talking about Kevin?"

"For now, yes. Let's talk about your father."

I sit up on the sofa. "Hand me my book bag."

Doctor Menner cocks his head to one side. "Your book bag?"

"Yes, please." My heart races, and I feel like I'm about to pass out. "I need to get something out of there. I want to show you—"

Doctor Menner gets up, retrieves my book bag from behind his desk, and opens up the flap.

"Under the books," I say.

Doctor Menner digs inside my book bag and draws out the plastic sandwich baggie with *the thing* inside.

"That's it."

He holds up the baggie to the light and peers at it. From where I'm sitting, I can see *the thing* inside and so can he. He unzips the baggie and pulls it out, pinched between his thumb and forefinger. The baggie floats out of his hand to the carpet, and he shakes open *the thing*. His eyes go wide when he sees the brown splotches.

Chapter 14

My father bolts out of Doctor Menner's office like a crazy person and dashes into the hallway. He doesn't even notice me sitting next to Doctor Menner's secretary, who's been watching me the whole time that Doctor Menner's been talking to him and Momma about the things I said he did to me when I was little, and probably to Hiro, too.

I hear Momma crying inside Doctor Menner's office, so I get up to look, but Doctor Menner's secretary tells me to sit still. Soon a couple of police officers show up and ask to see Doctor Menner. His secretary points at the door, and they march past us and walk into his office without knocking. One of the officers is a tall, fat Mexican named Lopez, and the other one—the one in charge—is a short, wiry Vietnamese guy named Nguyen. Neither of them looks very nice.

After a while, they call me inside and ask me lots of questions, making me repeat everything I told Doctor Menner, while Momma sits in a corner and sobs with her face in her hands. Doctor Menner hands them *the thing*, which is back inside the plastic baggie. Officer Nguyen tells us they're going to send it to a special lab to test the brown splotches to see whether it's really blood, and, if it is, they're going to find out whose blood it is.

After I finish, Lopez calls the police station on his walkie-talkie and tells them to look for my father, which gets me excited, because hopefully now they'll take him away forever so Momma and I can finally have some peace. Then they give us a ride home so I can show them where the box is buried. Finally, I take them to my room, pull out Hiro's mitt from under my bed, and tell them that they can keep it for their case. Momma falls to the floor when she sees it, and Lopez helps her out of my bedroom and into the living room.

Almost right away, another four officers in blue jumpsuits show up in a police van. Nguyen tells Momma and me to stay inside while two of the officers dig up the box with a machine they brought with them; he gives me permission to watch from the kitchen window. It only takes them around fifteen minutes to completely dig the box out of the ground. They pry it open and take everything out, piece by piece, separating it all into different coloured plastic bags, and putting tags on them. Then they put it all into the van.

The other two officers show Momma a warrant and spend the rest of the afternoon searching the whole house and the garage. In the end, they carry out a few more coloured bags, put them into the van, and drive away.

"The house will be under surveillance until we find your husband, Mrs Koba," Officer Nguyen says to Momma, who hasn't moved from the living room. "So you're safe to stay here."

Momma nods and looks at me with tears still streaming down her face. "I'm sorry, baby. I'm so sorry."

I roll my eyes and look away from her. Nguyen sits next to me on the sofa and squeezes my shoulder. "How are you holding up, my friend?"

"I'll be OK, thanks."

Nguyen looks nicer than he did earlier. He even smiles a little.

"Just make sure he never comes back," I whisper to him.

Nguyen stands and walks over to Lopez, who's hovering in the background, speaking in a low voice into his walkie-talkie. I catch a lady's voice on the radio say my father's name and Momma's head snaps up.

"If he tries to make contact, we'll know," Nguyen says. "Just go about your business like normal. We'll be watching and waiting."

That night Momma and I eat dinner in complete silence. She can't bring herself to look at me. Even when I talk to her, she just answers with a shake or a nod of her head and points at things and stuff. I'm only able to finish half my food and push my plate away.

"You're not mad at me for telling the police about Father, are you Momma?"

Momma looks at me for a moment and shakes her head.

"Then why aren't you talking to me?"

"I'm sorry, baby. I have no words yet. Everything is too confused in my head."

After my shower, I go straight to my room, turn off the lights, and jump into bed. It takes me a while to fall asleep since my mind is full of nervous thoughts about everything that happened today. I also wonder how long it's going to take for the police to find my father.

Finally, I decide to think about something else; otherwise, I'll be awake all night. So I think about Marilyn, about how her spirit is inside me, and about how I'm going to make sure that *this time* her life is not going to be as sad as her other life, and, as I think about all this, I start to doze off.

The next thing I know, my bed is shaking really hard. I open my eyes and find my father staring down at me in the dark, crazy-eyed, stinking of whiskey, and croaking, "What the *fuck* have you done, you little shit?" I scream and scream and scream until I nearly pass out and totally pee my jammies.

Before I know it, a bunch of police officers appear in my room with their guns pointed at my father. They order him to back away from me. Then they grab him, push his face against the wall, handcuff him, and haul him out of the house. Everything goes so fast, it takes me a while to understand that what I've been hoping for has finally happened. But it has; *I* made it happen. Now Momma and I are free.

The next morning, I junk my baseball uniform and begin to redecorate my room, starting by taping the picture of Marilyn to my dresser mirror.

—⁌—

Raphael
1970

—⁌—

וּבִקַּשְׁתֶּם אֹתִי, וּמְצָאתֶם: כִּי תִדְרְשֻׁנִי, בְּכָל-לְבַבְכֶם.

And you shall seek Me, and find Me, when you search
for Me with all your heart.

—Jeremiah 29:13

—〽—

An immigrant lad of twelve, soon to turn thirteen. High-strung, brilliant, devout—with sticky fingers. Pressured by his peers to conform. Urged by his parents to stand firm. Jerusalem; Los Angeles. Hebrew, French, Arabic, and now English.

Group training for his bar mitzvah with a bad-tempered sexton.

"Be careful with that scroll, Raphael. It's priceless."

"Sorry."

"Don't handle the silver like that. My grandfather didn't risk his life smuggling it out of Iraq only to have it manhandled by a spoiled adolescent. Show some respect."

"What did I do?"

"You're much too rough with things. Remember, you're not in Israel anymore. A little deference goes a long way."

Muffled giggles from classmates make his blood rise. There is an impatient tap on his shoulder from the sexton, and his knuckles turn white on the handles of the scroll. *It is a tree of life to those who hold fast to it;* those words are now a tortuous irony playing a repeating loop in his head.

Glancing back, his eyes come to rest again on the silver breast-plate, the crown, and the *yad*, glinting in the bright lights of the sanctuary. A tingling grows inside him like ants scratching his skin; sweat bathes his face and his hands jangle the silver as he dresses the sexton's precious family scroll and stores it in the ark, nestling it among the half-dozen others.

Later that evening, the image of the ritual silver burns in his mind as he picks at his food.

"Are you all right, son?"

"I'm not hungry, Abba. May I be excused?"

"Eat," his mother says. "The body needs fuel regardless of whether one feels hungry. You're excused once you've cleaned your plate."

The image of the silver breastplate bedevils him as he stumbles through his prayers after dinner. During his evening studies, the ghost of the yad blurs his vision, and his hands tremble over the pages of the Talmud as he tries to force it out of his mind. And when he finally covers his eyes with his hand to recite the Shema before seeking the oblivion of sleep, he cries out at the sight of the filigreed crown etched on the heel of his palm. He knows there is only one way to extinguish the burning in his blood, to obliterate those images from his mind:

A darkened sanctuary; the open ark; the ritual silver resting at the bottom of a discarded pillowcase; a quick taxi ride down-town; the cash in his pocket—for a moment—before he tosses the lot into a dumpster. *Relief at last.*

One week later, as he sits a trigonometry exam, two LAPD officers enter the classroom and exchange a few words with the teacher, who nods in his direction. Raphael raises his hand and stands as they approach him, his classmates wide-eyed and speech-less at the scene unfolding before them. One of the officers takes him gently by the arm and leads him out the door to face justice.

—⚏—

Ralph
1973

—⚏—

Chapter 1

"Welly, welly, well, doctor. What's it going to be then, eh?" Sixteen-year-old Raphael Dweck stands in front of an ornate wall mirror in Doctor Menner's office and adjusts his bowler hat, cocking it to one side and winking at himself. Then he spins on his heels to face his thirtysomething court-appointed psychiatrist and flashes him a crooked grin, more a grimace than a smile.

"Please have a seat, Mr Dweck."

Raphael takes three deliberate steps toward the brown leather sofa Doctor Menner reserves for his patients and plops into it, pushing his hat over his eyes and feigning sleep.

"Shall we begin?" Doctor Menner opens his steno pad, his pen poised above a blank page.

"So, what's it going to be, doc? Another hypno-session?"

"If you like." Without waiting for a response, Doctor Menner sets aside the steno pad and retrieves from atop his hyper-organised desk the pyramid-shaped prism he uses to induce hypnosis.

Raphael slips off his hat, adjusts his black felt *kippah* forward, and raises himself on his elbow. A lock of his longish, wavy black hair falls over one eye. He pushes it back into place with one hand and peers at the doctor. "If *I* like?"

"Yes, Mr Dweck, if *you* like."

"More like if *you* like, I think." Raphael winks at the doctor and sits up on the sofa, touching his forefinger to his eye and pointing it at the doctor.

Doctor Menner shifts in his seat and stares at the black-lacquered fingernail pointing at him.

"Whatever do you mean?"

"I mean, I think this is going to be our last session, doctor." Raphael pulls back his finger. He snatches his backpack from the floor and digs around in it.

Doctor Menner watches as Raphael extracts a miniature camera from the bag and sets it on the side table next to his larger Nikon.

"I don't understand, Mr Dweck." He points at the little camera. "What is that?"

"It's a camera, Seth. I *may* call you Seth, right? You can call me Ralph. It's only fair."

"Why, Mr Dweck?"

"Ralph."

"Sit back, please…Ralph. What's going through your mind today? Help me understand."

Raphael sits forward on the edge of the sofa and thrusts the upper half of his swimmer's body toward Doctor Menner.

"I would think after three years of *therapy*"—Raphael panto-mimes quotation marks in the air with his fingers—"I've earned the right to call you by your first name."

A sweat breaks out on Doctor Menner's forehead. He extracts a plaid handkerchief from the inside pocket of his tweed coat and absently passes it over his face. At that, Raphael flashes his teeth and scoots back.

"Now that that's settled"—Raphael rubs his palms against his jeans—"I'd like to tell you *exactly* what's been on my mind."

Doctor Menner nods and picks up his pad and pen, discreetly letting out a long and steady breath, a gesture not lost on Raphael. He inclines his head in Raphael's direction, his pen poised once again above the page.

"So, Seth, I've been thinking a lot this week about how much we trust each other."

"We who?"

"All of us!" Raphael waves his hands around the room. "People in society."

"Meaning?"

"Meaning…that to navigate society, we have to trust the people around us, people we know, strangers, everyone. I mean, we have no choice, do we?"

"I'm not sure I understand what you're getting at. Perhaps you could elaborate."

Raphael pushes up his hat with one finger and scratches his head. "You want me to elaborate?"

"Yes, please, so we can get to the bottom of things."

Raphael lets out a short laugh. "That *is* one of your favourite phrases, isn't it, Seth? 'The bottom of things'. It's a funny one, considering…"

Doctor Menner narrows his eyes at Raphael.

"Any*who*, getting back to *me*. I was saying we can't very well navigate society without trusting people—whether we like it or not. For example, we rely that the guy behind us on the escalator won't just give us a good shove, right? We trust that some numbnuts standing behind us at the crosswalk won't accidentally-on-purpose push us into the path of oncoming traffic. It's crazy, don't you think? No, don't say anything yet. The other day, I was getting blown by this dude in a suit behind one of those big green garbage bins in a back alley behind the Beverly Hills Police Station on Rexford. Can you imagine? In broad daylight! I think the dude was a lawyer. Anyway, I thought to myself, *how do you know this dude won't just bite down on your cock or yank off your yarbles!* Crazy, right?"

Raphael catches Doctor Menner glancing ever so quickly at the wall clock, and he leans forward on his knees, like a cat poised to pounce on a mouse. "You too, Seth."

"What *about* me?" Doctor Menner flips closed his empty notepad and sets it aside.

"You're not exempt from having to trust people. People like me."

"I never said I was."

"I mean, all this time, I've never once told my parents you've been feeling me up each time you put me under hypnosis."

Doctor Menner blinks at Raphael and leans forward in his chair. "I don't know what you're playing at, young man. But I'm not going to tolerate your false accusations."

Raphael smothers a yawn with the back of his hand, stands up, and stretches deliciously. "I have proof, Seth." He snatches the small camera from the side table. "You see, when I realised what you were doing, it's a few weeks now, I pinched this backpack-camera thing at the spy store on Melrose, switched it with one I had that looked a lot like it, except without the camera and the hidden compartment, of course, and made sure it was always sitting right there whenever we had a hypno-session"—Raphael points at the table across from the sofa—"which turned out to be the perfect place to capture all our intimate moments." He winks at the doctor, pulls some photos out of the hidden pocket inside his backpack, and shoves them into Doctor Menner's trembling hands.

The doctor leafs through the photographs, which clearly depict him removing Raphael's trousers, running his hands over his body, and masturbating above the young man. After a moment, the photographs slip out of his hands and fall to the floor.

"You can keep those." Raphael lights a cigarette and flicks the match across the room. "I have more. Consider them a souvenir, from our last session, that is."

The doctor's trembling intensifies, and he starts to cry. "I'm sorry, young man. I'm so very sorry." Streams of snot leak out his nose onto his upper lip. "Please...don't—"

"Don't what?" Raphael gathers up the photographs and places them on Doctor Menner's desk, then he takes a long drag on his cigarette and blows the smoke in Doctor Menner's face.

"Please, don't … my family, my reputation."

"Should have thought of that before, I guess." Raphael sniggers and slaps Doctor Menner on the back. "Don't worry, Seth. I'm not likely to say anything. After all, I can't say I didn't enjoy the attention."

Doctor Menner wipes his face with his handkerchief and looks up at Raphael, his brow furrowed, uncomprehending.

"I do have two conditions, though." Raphael crushes the cigarette underfoot, then pushes Doctor Menner against the back of his chair, one powerful hand pressed against each of his shoulders. Doctor Menner's eyes go wide, and he nods his head.

"First, this is our last session, *ever*. That means you'll have to tell my parents and the court that I'm cured, or whatever you guys say. That I'm not likely to steal from anyone again, especially considering I've finally paid back the *esnoga* for all the silver I pawned."

"Yes, I can do that. No worries!"

Raphael steps away from the doctor, removes his kippah, slips off his braces, and unbuttons his shirt, exposing his *tallit katan*.

"What are you doing?" Doctor Menner asks.

"I'm getting to my second condition."

He carefully folds his shirt and the tallit katan (reverently kissing the fringes), places them on Doctor Menner's desk, and unzips his fly.

"To bring my so-called therapy to an appropriate end, I think it's only fair if I get to bone you, hard." Raphael steps out of his trousers and stands completely naked in front of the doctor, save for a pair of black, steel-toed boots. "Don't you?"

The blood drains from Doctor Menner's face at the sight of Raphael, who grabs the Nikon and snaps his picture. The flash blinds Doctor Menner momentarily. As his vision clears, he sees Raphael pulling up his trousers and adjusting his braces.

"I couldn't resist," Raphael says with a bitter smirk. "You should have seen your face. I'll send you the picture once I develop it."

"You mean, you're not going to..."

"Oh, you thought I was serious?" Raphael hangs the Nikon around his neck and shakes his head. "I'm not going to violate a major commandment for a *ben-zona* like you. Not that you don't deserve it."

Doctor Menner retreats behind his desk and takes in a series of deep, calming breaths, glancing every so often in Raphael's direction.

Raphael checks his watch and picks up his backpack. "Don't imagine you're off the hook, doc. I may still report you to the police. Don't forget I have the evidence. Right now, though, it's almost time for *Abba* to pick me up. So, chop-chop, get your discharge notes ready."

—⁂—

Raphael follows his father Isaac Dweck to the parking garage. As they approach his Range Rover, Isaac unlocks it with the remote. Raphael climbs into the passenger seat, automatically handing his backpack to his father. Isaac opens it and briefly rummages through the contents, then passes it back to Raphael, who tosses it onto the back seat together with his Nikon. Neither of them says a word until they are well on their way up the Wilshire Corridor, flanked on both sides by the glittering residential towers, driving toward their synagogue in Westwood.

"I'm not exactly sure what happened back there." Isaac lowers the visor to block the glare of the afternoon sun.

Raphael removes his hat and sets it on the seat between them. He passes his hand through his hair and cranes his neck to peer at his reflection in the side-view mirror in an effort to buy time, thinking how he's going to respond to his father, a brilliant trial lawyer with a reputation for knowing people better than they know themselves.

"Your delayed response is telling." Isaac pointedly looks at Raphael for a moment before turning his attention back to the road.

"Sorry, Abba. I didn't realise you'd asked a question."

"Why did Doctor Menner abruptly end your therapy?"

"Like he said"—Raphael slouches in his seat—"he thinks I'm cured. So there's no further need for therapy. That's good news, isn't it?"

Isaac glances at Raphael and back at the road. "He didn't use the word *cured*. There *is* no cure for kleptomania."

"He said three years of talk therapy had finally broken the cycle of the compulsion, in his opinion. Same thing."

Isaac shakes his head and strokes his well-groomed salt-and-pepper beard. "Something's not right." He glances back at his son. "He seemed ... disturbed, somehow."

Raphael sits up and clears his throat. "Yes, I sensed that too, Abba. I could tell he wasn't feeling too well. You know, he was perspiring a lot, and he kept wiping his forehead with his handkerchief. Maybe he's having personal problems."

"What makes you think that? Did he say he was having personal problems?"

"Well, no. Or maybe he was sick or something."

"Maybe so." Isaac pulls the car into the turning lane as they approach their synagogue, a building constructed of honey-coloured stone to resemble the Old City of Jerusalem, and waits for the oncoming traffic to flow past before turning left into the underground car park. "Still"—he pulls into a space at the back, well away from the other cars—"I have a mind to call him."

"Abba, please." Raphael reaches into the back seat, unzips his backpack, and extracts his prayer book. "Let's talk about it after *Mincha.*"

Isaac's expression softens as he sees the prayer book in his son's hand. He squeezes his shoulder and nods. "After Mincha."

Raphael and his father make their way down a narrow corridor to the study hall. The room is full of school-age boys and those of their fathers who are able to take time off from work. Almost everyone is in position, ready for the prayer leader to kick off.

Isaac hurries to the front of the room to pray next to Rabbi Mordechai Sadot, while Raphael stands in the back, taking his time to clear his mind and concentrate by reciting the opening Psalm to himself from memory and meaning every word.

By the time he steps into his usual place next to his nemesis, the *hazzan's* son, Simon, who is the same age as Raphael, the group is already halfway through the silent version of the Amidah, the central prayer. Simon gives Raphael a discreet kick on the shin and winks at him. Raphael responds by stepping away and burying his face in his prayer book.

After prayers, the group quickly thins out, and those who are left step into the dining hall for coffee and biscuits. Isaac disappears with the rabbi into his office, and Raphael takes a seat in a corner of the dining hall, pulling out a library copy of *A Clockwork Orange* from his backpack and turning to the middle of the book.

Simon and the rabbi's thirteen-year-old son, Marc, approach Raphael, each of them nursing tiny paper cups brimming with Turkish coffee.

"That doesn't look like the Talmud to me," Simon says. "What do you think?" he asks Marc.

Raphael holds up the book at them. "It's Anthony Burgess. I get to read what I want as long as I study two pages of Talmud a day. Lucky me."

Simon leans forward and runs his finger over the top of the book. "And this is what you choose to read?"

"He probably stole it." Marc squints at the cover and shakes his head.

Raphael reaches up and takes hold of Simon's finger. Marc's face immediately darkens at the gesture, and Simon stoically raises an eyebrow at Raphael, extracting his finger from his grip.

Raphael grins salaciously at Simon.

"Look," Marc says to Simon, "his fingernails are painted black."

Simon shrugs. "I suppose it goes with the rest of his get-up."

"Seriously"—Raphael turns his back on Marc and holds out the book to Simon—"you should read this. It's great; much better than the film."

"The film?" Simon takes the book from Raphael and absently leafs through it, then hands it back to him and shakes his head. "I'm not allowed to read stuff like that. I don't know why you are."

"I suppose it's because I'm special." Raphael stuffs the book back into his backpack and pumps his eyebrows at both Simon and Marc.

Isaac steps into the room and waves. Raphael scoots back his chair, gets up from the table, and stretches, then inserts his arms through the straps of his backpack and adjusts it on his back. "Well, comrades"—he crumples his empty coffee cup and tosses it at the rubbish bin, missing it by six inches—"it's been real." Then he winks at Simon and Marc and jogs toward his father. "See you two at *Shacharit*."

Isaac ushers Raphael into Rabbi Sadot's office telling Raphael that he'll see him at home, then withdraws, closing the door behind him and leaving Raphael alone in the room with the rabbi, who is standing behind his desk peering into a well-worn tome, absently stroking his black, chest-length beard. Raphael removes his backpack, places it on a chair, and waits.

After a moment, Rabbi Sadot closes the tome and places it on his shelf, then points at the chair in front of his desk. Raphael waits by the chair until the rabbi is seated before he finally sits down. The rabbi leans forward and locks eyes with him.

"Your father tells me you're ... *cured*." He lingers on the word, then releases it quickly.

"That's what the doctor told him, Rabbi. He said the compulsion was broken."

"And is it?"

Raphael shifts in his seat, feeling unnerved by the fire in the rabbi's large, black eyes, evincing the incisor-like mind behind them. He looks down for a moment, then returns the rabbi's gaze.

"I'm still me, Rabbi."

Rabbi Sadot sits back.

"That's a clever response. But it doesn't answer my question, does it?"

Raphael draws a deep breath, then lets it out slowly. "If you're asking whether I'll ever steal again, I don't know. Right now I'm OK, I guess."

"I see." The rabbi narrows his eyes at Raphael. "Your father is concerned about the suddenness of this supposed cure."

"I know, Rabbi. He told me. But it's not all that sudden, is it? It's been three years."

The rabbi waves his hand. "He fears you may have had something to do with the doctor's sudden termination of your therapy, not that I'm much of a believer in such things."

"He wasn't a good man, Rabbi."

Rabbi Sadot holds his position, but there's a subtle dilation of his pupils that speaks volumes. After a moment, he says in a lowered voice, "Would you care to explain?"

Raphael slowly shakes his head.

The rabbi narrows his eyes at Raphael for a beat and nods. "As you wish." He picks up a pencil and scribbles something into a notepad. "We'll leave that for the time being."

"Thank you, Rabbi."

Rabbi Sadot pushes aside the notepad and clasps his hands.

"Shortly after you came to us, Raphael, your parents were concerned you were straying from tradition, that you were overeager to assimilate. They feared you'd lose your way."

"That was their fault!" Raphael blurts out. "They're the ones who—"

The rabbi holds up his hand. "*But*," he says, "I counselled them to allow you the freedom to develop, as long as you continued to study and observe the *mitzvot,* which you have done in large part. *Baruch Hashem."*

Raphael takes in a long breath and nods. "But ... ?"

"But, indeed ..." Rabbi Sadot strokes his beard and contemplates the young man sitting before him for what seems to Raphael an eternity, softly humming a familiar tune from the liturgy and passing his gaze over him from head to foot. "I'm not so sure what I proposed to your father is sustainable in the long term."

Raphael gets to his feet. "I don't agree, Rabbi. With respect, it's perfectly sustainable."

"How so?"

"I've held up my end of the bargain. You know that! I observe the *mitzvot* perfectly, better than anyone, morning to night. And I love it. I'm also a straight *A* student, I speak five languages, I'm a champion swimmer, national magazines have published my photos, and nobody in the whole school paints better than I do. Just ask any of my teachers."

"And you're modest and compassionate as well, yes?"

"What does modesty have to do with anything? I'm the best at everything I do. And I'm getting better."

"Yes, I suppose you are. But there's more to life than being the best." He picks up a thick, well-worn file from atop his desk and holds it aloft.

Raphael squints at the file. "What's that?"

Rabbi Sadot lowers it onto his desk, flips through the first few pages, and pulls out a photograph, which he slides to Raphael.

Raphael takes the photograph and finds himself staring at the image of a rugged-looking middle-aged woman with strong Levantine features burnished a deep brown by the desert sun. Raphael's brow spasms and he looks up at the rabbi. "Aunt Penina?"

Rabbi Sadot nods and strokes his beard as if he were stroking a cat.

Raphael looks again at the photograph of his estranged aunt, whom he hasn't seen in over five years. Her expression is hard, almost wild, and her deep-set, dark eyes stare out with an intensity Raphael finds difficult to bear. He places the photograph face down on the rabbi's desk and shudders.

The rabbi picks up the photograph and holds it up again. "This is not *just* your Aunt Penina." A tender expression transforms his face. He hands the photograph back to Raphael and whispers, "*This*, I believe, is your *salvation*."

Chapter 2

Raphael bursts through the front door of his family's Holmby Hills mansion and brushes past his older sister, Gabriella, who is just coming down the grand staircase to the foyer, a sky blue satchel slung over her shoulder.

"Rafi!" she says to his back as he rushes through the foyer.

He rounds the corner into the palatial drawing room and strides up to his father, who is sitting comfortably in a black leather recliner studying a tractate from the Talmud. "Abba, how could you?"

Isaac looks up at Raphael and closes the book. "Sit down, son."

Raphael shakes his head and drops into the matching leather love seat across from his father, then lowers his head into his hands for a second before looking back up at him. "Mitzpe Ramon, really? I mean, are you serious?"

Raphael's mother, Sylvie, rolls down the ramp into the living room in her wheelchair, engages the safety latch when she is still several feet away from the loveseat, and clears her throat. Raphael swings around and looks at her. "Did you know about this, Ima?" Sylvie meets his stare with her deep blue eyes, and Raphael averts his gaze. This is the first time she has looked at him in months.

"Your father and I agreed with the rabbi that you need a change of environment. We've been discussing this with him for several weeks now."

Raphael looks back up at her. "Weeks?"

"Yes, weeks. We don't feel Los Angeles is healthy for you at this point in your life. You'll need to leave, I'm afraid."

Isaac holds up his hand at Sylvie and looks at Raphael. "We came to our final decision today, thanks to the abrupt end of your therapy. The timing of that couldn't have been more fortuitous." Isaac rises to his full height and towers over Raphael. "The rabbi agrees it's best."

"I don't get it!" Raphael stands and faces off with his parents. "Jerusalem wasn't right, so you dragged me away from Saba and Savta and Uncle Shimshon, peace be upon him, and all my friends, and dropped me here in LA, where I didn't even speak the stupid language. And *now,* after eight years, you freaking want to send me back to Israel?"

Isaac points at Raphael. "Respect!"

"Yes," Sylvie shouts, "Respect your father; lower your voice."

"What's going on in here?" Gabriella steps into the living room. Tall, slim, and small breasted, with handsome Middle Eastern features, large, deep blue eyes, a strong aquiline nose, and dark wavy hair that she wears neatly pulled back into a thick ponytail, she looks like an eighteen-year-old clone of Sylvie.

"Ima and Abba, and Rabbi Mordechai," Raphael says, "they want to send me back to Israel."

"Israel?" Gabriella looks at her parents. "What's *that* about?" She steps over to Raphael and gives him a hug, which he gently shrugs off.

"Never mind, young lady," Sylvie says. "This has nothing to do with you."

"And not *just* Israel," Raphael says. "To Aunt Penina's place in Mitzpe Ramon!"

"Why there?" Gabriella asks. "Isn't that in the middle of nowhere?"

"Thank you!" Raphael says. "You see, Ima? You see, Abba? In the middle of *nowhere*. And, besides that, Aunt Penina totally *hates* us! She still blames Abba for what happened to Uncle Shimshon, peace be upon him."

"The rabbi agrees with your mother and me that Raphael should go back to Israel at this point and experience life from another perspective," Isaac says to Gabriella, ignoring Raphael's comment.

"You mean, from a poorer perspective," Raphael says.

Sylvie brings her hand down hard against the armrest of her wheelchair. "Away from all the distractions of a big city!" She wheels around to face Gabriella. "Your brother will become a part of another household for a while, a household that could use another man around."

"What do you mean *another man*?" Gabriella says. "Aunt Penina already has three sons!" She steps forward again and puts her arm around Raphael. "You can't just send him away like that! It's not right. Besides, if he goes now, he won't be able to claim deferral from military service."

Isaac and Sylvie exchange a glance that doesn't escape Gabriella's notice.

"Is *that* what this is about?" Gabriella says.

"Military service won't do your brother any harm." Sylvie wheels her chair to face Isaac. A fleeting wince of pain ripples across her face and quickly subsides.

"This is unbelievable." Raphael moves away from Gabriela and snatches up his backpack. "After all the progress I've made here, top of the class in *all* my subjects, intramural swimming champion, shortlisted for the National Young Artists award"—he points at his mother—"something *you* encouraged by the way, Madam Landscape Artist."

"Raphael, stop!" Isaac says.

Raphael faces his father and lowers his voice. "And nobody at the *esnoga*, *nobody* except Rabbi Mordechai, can hold a candle to me in the study of the Talmud. Not even you, Abba." He looks back and forth between his parents. "Please, Ima. Please, Abba, don't do this, I beg you. I have a future here. There's *nothing* for me in Israel."

"We're not going to debate this with you." Sylvie unlatches the safety on her wheelchair and rolls to her husband's side. "I'm afraid it's all settled."

Isaac places his hand on her shoulder. "Your mother's correct, son. We've arranged your flight after the High Holidays, and your cousin Assaf will be waiting for you at Savta's when you arrive in Jerusalem."

Raphael glares at both his parents. "Fine!" He pulls on his backpack and grabs his camera, hanging it around his neck, "But I *swear*, you'll regret this." He starts toward the foyer.

"Where are you going, young man?" Isaac says.

"To my art class! It's Wednesday, *remember*?"

"That's not for another two hours," Gabriella calls out. "We're serving dinner in ten minutes."

"I'm not hungry." And with that Raphael disappears into the foyer.

"Well, that went swimmingly," Gabriella says with a dismissive shake of her hair and storms out without waiting for a response.

She catches up with Raphael as he reaches the front gate and grabs hold of his backpack.

"What's the big idea!" He yanks the bag out of her hand.

Gabriella takes hold of his arm. "Don't fight them on this, Rafi," she says, her voice low and intense.

"Don't fight them? You freaking just told them you didn't think it was fair."

"I was a bit shocked is all. To be honest, though, I'm not sure whether it's fair or not."

"What do you mean?"

"They're our parents, remember? And they have the rabbi's support on this, too."

"So you *do* think they're right!"

"They're the people who are supposed to know what's best for us. Besides, you haven't exactly been the easiest person, what with the lying and stealing."

"That was only one time! And I've paid for that. Everything else has been perfect."

"I'm just saying, maybe Israel isn't such a bad idea. Think of it as a vacation. You'll get to spend time with Saba and Savta."

"Whatever!" Raphael pulls away from Gabriella and unlocks the gate.

"I'll pick you up after class," Gabriella calls out as he heads down the driveway, "on the steps of the art building. Wait for me!"

Raphael jogs down Mapleton Drive, past the hedges, walls, gates, and driveways of the several majestic estates lining either side of the road, forcefully kicking stray twigs and branches left by the gardeners into the gutter. He rounds the corner at Charing Cross Road East, hops onto the sidewalk, and picks up the pace, racing past the smaller mansions of that part of Holmby Hills, most of them either mock-Spanish or mock-Tudor, as he descends the hill toward UCLA.

Crossing the road at Hilgard, he accesses the campus via the sculpture garden outside the art centre. Then he takes his camera out of its case and makes his way across the university snapping pictures of his favourite landmarks as he goes: the world-class sculptures, the fountains, the courtyards, and the various hidden spots between buildings where he would often escape to read a book or have his lunch.

When he reaches the grass-covered quad between Royce Hall and Powell Library, the school's iconic Romanesque red brick buildings, he takes in the sight of them, a deep sadness welling inside. Scores of students crisscross the grass. Some of them smile at Raphael or nod a greeting as they pass.

Once the rush is over, and the square is relatively clear of people, he takes his time to frame shots of the facades and towers of the buildings set against the deep blue sky of the late afternoon, keen to preserve the memory of them. Then he runs up the stairs of Powell Library and snaps some pictures of the mosaics in the entryway before rushing off for a swim.

The lanes of the Olympic-sized swimming pool are all taken by the time he arrives in his black competition Speedos. He recognises one of the swimmers, a freckled redhead university student in red-and-white striped Speedos with an enviable butterfly stroke and an even better body. Kneeling at the head of the lane, Raphael waits until the swimmer reaches him and signals for him to stop by slapping the water. The swimmer grabs the edge of the deck, bringing himself upright and lifting his amber-coloured goggles.

"What's up, kid?" he asks, catching his breath.

"Mind if I share the lane with you? I'll give you to the middle of the pool before I start."

"Yeah, no problem. I've only got a couple more laps anyway. So you'll have it all to yourself."

Without waiting for a response, the swimmer kicks off, arching through the water with the grace of a dolphin. Raphael admires him from the pool's edge, broad back, muscular arms, small waist, before diving in and cutting through his wake with a ferocious Australian crawl, his fastest stroke. The swimmer makes room for him as they pass each other, and Raphael counters by edging toward him, taking any opportunity to brush against the swimmer's water-slicked body.

After a few more laps, the swimmer lifts himself out of the pool and quickly dries off. Then he ties his towel around his waist like a sarong and exits the wet area. Raphael climbs out and follows him into the locker room, which is empty at the moment, and watches from a corner bench as the swimmer strips off his Speedos and crosses the floor to the communal showers.

Raphael pokes his head into the shower room and finds the swimmer already lathering up at the far end. Peeling off his Speedos and kicking them to one side, Raphael crosses the blue-and-white tiled floor and takes the showerhead next to the swimmer, turning on the tap and running warm water over his hairy body.

The swimmer glances at him and looks around at the many available showerheads ranged around the room. "Don't tell me you want to share my showerhead, too," he says with a smirk.

"I don't mind," Raphael responds. "Do you?"

The swimmer laughs and splashes Raphael with some water. "You're very daring, kid. But no thanks."

Raphael shrugs and finishes washing up.

Afterwards, back in the locker room, as they finish changing into their street clothes, the swimmer breaks the silence.

"Where are you off to now?" he asks.

"I have a class in a half hour. I only came by for a quickie."

"A quickie, eh?"

"Yeah, a quick swim and whatever." Raphael winks at the swimmer and flashes a crooked smile.

"You don't look old enough to be taking classes here."

"I'm sixteen, nearly seventeen," Raphael says. "I'm taking college prep extension classes here. You know, like, for geniuses."

The swimmer barks a short laugh.

"No, seriously, I'm a genius."

"Ah, I see."

"But this is my last week. I'll be leaving the country soon. So you won't see me again. I mean, if you're up for something…" Raphael nods at a utility closet and raises his eyebrows expectantly.

The swimmer looks Raphael in the eye, and they stare at each other for a few moments, then he slowly lowers his gaze past Raphael's chin, neck, chest, stomach, then back up at Raphael's eyes. He glances around the room and takes Raphael by the arm.

Raphael's heart pounds hard at the touch of the swimmer's hand, and he moves toward the closet. But the swimmer holds his place. "I can't say I'm not flattered," the swimmer says in a low voice. "But I'm not a homo."

Raphael feels his stomach drop. "Neither am I. It's only a bit of fun, that's all."

"Listen, kid. Here's some advice: Be careful with who you proposition around here. Not everyone is as understanding as I am, if you get my drift. Someone might very well take offence and kick your teeth in."

Raphael pulls away from the swimmer. "Thanks. But I'm pretty good at reading people. I'm not your type; I get it." He digs his kippah out of his pocket and clips it into his hair, and grabs his backpack and camera.

The swimmer blinks at him.

"If you change your mind, I've got a class in the art centre," Raphael says over his shoulder as he swaggers away. "I finish at eight."

Raphael pulls open the glass door of the art centre and speeds down the empty hallway to the studio classroom where his life drawing class will be taking place. As it is still a half hour before the start of class, nobody has arrived yet. He strides across the room to his locker and takes out his easel, his sketchpad, and a box of pastel pencils and sets up in his favourite corner of the room, the one he considers optimal for capturing the models. Then he steps back into the hallway, runs up the steps to the mezzanine, and knocks on the office door of his art teacher and mentor, Shona Reilly.

After a moment, he pushes open the door to Shona's office and looks inside. He finds her speaking on the telephone, both elbows resting on her desk. She looks up and nods at him, signalling for him to take a seat. But he remains standing and waits while she finishes her conversation, taking the opportunity to admire her emerald green eyes and her long, straight auburn hair, which she pulls away from her face with a tarantula-shaped black hair claw.

Shona smiles at Raphael and mouths *I'm almost finished,* then turns her attention back to the telephone, which gives him a chance to examine the way her creamy coloured breasts rise out of her low-cut, white blouse accentuated by a thin rust-red cardigan, which she combines with a Catholic schoolgirl-style plaid skirt. He imagines, not for the first time, what she would look like naked. Then, realising he has gotten aroused, Raphael positions his backpack in front of his crotch, shuffles over to the sofa, and drops into it. After a moment, Shona hangs up and swivels her chair in his direction.

"Sorry to interrupt, Miss Reilly."

"What is it, Ralph?"

"I wanted to let you know that tonight's my last class. My parents are sending me to Israel in a couple of weeks. So, that's it. Sorry."

"But it's mid-course," Shona says, her voice pregnant with disappointment. "How long will you be gone?"

"Forever, I think."

"I'm so sorry to hear that. You're my best student. The youngest and the best! So much promise."

Raphael wraps his arms around his backpack and nods his head absently.

"I seriously believe you have a future in art if you keep at it. I don't think I'm telling you anything you don't already know, right?"

"Don't worry, Miss Reilly. I'll try to keep it up. I just wanted to thank you for everything. I've learned so much from you."

"That's sweet of you."

"No, honestly, I appreciate all your encouragement and support. I know my work is difficult to take sometimes."

Shona nods. "I'll never forget what you told me the first time we met last year—"

"*Whenever I paint, I'm both artist and exorcist.*"

"Yes, that's it. I think that explains a lot."

Raphael glances around Shona's office, and his eye comes to rest on a pair of antique silver candlesticks sitting on the highest shelf of her bookcase.

"What I didn't tell you," he says, looking back at her, "is that once all my demons are gone, I imagine I'll have nothing left to paint."

"Oh, yes?" She glances up at the candlesticks and furrows her brow. "And how do you feel about that?"

Raphael flashes a tight grin. "That's both my greatest hope… *and* my greatest fear." He points at the candlesticks. "Those are beautiful, by the way."

"They are indeed. They were my great-grandmother's. She brought them with her when she emigrated from Ireland. She gave them to my parents as a wedding gift."

"Was she Jewish?"

"Who? My great-grandmother? No, not at all. Why would you think that?"

"They look exactly like *Shabbat* candlesticks. You know, like, for the Sabbath. My grandparents have a pair back in Israel that look a lot like those."

"My great-grandmother was a Catholic as far as I know." She looks up at the candlesticks again and back at Raphael. "I've been keeping them safe for my mother ever since my father passed away."

Raphael and Shona stare at each other in the silence that follows. Their moment is interrupted by the chirping of her telephone.

Raphael grabs his backpack. "I'd best be heading to the studio to get ready for class."

Shona holds up a finger, picks up the telephone, and puts the caller on hold. Then she stands and smoothens out her skirt with a sweep of her hand. "I'll be down in about fifteen minutes."

Raphael nods. "Can I ask a favour, Miss Reilly?" He looks down at the floor for a moment and back up at her.

Shona cocks her head to one side.

Raphael shakes his head and takes a last glance at the candlesticks. "Never mind, Miss Reilly. It's cool. See you in a few."

Raphael races downstairs, the image of the two antique silver candlesticks burning in his mind's eye. He swaggers into the classroom, which by now is nearly full of his fellow students setting up their easels. The model, a hairless twenty-something albino, removes his robe and positions himself on the posing block. His eyes track Raphael as he crosses the room. Raphael sneaks a quick wink at him. The model responds by discreetly shifting to face Raphael's easel.

Shona enters and leans against her desk, surveying the room. Raphael moves past her and takes up his usual position. Once he has his pencils in place, he glances up and finds Shona staring straight at him. Averting his eyes, he turns his attention to his sketchpad.

Shona claps her hands. "Let's get started, shall we?"

Halfway through the session, Shona calls a break. The model grabs his robe and strolls over to Raphael, who steps away from his easel and sips water from a bottle. The model moves around to the other side of the easel, and his smile evaporates. He narrows his eyes at the sketchpad for a moment and looks at Raphael.

"What do you think?" Raphael looks past the model at Shona, who raises her head questioningly and crosses the room to join them.

The model points at the sketch, which is well on its way to being a finished drawing. "I don't get it."

"I sliced you open"—Raphael inclines his head toward the sketchpad—"from your left shoulder diagonally across your torso and down to your dangly bits."

Shona and the model peer at the drawing, which takes up the entire length and breadth of the sketchpad. The subject's face is contorted in an ecstatic grimace. One-half of its body, boldly drawn in thick black, dark blue, and dark green lines, reclines against an invisible wall. Its oversized scrotum, the focal point of the drawing, is carefully drawn in varying shades of purple and deep red, like an overripe fig. At the foot of the drawing lies the other half of the subject's body, crumpled into a foetal position. And above the whole scene, floating in the distance in the upper left corner of the drawing, is the subject's pudgy winged penis, looking all the world like a Raphaelite cherub. A group of Raphael's classmates gather around and stare at the drawing and whisper among themselves.

"That's quite an imagination you have, buddy." The model steps away from the drawing.

"Ralph never ceases to impress," Shona says. "But this is a life drawing class, people." She looks at Raphael. "Remember, you should be focusing on the model and drawing what you see."

Raphael steps up to his easel. "I never only draw what I see. I draw what I feel, which is *inspired* by what I see." He points at the drawing. "Anyway, it looks exactly like him, doesn't it?" He turns around and looks at his classmates, inclining his head toward the model, who has taken up his position on the block again. "Well, doesn't it?"

Some of his classmates nod their heads in agreement, others move back to their easels.

"What are those?" One of his classmates points at a pair of silver tubes that the subject is grasping in each of its hands, little yellow-red-orange flames emerging from the ends.

Shona glances at the drawing again, noticing the silver tubes for the first time, and quickly looks at Raphael, searching his face. Raphael averts his eyes and digs around in his backpack.

A few minutes before the end of class, Raphael breaks down his easel. Shona steps up to him and asks if something is wrong. He whispers that he doesn't feel well and prefers to leave early considering it's his last class. He promises to keep in touch, thanks her again for all her support, puts away his easel and the art supplies, and tiptoes out of the classroom.

Once outside, Raphael leans heavily against the door and closes his eyes for a moment, massaging the bridge of his nose. Then the image of the antique candlesticks in Shona's office comes back to his mind, and his hands go suddenly cold.

He moves away from the classroom, intending to walk down the hall toward the exit. But then he catches sight of the stairs to the mezzanine, and his heart starts to race. He estimates there are still five minutes before the end of class. He thinks he can probably make it up the stairs to Shona's office in about one minute, in another thirty seconds he could have the candlesticks in his backpack, and he'd have another two and a half minutes to get back downstairs and out of the building.

As his feet move him toward the staircase, he thinks of Shona and stops at the first step. *She's been so good to me; she's my friend,* he thinks. *Why would I do this to her?* But the image of the candlesticks burns all the brighter in his mind. The rate of his breathing increases and he leans against the wall to steady himself. He closes his eyes and whispers, "Help me, Hashem." *It's different when it's someone who deserves it,* he thinks. *But not Shona. Not Shona.* "Please, Hashem."

A hand touches his shoulder. He opens his eyes and suddenly finds himself inside Shona's office, inches away from her bookcase.

"What are you doing, Ralph?"

Raphael spins around and sees Shona. Her eyes are glistening.

He closes his eyes for a moment and whispers, "Baruch Hashem." Then he moves absently past her to the door.

"Do you need something?"

He stops at the door and turns around. "Yes, Miss Reilly, I actually think I *do* need something."

She stares at him, her eyes wide and questioning.

"I think I need salvation."

Raphael bolts out of the art centre and rushes past Gabriella, who is just coming up the steps.

"Rafi," she calls out.

Raphael halts mid-stride and whips around. "Oh, Gaby, sorry. I didn't see you. What are you doing here?"

Gabriella comes down the stairs, links arms with Raphael, and gives him a kiss on the cheek. "I told you I was going to pick you up, silly boy." She leads him toward the sculpture garden in the direction of the parking garage. "How did it go?"

"I said my goodbyes if that's what you mean."

"So you're agreed then?" She stops in front of Rodin's *L'homme qui marche* and peers at him. "You'll go to Israel?"

Raphael nods and pulls her along. "I'll go. Abba's probably right. Maybe it's for the best."

"Not just Abba. Remember, it's Ima decision too, and the rabbi's. They're all agreed."

Raphael holds up a hand. "I said I was going. So let's drop it, please."

Gabriella frowns and pulls Raphael around to face her. "I'm not dropping anything. When we get home, you're going to apologise to Abba and Ima, do you understand?"

"Apologise to them for what, pray tell?"

"For earlier tonight, of course. For your disrespect."

"What about *you*? You weren't exactly the meek, submissive daughter. In fact, if I remember it right—and I do—you were on *my* side."

"Don't worry about me. I've apologised. Worry about yourself."

Raphael kicks at the dirt. "What a total *balagan*." He reaches up and readjusts his kippah, then looks back at Gabriella, who is staring at him, waiting for an answer. "Yes, OK, I'll apologise." Glancing back at the art centre, he randomly recalls the story of Lot's wife. Then, linking arms with Gabriella once again, he says, "*Yalla*, let's go home."

As they cross the drive in the direction of the parking garage, a tall young man in a red tracksuit steps out of the shadows.

Raphael recognises the swimmer from earlier. He looks at Raphael and then at Gabriella.

"Oh, hey," Raphael says.

"Hey," the swimmer says. "What's up?"

Gabriella cuts her eyes at him. "Who is this, Rafi?"

Raphael forces a smile. "This is a friend from the aquatics centre."

The swimmer steps forward and holds out his hand at Gabriella. "Hi. I'm Eric."

"This is my sister," Raphael says, nodding at Gabriella.

Gabriella looks at Eric's outstretched hand and back up at him.

"Is this a bad time?" Eric asks.

"What's he doing here, Rafi?"

"You left these at the pool earlier." Eric reaches into his pocket and pulls out Raphael's black Speedos.

"Thanks," Raphael says, glancing at Gabriella and stuffing the swimsuit into his backpack.

Gabriella opens her mouth as if to say something, then closes her eyes and shakes her head.

"Anyway, bon voyage," Eric says to Raphael, arching an eyebrow at Gabriella.

"What was that all about?" Gabriella asks as Eric moves away from them down Circle Drive.

"I left my swimsuit at the pool. You heard him."

"How did he know to find you here?"

"I mentioned I had class here. What is it with you anyway? Can't a guy have friends?"

Gabriella grasps Raphael by the arm and pulls him in the direction of the car park. "We'll talk about this later."

Chapter 3

Raphael pokes his head into the living room. His father is sitting in his leather recliner, studying the Talmud, as he does every evening. But for the passage of a few hours, everything looks unchanged from when he was last in the room, except that his father is now wearing his dark blue satin housecoat and matching slippers.

"May I come in, Abba?" Raphael asks from the doorway.

Isaac looks at him over the top of the book and waves him into the room. Raphael walks over and offers the top of his head to his father, who places his hand on the crown of his head and utters a blessing, then kisses him on the forehead. Raphael sits on the sofa opposite him.

"I apologise, Abba. For earlier."

Isaac sets aside the book and sits up.

"I forgot myself and disrespected you and Ima. Please forgive me."

"Yes, I forgive you, son."

"Thank you, Abba." Raphael stands. "There's just one thing."

Isaac nods.

"I don't want to wait until after the High Holidays. I'm ready now."

"You mean—"

"For Israel; I want to go tomorrow."

Isaac shakes his head. "The arrangements, the flight, your aunt and cousins, everything is set for the Sunday after *Yom Kippur*."

"Please, Abba. Before I change my mind."

Isaac looks sharply at Raphael.

"I mean, I'd go anyway, since that's what you and Ima want. But, inside, I'm ready now. I think it's best if I go right away. Please, Abba."

"I'll need to speak with your mother."

"Speak with me about what?" Sylvie asks from the doorway.

Raphael and Isaac turn and see her tentatively poised in her wheelchair above the ramp, staring at them from the half-level above.

Raphael stands. "I'm ready to go to Israel now, Ima. I don't want to wait until after the High Holidays."

"I told him that all the arrangements are made," Isaac says. "Plus, I thought it would be good to spend Yom Kippur and his birthday together as a family."

"If you're going to send me away, what difference does one more Yom Kippur here make? Better I should observe it in Israel. And never mind about my birthday. If Aunt Penina isn't ready for me, I can always spend time with Saba and Savta in Jerusalem, and I can go to Aunt Penina's after."

Sylvie looks at Raphael, then at Isaac. "Let him go," she says, unlatching the brake and wheeling herself away from the doorway. "One Yom Kippur won't make a difference."

"She hates me, doesn't she?" Raphael says to his father.

Isaac looks at the empty doorway for a moment and looks back at Raphael. "She's tired, that's all. It's part of the condition."

Raphael nods and flashes a sad smile. After a moment, the smile disappears. "I want to go to the *mikveh* tomorrow, Abba, before Shacharit. And I need to speak with Rabbi Mordechai afterwards. Then I'll be ready to go."

Isaac hugs his son and holds him close for a few moments, then kisses him on his head.

"I love you, Abba."

"Goodnight, son."

—⚬—

Raphael finishes reciting *Grace after Meals* as he pushes into his bedroom after a quick dinner of leftovers. He closes the door behind him and surveys his room as if for the first time. He stares at the film posters on his wall, at the framed Dali and Francis Bacon reproductions, at the hand-painted bust of Richard Wagner on his dresser to which he has recently added a pair of fangs, and at his collection of vintage bowlers, trilbies, and top hats crenellated across the crown of his armoire.

He moves across the room with a heavy sigh, simultaneously sliding off his braces, unsnapping the buttons of his shirt, and exposing his tallit katan. Then he absently removes his shirt while running a finger over the books on his bookshelf. An empty space where he keeps his copy of *A Clockwork Orange* reminds him of his backpack. Spinning around, he casts about the room. Not seeing it, he heads for the door, pulls it open, and finds Gabriella on the other side, her clenched hand raised and ready to knock. They blink at each other and Gabriella holds up Raphael's backpack. "You left this in the study."

Raphael takes the backpack from her, withdraws into his bedroom, and tries to close the door. But Gabriella pushes inside.

"I'd like some privacy if you don't mind."

Gabriella points at the bag. "I didn't look inside of that."

Raphael tosses the backpack onto his bed with a shrug and removes his tallit katan.

"But if I had," Gabriella says, "what would I have found?"

"That's the million-dollar question, isn't it? What's in Raphael's backpack?"

Raphael kisses the fringes of his tallit katan and folds it carefully, placing it on a chair. Then he snatches up his backpack and lobs it at Gabriella, who catches it in her arms. "Go ahead and open it."

Gabriella looks down at the bag.

"Well, go on!"

She pushes the backpack back at him. "Tell me what's going on, Rafi. None of us knows anymore. Whenever you walk out that door, we never know what story you'll have when you come back. Nothing adds up. Like that guy tonight waiting for you in the dark. That wasn't really about your swimsuit, was it?"

Raphael takes the backpack out of Gabriella's hands and dumps the contents on his bed. He bends down and spreads it across his duvet, a couple of books here, two granola bars there, a bottle of water, a movie magazine, a pack of Kleenex, and a black wallet, which he picks up and holds out at her. "This one's mine." He tosses it back onto his bed. "You can search through the rest if you want. I'm going to finish changing."

Gabriella watches as Raphael steps into his closet for a few moments then re-emerges in his nightshirt and the white kippah he wears to bed. "Still here?"

"You haven't answered my question, Rafi. Why was that guy there to meet you tonight? I'll keep whatever it is a secret, I promise. I just need to know."

Raphael gathers up his things from atop his bed and stuffs it all into his backpack, save for his copy of *A Clockwork Orange*, which he tosses onto his nightstand. Then he turns to Gabriella. "You're totally paranoid, Gaby. The guy was there to bring me my swimsuit. That's it. So lay off and mind your own business."

Gabriella looks Raphael in the eye. He meets her stare and holds it for several seconds.

"I'm *glad* you're going to Israel," Gabriella says after a moment. "To Aunt Penina's."

"Good! Then you'll be happy to know I'm leaving tomorrow."

"Tomorrow? I thought it wasn't until after Yom Kippur."

"Surprise! Anyway, Abba agreed. He's making the arrangements."

"What about Ima?" Gabriella asks.

"What does she care anyway? She can't wait until I'm gone."

"That's not true!" Gabriella says. "She's devastated you're going."

"She's devastated I'm still here."

"That's an awful thing to say." Gabriella stares hard at Raphael. "I think going back to Israel will be good for you."

"I don't need any improving, thanks." Raphael moves to his stereo and flips it on. "I'm already the best."

Gabriella nods. "So you keep reminding us."

"I figure it doesn't really matter where I go. I'll always be the best. Especially in some backwater hellhole like Mitzpe Ramon. You'll see. I'll be taking over the place after a while."

Gabriella turns around and slowly walks to the door.

"You'll see," Raphael says again as she slips out of his room. He pushes shut the door behind her and locks it. "You'll all see."

Raphael pops an eight-track cassette of Wagner's *Das Rheingold* into his stereo, closes his eyes, and lets the first strains of the Prelude wash over him, pushing out of his mind all that has transpired throughout the day. He stays that way until the start of *Weia! Waga!* at which point he steps deep into his closet and pulls out his seven favourite canvases, which he has painted over the course of the last few months. He kisses each one of them and arranges them around his room. Then he sits on his bed, admiring each of them the way a parent does a precious child.

He focuses on the largest of the paintings, a self-portrait reminiscent of Michelangelo's *The Last Judgment*. In it, he floats naked in mid-air, high above an Olympic-size swimming pool, his arms wrapped protectively around a faceless male figure on one side and a faceless female figure on the other, against a star-filled sky out of which peer the disapproving faces of his immediate and extended family and the members of his community. On his head he wears the silver crown he stole from the synagogue, and around his neck hangs the matching silver breastplate. The look on his face is proud and arrogant, his mouth open, ready to answer his accusers. The painting takes him back to those early days following the theft when everyone in the congregation treated him like a pariah, everyone except the rabbi. He is jarred out of his concentration by an insistent knocking.

Opening the door to his bedroom, he is surprised to find his mother in the darkened hallway. She wheels herself forward until her knees touch his shins and extends her hands. Raphael hesitates a moment, then takes hold of them. They feel warm and moist compared with his own, which are cold and dry. He looks down at their grasped hands trying to remember the last time she touched him, when she suddenly squeezes them tight. His head snaps up, and he finds her staring at him, her eyes narrow and intense.

"I need to speak with you, Raphael," she says, her voice barely louder than a whisper.

Raphael nods and wheels her into his bedroom and sits on the bed opposite her. She lowers her head for a moment and sighs.

"Are you OK, Ima?"

Sylvie looks up, reaches out and squeezes his hands again. "Your father tells me that you think I hate you." Her voice is edged with pain.

Raphael locks eyes with his mother. "You do."

Sylvie holds Raphael's gaze for several seconds. She squeezes his hands again, this time more forcefully.

"I love you more than life itself, *motek sheli.*"

His mother's words of endearment are almost more than Raphael can bear. He pulls back his hands and sits up.

"You've been terrible to me, Ima. So cold, so mean."

"Raphael, stop."

Raphael scoots back on his bed away from his mother.

"Steady, *motek*," she says.

Raphael glances at his wall clock.

"Allow me to explain," she says

Raphael points at the clock. "I'm getting up early tomorrow. So please make it quick, Ima."

"Yes, yes…" Sylvie shakes her head. "After what happened at the *esnoga*—"

"You mean *three* years ago?"

"After what happened there," she repeats, "I was so ashamed, so disappointed in you. I never stopped loving you, of course. How could I? You're my son. My special son. But I struggled for a very long time to forgive you, for the shame you brought on all of us. It caused me so much pain."

Raphael chokes back the stinging tears that stand out in his eyes. But he holds his mother's intense gaze and listens to her without interrupting.

"I've never told anyone this before, not even your father. But the doctor recently told me he thinks my relapse and the acceleration of the disease may have resulted from all the stress I suffered during that horrible period of our lives."

Raphael looks down and wipes his face on the back of his sleeve and looks back up at her, determined not to own the guilt she seems to want to burden him with.

"*Motek*, I know very well how difficult it is to be an immigrant in a new country," she continues. "I've experienced it myself. First Israel, then America."

"You were two years old when you went to Israel, Ima. You were practically born there. That doesn't count."

"I didn't go of my own accord. My parents took me there. And they *never* learned to speak Hebrew. We spoke only French at home. For much of my childhood, I wished we would have stayed in Lyon. It wasn't easy for me, *motek*. It took me a long time to find my place. But I eventually did. And then your father brought us here to America, which wasn't easy for any of us. Not for Gabriella, not for me, not even for your father. But we've coped, we've adjusted. We've had to. We've had no other choice."

"What's your point, Ima?" He glances up again at the wall clock.

"My point is you've been blaming what you did at the *esnoga* on your father and me, for bringing you to America against your will. But that's completely on you." Her voice takes on a hard edge. "None of the rest of us who are in exactly the same position as you have resorted to theft, dishonesty, or chronic lying."

"That's all in the past, Ima."

"So you say."

"That's totally unfair, Ima! You have no proof of anything against me."

Sylvie holds up her hands. "A mother knows, *motek*. A mother knows. And then there are your outrageous eccentricities, what with your selection of reading material, these obscenities you paint"—she waves her hand at his paintings—"and the way you dress." And only Hashem knows what you get up to out there on the streets. The rabbi and your father have been willing to grant you these liberties and tolerate your strange behaviour in the hopes you'll change and become someone respectable. But not me. Not anymore. I love you, my son; I would give up my life for you. But you will not have my affection until you change."

"And sending me to Aunt Penina's is what's going to change me?"

"Only Hashem knows." Sylvie signals for Raphael to lean forward. He stares at her for a moment, then shakes his head and complies. Sylvie presses her lips to his forehead. "You're in His hands now."

Raphael lies back on his bed trembling with rage, his eyes tightly closed, his mother's harsh words still ringing in his ears. He focuses on his journey ahead, on what he remembers of Israel, in an effort to purge his mind of the black feelings her words provoked. He summons up the image of his beloved Savta, always so sweet to him, and of his old neighbourhood in Jerusalem. He recalls his drives to the Dead Sea with his Uncle Shimshon and his cousins to float on its oily surface under a burning sun. The cloudless sky, the hint of orange blossoms in the air, the bustle of the market, the smell of the spices, the prayers at the Kotel.

As his heart rate settles, he notices something odd hovering at the edge of his consciousness. At first, he finds it difficult to determine what it is, given that it is so far away. But as it moves closer, he can make out what looks like a floating head. The image terrifies him, but much as he wants to open his eyes and make it go away, he forces himself to look at the face as it speeds toward him, a woman's face with open and knowing eyes, the hard face of his Aunt Penina, the bitter, accusing, and tortured face of a soul without hope. Raphael sits up and opens his eyes, but he can still see her, hovering there, ever accusing.

He runs to the shower, spinning on the cold water tap to receive the full force of the stream over his trembling body. The frigid water shocks him back into full consciousness and sends his heart racing. He bends over and grasps his ankles and lets the water wash over his back for sixty seconds, then stands back up and arches into the stream, allowing it to pummel his face. As his trembling subsides, he spins on the hot water tap and finishes washing in the warming water, finally pushing away the image of Aunt Penina.

After his shower, Raphael puts the paintings away in his closet and climbs back into bed to recite the night-time Shema. When he finishes, he stays sitting for a moment, fiddling absently with the edge of his duvet and feeling thoroughly exhausted. Even though he knows the Shema is the last thing he should say before closing his eyes, he feels compelled to say something else. He looks up at the ceiling, then around his room, and then straight ahead.

"Hashem?" He pulls up his knees, wraps his arms around them, and sits that way for a bit. "Hashem?"

Raphael reaches up and touches his kippah with his fingertips. A warm sense of reassurance washes over him as he feels it on his head. He can't remember a time he ever slept without his head covered, out of respect for Hashem who, as the Talmud teaches, watches over us all hours of the day and all hours of the night, like a gardener who watches over a tender plant.

He takes up his tallit katan from his nightstand, kisses it, and sets it aside. Then he looks up again at the ceiling. "Hashem?"

After a few minutes of sitting in the dark silence, he shrugs and fluffs up his pillow before lying down and closing his eyes. Thirty seconds later he transitions from weary consciousness into a deep, dreamless sleep.

—␣␣—

The next morning, after immersing himself in the mikveh to ensure he is ritually pure for the start of his journey, Raphael changes into white cotton trousers and a white cotton shirt and walks alone the five blocks to the synagogue for morning prayers. The hazzan approaches Raphael as he finishes laying *tefillin* and offers him the honour of elevating the Torah scroll during the service, which Raphael readily accepts. He quickly moves into the study hall, head down, and slips into the row where his father is praying next to the rabbi.

Raphael ascends the platform at the start of the Torah service and kisses the scroll as he receives it from the stone-faced sexton, his lips lingering for several seconds on the embroidered vestments. Whether deliberate or not, Raphael recognises the scroll the sexton has selected as the very scroll he stripped of its precious silver three years before, and his chest goes tight. As customary, he carries it in a circuit around the room, followed by the rabbi and the hazzan, focusing his eyes on the floor rather than on the still-resentful congregation as they reach out hands and prayer books to touch the holy scroll, before he ascends the platform and sits to one side of the reading table.

The sexton removes the ritual silver from the scroll—the crowns, breastplate, and vestments (bringing back stinging memories of armed police officers bursting into his classroom)—after which Raphael stands and unrolls the scroll, four panels wide, on the reading table and waits until the hazzan finishes chanting. Then he holds high the scroll facing north as the hazzan calls out in Hebrew, *This is the Torah that Moses presented to the children of Israel.* He catches sight of Simon standing in the back row sticking out his tongue at him, and next to him he sees Simon's sidekick Marc Sadot looking away and shaking his head.

The rest of the service passes like a fog for Raphael; his thoughts are only of his quickly evaporating American life, accompanied by a chasm of anxiety for what lies ahead. But he keeps a brave face and chants the prayers with forced enthusiasm in an effort to keep his fears in check and hidden from the community.

At the conclusion of the service, the president of the community ascends the platform and pulls out his notes to make his usual morning announcements. When he finishes, he folds his notes, sets them aside, looks up at the congregation for a moment, and looks straight at Raphael.

"And, finally, I'd like to announce that our very own Raphael Dweck, who executed a perfect *levanta* for us this morning, will soon be returning to Israel."

Raphael turns his head and looks at his father and at the rabbi, both of whom stare straight ahead at the platform. He glances over his shoulder and sees Simon and Marc whispering to each other, then looks back up at the president.

"Raphael, we will all miss your energetic participation in our community, your quick wit, and your insightful arguments."

A general murmur of agreement rumbles through the community and Raphael looks down at the floor for a moment before lifting his head and nodding his thanks to the president.

As the service breaks up, Raphael makes his way to the back of the room, shaking hands with the various members of his community as he passes them. Simon and Marc intercept him when he reaches the door, and Simon gently pulls him aside by the arm.

"What's up with that, man?" Simon asks. "Israel?"

Raphael shrugs. "Let's just say I'm ready for a new challenge."

"I'll bet he got caught stealing again," Marc says.

Simon elbows Marc in the ribs, and Marc pushes him back. "Hey, that hurt!"

"Tell your girlfriend to mind her own business," Raphael says, indicating Marc with a tilt of his head.

"Girlfriend?" Marc says.

"Anyway," Raphael says to Simon, "I'm sure you'll be happy to be the best-looking guy in the community again, *gever*."

Rabbi Sadot passes them and asks Raphael to follow him as he disappears into the hallway.

"What do you mean?" Simon says.

Raphael winks at Simon. "See you when I see you!" He throws a sidelong glance at Marc. "Hope I never see *you* again, comrade."

He slips away from them and speeds down the narrow hall to the rabbi's office. The door is slightly ajar, and Raphael moves inside, closing it behind him. He is surprised to find the rabbi sitting on the sofa instead of behind his desk. The rabbi invites Raphael to sit next to him with a pat of his hand on the adjacent cushion. Raphael hesitates slightly before lowering himself next to the rabbi.

"I understand you wanted to speak with me," the rabbi says.

Raphael shifts left to look at the rabbi. "I'm leaving today, Rabbi."

"Yes, I'm aware. The question is why today?"

"I don't understand something, Rabbi. But I need for this to stay private, just between us, please."

Rabbi Sadot reclines against the back of the sofa, raises his eyebrows in agreement, and waits for Raphael to continue.

Raphael clears his throat, reaches for a glass of water on the table in front of the sofa, and takes a sip. After a moment, he sets the glass on the table and looks back at the rabbi. "After that time, you know, with the stealing and all that, I've done everything right. But it doesn't really work, does it, Rabbi?"

"What doesn't work?"

"I study and I pray, more than anyone I know. But I'm still bad inside."

Rabbi Sadot lifts his gaze at Ralph. "So I wasn't wrong, was I?"

Raphael looks down and shakes his head. "The compulsion is still there."

"Have you done something like what you did before?"

"No, Rabbi. But I want to. All the time! I ask Hashem to help me, but He doesn't. Last night I called out to Him. After the Shema."

"You called out to Him?"

"Yes, Rabbi. But He doesn't answer, does He? Not really."

"Hashem answers in other ways."

"I'm not sure He's really there, Rabbi." Raphael catches his breath as the words come out. "At least not for me."

Rabbi Sadot closes his eyes and pinches the bridge of his nose for a moment, then he opens them, leans forward, and whispers, "He's right here, young man. He's always right here. With me, with you, with all of us. Don't have any doubt about that."

"Then why doesn't He help me?"

"Hashem's help isn't always obvious. It will come to you. But it won't come to you here. Not with all the distractions you have around you. As you know, I've been giving this a lot of thought, and I'm convinced your answer will come to you in Israel. Trust me, young man. Trust me. And trust Hashem."

Chapter 4

Raphael pushes down the aisle of the 747 and finds his seat at the back of the plane two rows from the galley. Before sitting down, he pulls a makeup kit from his backpack and pops into the lavatory to quickly shave off his eyebrows and apply mascara. Then he returns to his row and slides next to the window, hoping no one will take the other two seats so he can recline across the whole bank.

After a few minutes, he spots a lanky young woman with a strawberry-blonde ponytail, a NASA-stencilled T-Shirt, and tight bell-bottom jeans headed in his direction, comparing her boarding pass with the numbers above the seats. A dark green roll-on suitcase trails in her wake. She pulls up alongside Raphael and squints at the number above the seat bank and at her boarding pass.

"Is this twenty-seven?" The young woman flashes Raphael a gap-toothed smile wrapped in silver braces.

Raphael nods.

She holds out her boarding pass at Raphael. "I think I've got the window."

Raphael scoots out and stands next to the young woman, who is about an inch taller than him. "Sorry, my fault," he says, noticing a nametag hanging around her neck in a plastic holder. The tag is topped with a red, white, and black logo that says *Tours of the Cross,* underneath which are the neatly calligraphed words *Joanie Smith.*

The young woman smiles again at Raphael. She lifts her suitcase into the overhead compartment, and Raphael follows her in as she scoots to the window seat, taking the middle seat next to her.

Once they are buckled in, the young woman offers her hand. "Hi, I'm Joanie."

Raphael points at her nametag. "I figured that." He glances at her hand and back at her face, which is covered in freckles. "I'm Ralph."

"Are you Jewish?" she asks, slowly drawing back her hand.

Raphael points at his kippah. "Guilty as charged."

Joanie lets out a short laugh and nervously jiggles her long legs. She glances out the window for a moment, and Raphael steals a quick peek at her breasts, which are small but shapely.

"I'm a born-again Christian," she says, looking back at Raphael.

Raphael nods and flashes a half-smile, turning a bit red.

Joanie points at a flow of chatty teenagers making their way down both aisles to the back of the plane, all wearing Tours of the Cross nametags. "We're part of a youth group from Fresno called The Faithful of Christ. We're off to Israel to see the places where the Lord walked. Have you ever been before?"

"Where? To Israel?" Raphael looks closely at Joanie, who has the gentlest, most beautiful light hazel eyes he has ever seen.

"Yes," Joanie says.

"I was born there, actually," Raphael says. "I'm going home."

"Really?"

"Yes, really. I'm originally from Jerusalem."

"That is *so* cool. You're, like, really special."

Raphael flashes his teeth and holds out his arm to Joanie, who looks down at it.

"What?" Joanie says.

"You can touch me if you want."

Joanie giggles at Raphael's little joke and spends the next thirty pre-takeoff minutes explaining her group's itinerary in detail. Raphael nods and smiles politely suddenly dreading the next fourteen hours.

As the plane pushes back from the terminal and starts taxiing toward the runway, Raphael excuses himself from Joanie's monologue and closes his eyes. Several minutes later, the plane speeds down the runway and lifts off. After about twenty minutes, he is awakened by Joanie, who is trying to climb over him to get to the lavatory. Raphael blinks a few times and sees that the plane has levelled off and the first drinks service has passed them up.

Raphael strolls around the cabin, grabs a cup of orange juice from the galley, and pokes his head into the first class cabin on the second level. He slips into an empty window seat and stretches out to sleep. After a while, he hears someone clear his throat and opens his eyes to find a gruff-looking, bearded flight attendant in his early thirties staring down at him. His thick eyebrows meet in the middle above an unnatural-looking snub nose as he narrows his eyes at Raphael.

"Is this your seat?" he asks.

Raphael sits up, quickly assessing the flight attendant, whose dark blue uniform is perfectly tailored and whose shoes are polished to a high shine.

"No, it's not."

"Then what are you doing in it?"

"It was empty. So, I figured, what's the harm?"

"Where's *your* seat?"

Raphael points downstairs.

"You have ten seconds to get out of first class before I call security."

Raphael stands and glares at the flight attendant. "You don't have to get nasty, *gever*." He notes the name *Uzi Shaked* on his tag and calculates the location of his wallet from the slight lift on the left-hand side of his jacket. "I can at least walk through the cabin, can't I?"

"Not in first class." He points at the stairs. "Now, go."

"Yes, your highness." Raphael bows to the flight attendant with an exaggerated flourish and heads for the stairs.

"I don't want to see you up here for the rest of the flight," the flight attendant calls out to him. "Is that clear?"

Raphael registers the comment without responding and descends the stairs.

"Hello again," Joanie says as Raphael slips back into his seat.

Raphael lifts his hand at her, and his mouth pulls up on one side into a half-smile. "Hey there."

"So," Joanie says, "I've been wondering…"

"Wondering what?"

"Whether you're a completed Jew?" Joanie flashes a broad smile, her braces glinting in the overhead light of the cabin.

"Sorry," Raphael says. "What exactly are you asking?"

"I'm asking if you're completed?"

"I don't understand the question."

"You're Jewish."

"Obviously." Raphael points again at his kippah.

"Right. So, what I'm asking is whether you're a completed Jew."

"Again, I don't get what you're asking. Completed how? Are you asking whether I'm circumcised? Or whether I'm a bar mitzvah?"

Joanie reddens and waves her hand. "No, neither of those. I meant, have you accepted Jesus, or Yeshua, as I think is what your people called him in Hebrew, as your Lord and Saviour."

"My people?"

"Jewish people."

Joanie pulls up one leg and beams a smile. "Our Lord Jesus was Jewish, too. Did you know that?"

Raphael looks at her with a deadpan expression. "I don't mean to be rude. But, are you really going to do this?"

"Do what?"

"The proselytizing."

"We're here on earth to spread the good news of Jesus to everyone. That's our mission. So, yes, absolutely. That's the reason the Lord placed us here together."

"Really?"

"Yes, I truly believe that."

"OK, fine. So, in answer to your question, yes, I do know that Jesus was Jewish. What about it?"

"We Christians believe he was the Jewish Messiah."

"Is there any other kind?"

Joanie lets out an exasperated sigh and continues, "So, when a Jew accepts Jesus as their Lord and Saviour, and as their Messiah, we consider them to be completed."

"You believe that Jesus is God, right?"

"Yes, we do. God the Son."

"How many of them are there?"

"What do you mean?" A deep crease appears between Joanie's yellow-red eyebrows.

"You said, Jesus is 'God the Son'. How many other Gods are there?"

"Well, there's God the Father, and there's Jesus, who is God the Son, and there's God the Holy Spirit."

"So there are three of them?"

"There are three, but they're also one."

"Yeah ... you know, that's the thing about us Jews. We're only allowed one God. So this three-in-one thing doesn't work. That's sort of blasphemy for us."

Joanie stiffens and shakes her head. "It's not like we're polytheists, if that's what you mean."

"No?"

"Of course not!"

"Also…" Raphael holds up his hand. He pulls a granola bar out of his pocket and tears open the pack, saying a quick blessing and munching on it.

Joanie crinkles her brow at him as he finishes his snack.

"Sorry for being rude," he says, wiping his mouth with a paper napkin. "I was totally starving."

"You were about to say something…"

Raphael suppresses an internal scream. "Oh, you mean, you want to keep talking about religion?"

Joanie nods. "Yes, please."

"OK, fine. So what I don't get is why *your* people would worship someone who practised a completely different religion from yourselves, and who, obviously, had different beliefs from your own."

"What do you mean '*different* beliefs'?"

"Jesus was perfect, right? According to you."

"According to the Bible."

"Yes, OK. But, I mean, you hold to the idea that everything Jesus did, everything he said, and everything he believed was perfect, right? He was infallible."

"That's what the Bible says."

"So then it logically follows that first-century Judaism is the only true religion, including all its beliefs and practices, if—as you believe—that was the religion Jesus followed. Right?"

Joanie narrows her eyes at Raphael.

"What did Jews in the first century believe, Joanie?" Raphael waits a moment for his words to hit before pressing on. "What books did they study? How and when did they pray? What did they eat? What did they avoid eating?"

Joanie glances across the cabin at her tour leader and back at Raphael. "I'm not an expert in first-century Judaism, sorry."

"Why not? If that's the religion your god followed, why don't you know more about it?"

After a moment of silence, Joanie smiles tightly and shakes her head. "I didn't mean for things to get heated, sorry. Let's call a truce, OK?"

"Sure," Raphael says with a slight lift of his shoulders. He looks back at the flight attendants who are pushing the meal cart up the aisle. "It seems like they're starting the food service anyway."

Joanie touches him lightly on the leg. "I'll be praying for you."

Raphael flashes Joanie a thumbs up.

After the meal service, the captain dims the overhead lights, and the cabin is plunged into near-total darkness. Raphael stretches out as best he can in his cramped seat and falls asleep. When he next opens his eyes, he finds Joanie resting her head on his shoulder, softly snoring. Glancing at his watch, he realises he has been out for nearly two hours.

Gently manoeuvring Joanie's head back onto her headrest, he unbuckles his seat belt and seeks out the lavatory at the back of the cabin. When he emerges, he glances around the corner into the galley, which is empty, and steps into it to poke around the snacks, inspecting the random packs of crisps, biscuits, nuts, raisins, and pocketing anything that bears the U *kosher* symbol.

As he is about to return to his seat, he spots a suit coat draped over the back of one of the seats the flight attendants use when they are relaxing in the galley. He glances over his shoulder, pulls on the lapel to look at the nametag, which says *Uzi Shaked*, and spits out the word *mamzer* under his breath. Shooting another quick look over his shoulder, he slips his hand into the inside pocket, his heart hammering in his chest, and lifts out Uzi's wallet. He swiftly replaces it with a square pack of Kit Kats and smoothens down the coat before stepping out of the galley. Strolling as nonchalantly as possible up the aisle opposite his, he crosses over at the front of the cabin and glides back down the other side.

When he reaches his row, he checks on Joanie to make sure she is still asleep. Then he pops opens the overhead compartment, unzips the side flap of her suitcase and, looking both ways to make sure nobody is looking, slips the wallet underneath a wad of socks. Realising he's been holding his breath for far too long, Raphael exhales, clicks shut the overhead compartment, returns to his seat and closes his eyes.

Just then the plane lurches violently, tossing screaming passengers, flight attendants, serving carts, dishes, and drinks about the cabin. Joanie wakes with a start and grasps Raphael's thigh, digging in her fingernails, and Raphael jerks away his leg. He glares at Joanie, who is hyperventilating, her face drained of colour. Raphael looks about the cabin and takes in the chaos unfolding around them.

"What's happening?" Joanie says.

Raphael glances at her and shakes his head. "Probably just bad turbulence." He passes his hand through his wet hair. His head and face are dripping sweat, and his clothes have soaked through.

A milkshake-smooth voice from the flight deck floats out of the public address system, confirming they have hit a rough patch and instructing the passengers to return to their seats. The plane continues to bounce over air pockets for several minutes before stabilising long enough for the flight attendants to attend to the general mess. They circulate through the cabin and verify there are no injuries.

Raphael dries his face and body with his bandana, then places it on the seat next to him to air dry. He checks his watch and, noticing it is already 7 p.m. Los Angeles time, pulls out his prayer book and flips the pages to the evening prayer service.

"Is that Hebrew?" Joanie points a trembling finger at the open book.

Raphael nods and holds it up. "Are you OK now?"

"I think so." Joanie looks away for a moment. "I really thought we were going to die; that was totally scary."

Raphael closes his prayer book. "Are you afraid to die?"

"Well … yes. Aren't you?"

"Let's talk about you."

Joanie glances across the cabin at the leader of her group, who is engaged in an intense conversation with his neighbour, then looks back at Raphael. "I guess I'm afraid of what happens afterwards. I mean, I believe and all that. But, still…"

"Still what?"

"There's still a lot I haven't done yet. I wouldn't want to go too soon, if you know what I mean."

"Like what?"

Joanie shakes his head and waves her hand at Raphael.

"What haven't you done yet?"

Joanie looks out the window. "Never mind," she mutters.

"Are you talking about sex?" Raphael whispers.

Joanie whips around in her seat. "Of course not. What's wrong with you? How can you even ask that?"

"How old are you?" Raphael asks calmly.

"Seventeen."

"Seventeen, really? And you're still a virgin? That's unbelievable."

"It's a sin to have sex before you're married. And I was saved when I was really young."

"You mean, you're waiting to get married before you have sex?"

"Yes, of course. It's what the Lord wants; it's what the Bible teaches."

"Oh." Raphael opens up his prayer book to the evening service again.

"What about you?" Joanie asks after a few moments of silence. "Have you, you know, had sex?"

Raphael shuts his prayer book. "Yes."

"How old are you?"

"I'm sixteen, nearly seventeen. But I've been having sex since I was fifteen."

"Seriously?" Joanie says.

"Yes, seriously. Loads and loads of it. But that's all we're going to talk about since we don't really know each other that well. Plus, you know, you're a girl."

"It's not a sin for a Jew to have sex before he's married?"

"It's complicated. Not as black and white as for you guys."

Joanie chews on her lower lip and nods her head tentatively.

Raphael holds up the prayer book. "I have to pray now. And I can't be interrupted once I start. Sorry. That's the rule."

"OK, I promise. But, I'd like to talk more about this with you, if that's all right. I'm interested in comparing Christian beliefs with Jewish ones. Maybe we can meet. We're going to be in Israel for three weeks."

Raphael shrugs. "We'll see." He points at his prayer book.

Joanie nods and pantomimes zipping her mouth shut and tossing aside the key.

Raphael turns back to his evening prayers and reads them to himself. As he reaches the last couple of passages, Uzi pulls up next to his seat accompanied by a massively built bearded redhead man in his mid-forties dressed in dark cotton trousers and a short-sleeve white button shirt.

"This is the one," Uzi says, pointing at Raphael.

The large man moves Uzi to one side and says, "Raphael Dweck?"

Raphael holds up a hand, turns the page in his prayer book, and starts in on the final blessing.

Uzi opens his mouth to say something, but the large man raises a hand and Uzi backs down. They wait until Raphael finishes and looks up at them.

"Raphael Dweck?" the large man repeats.

"What it is?" Raphael says.

Joanie peers out at the men from behind Raphael, and a hush descends over the cabin as all eyes focus on the unfolding scene.

"Come with me, please."

Raphael slides the prayer book into his seat pocket, unbuckles his seat belt, and follows the two men down the aisle into the galley.

"I'm Gideon Vered, head of Security," the tall man says, drawing the curtains.

"If it's about sitting in first class," Raphael says, "I already apologised to him for that." He points at Uzi.

"Don't get smart, kid," Uzi says.

Vered looks sharply at Uzi, who immediately shuts up.

"Mr Shaked here claims you stole his wallet."

"You were seen here in the galley," Uzi says.

"Again, you talk when you're supposed to remain quiet," Vered says to him.

"Sorry," Uzi says.

Vered points at the curtain, not taking his eyes off Raphael. "Wait outside, please."

Uzi shakes his head and exits the galley.

"I didn't take his wallet," Raphael says. "Now, may I please return to my seat, after you've embarrassed me in front of the whole world?"

"I'm afraid it's not as simple as that," Vered says.

"Why not? Because that prick said so?"

"His wallet was definitely stolen." Vered holds up a packet of Kit Kats. "Someone replaced it with this."

Raphael bursts out laughing when he sees the packet of Kit Kats in Vered's hand. "That's hilarious!" he says, once his laughter has subsided.

"I'm glad you're amused," Vered says, "All the more reason for searching you, the area around your seat, and your bags once the rest of passengers have deplaned."

"I'm telling you, I didn't take it. That guy's had a hard-on for me ever since I boarded this flight, and now he wants me to take the fall for this."

"I'll need to pat you down."

Raphael raises his arms and spreads his legs. "I'm going to expect a full apology from that guy after this is all over."

"Is everything OK?" Joanie asks when he returns to his seat.

"That flight attendant got it into his head that I stole his wallet," he responds. "I'm going to have to stay behind once you all get off so they can search my bags."

Once the plane has rolled to a stop, Vered reappears at Raphael's side and asks him to wait. Joanie slips past them, grabs her suitcase, and joins the rest of the passengers as they make their way down the aisles toward the exit.

When the last passenger clears the cabin, Vered orders Raphael to step aside, and he searches all around Raphael's seat and inside the seat pocket. Uzi hovers in the background, chewing his thumbnail.

Finding nothing, Vered asks Raphael to pull his backpack out of the overhead compartment and proceeds to empty the bag of all its contents onto the aisle seat, some of it bouncing onto the floor, and sifts through it all. After a couple of minutes, Vered straightens up to his full height and shakes his head at Uzi, who storms into the galley.

"You see," Raphael says, "No wallet! Are you satisfied now?"

"Pick up your things, kid," Vered says through clenched teeth.

"I know you're only doing your job," Raphael says in a lowered voice. "So, no hard feelings." He offers Vered his hand. "Just make sure Her Majesty over there apologises to me, personally." He points at the galley. "Otherwise, I'm lodging a complaint."

Chapter 5

Raphael grabs his backpack and camera and speeds down the aisle toward the exit door. The blistering heat of the afternoon radiating into the cabin forces him to step back for the briefest of moments. Then, setting his face, he lowers his head and steps out of the plane. He rushes down the stairs, runs past a young soldier standing at attention at the foot of the stairs holding his Uzi diagonally across his chest, and sprints across the tarmac to the white stucco terminal building.

Once inside, he swiftly clears immigration as a returning citizen and tracks down the luggage carousel that corresponds to his flight. Seeing that it hasn't yet started to circulate, he positions himself next to the chute and waits. Ten minutes later, the carousel makes a grinding noise and begins to turn.

Raphael recognises some of his fellow passengers approaching from the immigration hall. They congregate not far from him next to the luggage carousel. A few minutes later, a contingent of flight attendants passes through the luggage hall on their way to the exit. Raphael spots Uzi among the group, closely followed by Vered. Uzi glances toward the luggage carousel and, catching sight of Raphael, touches his index finger to his nose and thrusts it at him. Raphael responds by grabbing his crotch with one hand, pointing at it with the other, and winking at Uzi. Noticing the exchange, Vered shakes his head and urges Uzi toward the door with a push from behind. Raphael holds his ground until they've cleared the luggage area and turns back in time to see a few more bags drop onto the conveyor belt.

Joanie's tour group emerges *en masse* from the immigration hall, led by their tour guide, who marches them in holding high in the air a stick topped by a red-and-white striped ribbon. Joanie breaks away from the group and runs toward Raphael, pulling her roller behind her. She throws her arms around him and gives him a bear hug, briefly lifting him off the ground.

"Jeez," Raphael says once she's released him. "You'd think we hadn't seen each other in years."

"I was worried about you." Joanie searches Raphael's face.

"Everything's fine."

"Did they find the wallet?"

Raphael shrugs. "Hell if I know. I didn't have it."

"What do you suppose happened to it?"

"Someone stole it, I guess. There were over three hundred passengers on board. Could have been anyone."

"How awful."

Raphael indicates the luggage carousel with a lift of his head. "Anyway, I've been waiting here for a while. Nothing yet."

Joanie points at a full-size, well-worn green suitcase circulating away from them on the other side of the carousel. "That's mine."

"Go for it," Raphael says, "I'll watch this one for you." He pats Joanie's roll-on and winks at her.

Joanie flashes a thumbs up and sprints around to the other side of the carousel. As she bends forward to lift her suitcase off the conveyor belt, Raphael unzips the side pocket of Joanie's roll-on, slips his hand inside and grasps the wallet that is still under the socks. Joanie straightens and elevates her suitcase, victoriously beaming a broad smile at Raphael from across the room, and catches sight of Raphael zipping the side pocket closed. Her smile immediately evaporates. She slowly walks back to Raphael lugging her suitcase across the hall. When she reaches him, she takes hold of his wrist and guides him to a corner away from the crowds.

"What were you doing just now?" she asks, pointing at her roll-on.

"Doing you a favour," Raphael says, rubbing his wrist. "The zipper was open, so I closed it for you."

"It wasn't open."

"Sure it was."

Joanie shakes her head and looks away from Raphael for a moment, then looks back at him, her eyes brimming with tears. She unzips her bag and rummages through the compartment. After a few seconds of looking in and around the mass of socks stuffed inside, she zips it closed and stares at Raphael.

"What?" Raphael says.

"You stole that flight attendant's wallet, didn't you? You stole it and hid it in my bag."

"That's a horrible thing to say."

"Did you or didn't you?"

Raphael looks away for a beat and looks back at her. "The idiot deserved it."

"You didn't!"

"I'm afraid so." Raphael pats his back pocket with his hand.

"That is so messed up. How could you do that?"

"Like I said, he deserved it."

"Don't you even feel bad?"

"Why should I?"

"Because it's a sin! You know, *thou shalt not steal.* It's in the Ten Commandments. *Your* part of the book."

"Yeah, well, it's complicated."

"Sheesh!" Joanie stamps her foot. "I should turn you in."

"Be my guest."

"Seriously, I really should."

Raphael spots his suitcase circulating on the carousel and shoulders his backpack. "But, you're not going to, are you?"

Joanie surveys the crowd, which is starting to thin out. About half the members of her group have begun congregating around their leader, who looks across the hall at Joanie. He mouths the words *Is everything OK?* Joanie holds up a hand and nods, forcing a smile and looking back at Raphael with a pained expression on her face.

"I won't turn you in if you promise to hand it over to the airline desk over there." She lifts her head in the direction of the information booth at the back of the hall.

"How am I supposed to do that without incriminating myself? They already have a record of the accusation against me. I'd be practically admitting it if I showed up with it now, wouldn't I?"

"You can't just keep it."

"I have a better idea." Raphael digs the wallet out of his back pocket and pushes it into Joanie's sweating palm. "I'll head out to the arrivals area, and *you* turn it in."

"Me?"

"Tell them you found it or something. Don't give them any details. Say that you saw it lying on the ground as you were coming out of the plane and leave it at that. Then walk away."

Joanie looks at the wallet and back up at Raphael.

Raphael plants a wet kiss on Joanie's cheek and walks away. Swinging past the luggage carousel, he grabs his suitcase off the conveyor belt and speeds out of the baggage claim area.

When he emerges into the arrivals hall, he is confronted by a mass of humanity holding welcome signs in Hebrew, English, French, Spanish, and Arabic, and calling out people's names. He drags his suitcase past them into the coffee shop to the west of the entry doors and buys a sandwich, a packet of crisps, and some Turkish coffee. Then, after washing his hands at a micro sink using a battered tin wash cup, he positions himself at a table at the entrance of the coffee shop, where he can survey the masses of people entering and exiting the arrivals hall.

As he downs the last of his coffee, he spots Joanie's tour group entering the arrivals area, including Joanie, who trails behind. They gather at the far end of the hall next to a bronze statue of David Ben Gurion, and their tour leader pulls out a guitar and leads them in the singing of a happy-clappy song. Once they finish, they all close their eyes and bow their heads, their hands clasped in front of them.

Joanie drifts away from the group and strolls around the hall, taking in the sights around her, the signs in Hebrew, machine gun-toting soldiers not much older than herself, flocks of black-clad Chaddisim and their large families, groups of nuns and priests dressed in the habits of their various orders arriving as part of a religious pilgrimage. Suppressing a yawn with the back of her hand, she leans heavily against a hoarding across from the coffee shop where Raphael is sitting and closes her eyes. When she reopens them, their eyes meet, and Raphael lifts a hand and smiles. Joanie jogs over to Raphael, who stands to greet her.

"I would have thought you were long gone by now!" Joanie says.

"I was starving." Raphael sits back down, and Joanie joins him. "I'll be catching a cab to Jerusalem in a few minutes." He vigorously rubs his hands on his jeans, then leans forward and whispers, "Anyway, how did it go, you know, with the—"

"Let's forget about that, OK?" Joanie says, lightly touching Raphael's knee. "It's all taken care of."

"Thank you." Raphael drains the last of his coffee and pushes aside his tray.

"I still don't understand why you would do such an awful thing. But it's in the past now. I forgive you. It's what the Lord would want me to do."

"Got it." Raphael stands and stretches his legs. "I've got to get going, sorry. I need to get to my grandmother's before the Sabbath starts."

Joanie glances in the direction of her group and sees the leader speaking with the local Israeli coach driver. The rest of her group is starting to mobilise behind him. One of her friends waves and Joanie holds up a hand signalling her to wait, then she turns back to Raphael.

"I'd like to see you again," she says with a broad smile. "Like I said before, I'm here for three weeks. Maybe we can get together and, like, do something fun, and talk some more."

"That's going to be difficult." Raphael shoulders his pack and drapes his camera around his neck. "I'm only here for a couple of days, then I'm gone to the desert for a long time, and I don't mean for a holiday."

The smile disappears from Joanie's face, and Raphael holds out his hand to her.

"I guess this is where we part ways," he says.

Joanie looks at the extended hand. "Can I at least have your number?"

"I don't have one. But"—he pulls a small notepad out of his backpack and scribbles on it, then tears out the sheet and hands it to her—"that's my name: Ralph Dweck. And this"—he points at the sheet—"is where I'll be staying: Nachlaot here in Jerusalem, and after that, I'll be over a hundred miles away in a hellhole called Mitzpe Ramon. I've written the information in both English letters and in Hebrew. I don't know the addresses by memory, sorry. If you're able to make it to either of these places, just ask around, and most anyone should be able to point the way to me."

Joanie looks down at the little sheet of paper pinched between her fingers and back up at Raphael.

"I can't promise you anything," Raphael says. "You might be wasting a trip if you do actually make it to either of these places."

Joanie nods and puts the paper in her brown suede handbag. She takes Raphael's hand and holds it tight; then she pulls him toward her and hugs him. When she finally releases him, Raphael arches his brow at her and moves toward the door. Once outside, he lets out a long breath and joins the snaking taxi queue.

"I forgot to tell you…" a familiar voice calls out from behind him a few moments later.

Raphael turns and watches in disbelief as Joanie pushes through the grumbling queue to join him. "We're staying at the hostel in the Old City across from the Tower of David in case you want to come see me. It might be easier that way."

"We already said our goodbyes, didn't we?"

"Yes, but—"

"Look, miss, I like you and all that. So, please don't make me say or do anything I'm going to regret, all right? I *really* need some alone time."

"But I thought…because I helped you—"

"And I *appreciate* that. I really do. But, my life is completely turned upside down at the moment, and I need to make sense of things. So, *pretty please*, just leave me alone."

"Yes, OK. Sorry."

Raphael points at the tour group, which is slowly making its way out of the terminal building and headed in the direction of the coach park. "I think you'd better join your friends."

Chapter 6

The cab driver drops off Raphael in front of the Beit Knesset Ohavei Zion synagogue, and Raphael drags his suitcase into the winding lanes that make up his childhood neighbourhood of Nachlaot. The quarter is now nearly devoid of people in the lead-up to Shabbat. The few that are still around are busy closing up shop or hurrying home, their arms laden with bags overflowing with last-minute shopping.

Raphael navigates the narrow passages, hidden courtyards, and crumbling buildings in the waning light, past ancient homes, shops, *yeshivot*, cafes, and *shtiebels*, until he turns the familiar corner where the bakery that specialised in Syrian bread used to stand, now a pile of rubble, and unlatches the front gate of his *savta* and *saba*'s house. He pauses briefly to press his lips against the familiar cool metal of the ancient brass *mezuzah* his father's paternal grandparents brought with them from Syria in 1905 to what was then known as the Ottoman province of Palestine.

He pounds on the heavy wooden front door and waits for a bit, then knocks on it again. A moment later, the door swings open, and he finds himself suddenly enveloped in the enormous arms of his savta as she holds him close and kisses his head, whispering "motek, my little motek" over and over again. They stay that way for a while, then, guiding Raphael's fingers onto the large, stone mezuzah on the doorpost and kissing them with her moist lips, Savta leads him into the front room that serves as both reception and dining room. Raphael sets down his bags and is suddenly overwhelmed by the familiar aroma of Savta's Aleppo-inspired cooking as it wafts out of the kitchen, the memories of his lost childhood causing him to blink back the sting of profound emotion.

They sit on a well-worn leather sofa, and Raphael takes his beloved savta's hands in his and contemplates her, hardly believing he's finally looking at her after so long. Always more a mother to him than a grandmother, he marvels at how she doesn't seem to have aged in the five years since he last saw her at Uncle Shimshon's funeral, an eternity ago. She is dressed as ever in her cornflower-blue housedress with red trim, a colourful kitchen apron, and a finely-knit grey cardigan. He kisses her soft cheek, gazes lovingly into her deep-set, dark blue eyes, and caresses her wavy salt-and-pepper hair that she wears pinned up in a bun.

"It's good to have you back, motek," Savta says, gently squeezing his hand.

Raphael looks around the room and shakes his head.

"What is it, motek?"

"I don't want to go to Aunt Penina's, Savta. I'm happy to stay here with you. But over there, it's going to be torture."

"Let's talk about that later, motek."

"I'll go crazy, Savta, I know it. Plus, I haven't done anything wrong."

Savta shakes her head and kisses his hands. "Later," she whispers.

Tears pool in her eyes, and there's an ever-so-slight trembling of her head that makes Raphael's chest go tight. He dabs her cheeks with a handkerchief.

Savta stands and wipes her face on her apron. "I've prepared Shabbat dinner." She checks her watch. "That's not for another hour. Your cousin Yossi will be joining."

"Yossi?" Raphael is surprised to hear Savta mention the name of his twenty-year-old cousin, Uncle Shimshon and Aunt Penina's second son, the quiet one who used to disappear for hours without explanation and send his parents into a mad panic.

"The dear boy drives up from Mitzpe Ramon nearly every weekend and spends Shabbat with your saba and me so we won't feel so alone."

Savta presses a framed photograph of Aunt Penina and her three sons into Raphael's hands. "This is your cousin Yossi now." She points at the young man standing slightly apart from the rest. "This was taken under the big carob tree in front of the house this past July when Penina and the boys came for a visit. Yossi hired a professional photographer who spent all afternoon taking pictures of us, and of the house, and all around the neighbourhood. We felt like real celebrities that day."

Raphael examines his cousin's image. He looks to stand around the same height as Aunt Penina, who Raphael doesn't recall as being that tall, perhaps five feet five inches or so, with a wrestler's build, short and meaty. His panther-black hair is clipped short, and he is clean-shaven. Out of Aunt Penina's three boys, his complexion is the darkest, most likely from extended exposure to the desert sun. His lower lip is quite full, and his nose is aquiline, though not as prominent as Aunt Penina's or his brother Assaf's. But most noticeable are the thick black eyebrows that frame his large, clear hazel eyes, and the same inscrutable, serene expression that Raphael remembers from childhood.

He hands back the photograph to Savta.

"We'll do candles and *Kiddush* as soon as Yossi arrives." Savta moves toward the kitchen. "In the meantime, I must finish getting the table ready."

"Savta," Raphael says as she pulls a white tablecloth out of the cupboard. "Where's Saba? How is he?"

Savta shakes her head slowly and points at the darkened hallway off the living room. "Your saba might still be awake. He's in your Uncle Shimshon's room."

Raphael pads down the hall to the very back of the house. He hears a siren wailing in the distance, announcing the thirty-six minutes remaining before the start of Shabbat. Pausing at the door to Uncle Shimshon's old room, he listens for a moment. Then, hearing nothing, he eases it open, lightly grazing the mezuzah with his fingertips, and pokes his head into the room.

Inside he sees a hospital bed on which his grandfather is resting, eyes closed, looking thin and frail. His thick black hair has been replaced with wisps of grey; his once elegant nose now juts out of an emaciated, angular face, framed by a scraggly, unkempt beard. Raphael moves to his side and watches him sleep.

He thinks back to the last time he saw him, at Uncle Shimshon's funeral. After the service, Aunt Penina had lost her mind and had physically attacked Raphael's father. Saba had been able to pull her off him and shepherd her to a quiet corner where he calmed her down. At the time, the only signs of his illness were a tremor in his left arm and a stiffness in his left leg that made sitting for long periods uncomfortable for him. But he was still strong then, ever the unquestionable leader of the Dweck clan, commanding the love and respect of all members of the family. And although Aunt Penina continued to blame Raphael's father for Uncle Shimshon's early death in a cave-in at the clay mine where he worked, on that terrible day Saba was able to broker a fragile peace between them that was still holding. Barely.

Raphael takes Saba's thin hand and kisses it gently, then places it back on his chest. Saba's eyelids flutter, then they open wide, and he stares unfocused at the ceiling. Raphael passes his hand in front of his face, and Saba turns his head and blinks at Raphael.

"Hello, Saba."

Raphael caresses his arm. Saba glances down at Raphael's hand and blinks. Raphael gently strokes his beard, and Saba responds by closing his eyes and pressing his face against Raphael's palm, softly moving his cheek against his grandson's fingers, the way he used to when Raphael was a little boy. Raphael recalls how Saba would hum his favourite hymn to him at bedtime, which always helped him fall asleep. Remembering the tune, Raphael sings it now to his grandfather. When he finishes, he leans over and kisses his forehead, kisses each of his eyelids, and lovingly kisses him on the cheek before leaving the room and closing the door behind.

Raphael finds Savta sipping tea on the sofa, looking expectantly out the front window, her back turned to the hallway. The table is now set for Shabbat, adorned with a delicate white lace tablecloth, an arrangement of sunflowers, two large home-baked Sabbath loaves on a cutting board covered with an embroidered gold-yellow cover with white fringes, a silver kiddush cup brimming with wine, and, in the centre of the table, the antique candlesticks Savta and Saba received from Savta's grandmother on their wedding day. Raphael feels momentarily disoriented at the sight of them, recalling the ones in Shona's office, and experiencing a sudden mix of guilt and anger he finds difficult to place.

Turning away from the table, he joins Savta on the sofa and stares at her without saying a word. Savta continues looking out the window, occasionally glancing into her tea glass and absently swirling the liquid.

Raphael touches her wrist. "How long has Saba been that way, Savta?" His voice trembles with emotion.

Savta sets her glass on a side table and meets his gaze. "Your saba, he took to bed about a year ago. Before then, he hardly ever got up from his chair anymore, and he *never* left the house."

"He didn't recognise me, Savta."

"Your saba's gone, motek," she says softly. "He left us a few months ago. The doctor says it's some kind of accelerated dementia associated with the Parkinson's or perhaps with the medication. They don't really know which."

"Does Abba know about this?"

Savta looks at Raphael for a moment. "Of course he knows, motek. We speak on the telephone every day."

"He never mentioned it to me."

Savta lifts her shoulders in a vague shrug. "He didn't want to worry you, I suppose."

"If I knew, I would have come sooner."

Savta lets out a sigh. She rises from the sofa, carries her tea to the kitchen, then returns and sits at the table, lowering her head to her hands for a moment.

"This has been the worst time of our lives, motek, Saba's and mine. There's been nobody here for us. Neighbours, yes. The community, yes. But nobody in the family, except for your cousin Yossi, Baruch Hashem. If it weren't for Yossi, that sweet boy, I think I would have completely despaired. Your father calls every day, yes. But he hasn't come to see us in nearly three years."

Raphael sits next to Savta, takes her hands, and kisses them. Then he looks into her eyes. "Savta, I'm so sorry you and Saba have had to go through this alone. It's terrible to feel abandoned, I'm sure. But I'm here now."

"So am I," a man's voice says from the doorway. Raphael and Savta swing around and see Yossi standing there, holding a bouquet of yellow roses. He is dressed in the olive green off-duty military uniform of a tank unit sub-commander and a pair of black desert boots, with a shiny black Uzi submachine gun casually slung over his shoulder.

"Yossi, my boy!" Savta says, rising from the table. "*Shabbat shalom*! Come in, come in." She meets him halfway across the room, kisses him, and receives the flowers. "You remember your cousin Rafi, don't you?" She takes the flowers into the kitchen without waiting for an answer.

Raphael stands and raises his hand at Yossi, not quite sure what to say or do. Yossi strides across the room with a broad smile and, shifting his machine gun to his back, startles Raphael by throwing his muscular arms around him and hugging him, his face pressed against Raphael's neck. Raphael takes in the smell of Yossi's freshly laundered uniform, his recently shampooed, sun-warmed hair, and a musky hint of perspiration. "Welcome home, cousin," Yossi says, as he releases him from his embrace. "Shabbat shalom."

"Shabbat shalom." Raphael stares deep into his cousin's eyes and feels the bottom drop out of his stomach.

"I hear you're going to join us in Mitzpe Ramon." Yossi sets down his Uzi in the corner, never taking his eyes off Raphael.

"That's the plan," Raphael says, tracking Yossi's every move. "We'll see."

Yossi sits on the sofa, spreads himself out, and raises his eye-brows at Raphael. "You'll love it there. All wide-open spaces. You can see all the way to the horizon. And the colours, my God, when the sun sets, it's *a*-mazing."

Raphael stares at Yossi, mesmerised by his energy, half-listening to what he is saying.

"Don't worry about anything, cousin. I know the desert like I know myself. I'll show you around. If you're up for it, maybe we can even do a bit of camping."

Savta comes out of the kitchen with a crystal vase in which she has arranged the yellow roses and puts it on the table, then she hands Yossi a hair clip and a black felt kippah, which he affixes on his head.

"It's time," she says.

Yossi and Raphael join her at the table and put their arms around her as she lights the Shabbat candles and utters the bless-ing to usher in the Sabbath.

Once they've finished the initiatory blessings, Yossi picks up the kiddush cup and leads them down the hall into Saba's room.

They sing *Shalom Aleichem* at his bedside, each of them taking their turn to kiss him on his cheek and to tell him how much they love him. Then Yossi and Raphael sing *Eshet Chayil* to Savta, who beams with joy, looking from grandson to grandson as they honour her with the proverb that is usually sung by a husband to his wife on Shabbat.

Yossi and Raphael turn and look into each other's eyes, the way their fathers trained them from childhood and recite Psalm 1 in unison: *Happy is the man who does not heed the advice of the wicked, nor take his stand on the sinner's road...* Savta then places one hand on Saba's arm and takes Raphael and Yossi's hands in the other and recites the blessing for the sons, then Yossi and Raphael rest their hands on Savta's head and recite the blessing for the daughters.

Tears stream down Savta's face. Raphael puts his arm around her and holds her tight while Yossi takes the silver cup and raises it. He chants Kiddush, blesses and sips the sweet wine, and shares the cup with Savta and Raphael before dipping his finger into the wine and dabbing a bit of it onto Saba's trembling lips.

The three of them return to the kitchen and perform their ablutions before taking their places at the table to bless the bread. Against their protestations, Savta insists that her grandsons sit and allow her to serve them. Raphael and Yossi smile at each other sheepishly as Savta shuffles in and out of the kitchen, first with the cutlery, then with the dishes and wine glasses.

"You've grown a lot since we last saw you," Yossi says the next time she leaves the room.

"I should hope so. I was eleven years old. You look the same."

"Yeah, right." Yossi reaches over and playfully squeezes Raphael's bicep. "Are you working out?"

"Rafi's a champion swimmer," Savta says, as she emerges from the kitchen and places a steaming dinner plate in front of each of them piled high with saffron rice.

"A lot of good that's going to do me here." Raphael lowers his head to his dish and takes in the aroma of the freshly made rice.

"The regional council's putting in a swimming pool," Yossi says. "It should be ready in the spring. The high school's hoping to have a swim team this time next year."

"Like I said…" Raphael shrugs, tears off another piece of bread, and munches on it. "I'm turning seventeen in two weeks. I'll be done with high school in June."

"Save that sort of talk for later," Savta says, spooning generous servings of lamb stew with yellow split peas and dried limes on their plates. "Remember, it's Shabbat."

Yossi and Raphael apologise and spend the next twenty minutes alternating between singing Sabbath songs and gorging themselves on the stew, mopping it up with *za'atar*-spiced Syrian bread, while Savta sits back and watches them.

"Aren't you going to eat anything, Savta?" Yossi asks, pointing at the salad plate in front of her.

Raphael notices for the first time that Savta has not touched the half-portion of rice and stew she served herself. "Yes, Savta, eat something."

Savta shakes her head and slides away her plate.

"What's wrong?" Yossi and Raphael say at the same time. They glance at each other, then back at Savta.

"Nothing's wrong. I'm just thanking Hashem for the privilege of having my two favourite grandsons with me, sharing Shabbat. All of us together. Who knows when I'll have this opportunity again."

"What do you mean, Savta?" Raphael says. "Now that I'm back, we can do this every week."

"Don't be silly, Savta," Yossi slides the salad plate back toward her. "Eat with us. At least a little."

Savta flashes a sad smile at her grandsons and spends the next few minutes picking at her food while they mop up the last bits of stew in the silence that has descended over the room. Once they've finished, Savta pours onto their plates her signature cherry tomato salad with lemon-allspice dressing to round out the meal, which they polish off in a matter of minutes.

Yossi distributes prayer booklets, and they sing *Grace After Meals*, using the tune composed by his and Raphael's paternal great-grandfather, which Raphael hasn't heard in several years. Raphael stumbles over the words at the start as he adjusts to the nearly forgotten tune. Yossi adjusts his speed, allowing him to catch up and follow along, before bringing the home service to an energetic conclusion. Yossi, Raphael, and Savta then wish each other Shabbat Shalom and retire to the sofa to sip cardamom tea and nibble on fresh fruit.

"Tonight and tomorrow night," Savta says to Raphael, "you'll sleep in your old room with Yossi."

Raphael nods and glances at Yossi, whose focus is entirely on Savta. Even though Yossi is not the type of man Raphael would typically find physically attractive, he can't deny he feels drawn to him. Something in his eyes, or perhaps in his manner, the way he moves, or maybe the way he smells, something Raphael can't quite fathom, exhilarates him about Yossi. And as he ponders this, he finds suddenly frightening the thought of spending the night in the same room as him.

"And on Yom Rishon," Savta continues, "you will go with him to Mitzpe Ramon."

Yossi raises his eyebrows at Raphael. "Maybe we'll go back tomorrow night after *Havdalah*."

"Couldn't I stay here with you and Saba?" Raphael says. "That way you won't be alone. I could help with things here in the house. Plus, I could stay with Saba while you go out and run errands so you wouldn't have to worry about leaving him alone."

"No, motek. You must go to Mitzpe Ramon. That was already decided. Hashem will take care of us, as he always has. Come back next week for Shabbat."

"We can't next week, Savta," Yossi says. "I'm on duty. But we'll be here for Rosh Hashanah."

"*I'll* come next week," Raphael says. "I'll catch a bus or a *sherut*."

"We'll see, motek," Savta says.

"Fine, fine, we'll see." Raphael gathers up the empty tea glasses. "Thank you for the lovely dinner, Savta."

When he comes out of the kitchen, Raphael sees Savta and Yossi conferring in hushed voices. "I'm going to take a stroll around the neighbourhood," he announces. "Maybe I'll poke my gulliver into the Ades to say a prayer for Saba if it's still open. Would you like to come?" he asks Yossi.

"No, I'll stay here with Savta. You go ahead. I'll see you when you get back."

Raphael glances at Savta and raises his head questioningly. She shrugs at him, then smiles tenderly at Yossi and caresses his face with the back of her hand.

When Raphael returns after his walk, he finds the house already dark. He climbs the stairs to his old room and finds Yossi inside, still wearing his military trousers, but now bareheaded and barefoot and wearing a white tank top, busily arranging his clothes in the top right dresser drawer. Raphael is momentarily taken aback by how tiny the bedroom looks compared with his room back home in Los Angeles, so much smaller than he remembers it, especially in the dim light emanating from a Sabbath nightlight.

Yossi pivots to grab something out of his pack and catches Raphael staring at him from the doorway. He nods at Raphael and points at the beds, which, although they are pushed up against opposite walls, are only two arms' lengths from each other. "Take your pick," he says, his face an inscrutable mask.

Raphael notices his backpack and suitcase at the foot of the bed nearest the door and arches his brow at Yossi. He hangs his backpack on the wooden bedpost, then hauls his suitcase onto the hard mattress and flips it open, rummaging around inside until he finds his flannel pyjamas and night kippah.

Yossi strips off his tank top, and Raphael does a double-take at his hairy, muscular upper body and well-defined abdominals.

Yossi looks down at himself and back up at Raphael. "What is it?"

"Talk about working out." Raphael unbuttons his shirt and tosses it onto the bed, exposing his tallit katan.

Yossi nods. "Yeah, I do a bit of that."

Raphael turns away, carefully folds his tallit katan, and drapes it over a chair. "I'll bet you do," he says under his breath.

"What's that?"

"Nothing." Raphael unbuttons his jeans and looks over his shoulder at Yossi, who is staring at him, his tank top still hanging from his fingertips. "It's a little joke, *achi*, that's all," Raphael says.

Yossi nods and unbuttons his trousers. They fall to the ground, and he steps out of them. Raphael finds himself suddenly facing Yossi, who is wearing a pair of olive green bikini underpants. He blinks at Yossi's powerful-looking hairy legs.

"Oh, man." Raphael brings a hand to his mouth and chokes back a laugh. "You are one hairy gever."

Yossi frowns at Raphael.

"No offence, achi," Raphael says, doing his best to suppress his laughter. "I've just never seen anyone as hairy as you." He peels down his jeans and kicks them off into a corner of the room, then adjusts his blue-and-white striped boxer shorts. "I mean, I thought I was hairy." He tugs on his leg hairs.

"You are."

"Nothing like you." He retrieves his jeans and folds them. "Anyway, it doesn't matter. You're built like a brick shithouse anyway. I'd murder someone for a body like yours."

Raphael shuts his suitcase and slides it under the bed, then slips into his pyjamas. He sits on the edge of the bed to affix his night kippah with a soft clip and stares at Yossi, who is still standing in the middle of the room.

"I have to warn you," Yossi says.

"Warn me about what?"

"I sleep in the nude."

"Do you really?"

"Yeah. So you might want to turn away right now."

Raphael continues to look straight at Yossi, trying his best to look nonchalant despite the hammering of his heart, despite the shallowing of his breath. Yossi cocks his head to one side.

"Go on," Raphael croaks, his mouth now completely dry.

Yossi laughs and climbs into bed, slipping under the duvet. "*Meshuga*," he says, ducking under the duvet for a moment and emerging with his underpants dangling from his hands. He flings them at Raphael, who bats them away with a melodramatic shriek.

"Don't tell me you're shy," Raphael says when he recovers himself, eyeing the bikini in the corner and playing with the idea of keeping it for himself.

"I'm modest, not shy." Yossi raises himself up on one elbow. "There's a difference."

"What about when you're with your army unit? Don't you have to get naked in front of them?"

"That's different. Why are you so interested anyway?"

Raphael shrugs and slips under his duvet. "You were practically naked, already. I just wanted to see the rest. That's all."

Yossi stares at Raphael across the room, an ambivalent expression playing over his face. After a moment he shakes his head. "Meshuga," he repeats, then turns on his right side and faces the wall, drawing one of the pillows over his head.

Raphael takes a deep breath, hardly believing what has come out of his mouth and wondering what's going through Yossi's mind. Still, he can't get the image of Yossi's half-naked body out of his head, especially his well-muscled, hairy legs. He wonders how he's ever going to manage to fall asleep this close to Yossi, knowing he's completely naked right on the other side of the room under a thin duvet. The ache of desire takes hold of him.

Yossi pulls the pillow off his head and holds it against his chest. Raphael catches his breath. Yossi looks over his shoulder at Raphael and finds him looking at him out of half-closed eyes. He turns onto his left side and props up his head with the pillow.

"Still awake?" Yossi says.

"I can't sleep. Jet lag, I guess."

"Ah, of course."

"Are you coming with me to Shacharit tomorrow morning?"

Yossi closes his eyes and shakes his head. "I don't go for that stuff anymore. Not since Abba died."

"What does that have to do with anything?"

Yossi shrugs. "Abba was the religious one at home. And I never liked it much myself. So after he was gone…"

"What about tonight with Savta and Saba? Seemed like you were completely into it."

"I do it for them. Aside from that, I'm not interested."

Raphael sits up and crosses his legs Indian-style on the bed, pulling a pillow over his lap. "I can't live without it. It's in my blood."

"You're a funny one."

"What's funny about being religious? It's how we've survived throughout the centuries."

"Not about being religious." Yossi sits up and rests his back against the wall. "You. *You're* funny. First, you walk through the door fresh from saying prayers and dare me to strip naked in front of you. Then you invite me to Shacharit and tell me about how religious you are."

"What does one thing have to do with the other?"

"Isn't modesty part of being religious?"

Raphael smirks and leans forward. "I'm young and curious, that's all. And you have one of the nicest bodies I've ever seen. I wanted to see more. Nothing wrong with that, is there? It doesn't make me any less religious. It just makes me honest."

Yossi locks eyes with Raphael for several seconds. Raphael flashes a half-smile and winks at him.

"You're flirting with me, cousin," Yossi says, his face expressionless.

Raphael laughs. "I'm only playing with you, achi. Sorry, I didn't mean any disrespect."

"That's good to know."

"But, seriously, you do have a great body."

"I'm flattered, but not interested."

Raphael shrugs. "At least you're flattered. That's a start."

"Listen, achi," Yossi says. "You and I, we grew up together. We're practically brothers. Don't ever forget that."

Raphael stretches out his legs and rubs his hands against them to restore the circulation in them.

"Life isn't easy in Mitzpe Ramon," Yossi continues. "To survive there you're going to need a mentor, a *friend*. Someone to guide you, maybe even to protect you."

Raphael snorts and stretches out in bed. "I can take care of myself."

"I'm sure you can. But things will go easier for you if you have a friend, especially where my mother is concerned. Believe me."

"OK, fine," Raphael says, deliberately ignoring Yossi's comment about his mother. "We'll be friends."

Yossi nods and smiles tightly, then tosses off the duvet and, to Raphael's surprise, crosses the room completely naked and retrieves his underpants from the corner, shaking off the dust. Raphael raises himself up on one elbow and watches Yossi amble back across the room and climb into bed.

"Are we good?" Yossi asks after a few moments of silence.

Raphael takes in a deep breath and blinks at Yossi, who stares at the ceiling. "Yeah… Very good."

"Good."

"So what's next?"

"What's next?" Yossi looks over at Raphael.

Raphael nods slowly, dazed at how quickly Yossi has wrested control of the situation away from him.

"What's next is we're going to go to sleep now. Tomorrow morning, I guess you'll be praying at the Ades, and I'll spend

Shabbat morning with Savta and Saba. Then, when you get back, we'll have lunch. After lunch, we'll go for a nice long walk around the neighbourhood with Savta, drop in on a couple of neighbours, then we'll eat a light dinner of Savta's delicious *adafina*. You remember her adafina, I hope. Finally, we'll pray Havdalah with Savta and Saba, and then you and I will leave for Mitzpe Ramon."

"There's only one problem with that plan," Raphael says, now recovering himself and determined to regain control.

"What's that?"

"I'm not ready to go yet. I want to spend a little more time with Savta before we leave. Plus, I'd prefer if we drove in the daytime."

"OK, fine. We'll leave first thing Sunday morning at the crack of dawn." He dips under the duvet, turns his face to the wall and pulls the pillow over his head. "Goodnight, achi," comes his muffled voice from under the pillow.

Raphael stares at his back. After a few seconds, he turns away from Yossi and faces the door, in the direction of the Kotel, the Western Wall, covering his eyes with one hand. He meditates on Hashem, on the commandments, on the Kotel and the Temple Mount above it. Then he takes ten deep, focused breaths, and recites the Shema. When he has finished, he lies back and falls asleep to the sound of Yossi's gentle snoring.

Chapter 7

Raphael is momentarily blinded as he emerges from the cool darkness of the Ades synagogue into the late-morning sunlight. He stands blinking on the front steps, the flow of congregants moving around and past him onto the sidewalk and wishing him a Shabbat Shalom, and he wipes his watering eyes with his bandana.

Aside from a few stragglers here and there scurrying home for their Shabbat meals, the shimmering lanes of Nachlaot are deserted. Raphael looks across the road at the usually bustling Machane Yehuda market, now barricaded for Shabbat, and smiles at the sight of a dusty pair of calico street cats playing tug-of-war with a chicken's head. Before long, another cat comes along, its face scarred and missing half an ear, and wrests the ragged chicken head from them, then squeezes through a narrow opening at the bottom of the barricade into the market, carrying its prize between its teeth.

Raphael spins around at a clanging metal-on-metal racket. He sees the guest rabbi, a thin, black-suited man in his early thirties, securing the gate. The rabbi wraps a chain around the bars and slaps a padlock on it. He glances at Raphael and wishes him a Shabbat Shalom. Raphael lowers his sunglasses to make eye contact with the rabbi and returns the greeting. They exchange a few words about Raphael's family, whom the rabbi doesn't know as he recently moved to Jerusalem from Haifa. He assures Raphael that he and his wife will look in on Savta and Saba from time to time and invites him to spend the High Holidays at the Ades, promising to allocate to him the reading of the *Akedah*, the Binding of Isaac, on Rosh Hashanah. Raphael is thrilled to accept the honour, especially as the Akedah is one of his favourite passages in the Torah. The rabbi shakes his hand and hurries down the lane.

Trickles of sweat stream down the sides of Raphael's face as the hot sun reaches its zenith. His stomach rumbles, and he wonders why he's still standing in front of the synagogue. His thoughts turn to Yossi, who was still asleep when he got up to perform his morning ablutions. Even though he tried to keep the noise to a minimum while he dressed, he nevertheless banged around a bit, dragging his heavy suitcase out from under the bed. But Yossi continued to snore away, pushed up against the wall, the pillow over his head.

Up until now, by sheer force of will, he's been able to keep the image of Yossi's body out of his mind so as to allow himself to properly participate in morning prayers. But now that the service is over and he is facing the prospect of seeing Yossi again, the image of those powerful, hairy legs striding across the room within easy reaching distance of his fingers pushes its way back into his mind.

The thought of Yossi sets his heart to hammer. He falls back against the thick wall, feeling suddenly lightheaded as he replays the scene from last night in his mind. Hot tears of anger sting his eyes at the realisation that Yossi played him, and that he fell for it. He was off guard. That must be it. What with seeing Savta after so long, after finding out about Saba's deterioration and hearing about how kind Yossi has been. Then seeing for himself how loving Yossi was with them and with him, too. By the time he arrived back after his evening stroll, he was utterly under Yossi's spell, no longer in control. That *must* be it. But as attracted as he is to Yossi, regardless of how kind Yossi is to him, he swears he'll never allow him to play him like that again. From now on, he determines, *he'll* be in control of his relationship with Yossi.

When he swings open Savta's front gate, he is greeted by the meaty aroma of her adafina emanating from the house. As he expectantly steps through the front door, the bottom drops out of his stomach at the sight of Joanie Smith nervously pumping her long legs on the sofa. Savta is sitting across from her in one of the dining chairs, and Yossi, looking smart in a pair of khaki chinos and a crisply pressed white dress shirt, is leaning against the wall and staring down at her. They all look up as Raphael enters the room, and Joanie stands, a broad smile breaking out on her face.

"Ralph!" She crosses the room and throws her arms wide.

Raphael takes a step back. "What are you doing here?"

"You know this girl, Rafi?" Savta asks in Hebrew.

Yossi takes a tentative step in their direction.

Joanie frowns and looks over her shoulder at Savta, then back at Raphael. "You said I could come look for you," she says in a lowered voice, holding out the piece of paper on which Raphael had jotted down his details.

"It's OK, Savta," Raphael says. "She's someone I met on the plane."

Savta exchanges a glance with Yossi, who puts his arm around her shoulders and draws her close.

Raphael nods at Joanie and flashes a tight smile. "You caught me by surprise, that's all. It's Shabbat. You know, the Sabbath. For Jews."

"Oh, sorry. Everything was so quiet. I figured I might find you at home. Should I leave?"

"Stay for lunch," Yossi says.

Raphael shoots Yossi a look that Yossi bats away. Savta turns to Yossi and searches his face for a moment.

"There's plenty of food for us all, right, Savta?" Yossi says.

Savta looks first at Raphael, then at Joanie. "Yes, young lady, please stay. Be our guest."

Joanie raises her eyebrows at Raphael, and Raphael, surrendering to the inevitable, smiles at her and nods.

"I'm going to serve now," Savta says, moving to the kitchen.

"Thank you, ma'am," Joanie says.

"Let's sit," Yossi says, pulling out a chair at the table. "This one is yours," he says to Joanie.

Joanie obediently sits in the chair and flashes a smile at Yossi, a glint of metal from her braces reflecting the light streaming from the open window.

Raphael rolls his eyes and drops into the chair opposite Joanie.

"That's mine," Yossi says. "You sit here, please." He pats the chair next to Joanie and steps away from it.

Savta enters the room with the open pot of adafina and places it on the table.

"That smells delicious," Joanie says.

"It's called adafina," Savta says. "Sabbath stew. My grandmother's recipe. From Aleppo." She disappears back into the kitchen.

"Savta's adafina is legendary," Yossi says to Joanie, stepping over to where Raphael is sitting. "You're in for a treat." He taps Raphael on the shoulder and points at the chair next to Joanie. Raphael holds his place, determined not to give in to Yossi and planning his next move.

Savta returns with a bowl of chopped vegetables and places it on the table next to the steaming pot of adafina, then she sits in the chair to the left of Raphael.

"What's your friend's name again?" Yossi asks Raphael.

Raphael glances up at Yossi.

"I'm Joanie."

"Hi, Joanie. My name's Yossi."

Joanie extends her hand to Yossi who grasps it and pulls gently on it, lifting her out of her chair.

"Joanie, please sit here."

Raphael watches in amazement as Yossi guides Joanie into the chair next to him. A hot current of anger flows into his face, and he glares at Yossi, who calmly reaches for the decanter of red wine and pours a glass for each of them.

Yossi explains to Joanie the blessing for the wine, and they raise their glasses at his direction. The ritual reminds Raphael that as the oldest male, it's Yossi's place to lead, which calms him down and allows him to surrender to tradition. There would be plenty of time to assert himself with Yossi once Shabbat is over.

"That was so cool," Joanie says, as she and Raphael stroll the lanes of Nachlaot after lunch a few paces behind Savta and Yossi. "I've never seen anything Jewish before. You do that every week?"

"Yep, every week."

Raphael watches as Yossi and Savta stop to chat with a shrivelled old woman sitting on a bench under a massive carob tree. Her thinning white hair is dirty and unkempt and the multicoloured, embroidered poncho she wears is threadbare and full of holes. He stops walking to avoid being drawn into the conversation.

"I've been meaning to talk to you about the wallet," Joanie says.

Raphael blinks at her. "What wallet?"

Joanie reaches into her handbag and extracts the flight attendant's fat, brown patent leather wallet. "This one."

An unseen fist wallops Raphael in the chest, knocking the air out of him, and he grasps Joanie's wrist to steady himself. Joanie steps forward, closing the gap between them, now standing close enough for Raphael to smell the cardamom lingering on her breath from the tea, and deliberately shielding the wallet from anyone else's view. Raphael locks eyes with Joanie, forcing all expression from his face. Then he looks down at the shiny brown wallet in Joanie's trembling hand, his mind working at light speed.

"I'm sorry," Joanie says, her eyes moist. "I lost my nerve. I just couldn't do it."

Raphael grabs Joanie by the shoulders. "Listen to me." He looks over at Yossi and Savta, who are still chatting with the old woman. "We'll figure something out. You and me, OK?" Yossi straightens up and glances in their direction, and Raphael turns to block his view. He takes hold of Joanie's wrist once again, this time more gently, and smiles at her. "Put it back in your purse for now. OK?"

Joanie cocks her head and looks down at Raphael's hand.

"You're not angry?"

"No way." Raphael guides Joanie's hand toward her handbag. "I totally get it. Let's just deal with this later."

Joanie nods and pops the wallet back into her handbag. "When?"

Yossi calls out to them, asking them to join him and Savta under the carob tree. Raphael waves at him and turns back to Joanie.

"Can you get away tonight? We can meet at 9 p.m., right outside the gates of your hostel. We'll go someplace quiet and talk and stuff."

Joanie smiles. "I'd like that."

"But I need to spend some time with my family right now if that's all right with you. I haven't seen them in years. So…"

Joanie's smile evaporates. "You mean you want me to leave?"

"Yeah, if you don't mind. We'll have our time together tonight before I take off for Mitzpe Ramon in the morning. Just you and me."

"Hey, guys, seriously." Yossi moves in their direction. "Step it up!"

Raphael waves at Yossi and turns to Joanie. "I'll catch up with you later."

"But I have to thank your grandma for lunch. And Yossi, too. I can't just take off like that. They'll think I'm rude."

Raphael's chest tightens at the sound of his cousin's name in Joanie's metallic mouth. A flame ignites in his eyes, which he focuses on Joanie, ready to let loose a scathing retort when he is suddenly startled by a hand clamping down on his shoulder. He spins around and finds Yossi standing there, holding him fast.

"What's up with you two?" he says.

Raphael dips his shoulder and pivots away from Yossi.

"We were talking about something private," Joanie says.

Raphael's hand shoots up toward Joanie. "I'll handle this if you don't mind."

Yossi shakes his head at Raphael. "Looked more like you two were dancing."

"We were," Raphael says. "What's it to you?"

"I've got to get back to my hostel," Joanie says, looking at Raphael, who nods his agreement. "But first I want to thank your grandma for lunch."

Yossi extends his arm in the direction of Savta, and Joanie starts toward her. As she moves away, Yossi stares at her back for a moment. Then he sidles up to Raphael and whispers, "You're interested in this girl?"

Raphael turns and looks at Yossi. In the bright afternoon sunlight, Yossi's close-cropped hair is shiny and black, his sideburns groomed to right below his ears. His prominent eyebrows frame his soulful hazel eyes, his beautiful eyes. His nose is absolutely perfect, strong and prominent, but well-proportioned in comparison with the rest of his face. And his lips…his lips are full, dark red, and moist, hinting at pleasures to be given and received. Raphael finds himself wondering how Yossi is able to keep his lips so full and moist living in the harsh desert climate of Mitzpe Ramon. And suddenly, the thought of Mitzpe Ramon is no longer as daunting as it was before.

His eye travels down past Yossi's chin and his lovely Adam's apple to a thin gold chain that graces his powerful neck, now visible thanks to the fact Yossi hasn't fastened the top two buttons of the untucked white, linen shirt that looks so nice against his dark skin. By the time Raphael's eyes reach Yossi's chinos, his breathing has slowed…way…down. He is dazed by how fine they look on Yossi, how they hug his muscular legs, how they end right above his new white trainers, a hint of dark skin showing at the ankles.

Raphael looks back up at Yossi. His skin is glistening with perspiration that reflects the warm colours of the afternoon sun. He is close enough to kiss him. All he has to do is bend forward at the hips. And Yossi would probably let him just to trap him again. But Raphael is determined to keep control, to resist demonstrating further any visible signs of his attraction to Yossi.

"Why are you so interested anyway?" he asks. "Don't tell me you like her."

Yossi laughs and punches Raphael in the arm, then jogs in the direction of Savta, who is sitting on the bench next to her ancient neighbour, both of them shielding their eyes from the afternoon sun with their hands as they stare up at Joanie, who is gesticulating flamboyantly. Raphael lets out a groan, drags himself in their direction, and leans against the cool trunk of the carob tree. He remains quiet and alternates between staring at Yossi, who is standing behind Savta massaging her shoulders, and listening to Joanie drone on and on and on about how much she loved Savta's adafina, about how grateful she was for her hospitality, about how much she enjoyed the Jewish rituals, about how lovely her house is…praise Jesus.

After a while, Raphael tunes them out and focuses instead on the single tooth left in the old woman's mouth sticking up from her lower jaw, a yellowed claw emerging from a petrified sliver of redwood. He wonders why she hasn't just yanked it out.

Chapter 8

The night air feels thick and humid as Raphael pushes through the crowds jamming the Jaffa Road on his way up to the Old City. The streets, sidewalks, and plazas are heaving with people emerging from their Shabbat hibernation. There are street performers, and falafel vendors, and trinket sellers, and tourists and locals queuing to get into restaurants and Judaica shops. Amplified music blares from cracked speakers set up at Zion Square. Drivers lay on their horns, zigzagging to avoid collisions with pedestrians who jet across the road without regard for signs or signals.

Raphael breaks free of the press at the Shlomo Ha-Melech intersection and jogs up the hill rounding the ancient city wall, now dramatically illuminated with spotlights. He accesses the Old City through the Jaffa Gate and immediately has to dodge a stream of tourists passing under the ceremonial arch on their way to the street party raging on the Jaffa Road, then continues down the road toward Joanie's hostel. When he reaches the black iron gates, originally built to accommodate crusader-era pilgrims, Raphael checks his watch and sees that he's a quarter of an hour early for his meeting with Joanie.

Stepping into an Arab shisha lounge a few metres from the hostel, he orders some fresh mint tea and baklava and sits at a table below a speaker from which emanates the hypnotic voice of Fairuz singing an acoustic version of "Al Bostah," accompanied by an *oud*, a *buzuq*, and a *riqq*. The sound of a *mijwiz* floats high above the mix as a counterpoint to the melody, adding a sense of aching melancholy to the piece.

Raphael closes his eyes and breathes in the minty aroma of the tea, which mingles perfectly with the apple-scented smoke wafting through the air from several *nargilehs* being smoked around him.

He focuses on the words of the song, an ode to a lover's eyes in Arabic. The words transport him to earlier in the evening at Savta's.

He recalls staring across the double flame of the twisted Havdala candle into Yossi's eyes as they recited the blessing over the fire at Saba's bedside, while in the background behind them Savta caressed the forehead of their beloved grandfather. Yossi had stared at him through the flame and held his gaze. There was genuine affection in Yossi's eyes, and Raphael felt disarmed by it at that moment. And when they all hugged at the end of the ritual that brings Shabbat to an end, Yossi had pulled him close and kissed him on the cheek—an unexpected, lingering kiss—and whispered into his ear: "A good week, cousin."

Raphael had quickly excused himself once the ceremony was over and ascended the stairs to the upper floor to change into his evening clothes, a dark blue body shirt, tight, pegged black jeans tucked into a pair of black lace-up boots, and a set of red braces.

Pulling out his makeup kit, he'd peered at himself in the mirror, ready to apply some eyeliner, when Yossi entered the room and sat on the bed behind him. Raphael looked at his cousin's reflection in the mirror and studied his neutral expression. His lack of reaction bothered him.

"You all right?" Yossi had asked.

"Of course, I'm all right."

"Where are you going?"

"For a walk."

"To meet the American girl?"

Raphael had shaken his head.

"You said you wanted to spend more time with Savta. That's why I delayed our return to Mitzpe Ramon."

"Change of plans, sorry."

Raphael returned to drawing a perfect line under each eye with one expert sweep of his hand. He stepped back to check out the effect and felt satisfied at how the eyeliner made his blue eyes pop.

"What do you think?" he'd asked Yossi, spinning around to face him.

Yossi had stood and regarded Raphael, focusing first on his boots and looking up at the rest of his outfit. He'd stepped forward and gently tugged on the braces. "You're dressed like this for a date?"

Raphael had pushed away Yossi's hand. "I'm dressed like this because I like it."

Grabbing a black military-style beret out of his bag, Raphael had placed it on top of his kippah, securing it with a bobby pin. Out of the corner of his eye, he could see Yossi still staring at him.

"What are you looking at?"

"Has anyone ever told you that you can sometimes be a bit of an asshole?" There was no challenge in Yossi's voice.

Raphael felt a hot flash of anger blaze into his face. He whirled on his cousin, ready to respond with a blistering retort when he met his eye. But his expression was gentle. There was no arrogance, no anger. Only affection. The same warmth Raphael had seen in Yossi's eyes as they stared at each other across the flame. The effect on Raphael was unexpected and immediate. Emotion swelled inside him, bringing him close to breaking down in tears. Staggering backwards, he had felt the bureau at his back. His mind was a jumble. He struggled to find a reason for his inability to defend himself against Yossi's comment.

"I've gotta run," he had whispered hoarsely and bolted from the room.

Yossi's words played a loop in Raphael's head as he stumbled out of Savta's house into the darkness of the suffocating autumn night, and as he pressed through the surging crowds on his way to his rendezvous with Joanie. He imagined them emblazoned on the Old City walls, etched in fire by the finger of God Himself—*mene mene tekel upharsin*. He was Belshazzar the King, revelling amidst his plunder and stupid with arrogance, and Yossi was Darius the Mede moving in for the kill.

Yossi's words echo in his mind still as he sits nursing a glass of fast-cooling tea, enveloped in a cloud of blue smoke issuing forth from a half-dozen or so nargilehs, his chest aching at the memory of Yossi and his beautiful eyes.

The aromatic smoke roils around the cavernous shop and ascends to the vaulted ceiling. Raphael tilts back his head, following one smoke trail in particular, and deliberately focuses on it, working to regain control of himself. But the harder he tries, the stronger the image of Yossi staring at him from across the flame becomes.

Just then, the hypnotic rhythms of "Al Bostah" give way to the strident violins of a tune Raphael doesn't recognise. The sudden shift in the music jars him, and he sits up and blinks in the semi-darkness. The shop is now filled almost entirely by groups of young Arab men in their late teens and early twenties, each group huddled around a shared water pipe and conversing in hushed tones. He glances at his watch and speeds out of the shop.

In the distance, he sees Joanie sitting on a retaining wall next to her hostel, staring up at the Tower of David. She is wearing a red T-shirt, faded bell-bottom jeans, and a pair of red-and-white high-tops. Raphael glides up next to her and taps her on the shoulder; Joanie hops off the wall, a gloomy expression clouding her face.

"Sorry I'm late."

Joanie looks away from Raphael for a moment, then looks back at him. "I was scared you wouldn't come."

"Of course, I was coming. Actually, I was here already. Sitting over there having some tea." Raphael lifts his head at the shisha lounge. "I lost track of time, that's all."

Joanie nods.

"But, I'm here now."

Joanie flashes a shy smile. "That's cool." She looks at Raphael as if for the first time. "I like how you're dressed." She reaches up and touches Raphael's beret.

"Did you bring the thing?" Raphael asks.

"What thing?"

"You know. The thing you showed me this afternoon."

"Oh, yeah." Joanie pats her handbag. "It's in here."

"Good," Raphael says. "Come on. Follow me."

"Where are we going?"

"Somewhere private." He points at the Jaffa Gate. "That way."

They exit the city walls and take a shortcut down the hill and across the fields toward the start of King David Street. They pass the old Muslim cemetery on their right, which looks especially creepy in the dark, and Joanie grabs Raphael's hand, holding it tight as Raphael guides her up the street in the direction of the YMCA tower looming in the distance.

When they reach the King David Hotel, Raphael stops for a moment and tells Joanie the story of how Jewish resistance fighters blew it up when Palestine was still under British rule. Joanie responds by smiling and nodding, which irks Raphael. He turns on his heels and moves down the pavement running along the side of the hotel. Joanie chases after him and follows behind as Raphael passes the hotel gardens and turns into a dark, solitary park behind the hotel complex, in the centre of which is a roped-off archaeological excavation of first-century tombs. He strides across the grass and drops onto a bench under a large tree across from the site, stretching his legs out in front of him. Joanie catches up and sits next to him. They stay quiet for a while in the near-total silence of the park.

"I had a great time today at your grandma's," Joanie says, breaking the silence. "She's adorable."

Raphael looks at Joanie and nods. "That she is."

"Your cousin's nice, too. Before you got home, he showed me his machine gun."

"I'll bet he did."

"You're lucky to have such a loving family. I hate to say it, but mine are a bunch of ignorant rednecks."

Raphael scoots close to Joanie and leans against her. "Let's not talk about our families, OK? This is supposed to be about us."

Joanie goes suddenly quiet.

"You OK?" Raphael asks.

Joanie nods.

"Are you sure?"

"I think so."

"You know what we're doing here, right?"

"Sort of. Something about the wallet?"

"Nah, that can wait. Right now we're just getting to know each other better. That's what you wanted, isn't it?"

"I want us to be friends."

"Right." Raphael pulls a pack of Marlboros out of his back pocket and lights one up. "Want one?"

Joanie shakes her head and crinkles her nose. "I didn't know you smoked."

"I do lots of things." Raphael takes a long drag on his cigarette. He draws up his legs and sits Indian-style on the bench and blows a series of smoke rings. "Sure you don't want to try?"

"The body is God's temple," Joanie says. "It's a sin to pollute it."

Raphael chuckles. "Try it. Nobody will know."

"Maybe another time," Joanie says, fanning the smoke away with her hand. "Besides, I don't want them to smell it on me when I get back to the hostel."

"Suit yourself." Raphael stuffs the pack back into his pocket and takes another long drag. "So, Joanie," he says as he lets out the smoke, "we were talking about sex."

"We were?"

"Yes, we were. Yesterday on the plane, remember? You were surprised I'd had sex, and you told me you hadn't done it yet. Don't play dumb."

"I'm not playing dumb."

"Do you remember or don't you?"

Joanie looks away for a moment and looks back at Raphael. "Yes, of course, I remember."

"Good. Now, I want you to take a good look around at this park and tell me what you see."

Joanie looks around and shrugs. "I don't see anything. Just an empty park and those ruins over there."

"That's right, it's empty." Raphael put his hand on Joanie's leg. "It's just you and me."

Joanie looks down at Raphael's hand.

"You don't have to wonder what sex is like."

"I don't?"

Raphael tosses aside the cigarette, leans forward, and kisses Joanie on the cheek.

"It's a sin," Joanie whispers.

"So what," Raphael says as he takes Joanie's chin, pivots her head toward him, and kisses her on the mouth. Joanie closes her eyes and opens her mouth to receive Raphael's tongue.

As their passion builds, Raphael removes her T-shirt and unhooks her bra and buries his face in Joanie's small breasts. He unbuttons his jeans and guides Joanie's hand onto his underpants.

She responds by tentatively slipping her fingers between the elastic band and his hairy lower belly. Raphael reaches his other hand into her bag and extracts the flight attendant's wallet. Then he abruptly releases Joanie and backs away, leaving the young woman gasping for breath, searching Raphael's face for some explanation for the sudden end of their petting.

He retrieves her T-shirt from the grass and holds it out to her as she quickly puts her bra back on. She pulls the T-shirt over her head and stands to adjust her clothes, watching as Raphael lights another cigarette, her face darkening.

"How was that?" Raphael asks. "Good?"

"Why did you stop?"

"That was just a taster." Raphael takes a short drag on the cigarette and tosses it aside. "Let it settle in. Process it for a while. If you want more, let me know. If not, don't sweat it. You didn't do anything besides the kissing. So you have nothing to feel guilty about."

Joanie lunges forward and throws her arms around Raphael, kissing him again on the mouth. Raphael slips out of the embrace, wiping his mouth with the back of his hand, and holds up the wallet. Joanie screams and grabs for it, and Raphael puts it behind his back.

"So, here's the deal," Raphael says, stepping forward. "I'm not going to let you blackmail me with this."

"I wasn't blackmailing you."

"Don't kid yourself, Miss Born-Again Christian. You wanted to see me again, and this wallet was your insurance. That's why you didn't turn it in at the airport."

"That's not true."

"It *is* true. But what you didn't think about was that by *not* turning it in, you became an accomplice to theft. Now, *there's* something to feel guilty about."

Joanie sits on the bench and begins to sob.

"If I ever decide to see you again," Raphael says, "it'll be because I want to. Not because you have anything over me."

He pulls a bandana out of his pocket and wipes the wallet clean of fingerprints, then walks across the grass and pitches it into the excavation. He walks back to Joanie. "All gone." He holds out his bandana to Joanie, who takes it and wipes her face.

"You can keep that," Raphael says. "Consider it a souvenir."

Joanie leaps off the bench and punches him hard in the chest. "You jerk!"

"Hey, that hurt!" He massages his chest, wincing at the pain. "Are you crazy, or what?"

"You used me. Twice. Once at the airport and now."

He moves away from her. "I've got to go, sorry."

"What do you mean you've got to go? You're not planning on leaving me here like this, are you?"

Raphael shrugs. "Sorry. I'll wait for you."

Joanie grabs her handbag from the bench, her hands trembling as she shoulders it. She looks up at Raphael and shakes her head. "You're a real jerk, you know that?"

"Let's drop it, OK?" He turns his back on her and walks away. "I'll show you the way back, and we'll call it a night."

Joanie rushes him from behind and shoves him into one of the hedges. "Fuck you, asshole," she screams.

Raphael pulls himself out of the hedge, his forehead scratched and bleeding, and Joanie slugs him in the face, knocking him to the ground. She pounces on him and pummels him with her fists, screaming obscenities at him, and Raphael tries to fend her off with his hands. Just as she reaches for a large stone, three young men appear on the scene, grab her by the arms, and lift her off him. She kicks at them, screaming and cursing, and Raphael scrambles away, exiting the park and limping all the way back to Savta's.

Chapter 9

The sun bursts over the Judean Hills as Yossi's Saab station wagon skirts the slopes of Mount Scopus and starts its descent toward the Dead Sea. Raphael stares out the window at the tortured landscape, paying close attention to the Bedouin tents in the distance and the herds of goats foraging on the hillside.

As they head south along the edge of the Dead Sea, Yossi breaks the silence by pointing out the caves of Qumran and its partially excavated ruins and explains to Raphael about the Essene Community and the Dead Sea Scrolls. Raphael nods and rubs his chest, bruised purple where Joanie punched him. Yossi pulls to the side of the road.

"Why are we stopping?" Raphael asks.

"Let me see that." Yossi points at Raphael's chest.

After a moment of hesitation, Raphael unbuttons his shirt and pulls it open. Yossi lets out a whistle on seeing the bruise and palpates the area, making Raphael cry out. He pulls aside Raphael's hair and exposes the scratches on his forehead.

"Don't ask, please," Raphael says, backing away and buttoning his shirt.

"I wouldn't dream of it," Yossi says. "It's none of my business. Only, I think you're going to need to have Assaf examine that when we get to Mitzpe Ramon. It looks nasty. He's a medic."

Raphael nods and looks away from Yossi. "Thanks, achi."

He is thankful Savta didn't see him before they left for Mitzpe Ramon, having said his goodbyes to her the night before. She wouldn't have accepted his explanation of having gotten into a fight with some drunken tourists as easily as Yossi. Not that he imagined Yossi actually believed his story. But at least he hadn't pressed him for the truth.

Yossi pulls the car back on to the tarmac and urges it forward as fast as the winding road will allow.

"Why did we come this way?" Raphael asks as they pass the ancient hilltop fortress of *Masada* looming high above the shores of the Dead Sea. "Isn't this the long way round?"

"It's only thirty minutes more. The other highway is green all the way to Beersheba. I want your eyes to get used to seeing the desert."

"Gee, thanks." Raphael pulls a granola bar out of his backpack and offers half to Yossi, who finishes it off in two bites. He fishes out another one, unwraps it, and hands the whole thing to Yossi.

"Can I ask you a question?" Raphael says.

Yossi wipes his mouth with the back of his sleeve and takes a swig of water from a canteen. "Fire away."

"I was thinking about when we used to live here, all crammed together at Savta and Saba's like a big clan."

"What about it?"

"You used to disappear, and everyone would go mad looking for you, especially your mother."

Yossi laughs and presses down harder on the accelerator. "You remember that, do you?"

"Of course. I remember those crazy search parties your parents would organise to track you down, the whole family plus the neighbours, everyone out looking for you. Your mother was afraid you'd been kidnapped or killed or some other stupid thing."

Yossi nods. "She can be over-the-top sometimes, my Ima."

"Tell me about it. Like when she attacked Abba in front of everyone at Uncle Shimshon's funeral, peace be upon him."

"That was different."

"A different reason, yes. But, still, the same crazy reaction. Whenever we found you, or you decided to turn up, I remember she'd slap you down and drag you around the house by your hair and scream at you. But you didn't care. You always kept quiet and took whatever crap they gave you. The amazing thing was you'd do it all again, that disappearing act of yours." Raphael smirks. "We all thought you were retarded." Raphael regrets the comment the moment he says it.

Yossi urges the Saab toward Dimona and increases his speed to 110 kilometres per hour. He glances at Raphael, who is frowning at the floorboard. "What was your question?"

Raphael looks up at Yossi and, feeling a sudden urge to touch him, stretches his arm along the back of the seat stopping short of his shoulder. "Where would you go when you disappeared?" he asks. "And why would you take off?"

Yossi smiles. "That's two questions."

"I may have more, sorry."

"No worries. Sometimes I'd go to the children's zoo to feed the goats. Other times I'd wander the halls of *The Shuk* looking at the incredible variety of produce there. It seemed like those food stalls went on forever. Some of the vendors would give me samples to eat. That was fun. Most of the time, though, I'd find a park or a field to sit in and spend a few hours staring up at the sky."

"Oh!" Raphael says. "That's funny. Why?"

Yossi shrugs. "I was looking for Hashem." He glances at Raphael and looks back at the road.

"By staring at the sky?"

"I was a kid. What did I know? Abba and Uncle Isaac were always talking about Him, and I wanted to find Him. So that's what I did."

Yossi draws a deep breath and holds it for a moment, then lets it out slowly. "Honestly, cousin"—he lowers the sun visor to block the glare and slips on a pair of sunglasses—"I never was much of a believer. I prayed and all that. But I was never sure anyone was listening. Then after you lot left, and Abba dragged us to the edge of civilisation, and then the cave-in happened…"

"You can't blame that on God."

"I don't," Yossi says. "There is no God. You can't blame things on something that doesn't exist."

"You can't possibly know that. Just because bad things happen doesn't prove He doesn't exist."

"I'm not saying it does. I just don't believe there's anything out there other than the sky, the planets, and the stars in an expanding universe that one day will collapse back in on itself."

Raphael shakes his head and stares out the window as they speed past a sign that indicates they are 100 kilometres from Mitzpe Ramon.

"Anyway," Yossi says. "I still like looking up at the sky. Back in the day, the best views were in a park. Now I have the desert at my doorstep." A smile breaks out on his face. "You'll be able to take some great photos there with that camera of yours."

At the mention of his camera, Raphael pulls it off the backseat and snaps a few pictures of the passing landscape and a couple of Yossi driving.

"Now it's my turn," Yossi says.

"For what?"

"To ask a question."

Raphael slips the camera back into its case and nods.

"What's up with the stealing?"

Raphael narrows his eyes at Yossi. "How do you know about that?"

"People talk. Anyway, what's that about?"

Raphael shrugs. "I don't know. It just happens. Randomly sometimes. I see something, could be anything, and I get this itch to take it. The itch gets stronger until I think I'll go crazy. When the thing's finally in my hand, the itch goes away."

"And now?"

"It's better now." Raphael looks away from Yossi and stares out the window for a few seconds, then looks back at him. "Sometimes it still hits me, especially if someone pisses me off. But it's a lot better than before. I haven't stolen anything in a long time."

"Remind me not to piss you off." Yossi gives Raphael's arm an affectionate squeeze. "Anyway, I'm not into possessions. Feel free to take whatever you want."

They drive in silence through the desert, passing the eyesore of Dimona on their right and joining Highway 40 at Sde Boker heading south. After a few minutes, Raphael spots a complex of ruins on a hilltop overlooking the road. He readies his camera to snap a few pictures but changes his mind when he sees the determined expression on Yossi's face as he urges the car forward, clocking 120 kilometres per hour. Raphael slouches in his seat, pulls his hat over his eyes, and dozes off.

After what seems like a few minutes, he is lurched awake as Yossi abruptly reduces his speed and manoeuvres the car off the highway, mounting a narrow gravel road at the city limits of Mitzpe Ramon. Raphael pulls off his hat and rubs his eyes, focusing on a large iron structure in the distance toward which Yossi is guiding the car over the bumpy road. He straightens up as he recognises the gates of the cemetery in which the family interred Uncle Shimshon's personal effects in the absence of his body. Black memories from the funeral loop through his mind, transporting him to that day five years ago when the family and the entire Mitzpe Ramon mining community gathered graveside under the glare of the blistering desert sun in that awful cemetery in the middle of the wilderness. Aunt Penina had been inconsolable, on her knees and sobbing loudly, heaping handfuls of yellow dirt on her head, and spitting out curses at Raphael's father. It had taken her three sons and Saba several minutes to coax her off the ground, and several more to calm her in the Cadillac limousine Raphael's father had rented for the family.

Yossi parks outside the gates and hops out of the car, and Raphael follows him as he picks his way to the far end of the graveyard and stands in front of his father's headstone. Raphael pulls up next to him and reads the inscription, which gives no indication that the grave is empty, save for some clothes, a prayer shawl from which the officiating rabbi severed the fringes, and Uncle's Shimshon's prayer book, the one Saba gave him on the day he and his twin, Raphael's father, became Bnei Mitzvah.

Yossi looks up at the sky for a moment to collect himself and looks back at his father's headstone. He produces a blue-andwhite knit kippah from his breast pocket and recites *Kaddish*, the prayer for the dead. Raphael joins him, the two of them swaying gently in the empty cemetery. When they finish, each of them places a pebble on the headstone. Yossi kisses his fingers and touches the inscription, allowing them to linger there for a moment, then turns away and trudges out of the cemetery. Raphael follows a little behind.

Once outside the gates, Yossi hops up on the hood of his car and looks directly at Raphael for the first time in over an hour, the pupils of his hazel green eyes mere pinpoints in the bright morning light. "Ima still blames your father, you know."

"What on earth for?" Raphael clambers up next to him. "Abba was nowhere near here when it happened."

"That's the whole point. My father would have never moved us here if Uncle Isaac hadn't left for America. And this is where the accident happened."

"That's ridiculous."

"Maybe so. Still, be careful. Both with Ima and with Assaf as well."

"What about you?"

Yossi shakes his head. "Everyone's responsible for their actions, that's what I believe. But, that's me. Ima and Assaf think differently." Yossi pulls his keys from his pocket and slides off the hood of the car. "In any case, as I told you before, I'll be watching your back."

Raphael hops off the hood and slaps the dust from his trousers. "Thanks, but don't worry about me. I'm a big boy."

"I can see that." Yossi brushes aside Raphael's hair to expose his forehead. This time Raphael doesn't pull away. Instead, he closes his eyes and allows himself to feel the cool of Yossi's fingertips as they trace the outline of the scratches.

Moments later, when he opens his eyes, he finds Yossi staring into the distance, in the direction of the Ramon crater, the *makhtesh,* his face an unreadable mask obscuring any hint of emotion.

The silence is broken by the sound of a vehicle grinding across the gravel. They climb back into the car just as a beige military off-roader pulls up next to them. Yossi salutes the soldier driving the vehicle, and the soldier salutes back. He glances at Raphael, then nods at Yossi.

Chapter 10

The town of Mitzpe Ramon comes into view as Yossi enters the central traffic circle, with its collection of hastily assembled prefabricated concrete apartment blocks dramatically perched at the edge of the Makhtesh Ramon, the largest erosion crater in the Middle East.

"*Lasciate Ogni Speranza,*" Raphael says as they drive slowly around the traffic circle.

"I beg your pardon," Yossi says.

"It's Latin for 'Abandon all Hope.'"

Yossi shakes his head.

"You know, from *Dante's Inferno*. It's what the sign says over the Gates of Hell."

Silence.

"Never mind."

Yossi speeds down the access road toward the apartment blocks. "It's not that awful here once you adapt to it."

As they pull into the car park at the side of one of the blocks, they disturb a flock of Nubian ibexes, which scatter in the direction of the makhtesh. Raphael squeals with delight and jumps out of the car with his camera and follows after them, snapping pictures and tempting two baby ibexes toward him with a few weeds he yanks out of the cracked asphalt.

"Let's go," Yossi calls, smiling at his cousin's interest in the ibexes. "There are plenty of those around here."

Yossi carries Raphael's suitcase across the threshold of the apartment and sets it down in the foyer. Raphael trails behind. There are split nail holes on the doorpost where the mezuzah should be and Raphael points at it. Yossi shakes his head and waves Raphael into the dim, sparsely decorated living room. He tells Raphael to wait and disappears down the hall in search of his mother. Raphael moves to the window and pulls aside the heavy curtain to let in some light and finds the apartment faces another block only a few metres away. He cranks open the window and cranes his neck around the corner, catching a glimpse of the makhtesh and the expanse of desert beyond.

The sound of footsteps clicking toward him on the tile floor makes him turn around. Aunt Penina emerges from the hallway followed by Yossi, wearing a black, sleeveless housedress. Her kinky grey hair is pulled away from her face into a tight bun, which emphasises her high cheekbones, her sharp nose, her almond-shaped black eyes, and her thin dark lips. Her skin looks as brittle as crepe paper, sunbaked and withered by the harsh desert climate. She narrows her eyes at him, then glances at the open window.

"Hello, Aunt Penina."

Aunt Penina snaps her fingers at the open window, and Yossi crosses the room to close it and draw the curtains.

"This is a desert, in case you hadn't noticed," she says. "There's wind and dust. We keep the windows shut here."

Yossi stands next to Raphael. "He's only just arrived, Ima."

Aunt Penina strides past them and pulls the curtains even more tightly closed. "All the more reason. He should start learning how things are done here now."

Raphael suppresses the urge to snap at his aunt. "I'm sorry, Aunt Penina. It won't happen again." He takes a step toward her and kisses her on the cheek. "Thank you for having me."

Aunt Penina's head jerks in his direction, and she brings her hand to her cheek. She stares at him as if seeing him for the first time, then she reaches up and pulls aside his hair.

"What's this?" she asks.

"I lost my footing in the dark last night and fell into some bushes."

"Is that so?" Aunt Penina lets go of his hair.

"Assaf should examine him, Ima," Yossi says. "There's a bruise on his chest that I'm worried about."

"We don't need troublemakers here, young man. Do you understand?"

"Yes, Aunt Penina."

She stares hard at him, and Raphael averts his eyes.

"Show him where he'll be sleeping," she says to Yossi after a moment. "I'll set the table for lunch."

Raphael follows Yossi down the dark hallway, dragging his suitcase into a small room with a bunk bed, a dresser, a small writing desk, and a wooden bookcase containing a few textbooks, some action figures, and a collection of Matchbox cars.

"That one's yours." Yossi points at the lower bunk. "Tomer sleeps on the top." He slides open the bottom two drawers of the dresser, both of which are empty. "We cleared these for you."

Raphael nods and lifts the blanket on the bottom bunk, exposing the thin mattress and the roller springs on which it lies. "This is just brilliant," he says, dropping on to the bed and looking around the room.

Yossi sits next to him. "Mine's the same. I sleep on the bottom bunk, and Assaf sleeps on the top one."

"Why don't you people just move somewhere else?"

"Ima refuses to leave."

Raphael rolls his eyes and stands. He looks out the window at the apartment block opposite, noticing that the curtains are closed in all the other apartments as well, except for a couple on the top floor.

"What is it with your mother? I mean, I get that she blames my father and all that. But, why does she have to be so harsh?"

Yossi joins Raphael at the window, placing his hand on his shoulder and squeezing it. "Hang in there, achi. She'll eventually get used to your being here; then things will settle down. In the meantime, I'll watch your back."

They sit down with Aunt Penina to a lunch consisting of vegetable soup and a beef liver steak with a side of boiled cabbage. Raphael pokes at the steak with his knife and looks up at Aunt Penina.

"Is this meat kosher, Aunt Penina?"

"This is Israel," she says, slicing a piece of liver and holding it up at the end of her fork. "Everything is kosher." She pushes it into her mouth and chews on it.

"It's true," Yossi says, cutting into his steak. "All the meat here comes from the same source."

Raphael looks at the two of them as they focus on their food, then looks down at his plate, his stomach grumbling.

"Are you sure?" he asks Yossi, who nods and continues to eat.

After a moment's hesitation, Raphael recites a blessing over his food, pushes the plate with the steak to one side and eats the boiled cabbage. Aunt Penina frowns at Yossi, who holds up his hand and shakes his head. Raphael catches this out of the corner of his eye and takes a sip of the soup. They eat the rest of their meal in silence. When they finish, Yossi kisses his mother, who is trembling with rage, and he rises from the table, picking up his plates and cutlery.

"We each take our plates to the kitchen," he says over his shoulder as he moves out of the room.

"It's nearly noon," Aunt Penina calls out, tracking Raphael with her eyes as he follows Yossi into the kitchen.

Raphael puts the empty plates in the sink and places the one with the uneaten steak on the counter.

"That wasn't cool," Yossi whispers, lifting his head at the stiffening steak.

"What's not cool? I only eat kosher meat. If it's not from a kosher butcher, I'm not eating it. Simple as that. You don't expect me to break the commandments just because I'm joining an unobservant household, do you?" He points in the direction of the front door. "And on that subject, whose idea was it to rip the mezuzah off the doorpost?"

Yossi wraps aluminium foil around the plate with the steak and places it in the refrigerator. "All I can say is, from what I can tell, you're very selective about which commandments you observe and which ones you break. But that's a subject for another time. Right now I have to hurry. I've got to report for duty in a half hour."

"You're not going to leave me here alone with her, are you?"

"I have to. But I'll be back tomorrow afternoon. Assaf's around today and Tomer will be back from school in a couple of hours. So it won't be only you and her most of the time. Don't worry."

"What's to worry?" Aunt Penina says from the doorway, startling Yossi and Raphael.

"Nothing, Ima," Yossi says. "I was just filling Rafi in on things, that's all."

"Thank you for lunch, Aunt Penina. I'm sorry about the meat. But I only—"

"Yes, yes," Aunt Penina says, "I heard."

Yossi puts his arm around his mother and guides her back to the living room. Raphael sneaks past them, excusing himself, and heads back down the hallway to his room. He is in the middle of unpacking his suitcase, arranging his clothes on the bed for placement in the dresser and the closet, when Yossi steps into the room, now in full uniform, holding his beret in his hands. Raphael straightens and takes in the sight of Yossi looking more handsome than ever.

"I've just heard I'm off duty from Rosh Hashanah through Yom Kippur. So, if you're up for it, we can do a bit of touring, maybe an overnight in the makhtesh. I have a favourite spot I want to show you."

"Yes, sure. Why not."

"*Sababa*," he says with a smile. "I've got to run now."

Raphael watches Yossi disappear from the doorway, feeling an ache in his chest and wishing he'd given him a hug before he left.

He spends the next few minutes putting away his clothes and organising the bookshelf, moving Tomer's things to the bottom shelf to make room for his books. Then he tapes some of his photographs and drawings to the wall above the writing desk.

When he finishes, he pushes his empty suitcase under the bed and walks to the living room toting his backpack and camera. He finds Aunt Penina there, hovering over an antique wooden ironing board, an electric iron in one hand and a dripping plastic bottle in the other. A white shirt is draped over the board, and a half-dozen others hang behind her on some wooden pegs hammered into the dividing wall between the living room and the kitchen. She looks up at him for an instant, then turns her attention back to the shirt.

"I do this for extra money," she says, wiping her forehead with a yellow dishtowel. "The money your father sends us each month isn't enough to feed a dog."

"Where's the synagogue, Aunt Penina?" Raphael asks, not wishing to be drawn into a discussion about his aunt's finances, especially as it touches on his father. "I'd like to pray Mincha."

Aunt Penina sets down the iron and wipes her forehead again. "There's no synagogue here."

"Where do people pray?"

She picks up the iron and spits on it, making it sizzle. "I'm sure some of them do." Shifting the shirt to another angle, she attacks it again with the hot iron. "I'm not interested in that sort of thing."

She peels the shirt off the ironing board, hangs it on a vacant peg, and grabs another one. "Neither are my sons."

"Aunt Penina."

She places the next shirt on the ironing board and comes around to Raphael's side. "You're not here to ask questions, young man."

"Tell me why I *am* here, Aunt Penina."

"You're here to atone."

"For what?"

"For the sins of your father. For the death of my husband."

"I'm meant to be the scapegoat, am I?"

"Don't get cute with me."

Raphael takes a step toward his aunt. "I'm sorry about what happened to Uncle Shimshon, Aunt Penina, I honestly am. I loved him like I love my own father. But hating Abba and being mean to me won't bring him back."

"Thirty-nine years old," Aunt Penina says, raising her fist to the ceiling. "My husband was only thirty-nine years old, and then he was gone. Someone has to pay."

"We've all been paying, Aunt Penina. Five years already. When's it going to be enough?"

Aunt Penina slaps the ironing board, making it jump. "When I say it's enough." She glares at Raphael. "In the meantime, you'll behave yourself and do as you're told, for once in your life."

"Aunt Penina, with respect, I'm here until I turn eighteen. After that, I'm gone. That's one year. But while I'm here I refuse to live in a hell of your making just because you can't accept it was Uncle Shimshon's time to go."

"How dare you speak to me that way! I'm a grieving widow."

"I'm sorry, Aunt Penina, but if you cross me or try to make my life here more difficult than it already is, I promise you'll regret you ever laid eyes on me. I won't warn you again."

Raphael turns his back on his aunt and walks out the front door of the apartment, hardly believing what he said to her, mopping the sweat from his face with a bandana.

He crosses the car park, startling a small herd of foraging ibexes as he breezes past them on the way to some shops he saw when Yossi and he entered the town. He steps inside a hardware store and waits while a bony-chested, middle-aged salesman with thick black hair and leathery skin chats in a mix of French, Arabic, and broken Hebrew with a stout young man. After a while, Raphael raps his knuckles on the counter and addresses them in Hebrew.

"Excuse me, gents. Good afternoon."

The two men stare at Raphael.

"You're Penina Dweck's nephew, yes?" the salesman asks.

"Guilty as charged," Raphael says.

"Ah, yes," the younger man says. "We heard you were coming. From Assaf your cousin we heard this. Welcome to Mitzpe Ramon."

"How may we help you?" the salesman asks. "I'm Amir, by the way."

"And I'm Yona."

"Nice to meet you. I'm looking for somewhere to pray Mincha. My aunt didn't seem to know of any place."

Amir looks at his wristwatch. "There's a group that gathers in the school cafeteria after lunch at around one thirty. They don't always manage a *minyan*. If you hurry, you might make it."

"I'm going that way now," Yona says, pulling out his keys. "I'll give you a ride."

Raphael follows him out to his pickup. Yona pulls away from the hardware store and brings the truck around to head into town on the road running parallel to the edge of the makhtesh. As they pass Aunt Penina's apartment block, he rolls down the window and holds out his arm in the direction of the open desert. "If you ask me," he says, "the best place to pray is there, standing at the edge of the makhtesh, facing the desert as our ancestors did."

"Jerusalem's that way," Raphael says, pointing in the opposite direction. "We face the Kotel."

Yona lets out a laugh. "You can tell I don't pray much."

"You know what?" Raphael says. "Just let me off here, please."

"But the school's still blocks away at the end of the road," Yona says, slowing down.

"That's OK," Raphael says. "I like your idea better."

Raphael hops out of the truck, runs across the dirt, and scrambles onto the retaining wall overlooking the makhtesh. He catches his breath as he gazes out across the 500-metre deep chasm to the other side, which is over ten kilometres away, and at the expanse of purple, black, scarlet, and gold sand drifting between the jagged buttes spread out at his feet. In the distance, he can make out an empty, thin ribbon of road heading south toward Eilat and the Sinai beyond where Yossi and his tank brigade are training. The thought of Yossi evokes a deep feeling of loneliness in him.

His hand automatically goes to his camera, and he calms himself by framing shots of the makhtesh and some of the random ibexes precariously navigating the sheer cliff side. Then he finishes his last roll of film snapping a few shots of the squatty houses and Quonset huts that make up his new hometown.

Switching out his camera for his prayer book, he flips to the afternoon service, turns to face Jerusalem with the makhtesh at his back, and starts his recitation. As he prays, a scorching wind kicks up from the makhtesh, blowing dust everywhere. Raphael squints to keep the grit from getting into his eyes and speeds through the service, holding down his kippah to keep it from flying off. When he finishes, he glances in the direction of the concrete apartment blocks in the distance, where reality awaits him. Then, driven by the wind, he jogs back across the rock-strewn field and along the deserted street to Aunt Penina's.

When he walks through the front door, he finds Aunt Penina still ironing shirts. His twenty-three-year-old cousin, Assaf, is standing next to her, dressed in a khaki coloured Madei Aleph uniform of the IDF Medical Core, his cap folded and resting on his shoulder, held in place by an epaulette. They both look up at Raphael, which affords him the opportunity to examine Assaf's angular, humourless face. His deep-set, dark eyes are framed by thick black eyebrows, and a three-day stubble darkens his strong jawline. His close-clipped hair adds to the severity of his look.

"Hello, cousin," Raphael says from the doorway.

Assaf nods at him without a trace of emotion.

Aunt Penina turns her attention back to the ironing board, and Raphael catches a vague hint of a smile on her face. Assaf strides past him and moves down the hallway. "Come with me."

Raphael follows him into the bedroom. His photographs are no longer on the wall, and his books are on the bottom shelf. Tomer's things are back where they were when he arrived.

"Don't move things without asking," Assaf says.

"Where are my photos?"

"In the drawer that I assigned to you." Assaf taps the bottom drawer of the writing desk with his black boot.

Raphael opens the drawer and pulls out the photos. He holds them up to Assaf. "The corners are ripped, achi."

"And?"

"They weren't ripped before."

"Listen, my friend," Assaf says, using the English expression instead of the Hebrew word *chaver* and raising himself to his full height, "I want you to be clear on something."

"What's that?"

"I'm the head of this household. The house rules are my rules. Anyone that lives here has to follow my rules. That includes you."

Raphael studies Assaf's hard face. He senses behind those deep-set dark eyes a cauldron of intense emotion and a hint of danger held in check—just—by his years of training as an IDF commander. In that instant, Raphael realises that Assaf is not one to be crossed if he is going to survive the next year, even with Yossi's support.

"As long as I'm able to pray when I need to, eat what I can, read whatever books I want, sketch without being censored, and dress however I want, I'll obey whatever house rules there are."

A bitter laugh escapes Assaf's lips. He points at the ceiling. "By all means, pray to the empty sky whenever you like. And you can starve, as far as I'm concerned. As for the rest of it, I don't care: draw, read, dress like a clown. But if I ask you to do something or not to do something, you must obey me, without question. Understood?"

"Yes."

"Agreed?"

"Yes, agreed."

"Good. Now, take off your shirt."

"My shirt?"

Assaf snaps his fingers at Raphael. "Enough with the questions. Let me see the bruise."

Raphael unsnaps his shirt and tosses it onto the bed. "Yossi told you."

Assaf looks closely at the bruise. Then he presses hard on it, causing Raphael to scream and pull away. "Hey, that hurts!" He rubs the throbbing area and glowers at Assaf.

Assaf points at Raphael's chest. "That was made by someone's fist."

"What about it?"

"You told my mother you fell in the dark."

"More like pushed."

"You were in a fight?"

"Something like that."

"If she'd punched you a little harder, I would have recommended blood thinners just to be sure. But that's not likely to clot. Leave it alone, and it should fade in two to four weeks."

"You said *she*."

"Judging from the diameter of the injured area, that was caused by a woman's fist. Or a child's. But a child wouldn't have been able to reach that high, nor would a child have had the strength to inflict that level of injury. So, yes, *she*."

Raphael grabs his shirt and buttons it back up. "You're a regular Sherlock Holmes, aren't you?"

Assaf checks the scratches on Raphael's forehead and dresses them with supplies from his first aid kit.

"If you're going to get into fights here," Assaf says as he packs away the supplies, "stick to fighting with men."

Raphael avoids looking directly at Assaf, who seems to know everything. He peers at himself in the full-length mirror on the back of the door, pulling back his hair to examine his forehead.

Assaf snatches a lock of Raphael's hair. "It's time to cut this hippie mop of yours."

"No way." Raphael steps away. "I like my hair the way it is."

Assaf taps his index finger against Raphael's forehead. "This is the first test of our agreement." He pulls open the door, narrowly missing Raphael's nose, and disappears into the hallway.

Raphael steps into the hallway behind him, a smouldering anger intensifying inside as he watches his cousin's retreating figure. After a moment, he sets his teeth and follows him out the door, feeling suddenly helpless and hating him with every ounce of his being.

He spends the rest of the afternoon riding around with Assaf, first to Mitzpe Ramon's only hair salon. A Moroccan barber passes his clippers over Raphael's head, shearing off all his hair in less than three minutes. He swings Raphael's chair around to face the mirror, and Raphael suppresses a scream when he sees his reflection, imagining himself a concentration camp victim, with Assaf the Nazi guard standing behind him smiling sadistically and nodding his approval.

"Now you look like a proper Israeli," Assaf says once they are back in the car and on their way to a general store, where Assaf picks up dry goods, cleaning supplies, and new underclothes.

Lastly, they drive a half hour up the road to the meat supplier in Sde Boker. Assaf introduces Raphael to the butcher, a grizzled Yemeni in his fifties with shoulder-length sidelocks that remind Raphael of a pair of slinkies. He wears an embroidered felt kippah, and the elaborately-knotted fringes of his tallit katan poke through holes in the front of his blood-splattered apron. At Assaf's prompting, the butcher reassures Raphael the meat he supplies is indeed kosher, but that he can't afford to pay the inspection fee. Assaf then buys some chicken and a large pack of stewing lamb and shoves the bag of meat at Raphael.

"Thanks for that, I guess," Raphael says, breaking the silence halfway back to Mitzpe Ramon. "About the meat."

"You give a little; I'll give a little," Assaf responds. "That way, we'll all get along just fine."

Raphael arches an eyebrow at Assaf. "If you say so."

Assaf looks at Raphael, his face darkening. "One more thing, cousin."

"What's that?"

"If you ever threaten my mother again, I will break every bone in your body, drag you into the makhtesh, and bury you alive."

Chapter 11

They find Tomer watching TV in the front room when they arrive home. He jumps off the sofa, runs over to Raphael, and gives him a big hug and a kiss on the cheek. Assaf marches past them to the kitchen carrying a bag of groceries. Raphael wipes his face with the back of his hand and stares at his twelve-year-old cousin, who is dressed in a rumpled white button shirt and dark blue dress slacks. He is about two inches shorter than Raphael and around ten pounds heavier. His open, friendly face is round and pudgy, and his curly, dark hair is neatly trimmed. His skin is oddly pale for someone who lives in the middle of the desert, like the belly of a tortoise.

Tomer takes Raphael's hand and leads him to their shared bedroom. He plops next to him on the bottom bunk and rambles on excitedly, his eyes open with wonder at the sight of his American cousin sitting next to him.

"We're going to have so much fun," Tomer says. "Do you like Matchboxes?" He jumps to his feet and retrieves one of the miniature cars from the bookshelf and holds it out to Raphael. "This one's a vintage Corvette, my all-time favourite car." He grabs another. "And this one's a Ferrari. I can't decide which one I like more."

Raphael takes the Corvette from Tomer and turns it over in his hand, then returns it to him. "Sorry, I'm not really into cars."

"That's OK." Tomer places them on the shelf and bounces back onto the bunk next to Raphael. "There's loads of other stuff we can do, like feeding the ibexes and exploring and stuff, after the sun goes down a bit. I'm not allowed outside in the middle of the day on account of my sun allergy. But there's loads we can do indoors, like watch TV and play board games and cards. Anyway, during term time we'll be mostly in class during the week."

"You have a sun allergy?"

"Yeah, I get a bad rash that turns into blisters if the sun shines straight onto my skin. So I have to wear hats and long sleeves and sun cream and mostly stay indoors until after the sun goes down. It can get super boring. But now that you're here, we can do stuff together."

Raphael stands and looks at his younger cousin. "Most of what I like to do I do alone."

"Like what?"

"Like reading and taking pictures and sketching stuff." Raphael snatches his copy of *A Clockwork Orange* off the bottom shelf and hands it to Tomer. "This is my favourite book."

Tomer flips through the pages and hands it back to Raphael. "I can't read English, sorry. What sorts of things do you draw?"

"Things that scare people." He pulls his sketchpad out of the bottom drawer and sits next to Tomer. "Like this, for example." He shows Tomer a sketch of a dissected cat. Tomer wrinkles his nose and shakes his head. "Or this one." He shows Tomer a sketch of a cow giving birth to a boa constrictor, its face craned in the direction of the emerging snake and contorted in terror. Tomer pushes away the sketch and stands up.

"Why don't you draw normal stuff?"

"What's normal?"

"You know, like landscapes, or buildings, or portraits of people doing boring stuff like sitting in chairs with their legs crossed, or whatever." He points at the sketches in Raphael's hands. "That stuff's nasty."

Raphael shoves the sketchpad and a box of coloured pencils into his backpack. "I'm going for a walk. I'll catch you later on." He smiles at Tomer and pats him softly on the arm.

"Where are you going?" Tomer asks, the corners of his mouth curling down.

"I need to get out. I'm feeling a little cooped up in here."

"I didn't say anything wrong, did I? If I did, I'm sorry."

"No, honestly, I just need to get out for a bit."

Tomer follows Raphael into the living room. Assaf and Aunt Penina are sitting at the dining table, deep in conversation.

"Rafi's going for a walk," Tomer announces.

"I'm serving dinner at six," Aunt Penina says, directing her words at Raphael but looking at Assaf.

"Make sure you're here at five forty-five sharp," Assaf says, pointing his finger at Raphael.

Raphael checks his watch and flashes him a thumbs up, then runs out the door.

Outside, the wind has subsided to the point that there is no movement of air. Heat radiates off the cement surfaces of the buildings and the asphalt of the car park. The glare of the massive afternoon sun prompts Raphael to slip on a pair of sunglasses. He lights up a Marlboro and takes a long drag that makes his chest hurt. Opening his shirt, he checks the bruise, which is starting to turn greenish yellow at the edges, and he smoulders at the memory of Yossi prodding it under the pretext of a medical examination. "Screw him," he says out loud, and, tossing aside the cigarette, jogs toward the makhtesh, dodging a small gathering of ibexes on his way.

He climbs onto the wall, his legs dangling over the edge, and watches as the sun descends. The sight of the barren crater in the waning afternoon light evokes an empty feeling in him. He thinks about Yossi's offer to take him into it to spend the night and feels torn between his desire to be alone with Yossi and his fear of the dark and the emptiness of the makhtesh.

The orb of the sun spits out swirls of colour as it dips westward, painting the purpling sky with reds and oranges, and splashing the edges of the crater with an ever-changing palette. Raphael pulls out his pad and sketches furiously, trying to capture something of the devolving landscape as the colours intensify, and a warm wind kicks up from the desert floor. Glancing at his watch, he sees he has only five minutes to get home for dinner if he's going to maintain the peace with Assaf. So he stuffs his pad into his backpack, takes one last lingering look at the makhtesh, and sprints back to the apartment.

Aunt Penina serves chicken, rice, and boiled vegetables to Assaf and Tomer. She drops a plate in front of Raphael on which sits the cold liver steak he failed to eat at lunch; then she takes a seat at the table next to Assaf. Raphael glances at her and finds Assaf staring back at him. "You can finish that now," Assaf says.

Raphael looks down at the steak and fights the urge to shove it away, knowing that things could get much worse for him if he openly rebels against Assaf. After a moment, he utters a blessing over his meal, and eats it, ignoring the conversation between Aunt Penina and her sons. When he finishes, he thanks Aunt Penina, excuses himself from the table, and pads down the hall to his room, reciting *Grace After Meals* with a growing lump in his throat.

He sits on the lower bunk and thinks of Los Angeles, of his parents, and of Gabriella. He thinks about his dear savta and of his saba lying helpless in bed, fearing the worst for his beloved grandfather. And he thinks about Yossi, absent only a few hours, already missing him terribly. A sharp pain asserts itself in the middle of his stomach. He takes in a trembling breath, brings his hand to his flushed cheek, and takes a swipe at the tears that freely flow from his eyes.

"What's the matter?" comes a voice from the doorway.

Raphael jumps up as Tomer walks into the room, his face screwed up and questioning. He whips out a bandana from his back pocket and dries his face. "Hey, little man."

"You were crying."

Raphael snatches his prayer book from atop the writing desk and moves past Tomer toward the door. "I'm a little homesick, that's all."

"Where are you going *now*?"

"Outside. To pray. It's time for Arvit."

"What's that?"

"Evening prayers. You don't know about evening prayers?"

Tomer shakes his head and points in the direction of the front room. "He doesn't like it."

"Who? Assaf?"

Tomer nods. Raphael stares at his young cousin and feels moved at the sight of him, looking forlorn in the middle of his tiny, dimly lit bedroom, a hint of anxiety clouding his face. He steps forward and kisses Tomer on the forehead.

"You can come with me if you want. It's dark now, so you can go outside, right?"

"I don't know how to pray."

"You can just watch me." Raphael smiles and moves to the door. "Or not."

Tomer runs after him as he moves down the hall and emerges into the living room. Assaf and Aunt Penina are sitting on the sofa intently focused on a news broadcast. Assaf is leaning forward, his forehead a spasm of furrows, and Aunt Penina sits with her thin hand covering her mouth, her almond-shaped eyes widening.

"What is it?" Tomer asks.

Assaf holds up a hand and inclines further toward the TV set. A moment later, the broadcast switches to music, and he leans back into the sofa and exchanges a look with his mother. Tomer sits next to his mother and hugs her. She barely registers the gesture and shakes her head.

"There are troop movements," Assaf says to the room. "On the Egyptian border. On the Syrian border also."

"That's just routine, isn't it?" Raphael says. "There are always troop movements."

Assaf narrows his eyes at Raphael. "What would you know?"

"We heard reports about that before back in the states. It doesn't mean anything according to what we've heard."

"It means something," Aunt Penina says, her voice barely audible. She searches Assaf's face, the muscles of her jaw pulsating, her forehead creased and moist. "And with Yossi's unit operating so close to the Sinai."

The bottom of Raphael's stomach drops on hearing Yossi's name.

Assaf squeezes his mother hand. "Yossi will be fine, Ima." He looks back at the TV and sets his jaw.

"They wouldn't dare try anything," Raphael says. "They know they'd be wiped out *again*."

"Why is that?" Assaf snaps. "Because God's on our side?"

"Because Israel has the best army in the world," Raphael says. "And, that too."

Assaf stands and switches off the TV. "I wouldn't be so sure about that. Anyway, where are you going with that?" He points at the prayer book in Raphael's hand.

"Outside. It's time for Arvit."

"I want to go with him." Tomer jumps up from the sofa.

Assaf closes his eyes and pinches the bridge of his nose for a moment, then nods and waves them out the door.

Raphael marches across the scrub field to the retaining wall, with Tomer trailing behind. He climbs up and stares into the blackness of the makhtesh, the margins softly glowing in the silver light of the waning moon, a mere three days before the new month of Tishrei and the start of the Jewish New Year. Tomer watches him from below.

The sky pulsates with the light of a billion stars, a carpet of diamonds above their heads, the most intense night sky Raphael has ever seen. Forcing all distraction from his mind, he focuses on Hashem, on the eternity spread out above and before him, on the sound of his breathing. Then he turns to face Jerusalem, grasping the prayer book in his hand, and recites the evening prayers from memory.

He stands framed by the immensity of the star-filled sky, reciting the ancient words in a loud voice, delivering them to the empty streets of Mitzpe Ramon with the dramatic flair of a Shakespearean actor, his arms held out wide and beckoning to an unseen deity. He concludes with a closing hymn, which he softly croons; a soulful, heartfelt tune of his own composition. Once he finishes, he stands silently for a few moments, then reaches down and helps Tomer scramble onto the wall. They sit next to each other facing the parking lot, with the open desert at their back, and Raphael lights up one of his last Marlboros.

"That was beautiful," Tomer whispers after a while, wiping his face with the back of his hand.

Raphael smiles at Tomer and tousles his hair, then takes another drag on his cigarette.

"No, seriously," Tomer says. "I've never heard anyone pray like that before."

"I'm not just anyone."

Tomer sighs and kicks his feet against the wall. "Ima's worried about Yossi." He turns around to face the crater. "His unit operates in the Sinai. He's probably there right now."

Raphael glances over his shoulder. "They won't try anything. Believe me. They're just rattling swords."

"That's what everyone says. But Assaf thinks differently. I can tell. No matter what he says to Ima, he's worried, too."

"As I said before, even if they try something, we have plans in place. They won't make it one inch across the border. So don't worry so much." Raphael flicks his cigarette into the darkness and watches it sputter as it bounces off the cliff side into the makhtesh. "Listen, little man. Can you do me a favour?"

"Of course," Tomer says, a smile transforming his face into the face of an angel.

"Anything you hear Assaf or your mother say about me, I'd like for you to let me know."

"Oh..." The smile disappears from Tomer's face.

"I just don't want any surprises, that's all. Can you promise me that?"

"I don't know," Tomer says "I'm not sure that's right."

"I'm not asking you to do anything other than to let me know if they say anything about me. What's wrong with that?"

"It doesn't feel right, Rafi. Don't be mad, please."

Raphael stares at Tomer for a moment, unexpectedly moved by his cousin's vulnerability. He reaches out a hand and gently tousles his hair again. "That's OK, little man. Don't worry."

He hops off the wall and offers a hand to Tomer. They stroll back together to the apartment. When they reach the front of the building, Raphael puts his arm around Tomer's shoulder.

"Don't worry so much, little man. OK?" He kisses the top of Tomer's head. "Worrying never helps anyway."

Chapter 12

*R*aphael feels himself being dragged by one leg over the rock-strewn *desert floor, across dry creek beds, through nests of chaparral scrub and thorn-choked acacia bushes, and past scrambling lizards, scuttling scorpions, and hungry open-mouthed vipers with darting, pointed tongues. The hot desert wind screams through the sandstone canyon and flings grit against his face and into his nose and mouth. He opens his eyes for an instant and catches sight of the Milky Way throbbing across the sky, and he cries out to Hashem, even as the rocks shred his clothes and flay the skin off his back.*

Moments later he finds himself tumbling down the sides of a clay pit and landing in a pile of mush. He staggers to his feet and sees he is standing in the midst of a collection of dead bodies in various states of decay. Next to him lies the bloated corpse of Uncle Shimshon, his eyes a pair of opaque marbles shoved deep into a purple face, his mouth open and caked full of clay. Raphael screams and backs into the shadows, squishing through the mush of decaying humanity as loose dirt rains down on him. He raises his arms to shield his head, peers heavenward, and sees Assaf shovelling rubble into the pit, with Aunt Penina and Tomer standing on either side of him, expressionless as a pair of Byzantine icons. High above, a squadron of Israeli fighter jets screeches across the night sky heading toward Egypt and strafing the desert below. "I warned you," Assaf's voice echoes through the pit. "I warned you."

The ground beneath Raphael quivers. He glances down and suppresses a scream at the sight of the tattered flesh of the surrounding bodies rippling toward him in concentric circles. The quivering increases and becomes a shaking so intense he loses his balance and falls face down into the putrefaction. A thick sucking sound echoes through his head as he struggles out of the rancid porridge of macerated cadavers. Then, clawing his way to the side of the pit, he howls at Heaven asserting his innocence and demanding salvation, foam pouring forth from his mouth like that of a rabid bitch.

A pair of hands grasps his shoulders, and he struggles to get away. They yank him back and shake him. Flipping around, Raphael opens his eyes and finds himself staring into Yossi's face, his heart hammering and perspiration streaming down the sides of his face. He sits up and scans the room, desperate to establish his bearings. He sees Tomer peering at him from behind Yossi, who is dressed in his full combat uniform, in his stocking feet, his hair full of red dust. Closing his eyes, Raphael runs a hand over his damp scalp.

"Is he OK?" Tomer asks.

Yossi glances over his shoulder. "Seems he was having a nightmare." He sits on the edge of the bunk. "Is that right, achi?"

Raphael falls back against his pillow and draws a few deep breaths.

Yossi points at the door. "Fetch a glass of water, quick."

Tomer runs out of the room.

"Are you OK, achi?" Yossi squeezes Raphael's leg.

Raphael looks down at Yossi's hand and flashes a weak smile. "I'm so glad to see you; you have no idea. I thought I was going to fucking die."

"Die?"

Raphael narrows his eyes at the door and lowers his voice. "That Assaf's a complete dick, I swear. I don't know how you can live under the same roof as him."

Yossi shrugs. "He's strong, that's all."

"He's not strong. He's a bully."

Tomer runs into the room, hands Raphael a glass of lukewarm water and watches as he drains it in two gulps. Raphael pushes the empty glass back at him and asks for another.

Yossi scoots up to Raphael and looks directly into his eyes. "Listen to me, cousin. Suppress your inner asshole, and everyone will love you. Even Assaf."

"What about you?"

"What about me?"

Raphael stares at Yossi for a moment. "Never mind," he mutters.

Yossi backs away from Raphael and laughs. "You're a funny one, achi."

"It was only a question."

"You're right about that." Yossi rolls his head to work out a kink in his neck. "Anyway, switching gears, the good news is they've sent us home for the High Holidays. If I'm lucky, I may not have to report back until after *Sukkot*. So we'll have plenty of time to hang out before I'm called up again. Maybe we'll even take in that camping trip in the makhtesh I promised. He rubs Raphael's head and laughs. "I love the new haircut, by the way."

"What about Rosh Hashanah?" Raphael says, instinctively reaching up to fix his hair and finding nothing there but nubs.

"We'll go up to Jerusalem for Rosh Hashanah. So we can keep that date with Savta."

Tomer pops back into the room and hands Raphael a second glass of water. He sits on the bunk next to Yossi. Raphael takes a quick sip and puts it on the floor.

"What about the Egyptian troop movements?"

Yossi stands and stretches. "What about it?"

"Assaf and your mother are worried."

"It's true," Tomer says. "Ima was crying."

Yossi shakes his head. "If the Ministry isn't worrying, then why should we? It's not like the borders are undefended. We have people there. If they need us, they'll call."

"That's what I told Assaf," Raphael says.

"Anyway," Yossi says, looking down at himself and wrinkling his nose, "I've got to clean up. I've got some errands to run in Beersheba this morning. Are you interested in tagging along?"

"Hell, yes." Raphael jumps out of bed. "I'm all out of film, and I need to drop off some rolls for developing."

"Excellent," Yossi says, "I know just the place. We'll leave straight after breakfast."

—ᶸᶸᶸ—

Yossi speeds down the highway, and Raphael gazes out the side window at the passing landscape, which glows softly yellow in the early-morning light.

"I understand there was some trouble with my mother yesterday," Yossi says as they pass Sde Boker.

"Sort of." Raphael scoots down in his seat and stares at his trainers. "I asked her where I could pray, and then she fired off on me. She said I was here to atone for what happened to Uncle Shimshon in place of Abba and a bunch of nonsense like that. Then I lost it and warned her not to make my life difficult. I didn't mean to disrespect her, honestly. It just came out wrong. Then her guard dog, Assaf, threatened to kill me. It wasn't my best day."

Yossi reduces his speed as they approach the next settlement. "Here's the thing about Ima, achi, so you can understand how things are. Hopefully, it'll help."

Raphael inclines his head and waits as Yossi bites his lower lip for a moment, working out what he's about to say. Then he glances at Raphael.

"This is confidential, OK?"

"I'll take it to the grave, I swear."

Yossi nods slowly and looks back at the road. "Ima was always jealous of Abba's close relationship with Uncle Isaac."

"She was?"

"Completely. First, she wasn't thrilled about us living together at Savta's. She wanted Abba and her to get their own place. But Saba insisted the house was large enough for the whole family. So they stayed. And that pissed her off. But what really upset Ima was that Abba grew closer to your father after they married, and even closer after we kids were born. So when you guys left for Los Angeles, and Abba fell into a depression..." Yossi frowns and shakes his head.

Raphael sits up. "I know this story, remember? Uncle Shimshon was depressed, so he moved you guys out here."

"Actually, achi..."

"What?"

"Ima was the one who pushed for us relocate to Mitzpe Ramon. Her sister already lived here with her husband and their two kids."

Raphael slaps the dashboard. "So it's *her* fault you ended up here?"

Yossi nods.

"But yesterday you said Uncle Shimshon moved you guys here because we left for America."

"It's true. But it was at Ima's prompting. She thought the change would do us good, especially him. She saw it as an opportunity for us to make a fresh start as a family and for them as a couple."

"That's really screwed up, gever, you know that? Five years of scapegoating and guilting money out of my father when it was her fault all along."

"Try to see it from her side, achi. Despite all her good intentions, she lost the love of her life in a horrible accident. The fact they never recovered his body made it even worse. Ima's tortured by guilt. And at the same time, she's angry about the loss and doesn't know what to do with that anger. Somehow, she's focused it on your father."

"Great. And now that I'm here, she's focusing it on me."

"That will pass, I'm sure. What Ima needs from us, you included, is understanding and compassion."

"You're asking me to be her whipping boy?"

"Not at all. I'm asking you to be respectful and polite. If she crosses the line and abuses you, please don't react. Let me know, and I'll intervene. Same with Assaf. I'll be your buffer. If you follow my advice, things should settle down in a few weeks, I'm sure of it."

Yossi reaches over and squeezes Raphael's arm.

"Do you think you can do that?"

Raphael stares at the low-rise, shabby skyline of Beersheba looming in the distance and shrugs. "I'll do my best."

They drive for another few minutes past several ramshackle Bedouin settlements constructed at the side of the road. The smell of burning rubbish floats in through the air vent. Raphael flashes on his last drive through the Westside of Los Angeles with his father as they made their way to the airport, and he lets out a loud sigh.

"What is it?" Yossi asks.

"I'm feeling homesick, achi. It's only been a couple of days, and I'm already missing my old life in LA, my family, my school, my friends. This is hard."

Yossi nods and glances at Raphael. "I'll see what we can do to help make it bearable."

"Thanks, achi."

"Do you like movies?"

"Movies?"

"Yes, you know, Hollywood movies."

"Yeah, of course. I love them. Why?"

"My cousin Ari's the art teacher at the high school. He screens classic Hollywood movies at his place every week. It's like an informal cinema. He has a 16mm projector and a collection of films he rents from an outlet in Tel Aviv with a branch here in Beersheba; at the camera store we're headed to, in fact. A lot of those old movies are set in California. Maybe watching them will help you feel a little closer to home."

"I'm not so much into the classics. I'm more into modern stuff like Kubrick and Peckinpah."

"Ah, achi, you don't know what you're missing. Brando, James Dean, Montgomery Clift. You'll see."

A few minutes later Yossi pulls up in front of a shop with an extensive range of cameras displayed in the front window.

"This is it," he says, nodding at the shop.

"Aren't you going to park?"

"I've got a couple of errands to run," Yossi says. "I'll meet you for lunch at noon at that place." He points out a food stand across the road with a few outside picnic tables. "That'll give you a couple of hours to do your shopping and browse around."

Raphael frowns at the shop and scratches his head. "I only need to drop off some rolls and buy a couple more. It won't take long," he says. "Can't I come with you?"

"Nah, what I've got to do is boring. Plus, it's worth taking your time to have a look at all the equipment they have. If there's not enough to hold your attention, you can always check out the Old Town over there."

Raphael peers at the crumbling Ottoman-era buildings of the so-called Old Town off to the side of the commercial strip and arches his brow at Yossi. "If you say so." He grabs his backpack and climbs out of the car.

"If I finish early, I'll come straight back," Yossi says. "I promise."

The man behind the counter raises his head at the sound of jangling bells as Raphael pushes open the door and steps inside. The diverse range of cameras jammed into the shop startles Raphael, who stands staring, his mouth slightly open, at all the equipment in glass cases and on multitiered shelving that extends all the way to the back of the warehouse-like space.

"Welcome to heaven," the shopkeeper says with a smirk, sticking his pencil behind his ear.

"This is amazing," Raphael says.

"Who would've thought, right? In Beersheba of all places."

Raphael points at a vintage Leica 35mm resting on the counter. "May I?"

The man hands the camera to Raphael, who hefts it, then turns it over in his hands and stares through the lens. He frames a shot of the back room, noting the impressive range of movie cameras and projectors.

"What do you need with all this stuff?" Raphael hands back the Leica to the man.

"It's for the film and television industry. Storage space is cheaper in Beersheba than in Tel Aviv or Jerusalem."

"I thought this was a retail shop."

"This front section is retail." The man extends his hand toward the shelving behind him. "The rest is industry overflow. The full collection is in our warehouse at the edge of town, where rent is cheap as dirt."

"I see."

"How can I help you?" the shopkeeper asks.

An hour and a half later Yossi pokes his head into the shop and finds Raphael and the shopkeeper in the back going over the different parts of a 16mm movie camera. Raphael looks up and beams a smile.

"I thought I might still find you here," Yossi says.

"Welcome, gever," the shopkeeper says, straightening up and shaking Yossi's hand. "How's my best customer, Ari?"

"He's fine. He told me to let you know he'll be swinging by after Shabbat to drop off a couple of things. This one's my cousin, too." He inclines his head at Raphael. "He's recently arrived from America."

"Why didn't you say so?" the shopkeeper says to Raphael. "I would have rolled out the red carpet for you." He slaps Raphael on the back and heads to the front of the shop to attend to a newly arrived customer.

"This place is fantastic, achi," Raphael says.

"What did I tell you?" Yossi points at the camera in Raphael's hand. "That one's for making movies."

"Yeah, I know." Raphael frames Yossi through the lens and makes a buzzing sound pretending to film him.

Yossi laughs and holds up his palm at the camera. "Are you considering making the shift to film?"

Raphael sets aside the camera. "Never thought about it."

Yossi picks it up and holds it out to him. "Maybe you should. You say you love movies, right? You should try making your own. The light's perfect in the desert for that sort of thing. You can screen them at my cousin Ari's place."

"It's an expensive hobby, achi. Plus, I'd probably need access to editing equipment and stuff."

"We have all that here," the shopkeeper says from behind them. "I'd be happy to teach you how to use it when you're ready. The fundamentals aren't difficult."

"There, you see?" Yossi says, winking at the shopkeeper. "My friend here is happy to help."

"I wouldn't start with a 16mm, though," the shopkeeper says. He reaches for a smaller camera. "I recommend that you learn on this 8mm until you get the hang of it. If you end up liking it, you can upgrade."

"I'll even buy it for you," Yossi says. "And a bag full of film, too. Consider it an early birthday present."

Raphael takes the camera from the shopkeeper's hands and passes his hand over it, feeling an unexpected surge of happiness welling up inside. He looks at Yossi, who is smiling expectantly at him, and his eyes fill with tears.

"Thank you, achi," he says, his voice hoarse with emotion.

—⚱︎—

Later that night after dinner, Raphael and Yossi stroll along the highway to Ari's place in a converted warehouse wedged in Mitzpe Ramon's industrial zone at the edge of town. They crash on one of several beat-up sofas in his makeshift screening room and crack open a couple of beers while Ari sets up the projector and cues up the film they're going to watch.

"Where is everyone?" Raphael asks, stretching himself out lengthwise on the sofa, extending his legs across Yossi's knees.

"That's tomorrow night," Ari calls out in his gravelly voice. "This is a private screening for you by special request of Mr Tank Commander there."

"That's sub-commander," Yossi says.

"Whatever," Ari says with a chuckle.

He comes around in front of the sofa and raises his bottle to Raphael. "Anyway, consider this your official welcome to Mitzpe Ramon."

In his late twenties, a bit on the heavy side, with long side-burns and a receding hairline of kinky dark brown curls, Raphael finds that while Ari is not particularly attractive, he's somehow pleasant to look at.

Raphael sits up and clinks his bottle against Ari's and Yossi's.

Ari takes a swig from the bottle and wipes his mouth on his sleeve.

"Any cousin of Yossi's is a cousin of mine, especially one from Hollywood. That's what I say."

"I'm from Los Angeles, not Hollywood."

Ari takes another swig of beer and sets down his bottle on a side table. "Same diff. That's what I say."

Yossi pulls Raphael into a bear hug and rubs his head playfully. "This one's going to be the next Elia Kazan, I think."

"Oh, yes?" Ari says, dropping onto the sofa. "That's quite a comparison."

"He's already won awards."

"That was for my still photography, achi."

"If you have an eye for still photography," Ari says, "then you're light years ahead of the pack already."

"I bought him an 8mm camera this morning at Hanut Tzilum. He spent all afternoon wandering around town with it."

"I've shot five rolls already, mainly of the makhtesh and the ibexes, getting used to the camera and practising different techniques."

"Speaking of Elia Kazan," Ari says, draining the last of his beer and standing up, "tonight we're watching his *East of Eden*, again by special request." He nods at Yossi. "I also have copies of *Streetcar* and *On the Waterfront* that you can come and watch if you're interested."

"I chose *Eden* because it's set in California like we talked about," Yossi says. "Not to mention it's my favourite James Dean film."

"Cool," Raphael says, "let's do it."

Two hours later Ari brings up the lights and rewinds the film into the canister. Raphael sits staring at the blank screen, his face clouded over with a frown.

"What did you think?" Ari calls out.

Raphael shakes his head.

"What's up, achi?" Yossi says.

"It's based on the story of Cain and Abel from the Bible," Ari says, bringing over another couple of bottles of beer.

Raphael declines the beer and stands. "Thanks very much, gever."

"You're not leaving yet, are you?" Ari exchanges a glance with Yossi, who lifts his shoulders. "We can watch a different one if you want."

"Not tonight, thanks," Raphael says. He turns to Yossi. "Is it all right if we go now?"

"What was that all about?" Yossi asks as they walk along the empty highway back into town.

"That film," Raphael says. "That's my life." He kicks a piece of loose gravel into the darkness. "Nothing's ever good enough. Everything's always my fault."

He pulls up and stares around at the barren landscape.

"Steady, achi." Yossi rests his hand on his shoulder. "It was just a movie."

"That father, he was like Abba and Ima and Hashem all rolled into one. And I'm like that James Dean character, Cal, always trying to please and never getting it right." He pulls away from Yossi and drops to one knee. "That's why they sent me away. That's why I'm fucking here and not back home in LA."

Yossi kneels in the dirt next to Raphael. "Listen to me, achi. Forget all that. This is your home now. And I'm your family. Make the best of it and close the door on the past. Otherwise, you'll lose your mind. Like Ima, like Assaf, they can't let go, and look at them. They're consumed with anger and frustration. Don't let that be your reality. Fight regret as if you're fighting a mortal enemy. I'm right here with you."

Raphael stares into Yossi's shining eyes, which reflect the soft glow of the starlight, and lets his words wash over him.

Yossi lifts him to his feet, and Raphael puts his arms around him, taking in the scent of Yossi, feeling his moist breath on his neck, and surrendering. They remain that way for a few minutes. Then Yossi lifts Raphael's head.

"Better?" Yossi asks.

Raphael nods.

"Good stuff, achi." Yossi breaks into a run toward the town. "I'll race you back," he shouts over his shoulder.

Raphael watches as Yossi fades into a cloud of dust, feeling a sudden twinge of conscience at the realisation that he has neglected to say his evening prayers. Looking up at the sky, he offers an apology, then rattles off the evening service, dizzied by a sense of terror standing in the dark at the edge of the road.

A light wind kicks up from the south and blows around a bit of grit. Wrapping a bandana around his nose and mouth, Raphael sets his face toward the town and walks with his head down. As he moves along the highway, he reflects that he has utterly lost the battle against Yossi. And yet there is sweetness in the defeat. The question for him now is how he is going to hold onto it.

When he arrives at the apartment block, he finds Yossi sitting on the front steps, his car keys dangling from his fingers.

"I was about to go looking for you. What happened?"

Raphael sits next to Yossi and rests his body against his. "I forgot to recite Arvit before we went to Ari's. Plus, I needed some alone time. Sorry if I made you wait."

Yossi's head jerks up. "You forgot to pray? When's the last time that happened."

"That's the *first* time it's happened, achi." Raphael straightens up. "The first time. It was a little scary."

"You were distracted. Don't worry. If He's there, he'll forgive."

"I don't want to give it up, achi."

"No one's saying you have to."

"I appreciate everything you're doing for me. I honestly do. But please promise you won't pressure me to stop observing the *mitzvot*, to stop praying."

"Is that what you think this is all about?"

"It's happened to all of you out here. I don't want it to happen to me, no matter how bad things get. It's the only constant in my fucked-up life."

Yossi nods and stares out at the car park. "The only constant…"

"Yeah, the *only* one."

"The mitzvot."

"Yep."

Not Hashem?"

Raphael stands. "You got it."

Yossi lets out a long breath and crunches across the gravel toward the retaining wall overlooking the makhtesh, and Raphael follows. They startle a lone ibex standing sentry on the sheer edge of the cliff, and they watch it bound away.

"Life is full of surprises," Yossi says, lifting his head at the ibex as it vanishes into the crater. "Even for them."

"Especially for them," Raphael says. He pulls out a couple of cigarettes and hands one to Yossi. "We're not animals. We have minds. We can prepare for things."

Yossi laughs and lights up. "Don't kid yourself, achi. We're animals. And these things"—he holds up his cigarette—"are going to kill us one day if something or someone else doesn't kill us off before." He takes a drag and blows smoke over the dark crater.

"Gee, thanks." Raphael tosses his cigarette onto the ground and snuffs it out with his heel.

"That's *my* constant," Yossi says.

"What is? Death or the makhtesh?"

"Both, I guess."

"I'll stick with the mitzvot if it's all the same to you."

"Sure, why not. Anyway, I've got to go back to Beersheba tomorrow after lunch. Some friends from my unit and I are planning a tour of the north with a military guide around Rosh Hashanah time. Three or four days max."

"Can I come?"

"On the tour yes, of course. We'll stop over at Saba and Savta's for the *chag* and continue from there."

"I meant to Beersheba."

"Not this time, achi." Yossi flicks what's left of his cigarette into the darkness, and the two of them stroll to the apartment block. "You're OK with that, right?"

"To be honest, I'd rather go with you than stay here. But I suppose I need to start getting used to it."

"That's the spirit. And you have your movie camera."

They push into the darkened apartment, and Yossi unshoulders his machine gun and holds it at his side.

"Everything good?" Yossi whispers.

Raphael looks around the empty living room and back at Yossi. He pulls a tight smile and nods. Yossi squeezes his shoulder and moves down the dark hallway toward his bedroom. Raphael brings up his hand to the spot where Yossi touched him, still feeling the pressure of the squeeze, and watches as he turns left and disappears from view.

The next afternoon, Raphael heads over to the school library and works on a shooting script for a short film idea he has in mind. After a few hours, he packs up and heads back to the apartment, timing his return to coincide with Yossi's estimated arrival from Beersheba. He is surprised to find the front room and the kitchen empty so early in the day and wonders where everyone has gone.

Poking his head into his bedroom and Yossi's, he finds them both empty. Then he pads over to Aunt Penina's and, putting his ear to her door, he hears a faint whimpering coming from the other side.

"Aunt Penina?" he says.

The sound stops, and he hears a rustling followed by a soft thump.

He taps on the door, then pushes it open and finds Aunt Penina sitting in the dark with the curtains drawn, crying into a white handkerchief. She is dressed in a plain black housedress with her long, grey hair unpinned and unkempt. There is a red-and-black chequered nightshirt draped over her knees.

"Aunt Penina, what's wrong?"

He takes a couple of tentative steps into the bedroom, and Aunt Penina's hand shoots out, halting his forward movement. Recalling Yossi's admonition about showing her compassion, Raphael crosses the room and sits next to her on the bed. Aunt Penina tosses a sidelong glance at him and scoots a little away. Raphael responds by stroking her back. Her frame feels bony, like the shell of an armadillo. Aunt Penina dries her face with her handkerchief and straightens up.

"Was that Uncle Shimshon's?" Raphael whispers, reaching out to touch the nightshirt.

Aunt Penina nods and holds it to her chest.

"It was the last thing he wore before he left for the mines the day I lost him. It's all I have left of him."

"You have your memories, too."

Aunt Penina looks at Raphael and lowers the nightshirt. "Memories fade."

"And you have your sons."

"Sons are no substitute for a husband."

Raphael pulls back his hand. "I don't know what to say, Aunt Penina."

"Nobody asked you to say anything."

Raphael lets out a short, bitter laugh. "You should know by now, Aunt Penina, I speak my mind; sometimes out of turn like the other day, which I'm sorry about. But if something needs to be said, I say it."

"Well, save your words." Aunt Penina puts away her husband's nightshirt in a dresser. "There's nothing you or anyone else can say that will change anything."

"We're commanded to comfort those in mourning, Aunt Penina."

Aunt Penina whirls on Raphael. "Comfort?" she spits out. "It's all lies, all of it; *everything* you people say." She slaps the dresser with her open palm. "'Your happy memories of him will comfort you, Penina.'" She slaps it again. "'He's in a better place now,

Penina.'" She slaps it yet again. "'Everything happens for a reason, Penina.'"

"Everything *does* happen for a reason, Auntie."

"Tell me, smart boy, what's the reason? What's the reason the man I loved more than life itself, the father of my children, a man who never offended anyone and who observed all those so-called commandments you hold dear, why did he end up dead at thirty-nine under a mountain of clay?"

"I don't know," Raphael says.

"Who knows then? Tell me so I can ask them."

"Only Hashem knows."

Aunt Penina pulls a tight smile. "He and I aren't on speaking terms, in case you hadn't noticed."

"With respect, Aunt Penina, maybe you should be. It certainly would be better than this." Raphael waves his hand around the room. "It's over five years, and your anger hasn't subsided. That's not right."

"My anger is my comfort."

Raphael stands and shakes his head.

"Life is short, smart boy. I know it doesn't feel that way now when you're still young. But it speeds by, and we have no control over what happens. Some of us have no control even over what we feel. And feelings can be all-powerful and overwhelming."

Aunt Penina stares at Raphael, who has lowered his gaze to the floor. He looks up at the sound of the front door slamming. His eyes meet Aunt Penina's.

"That will be Assaf," Aunt Penina says softly, "back from the doctor's with Tomer."

"I hope it gets better for you, Aunt Penina."

She lifts her shoulder in a little shrug and shakes her head.

"Maybe we can talk again sometime," he says.

Aunt Penina's head snaps up. "Listen to me, you little pipsqueak," she hisses. "Don't think you can waltz in here and sweet talk me like you do everyone else. I know who you are and what you are."

"All I want is a truce, Aunt Penina. May we please have that, for everyone's sake? In exchange, I promise to keep out of your way. Please."

Aunt Penina stares hard at Raphael for a moment, then rolls her eyes and quickly nods her head.

Raphael steps forward and kisses his aunt on the forehead. She stiffens on the first contact of his lips, then relaxes and accepts the gesture. Their eyes meet again briefly, and each assesses the other, expert chess players staring at each other across the board, contemplating the end game. Then Raphael squeezes her hand and steps out of the room.

Chapter 13

The day before Rosh Hashanah, Yossi and Raphael pile into the back of a large transport truck, together with eight other members of Yossi's tank unit. All of them are dressed in their off-duty uniforms, except for Raphael, who wears a pair of army trousers and some old combat boots Yossi lent him, with a black lace-up shirt, a bone necklace, and a red bandana tied around his head. They drive caravan-style, with another two trucks behind them carrying twenty troops and a military tour guide. Yossi and his mates sing pop songs, smoke cigarettes, and tell off-colour jokes as the convoy makes its way up the Arabah Valley bordering Israel and Jordan toward the Dead Sea. Raphael sketches in his pad, occasionally glancing up to watch the group in mild amusement.

When they arrive at Masada at around four in the afternoon, they snack on almonds, dates, and energy bars, waiting for the sun to dip toward the horizon before attacking the hill on foot, making their way up the snake path to the summit. Yossi helps Raphael up the cliffside, walking behind him and steadying him as he catches his breath. The others hurl good-natured taunts at them down the side of the hill. But Yossi laughs it off, and he and

Raphael eventually pull themselves onto the summit and admire the tortured majesty of the desert, the Dead Sea, and Jordan in the distance, the distant red glow of Wadi Rum softly pulsating at the edge of the darkening eastern sky.

The tour guide leads them around the rubble of the ancient ruins, barely recognisable for the fortress palace it was two thousand years before. She explains how the compound came to be built, how Judean freedom fighters taking refuge in the abandoned fortress chose to commit suicide rather than submit to capture by the Romans. And she concludes the tour by reiterating to the soldiers the importance of Masada as a symbol of the modern state of Israel. "We will never surrender to our enemies."

Scores of hippie backpackers pour over the lip of the hill. Raphael leans against one of the crumbling walls to light a Marlboro and watches as the backpackers set up their collection of tents on various parts of the hilltop. As the sun dips below the horizon, they light fires in the middle of rings they build with stones with kindling they brought with them in their backpacks. Raphael turns away from them, stamps out his cigarette, and recites his evening prayers. Then he wanders back to look for Yossi and the other soldiers.

"Hey, handsome," a small-breasted woman in a granny dress with daisies braided into her long, blonde hair calls out in English from one of the groups. She stands and beckons Raphael over with a wave of her hand. The others giggle as Raphael strolls over and sits on the ground next to the woman, who introduces herself as Bright Moon. She grabs hold of Raphael's arm and snuggles up to him.

"Comfy, aren't we?" he says, sniffing at her hair, which smells a bit like freshly mown grass mixed with a hint of perspiration.

"She likes you," calls out a shirtless young man in cut-off jeans with a scruffy blonde beard. He is slightly older than Raphael, maybe eighteen, with bright blue eyes that sparkle in the firelight.

He holds out a joint to Raphael, who puts up his hand and shakes his head.

Bright Moon kisses Raphael on the cheek, then buries her face in his lap and nibbles at his thighs. He pushes away from her, and she falls into the dirt and remains there giggling. Raphael jumps up and stares down at her.

"Don't worry about her," the young man says. "She's just tripping." He holds out an empty palm. "Want a hit? It's windowpane."

"What's going on here?" a voice comes from behind Raphael. He turns and finds Yossi standing there; his machine gun slung over his shoulder.

"Shit," the young man says to the others in the group, who scramble to their feet and size up Yossi across the campfire.

"Nothing's going on," Raphael says. "I was hanging out with these guys for a bit."

"You know him?" says the young man with the beard.

"Yes, I know him." He looks down at Bright Moon, who is now rolling from side to side in the dirt babbling what sounds like a nursery rhyme. "You sure she's OK?"

"What's wrong with her?" Yossi asks Raphael in Hebrew.

"LSD, I think," Raphael whispers.

"She'll be fine," the young man says in broken Hebrew with a nervous giggle. "I won't let her launch herself off the hill or anything like that." He and the others drop back onto the dirt and resume passing around a joint.

Yossi shakes his head and walks away, and Raphael catches up with him. They hike across the top of the hill, now illuminated only by intense starlight, to join Yossi's troop, which has set up camp on the east side so as to have the best view of the sunrise. The group has already started preparing dinner over an open fire pit.

After a full meal of roasted chicken, vegetables, and hummus, they spend the next hour singing and trading stories about the war games they've been conducting in the Sinai. Raphael tunes them out and stares into the distance, contemplating with growing melancholy the sudden turn his life has taken in a matter of a few days, with Aunt Penina's words still echoing in his head.

Yossi sidles up next to him. "Are you all right?"

Raphael looks at him out of the corner of his eye. His dark thoughts lift at the sight of his cousin sitting so close. He rests his head against Yossi's shoulder. "I was feeling a bit lost. But, I'm better now."

Yossi rubs Raphael's head and smiles. "We all have our moments, achi."

The tour guide announces an end to the evening activities, and the group breaks up to unroll their sleeping bags, arranging them in a semi-circle around the campfire. Some of them wander to the edge of the hill to smoke a last cigarette before turning in for the night. Yossi hands Raphael a spare sleeping bag, and they set up next to each other a little distance from the others.

Raphael strips to his underpants and wriggles into his bag. "You're not sleeping nude tonight, are you?" he asks.

"Always," Yossi says with a smirk. Setting aside his machine gun, he unlaces his boots and strips off his uniform, rolling it into a makeshift pillow. Raphael watches him disappear into his sleeping bag. A moment later he emerges with his bikini underpants hanging from his fingertips. Raphael snatches at them, and Yossi holds them just out of his reach.

"What were you doing back there with those people, the hippies?"

"I wasn't doing anything."

Yossi moves his hand closer. Raphael takes a swipe at the underpants, and Yossi pulls back his hand again.

"You're not doing drugs, are you?"

"Hell no." Raphael lunges out, snatches Yossi's underpants out of his hand, and pulls them into his sleeping bag. "Yes!" he says and lets out a short laugh.

"Quiet, you two," a member of Yossi's troop hisses.

"What are you planning on doing with those?" Yossi whispers, pointing at the underpants.

Raphael brings them to his nose and sniffs. Then he winks at Yossi and flings them back at him. "Smells like sweaty balls."

"But you don't mind that, do you?"

Raphael scoots closer to Yossi until their sleeping bags are touching and he can just make out the scent of his cousin's body.

"I'm not interested in drugs, cousin," he whispers.

"I'm relieved to know that."

Raphael glances at the others for a moment and looks back at Yossi. "I'm interested in sex."

Yossi smirks. "Yes, I gathered that. Welcome to the club."

"No, what I mean is I can't get enough. Sometimes it scares me."

Yossi's face becomes serious, and he looks directly into Raphael's eye. "You're sixteen years old."

"Seventeen next week."

"OK, seventeen. The point is you're in your sexual prime. It's completely natural. There's no reason to be scared."

"You don't understand," Raphael whispers, moving even closer to his cousin. "I jerk off, like, five times a day. And, if I get the chance, I'll do it with just about anyone. Girls, guys. That can't be normal."

Yossi shrugs. "Some people are hornier than others, that's all." He reaches out and gently rubs Raphael's head. "Honestly, don't worry about it. It'll pass eventually. Try not to torture yourself over it."

Raphael blinks at Yossi, suddenly realising the accumulated tension in his neck and shoulders has subsided. "Thanks, achi. I've never told anybody that before."

"No worries. Anytime you feel like talking."

"What about you?"

Raphael's question hangs unanswered for a few seconds. After a moment, Yossi smiles and shakes his head. "That's for another time. Let's get some sleep."

—\\\\—

The screech of a whistle jolts Raphael awake as the tour guide rouses the group at five in the morning. Raphael and Yossi groggily creep out of their sleeping bags and gather with the others at the eastern retaining wall, where they wait as the black sky grows progressively lighter, glowing with the colours of the dawn.

Just before five-thirty, the sun explodes over the horizon, setting afire the Jordanian hills towering above the slick multi-hewed surface of the Dead Sea. As they stand at the cliff's edge snapping pictures and admiring the sight, they hear screaming from behind them. The young bearded man from the hippie camp comes running up, his face ashen and wracked by anxiety. He begs for their help to find Bright Moon.

The soldiers follow him back and fan out from the hippie camp over the top of the hill, searching among the ruins. Raphael tags along with Yossi, who clambers down into a dry cistern. As they search around the fallen boulders inside, they hear the sound of screaming echoing down into the chamber from outside. They climb back out of the cistern and see the entire contingent of soldiers and hippie campers gazing over the edge of the western cliff. They run to join the group and see two of the soldiers climbing down the shadowed side of the mountain toward a woman's body far below, twisted by the force of her fall onto the jagged rocks into what looks like a human pretzel, more a broken toy than a person.

The young bearded man, who turns out to be Bright Moon's stepbrother, is inconsolable and requires the strength of four soldiers to keep him from throwing himself off the cliff. They hold him down while Yossi runs back to the camp and returns with a syringe, which he plunges into the young man's arm. Within moments, his body goes limp.

It takes the balance of the morning to recover Bright Moon's body from the cliffside and for the air ambulance to arrive from Jerusalem. As it lands on the top of Masada, blowing sand and rocks everywhere, the soldiers rush toward it and load the sedated young man and his stepsister's body into it. A moment later it lifts off the mountain and heads toward the medical facility on Mount Scopus.

The experience leaves everyone in shock for several minutes, almost in a state of paralysis. Then, as the reality of her death sinks in, Bright Moon's companions stumble back to their camp to pick up their things, stopping occasionally to hug each other, and to sob over their lost comrade.

The soldiers wordlessly pack their gear. Once they've finished, Raphael and a couple of the religious soldiers step to one side and struggle through their delayed morning prayers before rejoining the rest for a quick lunch, none of them particularly hungry despite the twelve hours that have passed since their last meal. They hike back down the hill and pile into their respective transport trucks to make their way to their next stop, Jerusalem's Old City.

The rest of the day's activities are conducted half-heartedly, in mournful silence, save for a few basics recited by their guide. After the tour, which includes, to Raphael's surprise, a visit to the Church of the Holy Sepulchre and a couple of other Christian sights, the group enters a recently excavated tunnel complex reserved for the military, which lies beneath the Old City, to have a snack and discuss their itinerary following Rosh Hashanah.

—◊◊◊—

As Raphael and Yossi arrive at Savta's, they agree not to mention the incident on Masada so as not to disturb Savta's peace of mind during the holiday. For the first time in over five years, Yossi joins in for both the evening and morning prayer services at the Ades, and both he and Savta proudly watch Raphael chant the Binding of Isaac from the Torah scroll at the special invitation of the rabbi. Afterwards, they celebrate the holiday over a festive meal at Saba's bedside and spend the rest of the afternoon visiting with neighbours and friends. The following day, the boys bid farewell to their grandparents, promising to return the weekend after next for Yom Kippur and to celebrate Raphael's seventeenth birthday, which falls on the same day.

When they rejoin Yossi's unit for the rest of the tour, nobody mentions Masada, as if the incident never happened, which disturbs Raphael. Yossi shrugs it off, commenting that the soldiers see death all the time, and that they've learned it's best to get over such things quickly if only to retain their sanity. They spend the next few days touring the Carmel region, the Galilee, and the coast near the border with Lebanon.

As they convoy back to Mitzpe Ramon, Raphael sits in a corner of the truck pressed up against Yossi. He watches as Yossi enthusiastically exchanges with his comrades their plans for how they will be spending the balance of their holiday. Yossi pulls Raphael close and announces to the others their camping trip in the makhtesh, which draws playful catcalls and scattered applause. Raphael smiles at them and reflects that, despite the Masada incident, these past few days spent in Yossi's company have been the happiest of his entire life. His eyes well up and he turns to face the back of the truck. Fearful of what lies ahead, he utters a prayer, asking God for His mercy, promising to be a better person—and hoping that someone is listening on the other side.

Chapter 14

Yossi and Raphael stand at the edge of the yawning pit, its southern half caved in and eroded. It extends from side to side to the limits of their vision, and about three hundred metres across from where they stand baking in the afternoon sun, to the desert floor across from them. Yossi pulls a swig from his canteen and holds it out to Raphael, who stares into the pit, silent and unblinking. Yossi nudges him to get his attention and presses the canteen into his hand. Raphael takes a sip of the cool water and screws the cap back on.

Yossi extracts a prayer book from his backpack and flips to the last few pages. Standing with his legs wide apart, he recites: "You sweep people away in the sleep of death."

Raphael closes his eyes and takes in the sultry air, which carries the scent of acacia and wild herbs toasting in the heat. The words Yossi is reading provoke a surge of emotions he finds difficult to bear, and he battles to tune them out.

"In the morning, we are like fresh grass," Yossi continues, his voice level and calm, "but by evening we are dry and withered. We are consumed by your anger."

Raphael steps away from Yossi and kicks a baseball-size piece of sandstone, sending it tumbling into the very pit that crashed down on Uncle Shimshon five years ago, his remains forever encased in the clay before them.

The two of them remain quiet for a while, Yossi with his eyes closed, Raphael staring into the middle distance. The buzz of the late-afternoon cicadas drifts over the twisted landscape of the makhtesh, which brings Yossi back to himself. He stores the prayer book in his backpack and walks over to Raphael. Together they recite the Kaddish in memory of Uncle Shimshon.

"I still miss him," Yossi says, as they walk back to the car.

Raphael rubs Yossi's arm, but the gesture feels awkward to him. Yossi glances at him for a moment, then rounds the car to the driver's side and unlocks the door.

"What does it all mean?" Raphael blurts out.

Yossi looks blandly at him, standing at the open door.

"Seriously," Raphael says, "what the fuck does it all mean? Here today, gone tomorrow. Family, friends, love, hate, success, failure, money, poverty, war, peace. In the end, none of that matters, does it? We're just, like, what you said over there, grass that fades and dies."

"You're asking me?" Yossi says.

"Yes, I'm asking you. Because I sure as hell don't know."

Yossi shuts the car door and comes around to Raphael.

"I already told you what I think."

"I'm not asking you about God," Raphael says. "I'm asking you what all this means."

"It doesn't mean anything."

Raphael stares in the direction of the pit. "It should."

"But it doesn't. Not in any universal sense. At least that's what I think. That's what you asked me, right? For my opinion?"

"Yeah."

Yossi hops onto the hood of the car, and Raphael scrambles up next to him, reclining on the warm metal and taking in the desert air. He stares into the deepening blue of the cloudless expanse. The intensity of the light is diminishing, and the surrounding hills are taking on their first tinges of gold and ochre as the sun dips westward.

"We were raised to believe that everything happens for a reason, that there are no coincidences," Raphael says after several moments of silence. "Take me, for example. There were all these signs when I was born that supposedly meant I was special."

Yossi lays back on the hood and lets out a quiet laugh.

"I'm serious. You know I was born without a foreskin, right? Like Yaakov Avinu, and Yosef his son, and King David."

"So I've heard."

"Savta always told me it was a sign I was destined to be a leader of Israel. Ima used to believe that, too."

"I know."

"They said that when you put that together with the fact I was born on Yom Kippur and also that Abba descends from the line of Judah, it's clear I'm meant to be someone important."

"You mean like the Messiah?"

Raphael sits up. "Yes, exactly."

Yossi raises himself on one elbow and squints one eye against the glare of the afternoon sun. "And what do you think?"

"I used to believe it … before we left for Los Angeles. After that, everything changed. Nothing made sense anymore. The better I became at stuff, like art, and sports, and languages, the worse I became in other ways."

A distant, high-pitched sound breaks the silence of the desert, and they look up as five fighter jets appear above the rim of the makhtesh and screech across the sky heading south, leaving a thick trail of exhaust in their wake. Yossi and Raphael remain quiet a few seconds after the jets have disappeared. Once silence descends over the desert again, they look at each other. Raphael catches what he interprets as a flash of concern in Yossi's usually placid expression.

"We should move on." Yossi returns to the driver's side and pulls open the door. "It'll be dark in a couple of hours."

Raphael climbs into the car and stares back at the pit as they veer off the highway and travel off-road into the open desert. After jolting over sand and stones, and across ancient riverbeds coursing through multilayered mini canyons weathered away over aeons, they burst free of a forest of acacias into a large clearing at the edge of a running spring.

They work quickly to set up a two-man tent in the encroaching darkness a couple of metres away from the edge of a small pool created by the spring, near a circle of stones with the charred remains of a campfire. When they finish assembling the tent, Yossi sends Raphael to fill their canteens with water from the spring while he builds a fire in the stone circle and takes a few minutes to spray snake repellent around the perimeter of the clearing.

By the time they sit side by side roasting chicken and potatoes in the fire, darkness has enveloped the clearing save for a hint of electric purple and crimson from the twilight as it burns itself out at the western edge of the sky.

The disappearance of the sun is accompanied by a plunging of the temperature. Yossi and Raphael pull on their jackets. They huddle together and devour their dinner, chasing it with the cold spring water. Raphael watches Yossi dab the grease from his lips with a cloth napkin. The sight of his handsome cousin illuminated by the flickering campfire moves him, and he leans against him to savour the sense of closeness he feels in that moment.

"What did you think?" Yossi asks, folding the napkin and holding it out to Raphael.

Raphael rubs his mouth clean and tosses aside the napkin. "Best meal I've ever had." He pats his belly and burps.

Yossi lets out a ringing laugh and stands to work out the stiffness in his legs.

"Let's go for a hike," Yossi says, shouldering his machine gun.

"A hike?" Raphael looks around at the clearing and back at Yossi. "It's dark."

Yossi produces a pair of flashlights from his backpack and hands one to Raphael. "We have these. Plus, there are lots of stars up there." He points at the sky with his flashlight. "It won't seem as dark once your eyes adjust."

"What about snakes? Don't they come out at night?"

"Don't worry. Just stay close to me. We're not going that far." He points at a low ridge overlooking the clearing. "That's where we're headed."

Raphael grasps Yossi's arm as they pick their way across the clearing and ascend the ridge, accessing it via a switchback trail.

When they arrive at the summit, Raphael is surprised to see the crumbling ruins of an ancient Ottoman *caravanserai* spread out on the hilltop. It glows softly in the gentle starlight. Yossi sprints ahead and disappears into one of two intact watchtowers, ignoring Raphael's complaints at being left alone. A few seconds later he appears above the crenellated crown of the tower and calls for Raphael to join him.

Raphael jogs over and locates an opening at the base of the tower with an internal stone staircase spiralling upward. When he emerges at the top, he finds Yossi sitting on the crown smoking a cigarette, his back turned to him, legs dangling over the side of the tower. Yossi's machine gun is precariously balanced on the wall next to him.

"Come, sit," Yossi says, staring straight ahead into the darkness. "Right here." He slaps the wall.

Raphael hesitates a moment, then climbs onto the wall and regards his cousin out of the corner of his eye. Yossi taps a cigarette out of a pack of Dubeks, lights it with his, and hands it to Raphael.

Raphael inhales the harsh smoke deep into his lungs and ends up coughing and spluttering for the next couple of minutes.

"I forgot to warn you," Yossi says. "They're not Marlboros."

Raphael flicks the cigarette into the darkness. "How can you smoke that shit? It's nasty." He wipes his mouth on his sleeve.

"You can get used to anything." Yossi's left hand brushes against his machine gun, and he shifts so he is angled in its direction.

"Why are you always carrying that thing?"

"What thing?"

"That Uzi."

Yossi holds up the weapon with one hand and regards it with a glazed-over expression.

"It's not like you're on duty or anything," Raphael says.

Yossi takes a drag on his cigarette and looks at him. "It makes me feel safe. In control."

"You mean like a security blanket?"

"Something like that, I guess."

"You don't feel safe now?"

Yossi shakes his head. "Sorry. I'm feeling a bit edgy all of a sudden."

"Oh."

"You can never fully relax when you're on active duty. Even when you're given time off to recharge, it can end in any second." He shakes his head. "Like when those jets flew past earlier. I couldn't help thinking there might be a call-up."

"That's a bummer."

Yossi barks a short laugh. "It's not all bad. There are good things too, like the camaraderie, gaining confidence when facing danger, learning to defend yourself, feeling like you're a part of something larger. You'll see."

He holds out the weapon.

Raphael raises his hands. "No thanks."

"Go ahead, gever. I'll show you how to hold it."

"Seriously, no. That's not the kind of gun I like to play with."

"You're going to have to carry one of these next year when you're called up."

"I can wait."

"Take it." Yossi's voice takes on an edge that surprises Raphael. They stare at each other across the machine gun. Yossi's eyes are wide; his jaw is pulsating.

Raphael grabs the machine gun from Yossi, feeling the heat of anger coursing into his face. "Is that why we came here, achi? So you could bully me into playing soldier?" He turns the weapon over in his hands, finding it much heavier than he imagined. Then he places the butt against his shoulder and aims it into the darkness, his finger twitching on the trigger. "Is this what you want me to do?"

"Easy, there." Yossi takes the weapon out of Raphael's hands and places it back on the wall.

Raphael casts a sidelong glance at Yossi. "That wasn't cool."

"Sorry." Yossi taps out another cigarette and places it between his lips without lighting it. "Don't know what came over me."

They stay quiet for a while. Yossi looks up at the sky, his eyes shining in the starlight, and Raphael stares at his feet dangling over the edge, still hurt at the sudden change in Yossi's manner, and growing angrier at himself for even caring.

Yossi hops off the wall. "I'll be right back," he says, moving to the stairs.

"Where are you going?" Raphael asks.

"I've got to pee," Yossi says as he disappears into the stairwell.

A light wind sweeps across the desert. It whispers through the leaves of the acacias, causing the scrub brush to tremble and the shadows on the desert floor to shift. In the distance, a series of high-pitched, staccato *hee-hee-hee* cries from a pack of hyenas echoes off the walls of the makhtesh. Raphael freezes and peers into the darkness. As the sound dies away, he exhales and glances around him. His eye comes to rest on the Uzi that Yossi left on the ledge, and his chest goes tight at the memory of Yossi pressuring him to hold it. He tries to pry his eyes away, to force himself to look back at the desert, but the machine gun holds his gaze. An all-too familiar urge possesses him, and he watches with fear and elation as his hand moves toward the weapon and hefts it aloft. His heart pounds as his fingers play over the metal and come to rest on the pistol grip. Then with a quick backwards glance, he removes the magazine and empties it of its bullets.

When Yossi returns a few minutes later, he finds Raphael leaning against the wall smoking a cigarette.

"What took you?" Raphael asks.

"I went back to the camp and brought a couple of night vision binoculars."

He climbs back up on the wall and pats the place next to him. "Come up here."

Raphael flicks away his last Marlboro and sits next to Yossi, holding his arms tight across his chest.

"Listen," Yossi says, "I'm sorry about earlier. What do you say we reset?" He puts his arm around Raphael's neck and pulls him close, rubbing his cheek against his head. The remnants of Raphael's anger immediately evaporate. He kisses Yossi on the cheek and is pleased that Yossi accepts the gesture without pulling away or flinching.

Yossi releases Raphael and extends his hand. "Friends again?"

"Friends again," echoes Raphael, nervously feeling the rattle of the bullets in his jacket pocket against his flank and hoping for an opportunity to return them to the magazine as soon as possible. He takes Yossi's hand and kisses the back of it. Yossi pulls it back and grins at his cousin.

Yossi hands Raphael a pair of binoculars and spends the next half hour explaining to Raphael all about how the makhtesh was formed and pointing out the different plants and nocturnal animals that call it home. He shares with Raphael how he stumbled on the ruins of the caravanserai and the spring three years ago during one of his hikes and how this place soon became his sanctuary.

"I've never brought anyone here before," he concludes. "Consider yourself special."

"Yeah, thanks." Raphael looks at his watch and marks 10 p.m., keen to get back to the tent. "I could never be out here alone."

"No?"

Raphael shakes his head. "I'd find it way too scary, in the middle of nowhere, with snakes all around, completely vulnerable." He stares for a few moments into the void below and kicks his feet against the side of the tower. "I mean, don't get me wrong. I like being here with *you*."

"Well, that's a relief." Yossi points his cigarette heavenward. "But just look up there, achi. It's practically dripping starlight. Where have you ever seen anything as beautiful as that? Doesn't being out here makes you feel like one of the Patriarchs?"

"Right," Raphael says. "All we need is a burning bush."

Yossi smirks and takes another drag on his cigarette, its end glowing angrily in the darkness. "Or a pillar of fire."

"Or two million whingeing Israelites."

"OK, enough," Yossi says, swinging around and hopping off the wall. "How about if we get back to the camp? I'm absolutely knackered." He grabs his machine gun and starts for the stairs.

By the time they reach the camp, the temperature has dropped to ten degrees. Raphael stands shivering in the dark while Yossi arranges their things inside the tent. A few minutes later Yossi pokes his head out and beckons Raphael inside. As Raphael crawls in, he sees a fluorescent camp light set up in one corner of the tent, which is large enough for two people to sit inside without bumping their heads against the top, and wide enough for two people to sleep side by side, with about a foot of clearance on either side. The sleeping bags are zipped together.

What's up with this?" Raphael tugs at the unified bags and flashes a crooked smile.

"We're going to have to sleep together." Yossi peels off his T-shirt and blue jeans and places them to one side, remaining dressed in a pair of tight khaki briefs. "We'll keep each other warm by combining our body heat. Warmer than if we each sleep in individual sleeping bags, I mean."

"That's fine by me," Raphael says, stripping to his underpants and arranging his clothes in the opposite corner.

Yossi slides into the bag, and Raphael follows him inside. Yossi then zips it closed, pulling the top flap over them. He directs Raphael to face away from him, then wraps his arms around him and pulls him against his chest. Raphael's heart thumps hard at the sensation of Yossi's half-naked body pressed against his back.

"Everything all right?" Yossi asks in a low voice, his lips brushing against Raphael's neck.

"Everything's perfect," Raphael says, backing into Yossi and playfully grinding against him.

"Don't do that, please."

Raphael flips around to face Yossi. "You're still wearing your underpants," he says.

"What about it?"

"You said you always sleep in the nude."

"Normally, yes. But right now wouldn't be appropriate, would it?"

"I don't mind if you don't."

"But, I do."

"I'll take mine off, too." Raphael reaches down; Yossi's hand shoots out and pulls it back up by the wrist.

"Don't."

"Why not?"

"You're hard."

"So are you."

"We're not going to have sex, achi. I thought I was clear about that."

Yossi gently pulls Raphael's hand up and drapes his arm over his shoulder.

"I don't get it," Raphael says. "You bring me out here to the middle of nowhere, nobody around for miles, get into the same sleeping bag as me, hold me against your body after I confess that I love to have sex—with guys—and knowing perfectly well that I like you. And you don't have any intention of having sex with me?"

"That's right. We're not going to have sex. You need to learn not to sexualise all your relationships. You can start now."

Raphael stares at Yossi, wide-eyed, hardly believing what he is hearing.

"Can I at least hold you?"

Yossi shrugs. "Sure."

Raphael shakes his head and hugs Yossi close, burying his head against his neck, and Yossi returns the hug. The scent of his cousin's skin makes Raphael tremble and his eyes well up. They hold each other for a few quiet moments.

Raphael lifts his head and stares into his cousin's eyes, noticing that Yossi's eyes are moist. He kisses Yossi on the neck and peers again into Yossi's eyes, finding no hint of resistance. He passes his hand through Yossi's hair and presses his lips against his forehead, then slides down and kisses his cheek again and again. Then he releases Yossi and puts one hand on either side of his face and brings his mouth toward Yossi's mouth.

"No, achi," Yossi whispers, "not that."

"Please, Yossi," Raphael says, his hands still grasping his cousin's face. "Please let me kiss you. Just that."

"I'm sorry, achi."

"Why not? If it's like you said, if there aren't any rules, if nothing means anything, then what harm will it do? Nobody will know, except us."

"I can't."

"But, I—" Raphael lets go of Yossi's face and breaks out in tears. "Don't make me say it, achi, please."

Yossi pulls up Raphael's face by the chin. "What is it?"

Raphael shakes his head. "Just one kiss, Yossi, please. Then we can go to sleep. I'll never ask you for anything ever again. I promise."

"But, why?"

"Because I fucking love you, you goddamned motherfucker. That's why."

Raphael explodes out of the sleeping bag and rushes out of the tent. Yossi pulls on his clothes and his boots, grabs a coat, and chases after him. He finds him curled up on the front seat of the car, sobbing.

"Leave me alone," Raphael screams as Yossi opens the door. "I begged you not to make me say it, but you had to push me, didn't you? You just had to push me."

"Come back to the tent, achi."

"No way, I'm not going back there with you. Just bring me my sleeping bag. I'll sleep in here."

"Come on, achi. Let me explain."

Raphael sits up and glowers at Yossi. "If you have anything to explain, do it now. But I'm not going back to the tent."

Yossi climbs into the car and sits next to Raphael, who scrambles away and huddles against the opposite door. Yossi drums his fingers on the dashboard for a few seconds, then looks at Raphael.

"I have a girlfriend. That's why I can't let you kiss me on the mouth. It wouldn't be right."

"Since when do you have a girlfriend?" Raphael spits out. "I never heard anything about that. As far as everyone is concerned, you're as asexual as an earthworm." He kicks at Yossi's crotch with his bare foot. "But we know better, don't we?" A bitter laugh escapes his lips.

"I haven't told anyone about her because they wouldn't approve. Her name's Alina; she lives a few miles south of Beersheba with her family. She's who I went to see when we were there last week." He pauses for a moment. "She's Bedouin."

Raphael slaps the side of his head. "Wait, what? You're dating an Arab girl?"

Yossi nods and runs his hand through his hair.

"And you're keeping this big romance a secret because, what, you're afraid what people will think?"

"Our families would disown us if they found out."

"Oh, right, I get it now. You're a coward."

"It's not that." Yossi turns away from Raphael and stares out at the running spring. "You don't understand how it is. How things work around here. Socially, I mean."

"Guess not."

They stay quiet for a few minutes, their breath condensing in the frigid air of the car. Raphael rubs his arms to generate some warmth, and Yossi hands him his coat.

"So, let me ask you," Raphael says, slipping on the coat and flashing on the bullets in the side pocket. "If you didn't have a girlfriend, this Alina *ptitsa*, what would've happened in there just now?" He jerks a thumb in the direction of the tent. "Would you have let me kiss you?"

"I don't know."

Raphael slaps the dashboard and turns away, struggling to hold back tears. "I still love you, you fucker. I've never loved anyone before. You're the first."

"I'm sorry."

"It hurts."

"I know."

Raphael whirls on Yossi. "I *hate* you."

"Shall we go back to the tent?"

"Fuck you."

"Come on, gever. Don't be like that."

"Leave me alone, will you?"

Yossi tugs Raphael's elbow. But Raphael pulls away and crosses his arms over his chest.

"Come back to the tent."

"I told you, I'm sleeping in here. Just bring me my sleeping bag."

"It's going to get a lot colder. Are you sure?"

"Of course, I'm sure. I'd rather freeze into a block of ice than spend another minute in there with you."

Chapter 15

Raphael refuses to eat anything Yossi prepares for breakfast. Instead, he digs a pair of stale granola bars out of his backpack and perches on a boulder a few metres away from the campsite to eat them, forcing them down his throat with some metallic-tasting water he sucks out of his canteen. Yossi calls out to him as he finishes breaking down the tent, and the two of them drive back to Mitzpe Ramon in silence.

When they arrive home, Raphael leaps out of the car and sprints to the apartment, running past Aunt Penina and Tomer, who are sitting on the sofa watching TV. He closes the door to his room and climbs into his bunk. A few moments later, Yossi enters the room toting his machine gun and closes the door behind him. Raphael rolls over and faces the wall.

"I'm sorry, achi," Yossi says, placing his weapon on the dresser.

"Don't call me that."

"Honestly, I didn't mean to hurt you."

Raphael sits up. "Don't worry about me, OK? I'll be fine." He stands and faces off with Yossi. "In fact, I'll be more than fine."

"Yom Kippur starts tomorrow evening."

"Yeah, so?"

"So, I'm asking you to forgive me. That's how it works, doesn't it?"

"Yes, OK, I forgive you. I *forgive* you. I just need some time to myself."

"I get that." Yossi offers Raphael his hand. "But, let's not leave things like this. I want us to start over again. Tomorrow night at Savta's when we light candles."

They are interrupted by an insistent knocking on the door. Yossi pulls it open, and Tomer sticks his head inside.

"Are you guys all right?"

"We're just having a chat, motek," Yossi says. "Come back in five."

"We were just finishing," Raphael says, pushing past Yossi and slipping out the door. "The room's all yours."

Raphael locks himself in the bathroom and sits on the toilet. He lowers his head to his hands, massaging his temples with his thumbs to relieve the accumulated tension threatening to trigger a migraine, and rests his elbows on his knees. He soon falls asleep to the sound of a steady drip from the bathtub faucet.

The roar of a car engine outside wakes him. He stands on the edge of the tub and looks out the window in time to see Yossi manoeuvring his car onto the slip road. Raphael remains looking out the window until after Yossi's car has disappeared down the highway in the direction of Beersheba.

After saying his afternoon prayers at the edge of the makhtesh, Raphael sits on the wall and smokes a Dubek in the burning sun. Thoughts of Yossi provoke a profound, empty feeling in the pit of his stomach. Slipping on a pair of Wayfarers to guard against the glare, he replays in his head the events of the night before, allowing himself to relive his emotions, the anticipation, excitement, ardour, love, rejection, disappointment, betrayal, anger, and hate, all experienced within the course of a few hours. He'd hoped Yossi would be his salvation, his key to surviving this year in hell. Now he knows he's on his own despite Yossi's offer to start over. After everything that has happened, he can't see how to dial back his feelings for him.

Hopping off the wall, he stamps out the cigarette and heads down the road in the direction of the school, keen to spend the afternoon reading in the peace of the library. As he rounds the corner, the school buildings in sight, an unexpected surge of sadness hits him, and he moves into the shadow of a con-crete apartment block to battle back tears. Wiping his face with his bandana, the thought of Yossi's confession about Alina reignites his anger. He kicks at a mound of dirt sending a spray of pebbles into the dirt-choked gutter and strides down the deserted road. Yossi had fooled him once before. He had promised himself he wouldn't let it happen again. But he'd allowed Yossi to fool him a second time. He had gotten what he deserved.

When he arrives at the school, he finds it locked for the holiday, with nobody in sight, not even a janitor who might be able to let him inside. He makes a circuit around the complex, testing each door, the noonday sun pounding down on him. Sweat streams into his eyes and down the sides of his face, leaving tracks in the yellow dust that has adhered to his skin. He lets loose a loud kick at the last door and darts to a nearby date palm to take shelter against the sun. The shadow it casts barely covers his head, let alone his body. So he moves away and heads in the direction of the highway.

A few minutes later, he is sitting in a dingy coffee shop at the edge of town, sipping thick Turkish coffee from a permanently stained plastic cup and trying to read a book. The proprietress, a leathery Yemeni woman with waist-length, sun-damaged hair, flashes a gap-toothed smile at him every so often as she alternates between wiping down the Formica counter and obsessing over the cash in the till. Raphael spins his chair around to face the wall and spends the rest of the afternoon deciphering Hermann Hesse's *Demian* in German.

When he finally emerges from the coffee shop, he is surprised to see that the sun has started its descent. He checks his watch and, realising it's nearly 5 p.m., sprints back to the apartment in time to join Aunt Penina and Tomer for dinner. Aunt Penina engages Tomer in family chit-chat, and Raphael tries his best to participate despite the sour looks Aunt Penina tosses in his direction. He glances at Yossi's empty chair and swallows hard, painfully feeling his absence, ready to forgive him for everything that happened in the makhtesh, if only he could have him near.

After dinner, the three of them gather to watch the six o'clock news, Aunt Penina and Tomer on the couch, and Raphael sitting backwards on one of the dining chairs. There is some mention of Syrian troop movements, but nothing of the situation on the border with Egypt. When questioned about the country's readiness, a military spokesman assures a reporter that the country's borders are adequately defended. The program then shifts to coverage of local news, including the ongoing holiday festivities around the country. Aunt Penina sighs heavily and switches the channel to a soap opera, then settles back into the sofa. Tomer kisses her on the cheek then rests his head in her lap, and Aunt Penina strokes his hair.

At around 7 p.m., Yossi pushes open the front door, spots Raphael, and points at him. "There's my man," he says in English.

Raphael leaps to his feet at the sight of his cousin, knocking over the dining chair in the process. Tomer rushes over and rescues the chair, setting it upright.

"Look at what I found wandering around outside." Yossi steps aside, and Joanie Smith slinks into the apartment, rubbing her hands on her bell-bottom jeans.

"No," Raphael whispers. He steps back, the smile disappearing from his face.

"Come in, come in." Yossi pulls Joanie by the crook of her arm into the middle of the room. "Don't be shy." He inclines his head at Raphael. "You remember my cousin Raphael, right?" He winks at Joanie.

Joanie smiles at Raphael and raises her hand. "Hi, Ralph."

Raphael raises his hand back at Joanie. "Hey."

"Yossi, who is this girl?" Aunt Penina asks in Hebrew.

"Ima, this is Joanie, Rafi's American friend. I met her at Savta's the weekend he arrived."

"What are you doing here?" Raphael asks.

Joanie holds up the piece of paper Raphael gave her at the airport. "You told me how to find you, remember? I caught a bus from Tel Aviv this morning. I hadn't realised it was so far."

"Now, you two"—Yossi leads Joanie over to Raphael—"give each other a proper greeting. A handshake? Maybe a hug?"

Raphael shakes his head at Yossi, then smiles tightly at Joanie and holds out his hand. Joanie steps forward and hugs him tight.

"He made me tell him everything," she whispers in Raphael's ear.

Raphael disengages from the hug and takes a step away from Joanie. "Weren't you supposed to be gone by now?"

"We go back day after tomorrow. I needed to see you before I left."

"I found her at the gas station," Yossi says, "She was asking some random people about you. It's lucky I stopped for fuel."

"Yeah, lucky," Raphael says.

Aunt Penina crosses the room to the dining table. "Have you had dinner, young lady?" She pats the back of one of the chairs. "Sit here with Yossi. I made some nice lamb." She walks into the kitchen mumbling to herself.

Joanie shrugs and sits at the table. "Thank you, ma'am," she calls out to the kitchen.

Yossi drags Raphael's chair to the table and points at it. "Sit with us, with your friend."

Raphael sits at the table, exchanging awkward glances with Yossi and Joanie as Aunt Penina serves them. When she finishes, she kisses Yossi on the top of his head and withdraws with Tomer to their bedrooms.

"Joanie and I had a nice long chat." Yossi picks up a braised shank and examines it for a moment before taking a bite.

Joanie nods and looks away from Raphael.

"When was that?" Raphael asks.

"Over coffee," Joanie says. She raises her eyebrows at Yossi, who responds by nodding and taking a sip of wine.

"When did you have coffee? I thought you just ran into each other at the gas station."

"That's right," Yossi says. He wipes his mouth with his napkin and pushes his plate away. "Then I took her for a coffee."

Joanie nods at Raphael. "He knows about the wallet."

Raphael looks at Yossi, who stares back at him.

"He made me tell him," Joanie says.

"Is that all?" Raphael asks, still staring at Yossi.

"He made me tell him about what happened in the park, too."

Raphael lowers his hand under the table and punches Yossi's knee. But Yossi doesn't flinch.

"Tomorrow we're going to Jerusalem to spend Yom Kippur, the Jewish New Year, with our grandparents," Yossi says to Joanie. "It's Rafi's seventeenth birthday as well."

"It is?" Joanie says, a smile breaking out on her face.

"We'll drop you off in Tel Aviv on our way there." He points at the sofa. "Tonight you'll sleep there. We'll make up a bed for you. It should be comfortable enough."

"Thanks."

Yossi picks up the dishes and takes them into the kitchen.

"I'm really sorry about that, Ralph," Joanie whispers. "It's like he knew everything already."

"What are you doing here anyway?"

"I had to see you…to ask your forgiveness for everything, for not turning in the wallet, and especially for what happened the other night in the park. I lost my temper badly, which was wrong; plus, I injured you."

"You came all the way from Tel Aviv to tell me that?"

"It's what the Lord would want me to do. Do you forgive me?"

"Sure. I forgive you."

Joanie peers into Raphael's eyes. "Also, I wanted you to know that I've already forgiven *you* for the stuff you did to me, which was pretty rotten."

Raphael nods.

Joanie frowns at him. "I mean, you ruined this trip for me." She pauses, waiting for some reaction from Raphael. "This was supposed to be the trip of a lifetime, and I was so excited to meet one of the Lord's people on the plane. I thought I'd made a new friend. Then you went and practically framed me for something I didn't do. I didn't deserve that."

Joanie's hands start to tremble, and her eyes well up with tears.

"I'm sorry," Raphael says, looking at her hands.

She wipes her face on her jacket sleeve. "I forgive you for that."

Yossi steps out of the kitchen and squeezes Raphael's shoulder. "May we have a word?"

Raphael nods, still looking at Joanie.

"Make yourself comfortable, Joanie." Yossi flips on the TV and nods at the sofa. "We'll be back in a few minutes."

Raphael follows Yossi out the door. They trudge across the parking lot to the edge of the makhtesh and climb onto the wall. Yossi pulls a brand new pack of Marlboros out of his breast pocket and taps out a cigarette.

"I picked up a carton of these in Beersheba today," Yossi says, lighting the cigarette and handing it to Raphael, who flashes a half-smile. "It was supposed to be a surprise. A peace offering."

"Thank you."

Yossi lights one for himself and takes a deep drag on it. He stares into the makhtesh and exhales a trail of smoke into the darkness.

"You told me you hadn't stolen anything in a long time," Yossi says after a moment.

"I told you, I have a condition—"

"That's what made you steal the wallet, I get that. But lying to me isn't part of the condition, is it?"

"I don't know. It might be related."

"And putting the wallet you stole in your friend's bag and leaving her with it at the airport was just you being an asshole."

Raphael looks sidelong at Yossi.

Yossi looks directly at Raphael, a stern expression on his face. "Shall I run down the list of everything else?"

Raphael flicks the cigarette into the makhtesh and shakes his head. "I'm sorry, achi. For everything. I'm trying to change."

"Change what? Being a thief or being an asshole?"

"Both."

"Try harder, cousin."

Raphael nods.

"Do whatever you need to do. But don't let yourself go into adulthood with either. It's a lethal combination that will destroy you and those around you."

"I said I'm trying," Raphael screams. "I've been trying my whole goddamned life."

"Steady, achi." Yossi glances back at the apartment block, then leans in closely toward him. "Listen, if you *really* want to get better, it's important that you trust somebody with this. If not me, then someone else. It's the only way you're going to beat it."

"I'll *never* beat it, achi." Tears stand out in Raphael's eyes, and he wipes them with the back of his hand. "There's no cure for what I have." He jerks his thumb at the sky. "And *He's* no help."

"All the more reason to keep someone down here in the loop." Yossi extinguishes his cigarette on the wall, puts his arm around Raphael, and pulls him close. Raphael rests his head against Yossi's chest and closes his eyes.

"Let's trust each other, achi," Yossi whispers. He removes Raphael's kippah and kisses the top of his head, then he presses it into Raphael's hand. "There's nothing like the closeness of mutual trust between two people who care for each other." He kisses Raphael's head again. "It's a million times better than sex."

Raphael looks into Yossi's eyes. "What about Alina?"

Yossi shakes his head. "I don't know, achi. Things are complicated. Let's talk about that some other time. We have a whole year ahead of us."

"OK, sure."

"Anyway, think about it. I'm here for you one hundred per cent."

Yossi hops off the wall and walks back to the apartment. "In the meantime," he calls out, "we have our trip to Savta's tomorrow for Yom Kippur and your birthday as well. I'm even planning on fasting this year, if you can believe that."

"Seriously?" Raphael says, catching up with him.

"Yes, seriously," Yossi says, his hand poised on the door to the complex. "I want this to be a fresh start for us, a year to remember."

They find Joanie asleep on the sofa in front of a humming test pattern on the TV, her head leaning back, her mouth open. Yossi pulls a couple of pillows and a sheet from the linen cupboard in the hallway and hands them to Raphael and gives him a goodnight hug.

Raphael returns to the living room and places the pillows at one end of the sofa. He stands over Joanie, considering how best to move her into a horizontal position without waking her up. Sensing Raphael's presence, Joanie opens her eyes.

"Where did you go?" she asks. "I didn't get you into trouble, did I?"

Raphael sits next to her. "No, everything's cool. We just had a few things to sort out."

Joanie's face brightens, and she opens wide her clear hazel green eyes. "Praise God for that."

Raphael stands. "Those are for you." He points at the pillows. "Here's something to cover yourself with in case you need it." He hands the sheet to Joanie and moves away. "Feel free to grab something out of the fridge if you get hungry. I'm sure my aunt won't mind."

"You're not going to bed yet, are you?"

"I'm tired. We have to be up early tomorrow."

"But I wanted to finish our conversation from earlier at the dinner table."

"Was there more?"

Joanie nods and pats the sofa. Raphael drags himself over to her and drops onto it with a soft thud.

"Now that you've forgiven me and I've forgiven you," Joanie says, "I was hoping we might be friends."

"That would be kind of difficult, wouldn't it? With you in California and me in Israel."

"We could stay in touch and write to each other. And then, maybe I could come back in the summer to see you."

Raphael closes his eyes and massages the bridge of his nose.

"We still have lots to talk about," she says.

"Listen, Joanie…" Raphael opens his eyes and touches her arm.

Joanie chews her lower lip for a moment. "I know you don't like me, Ralph." She looks down at her knees and rubs her hands against them. "Not the way I like you. But"—she looks back up at him—"the other night, in the park…"

"Let's forget about that. What I did wasn't cool. I don't mind us being friends and everything. But my life is way too mixed up at the moment for anything more than that. So, if you don't mind, let's call it a night. We can talk more in the morning." He gives Joanie a quick hug, then pads away quickly down the hallway to his room.

Chapter 16

Everyone in the Ades is dressed in white and smiling at him: Savta in the back of the sanctuary with the other women; beautiful Yossi in the front row; the young bearded rabbi and his grizzled sexton standing to one side of the reading platform. Raphael turns, looks through the closed doors of the ark, and sees the Torah scrolls glowing inside. The room vibrates with the murmur of prayers issuing from a thousand unseen mouths.

Turning to face the congregation, Raphael extends his arms to the ceiling. Light emanates from his body, blinding multihued rays that fill every crevice of this house of prayer. I am the sun, Raphael hears, these people are my planets, and the Ades is my universe.

"Oh, earth, earth, earth," he cries, "hear the word of Adonai."

At the mention of the divine name, the congregation reaches out to Raphael, and he begins to float. He rises above them like a helium-filled balloon, propelled upward by a rush of photons. As the final blast of the shofar thunders through Jerusalem, he shoots through the ceiling, arcing across the sky like a shooting star, and crashing into the blinding corona of the sun.

—⁓—

"Something's happened, Rafi. Assaf's here. Hurry!"

Raphael peers at Tomer out of half-closed eyes and is blinded by stabbing light blazing into the room from the window. He drags a pillow over his face and sees red-and-black spots floating behind his closed eyes.

"Hurry, Rafi."

Tomer's muffled voice intensifies as he yanks the pillow out of Raphael's grasp. Raphael groans and sits up, rubbing his eyes.

"What's the big emergency, little man?"

"Assaf's talking to Yossi." Tomer's face contorts into spasms of anxiety. "Ima's crying."

Raphael tosses aside his blanket and runs down the hall, followed by Tomer. He finds Assaf and Yossi in the living room conversing intensely in hushed tones. Aunt Penina hovers in the kitchen doorway covering her mouth with a clenched fist. Tomer runs to her, and she wraps her arms around him.

"What's going on?" Raphael asks, approaching his cousins.

Assaf's arm shoots out at him. "Step away. We're having a family discussion. Go join your American friend outside."

"I'm part of this family too," Raphael snaps.

"Brother, please." Yossi taps Assaf's arm, and Assaf lowers it. "Assaf's heard some rumours about the Egyptian troop movements."

"I knew it," Aunt Penina says. "I just knew it."

"Ima, please," Assaf says.

"Rumours about what?" Raphael asks.

"Assaf thinks Egypt might be preparing to attack," Yossi says.

"That's enough." Assaf glares at Yossi. "You've said enough."

"That's ridiculous. You're totally paranoid." Raphael strides to the TV and switches it on. "Look"—he flips between channels—"nothing." He jerks his thumb at the TV. "Don't you think they'd mention something if Egypt were about to attack? And what about you guys? You're on holiday, for God's sake. If we were under threat, you definitely wouldn't be standing here speculating like a couple of hysterical hausfraus. You'd be mobilised by now."

"I said *enough*," Assaf yells. "The point is, Yossi's not going to Jerusalem today."

"Why the hell not?" Raphael asks.

"I want him to stay close to home until I feel more certain of things."

"Oh, so this is about your feelings, is it?"

"Don't defy him, Rafi," Yossi says.

"That spokesman from the Ministry on the news last night said the borders are well-defended," Raphael says. "He said there's nothing to worry about. Ask Aunt Penina. She heard."

"I'm staying, achi," Yossi says in a calm voice.

Assaf raises himself to his full height and nods at Yossi. Then he gently takes his mother by the wrist and leads her and Tomer down the hallway.

"Don't do this to me, achi," Raphael says, his voice catching in his throat. "You promised Savta; you promised me."

Yossi squeezes his shoulder. "Don't worry about Savta. I'll call her and explain everything. But, I have to obey Assaf."

Raphael shakes him off. "But this was meant to be a special time for us. That's what you said. 'A fresh start' is what you freaking said." He punches the wall and turns away from Yossi, his knuckles throbbing. "Nothing's even *happening*. Assaf's just being paranoid."

Spotting a pack of Dubeks on the dining table, Raphael snatches them up and wrestles out a crumpled cigarette.

"I'm sorry, achi. I'll make it up to you, I promise." Yossi checks his wristwatch. "There's a bus bound for Jerusalem in twenty minutes. Your friend Joanie's already outside. Fetch your things. I'll pack something for you to eat in the meantime."

Tears stream down Raphael's face as he lights the cigarette with trembling hands.

"Don't smoke in here, achi."

Raphael pushes past Yossi, knocking him into the dining table, and strides out of the room. "I'll smoke wherever I please."

He pushes into his bedroom and finds it empty, wondering for a moment where Assaf has taken Tomer. Yanking open the lower drawer, he pulls out a change of clothes and stuffs it into his backpack, the cigarette still clenched between his teeth. Then he selects a couple of books and packs them away as well. Scanning the room one last time, he spots his movie camera on the writing desk and drops it into the drawer with a thud before shoving it closed with his foot.

Yossi pokes his head through the doorway. "Achi, I asked you not to smoke in here."

"Fuck off," Raphael spits out. "I'm leaving now anyway."

Yossi's eyes ignite. He raises his hand at Raphael, and Raphael responds by holding up his chin at him, daring him to strike. Yossi's face instantly softens, and he retreats into the hallway. Raphael listens at the door and hears the click of the bathroom door. Then, shouldering his backpack, he flicks the cigarette across the room and runs down the hall to the front door.

—∿—

Raphael and Joanie ride most of the way to Jerusalem in silence. The bus makes frequent stops to pick up both civilians and soldiers on their way home for Yom Kippur, which starts at sundown. The bus reverberates with excited chatter. Raphael stares out the window at the passing landscape as it changes from the yellow dirt of the barren desert to the grassland of the Upper Negev. The bus passes a long stretch of farmland, then ascends the pine-covered Judean Hills toward Jerusalem.

Unmoved by Joanie's impassioned protestations as they disembark at Jerusalem's Central Bus Station, Raphael points her in the direction of the Tel Aviv-bound bus, half-heartedly promising to write to her, and hops a cab to Nachlaot. The cab driver drops him off across from the Machane Yehuda market, now shuttered for Yom Kippur, and Raphael enters the nearly deserted lanes of Nachlaot.

As he rounds the corner and approaches Savta's house, he finds her dozing on her front porch in one of her rickety dining chairs. He tiptoes up and gives her a peck on the cheek. Bringing her hand to her face, she opens her eyes and beams a smile at the sight of her grandson. She struggles to her feet and envelops him in her big, pillow-soft arms, covering him in wet kisses, then lifts her head and surveys the walkway, expectation etched on her face.

"Yossi didn't call you, Savta?"

"Call me?" Savta looks at Raphael. "When?"

"Today, Savta. He said he was going to call you to explain."

Savta shakes her head. "What's to explain?"

"He isn't coming." Raphael drops onto the porch and kicks his legs out in front of him. "Assaf's convinced him that Egypt might attack, or something like that. He ordered him to stay in Mitzpe Ramon."

Savta stares at the walkway for a moment as if still expecting to see Yossi appear. Then she turns and hobbles past Raphael into the house. He follows her carrying the dining room chair and puts it back into its place. Savta stands in the middle of the room, biting her knuckle and mumbling something to herself. Raphael puts his arm around her.

"Are you feeling OK, Savta?"

She looks at him, tears welling in her eyes. "I'm fine, Rafi." She glances at the wall clock and moves to the kitchen. "I have to serve; the fast is starting soon."

They eat their final meal in silence. Every so often, Raphael catches Savta moving her lips as if she were in a conversation with someone unseen.

"I feel terrible, Savta," Raphael says as they start the final course. "I was cross with Yossi for not coming."

Savta blinks at him, then stares into the salad bowl in front of her. "This is the first time he's missed spending Yom Kippur with us."

Raphael's mouth goes suddenly dry. He picks up his glass with a trembling hand and takes a quick sip of water. "He said he didn't have a choice, Savta."

"How strange he didn't call." Savta glances at the telephone and looks back at Raphael. "It's not like him." She looks again at the clock.

"There are five minutes left before the start of the fast, Savta. I'll call him."

Raphael dials Aunt Penina's number, his heart pounding, and listens anxiously as the telephone rings and rings. He hangs up and tries again. Seeing that he has only one minute left before the start of Yom Kippur, he puts down the receiver and shrugs at Savta, who stands ready to light the candles to initiate the holiday.

Afterwards, Raphael and Savta enter Saba's room and recite a blessing at his bedside, then Raphael readies himself for Kol Nidre at the Ades. As he crosses the living room to the front door, the telephone rings. He and Savta look at the telephone and then at each other.

"Ignore it, Savta. Nobody we know would call after the start of the holiday."

They stare at the telephone until it stops ringing. Raphael hugs his grandmother and leaves for the service.

The next morning, the air over Nachlaot is split by a loud rising and falling siren, which continues non-stop. Raphael runs down the stairs and nearly collides with Savta as she emerges from the hallway. The two of them step out of the house and see a stream of soldiers running through the lanes of Nachlaot. A male voice booms out of a nearby loudspeaker announcing a mobilisation of all active military personnel, and ordering any remaining civilians to remain indoors until further notice.

"Get inside, Savta," Raphael shouts over the noise. "I'll be back."

Raphael dashes into the crowd and asks a passing soldier what's happening.

"Didn't you hear what they said?" the soldier answers, shifting his machine gun to his other shoulder. "If you're not being called up, get yourself back home." He picks up his pace to catch up with the others. "And start praying."

Raphael runs to the Ades. When he steps inside, he finds it empty save for a few old men murmuring their prayers. He glides up the side row looking for the rabbi and finds the sexton sitting behind the reading platform hovering over a prayer book. Raphael clears his throat, and the sexton looks up at him.

"Where's the rabbi?" Raphael whispers in his ear.

The sexton pulls his prayer shawl over his head and continues praying. Raphael straightens up and looks out at the sparse congregation, the wailing of the sirens penetrating the usually calm atmosphere of the sanctuary, and he decides to return to Savta's.

Battling through the flow of military personnel, he reaches Savta's house ten minutes later. She rises from the sofa when she sees him.

"The country's under attack," she whispers. "Vered from next door told me. Her son works for the Ministry of Defence. He called her this morning and told her to stay home."

Raphael drops onto the sofa and rakes his hair with his fingers, ripping off his kippah in the process. "I feel so stupid, Savta. I told them that Assaf was paranoid. But he was right."

"They'll have been called up by now," Savta says staring out the window at the last few stragglers running past. "Assaf to the north; Yossi to the Sinai."

At the mention of his cousin's name, Raphael flashes on Yossi's machine gun, now empty of bullets, and his chest goes tight. He rushes across the room and reaches for the telephone.

"No, Rafi," Savta says, placing her hand on Raphael's fingers as he dials Aunt Penina's number and hangs up the receiver. "After Havdalah."

Raphael picks up the telephone and backs away from Savta. "But I have to warn him, Savta. It can't wait?"

"Warn who? What are you talking about?"

Raphael's hands shake, and he starts to cry. "I did a terrible thing, Savta." He tries to dial Aunt Penina's number, but his fingers stick in the dial pad, and he drops the telephone onto the carpet. "I have to warn Yossi." Picking it up, he carries it to the dining table, stretching the cord to its limit. He tries dialling again and reaches a recording announcing all circuits are busy. He slams down the receiver, lowers his head to the table, and sobs.

"Rafi," Savta says, her eyes widening at the sight of his desperation, "what have you done?"

"I took the bullets out of Yossi's machine gun, Savta. I was upset with him. And when I saw his gun..."

"Rafi," Savta cries, "how could you do such a thing?"

"I was angry, Savta. But I never thought anything like this was going to happen." Raphael goes to the window and looks out at the empty lane. "If I could just warn him..."

Savta shakes her head and sits on the sofa. Bringing her hands to her face, she starts to weep. Raphael rushes to her side and caresses her arm.

"I'm so sorry, Savta. I didn't mean for any of this to happen."

Savta slowly lowers her hands, dabs at her face with her apron, and stares at Raphael with a hard expression. "You've always been a brilliant child, Rafi. So many gifts. But you're also destructive. I told your parents they should give you time, that you'd grow out of it. But now I see you never will." Savta rises from the sofa. "I'm ashamed to be your grandmother."

Savta's words are an icepick through Raphael's heart. "But it was only a stupid prank, Savta."

"How dare you say that?" Savta stares at him as if he were a stranger. "What you did was an act of sabotage with potentially deadly consequences."

The telephone rings. Raphael leaps toward it. Savta holds out her hand at him and picks it up. Raphael watches her as she listens to the caller, the expression on her face changing from anger to concern, and then to shock. She lets out a muffled scream, then mumbles a few words of thanks to the caller and hangs up.

"Savta, what is it?"

"That was the president of the council in Mitzpe Ramon," Savta whispers, staring at the telephone. "He's been calling since yesterday." She looks up at Raphael. "There's been an accident."

"What kind of an accident?"

"A fire." Savta sits at the table. "There was a fire. At Penina's."

Raphael thinks back. *Don't smoke in here,* Yossi had said.

"Penina is badly burned," Savta says. She brings a trembling hand to her mouth. "Three-quarters of her body, the man said. She may not survive."

Raphael remembers the cigarette—in the bedroom.

"Assaf and Yossi were at the hospital all night; they had to leave this morning when the call-up happened."

Yossi had raised his hand at him, and he had dared Yossi to strike him. He had flicked the burning cigarette across the room.

As if hearing his thoughts, Savta turns her head to Raphael and finally says the words she feared to utter: "Little Tomer. He's gone."

Raphael collapses to the ground and screams, as the image of the burning cigarette igniting the bed sheets, fire spreading through the apartment, bores into his mind. "It's my fault," he cries. "It's my fault."

Savta stands and watches him with a horrified look as he tears at his hair and sobs. The thought of his cousin Tomer burning to death is simply too much for him to bear. Scrambling off the floor, he screams, "Everything is my fault. I'm a terrible person. I'm the one who should be dead." Spotting a steak knife on the dining table, he grabs it and holds it over his heart.

"No, Rafi," Savta screams. She tries to snatch the knife out of his hands.

Raphael blinks at her, then hurls the knife away across the room and launches himself at the wall separating the dining room from the kitchen. "I'm sorry," he wails, knocking his head again and again against the plasterboard. "I'm so goddam fucking sorry," he whimpers as he blacks out and slides to the floor, leaving a stripe of blood on the wall.

—⧢—

Marilyn and Jimmy

1982

—⧢—

—⟋⟍—

Tuesday, 11 November 1982

United States Penitentiary, Tucson

"In Los Angeles, you see a lot of freaks. Star freaks; junkie freaks; queer freaks; straight freaks; religious freaks; red, yellow, black, and white-ass freaks." The Prisoner stares at a fuzzy brown spider creeping across an intricate web occupying a corner of the cracked concrete ceiling. "But the worst of them are the *normal* freaks."

"Why's that?"

The Prisoner glances down at his cellmate, Klein, who is lying face up on his bunk dressed only in a pair of blue-and-white striped boxer shorts. He notes for the first time that Klein's belly button is an outie. He also notices the contrast between the kinky black hair that covers his thin legs and his smooth, bony upper body.

"Because, dearie, the normal ones are so fucking boring," the Prisoner answers.

He climbs down from his bunk and shoots a quick glance through the bars at the empty corridor, then sits next to Klein.

He passes a hand over the soft, cinnamon-coloured skin of his stomach and feels the edge of his ribcage as he moves his hand upward. Klein closes his eyes expectantly.

"What kind of freak were you?" Klein asks after a moment.

The Prisoner sniggers. "*I* wasn't a freak." His hand glides up to Klein's left nipple and kneads it for a few seconds. Klein rolls his eyes into his head and grins.

"I was a world unto myself."

—⁂—

Wednesday, 4 August 1982

It's a blistering summer afternoon in Hollywood. The boulevard is seething with tourists and derelicts jostling past each other on the jammed pavement amidst the usual glitz and garbage. On the corner of Hollywood and Highland, a sunburnt middle-aged Hispanic woman with Frida Kahlo braids, wearing a white dress and a red poncho, perches on a fire hydrant selling *Maps to the Stars' Homes*. She's been sitting on this same fucking fire hydrant selling the same magazine for the past twenty-five years and can spot an interested buyer three blocks away.

On this particular scorcher of a day, she spies a pair of shapely legs through the crowds, draped in a knee-length red satin skirt, hugged by black fishnet stockings, and set in impatiently tapping stiletto heels, waiting at the crosswalk to traverse Highland. The crowd surges forward after the tail-end of a mass of cars inches past the intersection. The woman readies herself to hawk her magazine as the legs move in her direction.

The crowd mounts the pavement on the woman's side of the street as the traffic signal changes to green. It parts to reveal the owner of the legs, a young and curvy creature with shoulder-length platinum blonde hair, styled into elaborate retro waves that frame a heavily powdered, angular face.

The blond creature sashays up to the woman on the fire hydrant and yanks a copy of *Maps to the Stars' Homes* out of her grasp with its elegantly manicured hands. Flipping to the index, it runs a red lacquered fingernail down an alphabetical list of names and stops at the listing *Marilyn Monroe/Joe DiMaggio Honeymoon House*. Then, flicking a five-dollar bill at the woman, the creature saunters down the boulevard in the direction of the Chinese Theatre.

Later that night, the creature struggles through a hedge-row surrounding a large estate, careful not to tear the pink satin evening gown it has changed into. Its spike heels catch in the dirt and it stumbles to its knees. Picking itself off the ground, the creature pulls them off and hobbles through a break in the greenery the rest of the way to the house. It tests the doors on the ground floor and finds them all locked. Then it jiggles the windows and, finding one in the back of the building that is unlatched, pushes it open and climbs into the darkened house.

The creature glides through the kitchen and across the foyer, then mounts a circular staircase and ascends to the next floor, where it finds a long hallway. Tiptoeing from door to door, it listens briefly at each one, then stops at the end of the hall outside a door from which emanates a high-pitched humming. Finding the door unlocked, the creature pushes it open slowly.

Through the open door, the creature sees a shaggy young man in a tattered nightshirt passed out in an easy chair in front of a TV set, which is broadcasting the end-of-programming test pattern. Lunging forward, the creature throws itself at the young man's bare feet and hugs his legs.

"Joe, wake up," the creature says in a hoarse voice.

The young man stirs.

"I'm back, Joe. I've come back."

The young man wakes up and blinks at the creature, then force-fully pushes it away, sending it tumbling backwards.

"What the—?" The young man rises to his full height.

"No, Joe." The creature scrambles to its feet and smoothens its evening gown. "It's me—Marilyn. I'm back."

The creature slinks forward, a pouty smile on its face, its arms thrown open, ready to embrace the young man, who takes a step backwards and bumps into the chair, his eyes growing wide.

"Don't you recognise your Marilyn anymore, Joe?" it purrs.

As the creature reaches the young man with its cherry-red lips puckered for a kiss, he pulls back his fist and hammers the creature in the face.

Through closed eyes, the creature hears the wail of a siren and the squawk of a police radio. Its head pulsates with sick waves of pain that move in and out like an ocean tide. Streams of sweet-salty stickiness leak into its mouth. It cries out as its nose bumps against a hard surface.

"Shut up, you," a deep male voice rings out.

The creature pries open one eye and finds itself slumped on the back seat of a squad car, its hands cuffed behind its back with ever-tightening metal restraints that dig into its wrists. It groans as it sits up and looks out the window at the palm-lined streets speeding past the window.

A moustachioed, black police officer in the passenger seat whips around and glowers at the creature through the grate.

"I said shut the fuck up."

The squad car jerks to a stop in front of the Beverly Hills Police Station, and the moustachioed officer roughly hustles the creature into the hands of a pair of waiting bailiffs. They drag the creature inside and downstairs into the bowels of the building where they yank off its earrings, strip off its gown, and process it into a holding cell in the male section of the jail.

The next afternoon, following swift post-arraignment negotiations between a public defender and an assistant district attorney, the creature stands at the counsel table in a small courtroom of the Beverly Hills Municipal Court, its bruised face now scrubbed clean of blood and makeup, its hair pulled back into a ponytail.

Besides the court personnel, the creature's parents, Yoshi and Tomoko, are the only people in the courtroom. Tomoko sits in the front row leaning forward trying to make out what the judge is saying. Yoshi sits in the back of the room with his arms crossed, looking out the window at a red brick wall.

"Clyde Koba," the judge says, alternating between staring at Clyde over the top of his half-glasses and reading from Clyde's court file, "based on your plea of no contest, this court finds you guilty of criminal trespass, which is a misdemeanour."

Clyde raps his fist against the counsel table. His public defender's head snaps in his direction, and she touches his shoulder, but Clyde shakes her off.

"Your honour."

The judge puts down Clyde's file and looks at his public defender. Yoshi flashes an angry look at Clyde and shakes his head.

"What is it, Mr Koba?"

"I just wanted to say, for the gazillionth time, that my name is *not* Clyde Koba. It's Marilyn Monroe."

The judge removes his glasses and sets them to one side of the file.

"Yes, Mr Koba. I think you've made that abundantly clear to this court. That's why, considering this is your first and hopefully your last offence as an adult, I'm going to suspend your sentence of one year in the county jail and place you under the guardianship of your mother and the Probation Department, on the condition that you undergo a year of psychiatric therapy."

"I don't need therapy."

Clyde's public defender nudges Clyde with her elbow. Clyde stamps his foot and looks down at the table, tears coursing down his face.

"Everything all right there?" the judge asks.

Clyde crosses his arms, shuts his eyes, and softly hums a tune.

"Yes, your honour. Apologies," Clyde's public defender says.

The judge nods, scribbles something on a piece of paper and hands it to his clerk together with Clyde's file.

"I've made a referral to Doctor Seth Menner, as I see he treated your client after his juvenile incident. Good luck."

The judge raps his gavel and speeds out of the courtroom.

Clyde turns around and hugs Tomoko over the bar as his public defender waits to one side.

"Clear the courtroom, please," the bailiff calls out.

Yoshi leaps out of his seat and storms out of the courtroom.

Several days later Clyde finds himself back on Doctor Menner's brown leather sofa, on his back and staring at the ceiling.

"It's really quite obvious, Doctor."

"What's obvious?"

"Look"—Clyde sits up—"I was born on August 5, 1962, just after midnight."

"Uh huh." Doctor Menner looks down at Clyde's red lacquered toenails, which peek through a pair of open-toe heels. "And the significance of that is?"

"Well, isn't it fuckingly obvious? I was *born* on August 5, 1962. Marilyn Monroe *died* on the same day, at the same time. All things are recycled. Ergo, I am Marilyn Monroe. It's as plain as Mona Lisa's tits, Doctor."

—⁓—

"My opinion is your son is suffering from a near-total rejection of self," Doctor Menner explains to Yoshi and Tomoko in his office two weeks later. "He rejects his race and thus wants desperately to be Caucasian; he rejects his sexuality and thus wishes to be a woman so his attraction to men may be acceptable."

"His attraction to men?" Yoshi says. "Excuse me?"

Tomoko stares at her hands, which sit clasped in her lap.

"Mr Koba, Marilyn Monroe is, to your son, the embodiment of the perfect white woman. Thus, his fixation with the star."

"Oh, Jesus fucks Christ. Now I've heard everything." Yoshi stands up. "You know, you guys really earn your money, I tell you."

Tomoko pulls at his shirt, and he slumps back into his chair.

"Maybe he actually *believes* he's Marilyn Monroe," Yoshi says. "Did that ever occur to you? There *is* a family history of mental illness, you know."

"Doctor, this is tearing our family apart," Tomoko says.

"We're ready to sign papers," Yoshi blurts out.

"What papers are those, Mr Koba?"

"You know, to lock him away. He's obviously sick. And we can't take care of him."

Tomoko's head snaps up. "Oh, Yoshi, no."

"Besides, my parole officer's only just allowed me to move back in."

"What does that have to do with anything, Mr Koba?" Doctor Menner removes his glasses and sets them on the desk.

"Things might get heated. You know, normal-like, but heated. I wouldn't want my PO to get the wrong idea, if you know what I mean."

Doctor Menner glances at Tomoko, who averts her eyes and dabs at them with a handkerchief.

"All parents argue with their kids," Yoshi continues. "They got the wrong idea the last time. I wouldn't want them to make another mistake."

Doctor Menner pushes away from his desk and stands. "Your son's condition doesn't warrant commitment, Mr Koba. At least not yet."

He comes around to their side and hands Tomoko a business card. "I'm going to recommend a therapy group I moderate twice a week in the evenings, on Mondays and Thursdays. We meet on campus at USC. I think your son may benefit from it."

"Thank you, Doctor." Tomoko peers at the card and pops it into her purse. "Thank you for everything you're doing."

"I'd like a word with your husband if you don't mind, Mrs Koba."

Tomoko nods and slips out of the office.

"Mr Koba, with respect."

"Spit it out, Doc."

"I question the wisdom of letting you back into the home, given the history."

Yoshi stands. "Is that all?"

"You're a volatile man, Mr Koba. Your son needs understanding, not an iron fist."

"He's twenty years old. He's the one who should be out of the house fending for himself. That's what'll fix him, in my opinion. Not any of this therapy business."

"Be very careful, Mr Koba."

—៣ヽ—

Clyde follows Doctor Menner into a large classroom in which twelve empty chairs are arranged in a circle. A diverse group of around ten people, composed of both men and woman in their twenties and thirties, mills about socialising, drinking coffee, and munching on glazed doughnuts.

Spotting a large mirror at the end of the room, Clyde breaks away from Doctor Menner and approaches it. He admires his blonde curls; he pivots from side to side checking out how his ass looks in his tight pegged jeans; he kicks up one of his heels and blows a kiss at himself. Then he fluffs the frills of his white chiffon blouse and freshens up his lipstick.

Doctor Menner draws near and takes Clyde gently by the arm.

"What do you see in there?" he whispers to Clyde.

Clyde starts and blinks at the doctor, then averts his eyes.

"I see Marilyn, of course." Clyde turns back to the mirror and peers into it.

Doctor Menner looks at Clyde's reflection and nods.

"Now then," Doctor Menner calls out to the group after a moment. "Let's begin, shall we?"

The people move to the chairs, and Doctor Menner guides Clyde to the chair next to his. Clyde sits with his legs closed tightly and places his clutch purse on his lap. He looks around at the people and frowns at Doctor Menner. Then he pulls out a pair of round vintage Chanel sunglasses from his purse and slips them on.

"Sunglasses won't help, darling," whispers a young man sitting to Clyde's left with springy shoulder-length strawberry-blonde locks.

Clyde glances at him out of the corner of his eye and leans in his direction. "Why don't you go fuck yourself, Tiny Tim," he whispers back.

Doctor Menner taps Clyde on the shoulder and points at the sunglasses. Clyde rakes them off his face and tosses them into his purse. He looks around at the group, which is now assembled in the chairs quietly waiting for Doctor Menner to begin.

"I'd like you all to meet someone who will be joining us for the first time," Doctor Menner says.

Clyde's heart jumps the moment he hears those words. He closes his eyes for a moment and pulls himself together. Then he looks up and sees everyone in the group is looking at him

"This is—" Doctor Menner turns to Clyde. "Well, why don't you introduce yourself to everyone."

Clyde shoots a glance at Doctor Menner, who nods at him.

"All right," Clyde says.

He looks back at the group and clears his throat. "I really don't know why I'm here," he begins in a soft voice.

"I'm with her, Doc," says a young man with long brown hair and a beard sitting across from him. "I don't know why I'm here either."

The others look at the young man and murmur among themselves.

"That's perfectly fine," Doctor Menner says. "We're all here to help each other."

Most everyone in the group nods and smiles at Clyde, who glances at Doctor Menner with a puzzled look. Doctor Menner squeezes Clyde's hand.

"Now then," Doctor Menner says, "tell us your name."

"OK, fine." Clyde sits up. "I'm Marilyn—"

"Your real name, please," Doctor Menner says.

Clyde looks questioningly at Doctor Menner for a moment. Doctor Menner smiles and nods. "Go ahead."

"Oh ..." Clyde's face brightens; his frown morphs into a toothy smile. "Oh, yes, thank you, Doctor." He turns to the group. "My *real* name is Norma Jean Baker. But my professional name is, of course, Marilyn Monroe."

A smile plays on Doctor Menner's lips.

"All right, thank you. Now then, let's all proceed to introduce ourselves. Be sure to mention a little something about yourself when it's your turn."

He turns to a sallow young man with slicked-back black hair and thick sideburns sitting to his right. "We'll begin at this end."

"Hello, all," the young man says in a rumbling, southern drawl, "I'm Elvis Aaron Presley." He turns to Clyde. "Welcome, and God bless you, even though I don't believe you're Marilyn."

"I don't give a fly's twat what you believe," Clyde snaps.

The others laugh at the exchange.

"I knew Marilyn," the Elvis clone says. "She wouldn't have used that kind of language."

"Next, please," Doctor Menner says, scribbling something in his notepad.

The man to the left of Elvis stands up. He looks to be in his early twenties with long bushy brown hair, wearing an off-white pirate shirt, faded blue jeans, and a pair of brown leather sandals. He raises his hand at Clyde. "Hey there, welcome. I'm Jim, the

Lizard King. And"—he looks at the others—"I still think you people are strange. Real fucking strange."

"You're normal?" the young man across from Clyde blurts out.

The others applaud and yell down the Lizard King, who sneers at them and sits, tightly crossing his arms.

"Please," Doctor Menner calls out as he scribbles into his notepad, "settle down, people. You know the rules. No talking out of turn."

A heavily made-up woman in her late thirties with tease-damaged brown hair and dangly metal earrings yells out of turn: "I'm Madonna." She points at Clyde. "And I think your hair looks ridiculous."

Clyde blinks at her. "What?"

Doctor Menner flips shut the notebook and frowns at Madonna. "Was that necessary?"

"You always tell us we should say whatever we feel," Madonna says.

"What did that slut fucking say to me?" Clyde asks Doctor Menner.

"I think her hair looks great," the young man across from Clyde says.

"Yeah, you would." Madonna peers into a compact mirror and touches up her makeup. "I think Jesus wants to get into Marilyn's panties." She snaps shut the compact.

"Hang on," the young man says. "I never claimed I was Jesus. What I said was that his spirit guides me."

"Oh, my God," Clyde leaps out of his chair, knocking it over. "You're all fucking crazy." He rushes out of the room.

Doctor Menner runs after him and finds him halfway down the hallway at the lift repeatedly pushing the buttons. "Clyde, wait."

Clyde glares at Doctor Menner, then kicks the lift door and disappears into the emergency exit at the end of the hallway.

Doctor Menner chases after him and sees Clyde speeding down the stairwell, already several floors away.

"Clyde, come back," he calls, running down the stairs. "Clyde, please."

Clyde halts and whirls around as Doctor Menner reaches him, streaming sweat and huffapuffing.

"I am never coming back to this madhouse. Do you hear me?" Clyde yells, poking Doctor Menner in the chest. "I'm not crazy, and I'm not going to let you make me crazy."

"Listen, Clyde," Doctor Menner says, squeegeeing the sweat off his bald head with his fingers. "If you prefer, we can go back to the hypnosis, to working one-on-one—"

"No," Clyde screams. "And don't you ever call me by that other name again. My name is Marilyn, Marilyn Monroe! And I'm going to make sure the whole goddam world knows it."

Clyde spins around, and a dazed Doctor Menner watches as he sprints the rest of the way down the stairwell and out of the building.

"Where'd she go, Doc?"

Doctor Menner turns around and sees Jesus standing on the landing above him. Letting out a groan, Doctor Menner sits on one of the steps and lowers his head into his hands.

—⁂—

Clyde steps off an RTD bus at Hollywood and Vine, a dark, intense expression clouding his face. He strolls aimlessly down the crowded pavement, absently swinging his purse and fighting back tears.

He stops in front of a storefront window crammed full of cheap plastic mannequins wearing sexy lingerie and sees the image of Marilyn reflected in the glass. She waves at him and smiles. Clyde nods and dabs at his eyes with a Kleenex, then resumes his stroll, smiling and coyly waving at passers-by who give him wide berth.

Passing an old revival cinema on Hollywood near Wilcox, Clyde abruptly pulls up in front of the marquee and sees a poster announcing *The Misfits,* starring Marilyn Monroe and Clark Gable. He squeals with excitement, quickly fumbles a few bills out of his purse and steps up to the old-style wooden ticket booth. He peers inside and sees a clean-shaven olive-skinned man in his mid-twenties lost in a book.

"One, please," Clyde says through the grate.

The attendant looks up at Clyde, leans forward, and presses the intercom button. The attendant's thick black eyebrows set off his intense blue eyes.

"It started a half hour ago," the young man says.

"Well, then, hurry up and sell me the fucking ticket," Clyde snaps. He glances at his watch and frowns.

The attendant sets aside his book and narrows his eyes at Clyde, the side of his mouth pulling back into a crooked smile.

"Pretty please," Clyde says. He blows a kiss at the attendant, who pantomimes catching it in the air and dropping it in his breast pocket. Then he punches out the ticket.

Clyde shimmies into the dark, sparsely occupied cinema, which reeks of piss and stale popcorn, and sits in the very centre, holding his legs tightly together and placing his purse on his lap to avoid touching the sticky threadbare seats. He looks up and watches as the famous "Mustang Scene" plays out on the screen. Clyde follows every one of Marilyn's expressions with painstaking concentration, quietly miming every line of dialogue with flawless precision. Every so often, the sound of laboured breathing behind him breaks his focus. Whipping around, he sees a skinny, pimply faced man sitting behind him with his black joggers pulled down to his ankles, masturbating over a half-full bucket of popcorn.

"Do you mind taking your cock elsewhere," Clyde yells. "We're trying to watch a movie here."

The man pulls up his joggers and shuffles away.

"Jesus!" Clyde watches the man sit behind another patron and restart his strange courting ritual. "Some people are so rude."

Turning around, he settles back into watching the film.

As the final credits roll, he dabs a few tears from his eyes and lets out a loud sigh. He glances around the vast, empty auditorium when the house lights come up. A desiccated black usher with a snowy-white afro props open the back doors and shuffles down the aisle half-heartedly, dragging a broom behind him.

Clyde glances at his watch. "Monkey shit!" he screams and dashes out.

"Where are you off to?" someone says as he bursts out of the lobby and speeds past the ticket booth.

Clyde pulls up and sees the attendant from earlier reclining against an outside wall smoking a cigarette and flashing a half-grin at him.

"A casting call maybe?" He blows a series of smoke rings and pumps his eyebrows at Clyde.

"I beg your pardon?" Clyde wrinkles his nose at the sight of the attendant's hairy arms showing below the sleeves of his dark blue shirt, which are rolled up to right below his elbows.

"Looks like you're in a hurry. I thought you might be going to a casting call, like half the people in this city."

Clyde steps up to the young man, waving his hand to disperse the smoke. "I don't *do* casting calls anymore."

"No?"

"Not at my level." Clyde points at the movie poster in the glass case next to the young man.

The young man glances at the poster, then back at Clyde and arches an eyebrow. "That's you?"

Clyde nods and strikes a pose next to the poster.

"You're Marilyn Monroe?"

"In the flesh, baby."

The young man drops his cigarette to the pavement, crushes it underfoot, and holds his hand out to Clyde. "Nice to meet you, Marilyn. I'm Ralph."

Clyde looks at Ralph's hand and back up at him.

"I'm a graduate film student." Ralph lowers his hand. He takes a step toward Clyde and pumps his eyebrows at him again.

"What about it?"

"Maybe you'd like to get together sometime and talk movies."

Feeling Ralph a bit too close for comfort, close enough, in fact, to smell the musky-sweet scent of his skin, Clyde blinks at him and stumbles backwards. Checking his watch, he lets out a hoarse little scream, then spins around and dashes down the pavement.

Ralph cocks his head to one side and watches Clyde dash down Hollywood Boulevard, slaloming around the tourists meandering west along the Walk of Fame toward Mann's Chinese Theatre. When he disappears around the corner at Cahuenga Boulevard, Ralph returns to the ticket booth and shuffles through a stack of Los Angeles Herald-Examiners set aside for recycling. A few minutes later he's scanning an article reporting the attempted burglary of the Marilyn Monroe/Joe DiMaggio "honeymoon house" in Beverly Hills by a deranged fan, illustrated by a photo of the modest-looking house, a stock photo of Marilyn and DiMaggio in a booth at the Brown Derby, and a grainy image of Clyde in the courtroom sitting next to his public defender. Ralph looks up and gazes out at the boulevard for a moment, then folds the newspaper and stuffs it into his book bag.

—⁓—

Clyde leaps out of a lumbering RTD bus as it pulls up outside the block-size, windowless concrete Pacific Telephone Exchange Building, reaching into his purse at the same time. He pulls out his company ID and sprints past a security guard into the employee entrance.

As he gallops past numerous manned operator bays, his co-workers raise their heads and exchange disapproving glances as he speeds by. Stopping behind a forty-something redhead with a pinched face and black cat-eye glasses, he pulls off her headset.

"Your shift started over a half hour ago." The redhead stands and straightens her hair. "Where were you?"

Clyde shoves her aside, slips on the headset, and sits at the console. The redhead storms off down the aisle, and Clyde struggles to catch his breath.

"My God!" A Filipina co-worker at the next console hands him a few pieces of tissue paper. "What happened to you?"

Clyde snatches the paper out of her hands and wipes his face, nodding a thank you.

"No, not you, sir," the co-worker says into her mouthpiece. "I'm sorry."

"This is the operator," Clyde says into his mouthpiece, breathing heavily. "How may I help you?"

A few minutes later, Clyde's supervisor marches up to him, followed by a prim young woman in a pink-and-white summer dress. The heads of several operators pop up over their consoles and watch as the supervisor taps Clyde on the shoulder. Clyde looks up at him.

"One moment, please, ma'am," Clyde says into the mouthpiece.

The supervisor signals with his forefinger for Clyde to follow him. The young woman in the pink dress slides into the chair as Clyde rises, and she slips on the headset. Clyde follows his supervisor, who is walking several paces ahead, down the aisle.

Clyde's Filipina co-worker mouths *What's up?* to Miss Pink Dress, who responds by drawing her thumb across her throat.

Thirty minutes later Clyde emerges from the building carrying a pink slip and his final pay cheque in his hand. He drags himself to the bus stop and waits for the next bus to Pasadena.

The bus drops him off at Fair Oaks and Washington, and he walks a few blocks home. He halts a moment when he sees his father's truck parked in the driveway, feeling his heartbeat in his throat, then walks past it and enters the house. Glancing into the living room as he glides by, he sees his parents sitting on the sofa in front of the TV, which is broadcasting a baseball game. His mother is knitting a blanket, and his father is listing to one side, bleary-eyed and drooling, a half-consumed bottle of whiskey on the coffee table in front of him.

Clyde pads quickly down the hallway to his bedroom, which he has converted into a veritable shrine to Marilyn Monroe, filled with photos, memorabilia, trinkets, and a plaster bust of Marilyn atop a candlelit altar. He pushes the door closed, throws himself on his bed, hugging a life-sized Marilyn pillow to his chest, and sobs.

Yoshi sits up and glances around. "What was that?" He wipes his mouth with the back of his hand and blinks at the TV. Tomoko sets aside her knitting and stands. Yoshi glances at the grandfather clock. "What's he doing home so early? Why the hell isn't he at work?"

Tomoko moves to the door.

"It's a miracle he still has a job."

"Yoshi, please," Tomoko says, "Don't raise your voice so." She moves down the hall and listens at Clyde's door for a moment, then knocks softly.

"Go away," comes Clyde's muffled voice from the other side.

"I'll raise my voice in my own house if I want to raise my voice," Yoshi roars from the living room.

Tomoko knocks again, this time more forcefully.

"Go away," Clyde screams, "leave me alone."

Tomoko opens the door, glides to Clyde's bedside and sits on the edge of his bed. She strokes his back softly, and Clyde sits up and embraces her.

"Please, go away," Clyde whimpers over his mother's shoulders.

Tomoko holds him tightly and rocks with him. "What is it, my baby? What's happened?"

Yoshi staggers up to the partially open door and eavesdrops from the hallway.

"I'm not going back to that stupid therapy group, Momma."

Tomoko releases Clyde. "What do you mean?" She stares at him, her eyes wide. "You *have* to go. The judge ordered it. It's part of your probation."

Clyde scoots away from her and sits against the wall, pulling up his knees and hugging them. "I don't care, Momma. Those people were all crazy. They were making fun of me."

Tomoko frowns and looks over her shoulder at the door, then she turns back to Clyde. "What about work?" she whispers. "Didn't your shift start already?"

Clyde grabs the remote control from his nightstand and switches on the TV. "I'm not going back there either. I want to rest."

"That's it!" Yoshi bursts through the doorway. "I'm sick of all this! I've had it!" He strides to the middle of the room. "We've all had it with you."

"Don't yell at me!" Clyde screams. "Momma, tell him not to—"

Tomoko stands. "Yoshi, please."

"You keep out of this." Yoshi shakes an unsteady finger in her face. "You made him like this." He lurches forward and pulls Tomoko away from Clyde's bedside.

"Leave my momma alone, you drunken pig." Clyde leaps from the bed and stands eye-to-eye with Yoshi.

Yoshi slaps Clyde to the ground and kicks him.

"Get out of my room, you mutha fucka!" Clyde screeches.

"*Your* room?" Yoshi rakes his dirty fingernails along the wall, tearing through a line of Marilyn photos.

"What are you doing?" screams Clyde.

Yoshi attacks a display case filled with Marilyn memorabilia, grabbing armfuls of knickknacks and magazines and throwing them on the floor.

"Stop it! Stop, you pig, you pig!"

Clyde scrambles to his feet, grabbing for the magazines that Yoshi is shredding, and Yoshi kicks him back down while Tomoko blubbers at the door. Yoshi launches himself at the bust of Marilyn. He hefts it off the altar and slams it against the wall. Clyde screams as if mortally wounded. He crawls across the floor trying to salvage the pieces as shattered plaster rains down on him.

Yoshi grabs him by the hair. "Get out of my house, you freak!" He half-pulls, half-drags Clyde out of the room. Teary Tomoko slinks behind boo-hoo-hooing as Yoshi pulls, pushes, and kicks Clyde down the hallway.

"Ahhh! Ow! Let go of me." Clyde yanks himself away from Yoshi and struggles to his feet. "Momma, call someone, please. Call his fucking PO."

Yoshi smacks Clyde back to the ground and hauls him by one arm toward the front door.

"Please, Yoshi, don't…" Tomoko whimpers from a safe distance. "He's sick. My baby's sick."

Clyde breaks loose in the foyer and runs into the living room, accidentally crashing into the coffee table and knocking over the bottle of whisky, spilling its contents on the carpet. He snatches up the bottle and holds it over his head as Yoshi approaches.

"Don't come one step nearer, you good for shit drunk. I'll kill you. I swear to the spirits of your parents, I'll crack open your piece-of-shit head once and for all.

Yoshi bats the bottle out of Clyde's hand. It flies across the room and explodes against the wall. Clyde collapses to the whiskey-sodden carpet. Yoshi drags him to the front door and pushes him out of the house on to the front porch. Tomoko tries to follow, but Yoshi yanks her back inside and slams the door. After a moment, the door swings open, and Clyde's purse comes flying out, hitting him in the head.

Bruised and dazed, Clyde struggles to his feet, steadying himself for a moment against the stucco. He straightens his ripped and tattered blouse and fixes his hair. Then, stepping back from the house, he screams, "I'm a star! Do you hear me? You can't treat a star like that."

A few neighbours step outside and assemble on the pavement across the road. Others pull aside their curtains and peer out their windows wagging their heads. Tomoko looks out the front window at Clyde; tears stream down her face as she watches him hobble past the neighbours and down the street toward the bus stop.

—◉—

Clyde alights in front of a petrol station on Sunset Boulevard and heads for the ladies' room, where he washes his face and reapplies his makeup. He covers the bruises and scratches with heavy foundation. Then he carefully pencils in his eyebrows, emphasising the beauty mark on his cheek with the eyebrow pencil. Finally, he digs his favourite cherry-red lipstick out of his purse and draws on his lips. Stepping back to examine the overall look, he sees Marilyn reflected in the mirror. He giggles and waves at her, then, puckering up, he blows a kiss at the mirror.

Sunset Boulevard is throbbing with activity in the sultry air of the late summer evening, and Clyde strolls along it softly humming Judy Garland's *Who Cares*. He sashays past a group of grime-covered vagrants of various ages sitting against a wall outside a cheque cashing store and heads toward the door.

"Oooh, wee," says the largest of the vagrants, "ain't she a sweet one!"

His friends laugh it up and whistle at Clyde, who ignores them and steps inside. A few minutes later, Clyde exits the store counting a wad of cash.

"Got any for me, sweet thing?" the vagrant says.

"Go fuck yourself," Clyde snaps.

The vagrant grabs his crotch. "I'd rather fuck you, pumpkin." He lifts his head at Clyde and winks. The vagrants fall over themselves laughing.

Clyde moves swiftly down the pavement. A block away, he turns into a narrow, poorly illuminated and rubbish-strewn alley and picks his way through the debris, still counting the cash. He trips over a sleeping derelict and falls to the pavement.

"Hey, what's the big deal?" the grizzled derelict says through his toothless mouth.

Clyde whips around and sees someone who looks like Popeye crawling toward him on his hands and knees, hungrily eyeing the cash.

"Hey!" Popeye points a trembling, dirt-caked finger at Clyde. "Ain't you some kind of movie star?"

Clyde sits up and smiles. "You recognise me?" He lightly touches his blouse.

"Yeah, sure I do." Popeye crawls up to Clyde, close enough for Clyde to smell raw onions on his breath, and Clyde brings a hand to his nose.

"You're...wait, don't tell me." Popeye snaps his fingers. "You're—"

"Marilyn..." Clyde whispers.

"That's it," Popeye says. "Marilyn, yeah." He reaches out to Clyde. "Nice to meet you, Marilyn."

Clyde straightens up and smiles, then hands Popeye half the cash.

The derelict gasps and fans out the notes in his hand like a deck of playing cards; then he looks up at Clyde and beams a gummy smile. "Gee, thanks, lady."

"Thank *you*." Clyde stands. "You're very kind."

He brushes himself off and strides out of the alley, emerging onto Hollywood Boulevard, which is jammed with traffic as *cholos* cruise the boulevard in their lowriders.

A tired and more subdued Clyde wanders along the pavement, jostled by groups of tourists and teenagers out for the night. Every so often, pairs of mounted police approach, forcing Clyde to step into the gutter to make way for them. Seeing the Chinese Theatre looming in the distance, Clyde crosses the street at the next intersection and heads toward it.

Outside the iconic façade, he sees a half-dozen Japanese tourists gleefully snapping pictures of each other next to a life-size cutout of Marilyn Monroe. Clyde stands in front of the cutout and strikes a pose, kicking up one leg and puckering his lips at the tourists who complain among themselves and move on, shaking their heads. Clyde frowns and trudges away, glancing at the celebrity handprints pressed into the cement before crossing the boulevard and heading east, occasionally stopping to read the inscribed terrazzo and brass stars embedded in the pavement along Hollywood's Walk of Fame.

A block away from the Chinese Theatre, he sees a round-the-block queue of bored leather-clad patrons waiting outside a rock club. Loud music pours out the open doors of the club. Catcalls erupt from the crowd as Clyde struts past in time to the beat of the music. One of the patrons sticks out his foot, and Clyde pulls up short in time to avoid tripping. He snaps his fingers at the patron, who laughs and bows to Clyde as if to royalty, and the others cheer and applaud. A smile breaks out on Clyde's lips, and he saunters away hugging his purse to his chest.

As he reaches Marilyn's star, Clyde sees a small group of fans kneeling around it in a semi-circle. They reverently light memorial candles set in shot glasses, placing them on and around the star. Clyde strikes a pose at the head of the star, but they ignore him. He walks up to a young, barefoot woman in a plain white granny dress and asks her for a candle. She lights one and hands it to him. Clyde carries it a few blocks away to Vine, kneels in front of Clark Gable's star, and places the candle in the centre. Then he kisses the star and chants *Namu Myōhō Renge Kyō* ten times before returning to Hollywood Boulevard and resuming his sojourn.

He reaches a building at the southeast corner of Hollywood and Wilcox on which someone has painted a colourful mural of an audience seated inside a darkened, old-time movie theatre staring out at the street. In the audience are dozens of film legends from Hollywood's Golden Age, including Charlie Chaplin, James Dean, Marilyn Monroe, and Clarke Gable. Clyde smiles and waves at the mural.

"Marilyn, dear," calls Charlie Chaplin from the mural, "What are you doing down there?" He points at an empty seat where Marilyn was sitting a moment before.

"Hello, Charles." Clyde curtsies. "I'm simply taking an evening stroll."

"Come join us," calls Oliver Hardy from the back row. "The show's about to begin."

The others nod in agreement.

"Oh, thank you. Thank you all so much." Clyde giggles and fans himself with his purse. "But, I'm afraid I have a prior engagement."

A passing group of predatory teenagers dressed in chinos, wife beaters, and hairnets spot Clyde talking to the mural.

"Look at *that* one," one of the predators says. He spits in Clyde's direction.

The group crosses over to Clyde's side of the road, and Clyde snaps out of his daydream as they swagger toward him. One of them breaks from the group and steps up to Clyde.

"Hey, you," he says, forcefully tapping Clyde on the chest.

Clyde drops back, noticing an angry red scar running from the young tough's ear to the side of his mouth.

"Who you talking to, princess?"

Clyde looks past him at the others jostling in the background. He puffs up his chest and lunges forward, closing the gap between them. "The name's Marilyn, wise ass."

Momentarily startled, Scarface retreats a couple of steps, and the others erupt into peals of laughter, slapping each other on their backs and pointing at him. Scarface reddens and draws his fist at Clyde. Suddenly, from out of the shadows, an athletic-looking man in his mid-twenties wearing black jeans and a black T-shirt swoops in between Scarface and Clyde and flicks open a switchblade.

"Now, you're not going to hit a lady, are you?" He waves the sharp end of the switchblade at Scarface and raises his head at him.

Scarface pulls back. "Hit her?" He glowers at the knife. "I'm gonna kick that bitch's ass."

The young man in black jumps forward and takes a swipe at the air with the knife. "You'll have to kick mine first, gever."

Scarface stumbles back, angrily eyeing the knife. One of his friends breaks away from the group and takes him by the arm. "Come on, *homes*, let's go. They're just a couple of sick fags."

Scarface shakes off his friend and spits on the ground. "They've probably got AIDS anyway." He swaggers back to the group with his friend. They walk back toward the boulevard screaming insults as they go. As they round the corner, Scarface stoops to pick up a beer bottle and hurls it at Clyde's champion. It smashes into the pavement a metre away from him. The young man turns to see Clyde walking away, already halfway down the block to Selma. He grabs his backpack off the pavement and chases after him.

"Hey, don't I even get a thank you?" he shouts.

"For what?" Clyde says over his shoulder as the young man pulls up alongside him.

"Are you kidding me? Those guys would have torn you up."

Clyde lets out a short laugh and picks up his pace. "What are you, my personal Superman?"

"Wait up! I—"

Clyde halts and whips around.

"Beat it, buster. This girl can take care of herself."

The young man frowns and rakes his fingers through his short black hair. "You don't remember me, do you?"

"Should I?"

"You're Marilyn."

Clyde flips open his hand and passes it from his head to his knee. "Obviously."

The young man grins. "You really don't remember me, do you?"

Clyde takes a step back and peers at him, his head cocked to one side. He extends his forefinger at him and twirls it in the air. "Turn around for a second."

The young man shrugs and turns.

"There, stop," Clyde says once the young man's back is facing him. He sizes him up carefully, feeling a sudden flutter inside at the sight of his broad shoulders, shapely backside, and strong legs.

"No," Clyde says after a moment. "I don't believe we've met."

"We *have*."

"No, we haven't." Clyde slinks toward him and taps his thigh. "I could never forget an ass like that."

The young man turns around slowly, a smile breaking out on his face.

"Thanks."

Clyde flashes his teeth. "Don't mention it."

They stroll south together in the direction of Sunset Boulevard.

"We really have met, you know," the young man says as they reach Sunset. "You don't remember because you were too busy looking at someone else."

Clyde stops and shakes his head. "And who was that?"

"Yourself." A twisted half-smile breaks out on the young man's face.

Clyde glances sidelong at the young man. "Where exactly *did* we meet?"

"At the movie theatre this afternoon. The one up the road there." He jerks his thumb toward Hollywood Boulevard. "My name's Ralph, remember?" He extends his hand toward Clyde.

Clyde glares at Ralph. "You're the flirty guy with the hairy arms? Goodbye." He spins on his heels and storms away.

"No, wait." Ralph follows close behind.

"Get away from me," Clyde shouts, weaving in and out of groups of people buzzing up and down the pavement bordering Sunset Boulevard.

Once they break free of the crowd, Ralph catches up to Clyde and takes him by the arm.

"Stop grabbing me." Clyde shakes him off. "Who the hell do you think you are?"

"Sorry!" Ralph holds up his hands. "I did ask you to wait."

"Wait for what?"

"I'm the guy who just saved your life, remember?"

"You're the guy who sells tickets at a flea-bitten movie house. Marilyn doesn't do the help, sorry."

Ralph narrows his eyes at Clyde. "Sure she does."

"What?"

"Marilyn does everyone."

"Why, you rude bastard!" Clyde steps forward and raises his hand at Ralph.

Ralph smirks and lifts his cheek at Clyde. "Go ahead, slap me hard. Then let me buy you a drink."

Clyde lowers his hand and shakes his head. "What kind of crazy sicko are you?"

"The kind that believes you're who you claim to be," Ralph says.

Clyde stares at Ralph, opens his mouth to say something, then rolls his eyes and looks away.

"Admit it," Ralph says, "It's not easy for people to accept you for who you are. Am I right?"

"One day they will," Clyde says.

"But they don't now. Right?"

"So what?"

"So you shouldn't alienate someone who's ready to accept you *now*."

Clyde blinks at Ralph.

Ralph touches his arm. "At least accept my friendship, Marilyn. That's a start."

Clyde glances at Ralph's hand.

"It's not easy finding a friend in this insane town." Ralph squeezes Clyde's arm and smiles at him. "Let *me* be your friend."

Clyde searches Ralph's face, slowly lowering his guard as he takes in the intense gaze of the young man's dark blue eyes. "And what, in your playbook, do *friends* do?"

"Well, let's see…" Ralph looks around the boulevard. "I think new friends should seal their relationship over a cold beer or three." He points at a nearby club flying a rainbow flag with a lineup of Harley Davidsons parked outside and jogs toward it. "This place looks promising."

Clyde releases a breath and runs after him.

—m—

Clyde sits squeezed against a wall in a corner of the dimly lit, smoke-choked bar, which is jammed elbow-to-elbow with lesbian bikers dressed in leather and bristling with chains. He fidgets nervously and glances around at the crowd as it roils and undulates in time to deafening disco music.

A freckled, muscular woman with a pair of reflective aviator sunglasses pushed up onto her slicked-back auburn hair emerges from the jam and squeezes her way toward Clyde. She hops on a suddenly free stool opposite him and hungrily eyes him, reaching down to unbutton the top of her cut-off blue jean shirt to expose the cleavage of her enormous breasts. Clyde rolls his eyes and scans the crowd.

Ralph approaches with two sloshing mugs of beer in one hand and two brimming shot glasses in the other. He comes around to Clyde's side of the table, shoves away a pair of women engaged in a lip wrestling contest to make room for himself, and drops a mug in front of Clyde. The two women hardly notice the interruption and carry on tonguing each other. Ralph empties one of the shot glasses into Clyde's beer mug. Clyde sniffs at the concoction and pulls a face.

"Isn't this place great?" Ralph shouts over the music.

Clyde arches an eyebrow and glances around, unintentionally making eye contact with the muscular woman from earlier who winks at him. Clyde smiles weakly and winks back. He pulls a hand-painted silk fan out of his purse.

"It's got loads of atmosphere." Ralph knocks back a shot of tequila and chases it with some beer.

"Must be the second-hand smoke." Clyde fans himself vigorously.

"Maybe so." Ralph pulls a pack of Marlboros out of his backpack and taps out a cigarette. He lights it with what looks to Clyde like a diamond-encrusted silver lighter.

"So anyway"—Clyde stares at the lighter as Ralph snaps it shut and puts it back in his pocket—"what's a graduate film student doing working at a cheap little movie theatre anyway?"

Ralph grins and blows tiny smoke rings through big smoke rings. "Are you seriously asking me that?" He places his cigarette in an ashtray.

Clyde narrows his eyes at Ralph. "It's a fair question. Graduate school's expensive; poor people can't afford that. Punching tickets at some no-name movie theatre is a kid's job that probably doesn't pay much—and you're obviously not a young kid—or a seventy-something retiree with nothing to do, for that matter."

"I'm a sucker for old films. What can I say?"

"So am I. But I'd never work in a place like that." Clyde takes a sip from his mug and processes the heady mix of beer and tequila, trying to decide whether he likes it or not. "Besides, I would think you'd be too busy with working on film projects and stuff to be wasting your time with some stupid, mindless job."

Ralph shrugs and downs some beer. "We wouldn't have met if it weren't for that stupid, mindless job."

As the beer and tequila work their way to Clyde's head, he finds himself discreetly admiring Ralph's athletic build, his broad shoulders and muscular arms, the way his powerful-looking legs fill out his tight black jeans, how his straight white teeth flash in the black light. Sensing a mellowing of Clyde's mood, Ralph rests his thigh against Clyde's, and Clyde scoots into the warm pressure of the contact.

"Anyway, speaking of film projects"—Ralph lowers his head to Clyde's shoulder and speaks in a confidential tone—"I have an idea for one."

Clyde looks at him. "Do you really?"

"Can I pitch it to you?"

"You want to pitch a film project to me?" Clyde says.

"If that's OK."

"Knock yourself out."

"What if *you* were to meet another someone from back in the day, only now in 1982."

"Who, me?"

"Yes, you—Marilyn Monroe."

"What do you mean 'another someone'?"

"Another film star."

"Like who?"

"Like anyone, a guy. But someone dead."

"How can I meet someone dead?"

"Back from the dead, I mean. Like you."

Clyde shakes his head and takes a sip of his beer. "Sounds silly to me."

Ralph frowns and takes a drag on his cigarette. "Stay with me on this. Let's say that you and someone else really iconic—someone

who died young, like Sal Mineo or James Dean or Valentino—
what if you were to meet each other *now* in 1982."

"You mean like someone reincarnated?"

"Yeah, something like that. Personally, my vote would be for
James Dean. But you can pick whomever you want."

"I like James Dean, too."

"Great! So, imagine it: Marilyn Monroe and James Dean meet
in this life, and together they work out how to convince the world
of who they really are."

"OK …" Clyde says. "Then what happens?"

"I have no idea." Ralph grins and blows a long stream of
smoke at the ceiling. "That would be the fun bit of making
the film, playing it out and seeing how people react, like a
kind of semi-scripted documentary. You'd play yourself, of
course, and I'd play the part of the guy who thinks he's James
Dean come back from the dead. And I'd write, direct, and film
it all."

"Only I wouldn't be acting, of course. Because I *am* Marilyn. I
don't just think I am."

"Of course."

Clyde looks around at the crowd for a moment and looks back
at Ralph. "I'd have to talk about it with my people."

"Fine. But the way I see it, Marilyn, it's a win-win," Ralph says.
"It would give you a chance to convince the world of who you
really are—we'll have to work that bit out—and I'll have a fasci-
nating film project for my master's thesis."

Clyde stares at Ralph for a moment, then looks at his watch.
"I'll think about it and let you know. Right now, though, I've got
to get going. It's getting late."

"Rushing off again, eh?" Ralph sucks the last few drops of beer
from his mug, then turns it upside down and flashes an exaggerated pout at Clyde. "All gone."

They exit the bar and stand next to the long row of Harleys.
The air is full of dust from the hot Santa Ana winds that have

kicked up in the time they've been inside. Rubbish tumbles across the now-deserted pavement.

Clyde stares out at the boulevard. "Well, anyway...thanks." He shoulders his purse and smiles at Ralph. "I had a nice time, after all."

"No, thank *you*. I'm sure it was a great sacrifice for a celebrity of your standing."

"It was. But I had fun. Anyway... Bye, Jimmy." He runs a finger through the hairs on Ralph's arm. "I *may* call you Jimmy, right?"

"Why 'Jimmy'?"

"You know, James Dean...Jimmy Dean. It's nicer than that other name."

Ralph smiles. "Sure, why not?"

"Bye, Jimmy." Clyde kisses Ralph's cheek and moves away.

"Marilyn," Ralph says.

Clyde turns around.

"Where are you going?"

Clyde looks past Ralph for a moment and absently watches a new flow of patrons entering and exiting the club, then he looks back at Ralph and shrugs, feeling a lump rising in his throat. "I don't know."

Ralph approaches him. "Do you live around here?"

"I, uh... No, I don't." He looks around. "I guess I'm sort of..."

"I see." Ralph lightly touches Clyde's arm. "Look, why don't you stay at my place until—"

Clyde arches an eyebrow. "Is there room?"

"Sure, plenty of room. You can have your own bed and everything. I promise, no funny stuff. Strictly friends. And no pressures about the film."

"Well, yeah...it's not like I have a lot of choice in the matter. I mean, after all, who ever heard of Marilyn Monroe sleeping rough?"

"Exactly, good. Then, it's done." Ralph takes Clyde by the hand. "Come on, let's go." He leads him to a black Nissan 300ZX parked at the kerb next to an expired metre halfway up Wilcox. A parking citation pinned under one of the wipers flutters in the wind. Ralph snatches it off the windscreen, turns it into confetti, and tosses the pieces into the wind.

Clyde lets out a hoarse little scream. "What are you doing? Are you crazy? What if the owner sees you?"

Ralph pulls a set of keys out of his pocket and jangles them in front of Clyde's nose. "I *am* the owner."

—◊—

Clyde follows Ralph into a dimly lit, spacious, cluttered loft apartment with cathedral ceilings, brick walls, unpolished wood floors, and a mismatched collection of oriental rugs.

"Be right back." Ralph drops his backpack on a red velour ottoman and heads straight to a doorway at the far end of the room. "Make yourself at home," he says over his shoulder.

Clyde finds the dimmer switch on the wall and increases the lighting, then wanders around the apartment examining Ralph's collection of expensive gadgets, cameras and film equipment, musical instruments, state-of-the-art computers, and movie posters. A massive mirror mounted on a far wall catches Clyde's attention. He strolls toward it, passing what looks like a table shrine on top of which sits a single burning votive candle next to a silver-framed photograph of a sallow-skinned boy. Hanging on the wall above the shrine are two black-framed photographs, one of a swarthy young man in a dark green military uniform and one of a sombre-faced woman wearing a dark blue blouse, her black, kinky hair pinned into a bun.

Ralph walks back into the room carrying a couple of bottles of San Pellegrino.

"My God," Clyde says, disengaging from the table shrine, "this place is fantastic."

"Thanks." Ralphs sets the bottles on the coffee table. "Welcome to my sanctuary."

"Where did you get all this stuff?"

"As you can see, I'm no Robin Hood." He takes the beer mugs from the biker bar out of his backpack and finds a place for them on a shelf. Clyde lets out a gasp and stares at him in disbelief.

"You didn't *steal* this stuff, did you?"

"Not all of it; just most of it."

Clyde holds his purse tight against his chest.

"What?" Ralph says.

"Stealing's disgusting." Clyde looks around the room and shakes his head.

"Is it?"

"Don't tell me," Clyde says, "you grew up penniless and had to steal to survive. Boo hoo hoo. Poor little victim."

"Nope, that's not it at all." He takes a sip from one of the bottles and sets it down noisily on the table.

"So...you're what?" Clyde says. "Full-time student; part-time thief?"

"No, actually, I'm both a full-time student *and* a full-time thief. They're two of my lifelong obsessions, and I'm excellent at both."

Clyde snorts. "Are you really?"

"Yep."

"And all this time nobody's ever caught you?"

"Only once when I was a kid."

Clyde kicks Ralph's shin. "Only once, my ass. If you got caught, how excellent can you be?"

"The only reason I got caught *that time* was because I broke the cardinal rule of theft."

"You turned yourself in?"

"Ha ha. No; but just about. I stole something from people I knew."

"What kind of something?"

"Antique silver. Priceless stuff. By the time they figured out it was me, I'd already pawned it at some hole-in-the-wall shop downtown."

Clyde rolls his eyes. "Why are you even telling me all this? I'm a total stranger."

"Because you're my friend, and friends trust each other."

Clyde leans in and says in the breathy voice, "Jimmy?" He traces an infinity sign on Ralph's hairy arm. "I hope you won't be offended if I say I think you're full of ca-ca. You might trust me, but I sure as shit don't trust you. Even less now than before."

Ralph pulls back his arm. "You will one day, I hope."

"It's not likely." Clyde gazes into the electric blue of Ralph's eyes, which are still shining from the alcohol. "I haven't found anyone I could trust in twenty years. But you're welcome to try."

Clyde moves away from Ralph and drops into the sofa, exhausted from the day. Ralph sits next to him and kicks off his trainers.

"So you're a fucking thief…" Clyde echoes after a moment. "Just my luck."

"Yep." Ralph stretches deliciously and drapes his legs across Clyde's lap. "I also practice a bit of credit card fraud, some forgery, and occasionally I pass bad checks."

"Uh, huh…" Clyde pushes off Ralph's legs and stands. "Your family must be mighty proud of you."

"They don't know about it. Except for that time about the silver." He stares at the ceiling. "It was a big deal. Court, probation, even counselling."

"A lot of good *that* did you…" Clyde sits opposite Ralph in an alligator skin club chair.

"Yeah, tell me about it," Ralph says.

Clyde pulls out his fan and flips it open. "Why do you do it?"

"What, the stealing? It's an impulse. You know how some people *buy* things on impulse, right? They see something they like, and they buy it whether they can afford it or not. Other people eat on impulse. Other peoples are mean or sarcastic to the people they love on impulse."

Clyde nods.

"I steal on impulse whether I need what I'm taking or not. Simple as that."

"Don't you ever feel guilty?"

"At first I did. Each time I swore I'd never steal again. But I'd always end up doing it again anyway." He sits up. "I used to be religious; I hoped God would help me stop."

"But he didn't," Clyde whispers.

Ralphs spreads his hands at his collection of stolen objects and shrugs. "There is no God."

Clyde jumps to his feet. "How could you ever possibly know that? Even Einstein believed in God. Are you smarter than him?"

"I don't know. Maybe. Anyway, I don't feel guilty anymore. I wouldn't be able to live that way. I've purposely seared my conscience."

Clyde stares at Ralph and shakes his head. Then, as if heeding some unheard call, he disengages from the conversation and wanders away. Ralph studies him as he strolls aimlessly around the loft.

Circling back when he reaches a wall of books, Clyde cuts his eyes at something over Ralph's shoulder. Ralph turns to see what Clyde is looking at, and his heart jumps at the blur of Clyde speeding past him.

Clyde pulls up in front of the large mirror and reaches out a hand. Ralph approaches from behind and watches as Clyde giggles and strikes a few random poses, kicking up his leg and checking out his ass in the mirror. He concludes by blowing a kiss at his reflection and turning around, smiling playfully at Ralph.

"I think I like it here."

Ralph draws a deep breath and nods. "OK ... fine. As they say: '*Mi casa es su casa*'. Grab your purse. I'll show you where you'll be sleeping."

Clyde follows him across the main room toward a staircase leading up to the mezzanine.

"What's this?" Clyde asks as they pass the table with the photographs.

"That's my memorial shrine."

Clyde stops and passes his finger along the edge of the table. "Who are these people?"

"They're my victims." Ralph picks up the photograph of the young boy and stares at it. "People I hurt badly."

Clyde examines the photos on the wall.

"This is both a memorial to each of them and a reminder," Ralph says.

Clyde looks at Ralph. "A reminder of what?"

"To be careful with people, I guess." He shrugs and places the photo of the boy back on the table. "Stealing's one thing. Hurting people is another."

Clyde barks a short laugh.

"What's so funny?"

"I don't see a difference, sorry. When you steal something, you're hurting the owner and maybe other people too, especially if you steal something they cherish. That's the case regardless of whether you're Robin Hood or Jesse James."

Ralph blinks at Clyde. "I never made you out to be a moralist."

"You don't know me at all, Jimmy."

"Guess not."

"What if I were to turn you in?"

Ralph shrugs. "If you do, you do; I guess I'd deserve it. But I don't think you will."

Clyde shakes his head. "Anyway…" He inclines his head at the shrine. "Who are they exactly?"

"I'll tell you some other time when we know each other a little better." Ralph moves to the staircase. "Come on; it's getting late." He races upstairs.

Clyde trudges up the stairs to the mezzanine on which is positioned a king-size waterbed with a black-lacquered headboard, a matching chest of drawers, and a writing table. Ralph flips on the recessed lighting and nods at an illuminated opening in the back wall.

"You can sleep inside there. It's a kind of guest hutch. It should be comfortable enough."

Clyde drops to his knees in front of the hutch and peers inside. He sees a clean, dressed twin mattress that extends well into the wall and a couple of puffy pillows. A mixed media mural of shattered mirrors and pornographic images covers the walls and ceiling of the hutch. Clyde glances back at Ralph, who is unbuttoning his jeans.

"Inside here?"

"Yep, crawl in there when you're ready to hit the sack. Ignore the dirty pictures. They're courtesy of my last guest."

Ralph strips to his briefs and Clyde averts his eyes and looks back into the hutch. "Uh...I don't know. I might never fall asleep." He crawls inside the hutch, which is barely large enough for him to sit up without banging his head against the ceiling, and tests the mattress. "I'll try my best." He pokes his head out of the hutch, his eyes tightly shut. "Goodnight, Jimmy. Thank you." Then he pulls back inside. A few moments later his blouse flies out of the opening, followed by a brassiere and a pair of jeans.

Ralph dims the lights. He moves to a CD player and plays *Siegfried* at low volume. Clyde pokes his head out of the hutch again and watches as Ralph slips on a pair of tortoiseshell horn-rimmed glasses and sits at his writing desk. He reaches into the bottom drawer and pulls out a metal strongbox that he places on the desk. Then he extracts a notebook from the box and writes in it.

"What are you doing?" Clyde asks.

Ralph jumps, and the pen clatters out of his hand. "Jesus H Christ, you scared me." He retrieves the pen and looks over his shoulder at Clyde. "I'm starting work on the treatment for the film project we talked about."

"You were serious about that?"

Ralph swings around and faces Clyde. "Of course I was. I think it's a great idea. Don't you?"

"Maybe your treatment should be about stealing stuff instead. I once heard the best stuff to write about is the stuff you know best. You don't know anything about what it's like to be rein-carnated. But you obviously know *a lot* about being a thief. So maybe you should just make it about that and leave me out of it. I can find some other way of getting people to recognise me."

Ralph stares at Clyde, then lowers his gaze to the floor. After a moment, he looks up at Clyde. "What if I really *do* believe I'm James Dean reincarnated?"

Clyde narrows his eyes at Ralph. "Do you?"

Ralph shrugs. "It's possible, isn't it?"

Clyde sits up. "Everything is recycled; that's what I believe. Even people. So, yes, it's possible. But there has to be some evidence. You can't just wake up one day and say: 'Hey, I think I'm the reincarnation of James Dean'. That would be *crazy*."

Ralph scratches his head with his pen. "What sort of evidence?"

Clyde yawns and rubs his eyes. "I don't know, Jimmy. You'll have to work that out yourself."

Ralph nods and turns back to his writing.

"Jimmy?"

"Yes?"

"I didn't mean that I think you're crazy. I just think you're con-fused, you know, with the stealing and all that."

Ralph pulls a tight smile, his back still turned to Clyde. "Thank you."

"See you tomorrow, Jimmy."

"Yes. Goodnight."

Clyde crawls back into the hutch, and Ralph sits for a few moments staring at his notebook. Then he flips it shut and turns off the lights.

―⁓―

Clyde finds himself in a vast, black formless space. His face is plas-tered in white pancake and rouge, his hair is perfectly coifed, and he is dressed in a floor-length pink satin evening gown that hangs off his shoulders.

Suddenly, Ralph materialises from out of nowhere and strides up to within inches of his face. He rips off Clyde's evening gown with a single, violent tug, leaving him standing naked and trembling. Clyde raises his arms defensively, and Ralph vanishes.

A massive full-length mirror appears in the distance, and Clyde glides toward it, propelled by an internal force he is unable to resist. Marilyn's reflection greets him with a coy smile and a kiss that she blows at him. Clyde reaches out to touch the reflection. As his fingers touch the glass, it explodes, shattering into pieces. One of the shards flies into his eye.

—〰—

Ralph hears Clyde scream and sits bolt upright in bed. The scream is swallowed up by the night and is replaced by a deathly silence. Ralph waits expectantly in the darkness.

—〰—

An insistent knocking jars Clyde awake. He pries open his lids and finds himself staring at his bleary-eyed reflection in the mirrors that decorate the roof of the hutch. Letting out a groan, he rolls over on his side, pulling the sheet over his head.

"Good morning! Marilyn! Hello!"

Clyde pokes his sheet-shrouded head out of the hutch. "I forgot where I was for a second," comes his muffled voice.

Ralph lifts the sheet and smiles at him. "Hi."

"Good morning."

Clyde sits up and sees that Ralph is smartly dressed in a crisp white button shirt rolled up to his elbows, a pair of Levi 501s cuffed to show his bare ankles and a pair of brown Sperry boat shoes.

"I'm off to class. There's food in the fridge. Um, what else, what else…? Oh, yeah. Help yourself to the TV or the video player." He points at his nightstand. "There's the remote."

Clyde hugs his legs against his chest and watches Ralph gather his things and place them into his backpack. "What time will you be back?"

"Around three." Ralph puts his arms through the straps of his backpack. "OK?"

"Jimmy?"

"Yeah?"

"Thank you for everything."

"Sure thing, Marilyn." Ralph winks at Clyde and moves to the stairs.

—⁂—

Clyde approaches Ralph's writing table balancing a bowl of Fruit Loops and milk in his hand. He sets down the bowl and pulls the strongbox out of the bottom drawer. Finding it locked, he places it back inside. Then he strolls to the telephone on Ralph's nightstand and dials a number. Hearing his father answer, he listens for a beat and puts it down. He stares at the telephone for a moment and picks it up again, his finger hovering over the dial pad. Then he redials the number.

"It's me," Clyde says when his father answers.

After a moment of silence, his father says, "Stop calling here." Then the phone goes dead.

Clyde dials the number again.

"I said stop calling, God damn it!"

"Put Momma on the phone."

"We don't want to know anything about you. You're on your own now."

"You're not getting away with this; I hope you know that," Clyde says. "One of these days when you least expect it, I'll come looking for you, and you and I are going to have it out once and for all."

"I should feel threatened by a sissy, should I?"

"It's not a threat, Yoshi. It's a promise. And when Marilyn makes a promise, you'd better damned well know she keeps it."

"I'm shaking in my boots."

"Take care of Momma," Clyde says after a moment. Then he puts down the phone and curls up on Ralph's bed to decompress from the pent-up emotion provoked by the telephone call, clearing his mind of everything and focusing on a single point of light in the middle of his head.

Namu Myōhō Renge Kyō
Namu Myōhō Renge Kyō
Namu Myōhō Renge Kyō

Once his heart rate has returned to normal, he sits up and looks around the room. He spots Ralph's stereo and tunes it to a rock music station, then dances over to Ralph's dresser and rifles through the drawers.

His fingers make hard contact with a photo album hidden under a stack of white T-shirts in the bottom drawer. He takes it to Ralph's bed and pages through it, and his breath catches at the sight of a younger Ralph wearing sidelocks and a skull cap. He brings the album closer and goes more slowly through the pages, which portray a life of affluence, including trips abroad, mansions, maids, sports cars.

Toward the back of the album, he finds a large photo of Ralph in a military uniform and peers at it for several seconds. There is something strangely familiar about Ralph's expression. Devilish smile, soulful eyes, a lock of wavy hair hanging over one eye. He flips to the front of the album and regurgitates his Fruit Loops in a shock of recognition at the sight of young Ralph in a family portrait standing next to a tall man with a smartly trimmed black beard and kind blue eyes. He is instantly transported to that afternoon in Doctor Menner's clinic in Beverly Hills when the handsome Jewish boy and his father stepped out of Doctor Menner's office, and the boy snapped a picture of him. Ralph was that boy.

Clyde pushes the album away and stares at it, swallowing hard, wrapping his arms around himself in a protective self-hug, his mind a jumble. He wonders whether Ralph remembers him and as quickly dismisses the thought. It's been too many years. Both of them have changed so much, especially him. Then again, it seems too much of a coincidence that their paths would have crossed again now that he is back in treatment with Doctor Menner. Or maybe not. And what was Ralph doing at Doctor Menner's anyway? Clyde pitches forward and passes his fingers over the album, tempted to open it again. Then he shakes his head and hefts it onto the nightstand. Feeling the need to reset the chaotic tangle of thoughts and emotions coursing through his mind, he snatches up the remote control and points it at the TV.

He flips through the channels and finds a colourised version of *Whatever Happened to Baby Jane* airing on Channel 5. Fluffing up the pillows, he makes himself comfortable and settles into watching a movie he's seen countless times, so many times, in fact, he can recite all the lines from memory. Right at the part where Baby Jane serves her wheelchair-bound sister Blanche a dead rat for lunch, the bit where Blanche screeches in horror and Baby Jane giggles in her bedroom, Clyde gasps and clasps a hand over his mouth to suppress a scream. He crawls forward to the foot of the bed and studies Blanche as if for the first time, having always paid more attention to Baby Jane than to her boring sister. Caterpillar thick eyebrows, pinned up mousy hair, eternally tortured expression, and ... wheelchair ... wheelchair ... wheelchair.

His head pivots from the TV to the photo album on the nightstand, which he blinks at for a beat before creeping toward it and flipping it open. Turning once again to the family portrait, he removes it from the protective plastic and examines it, paying close attention to the other people in the photo: a pretty young woman with a toothy smile standing next to Ralph that Clyde reckons is his sister, and a thin woman with her hair pinned up in a tight bun—sitting in a *wheelchair*. He peers at the woman and feels his heart racing. She is staring off to one side with half-closed eyes, her hands clasped tightly on her blanket-covered lap.

Clyde narrows his eyes at the photo and traces a line with his finger from the wheelchair-bound woman to Ralph and pauses for a moment. Then he leaps out of bed and races downstairs with the photo in his hand. He dashes up to the table shrine and compares the woman in the family portrait with the one on the wall above the shrine. It's the same woman, only much younger, with a full face and intense dark eyes, and her hair pinned up the same way.

—※—

Ralph arrives home in the afternoon and finds Clyde sitting on the bed watching TV, dressed in a transparent, pink nightgown. Clyde smiles when he sees him.

"Am I glad you're home!" Clyde scoots to one side and taps the bed.

Ralph sets his backpack on his writing desk, noting that the bottom drawer is slightly open. "I was afraid you wouldn't be here," he says.

Clyde slaps the bed. "Sit here and watch *Sacred Places* with me."

Ralphs kicks off his shoes and sits next to Clyde, who nuzzles up to him and rests his head on his shoulders.

"It's a show about people who get in touch with God by making pilgrimages to the holy places in their religions. You know, Muslims go to Mecca, Hindus bathe in the Ganges, Catholics go to Rome, Jews pray toward—"

"I don't believe in God."

"Don't be silly, Jimmy. Don't you see?" He shakes his finger at the TV. "It's obvious those people tap into some kind of higher power at those places."

"So what?"

"So, I was thinking, *we* should go to *our* sacred places. We should make pilgrimages to the places that were important to me in my past life and to the places that are important to you, whatever they are. Maybe that way we can get empowered."

Ralph tries to read Clyde's face but finds it difficult to see past the plastered-on smile and heavy makeup.

"That's not a half-bad idea," Ralph says. "I can incorporate it into the treatment I'm writing."

"Not for your film, silly. I mean it's something we should do *anyway*. To empower ourselves, to make ourselves better people, you know. To make us stronger to deal with the stuff we might need to take care of."

"Like what kind of stuff exactly?"

Clyde shrugs. "Any stuff. Personal stuff."

"Right," Ralph says. "Well, I still think it would work nicely with my film idea. We'll go to the Marilyn places and to the James Dean places and film our reactions, and anything else that happens while we're there."

"What'll that do?"

"I don't know. We'll see. It might be a load of crap. Or it might be fantastic. At any rate, it can't hurt. And it might even be fun, especially for you. You haven't been in front of a camera for a while."

Clyde stretches out on the bed and closes his eyes. "I'm not looking to be in front of a camera, Jimmy. I'm retired now."

Ralph stretches out next to him. "Please, Marilyn, it'll be perfect, you and I can experience our…'sacred places' together like you want. And I'll record it all. I'll even use a compact video camera to be as unobtrusive as possible. You'll get what you want, and I'll get what I want."

Clyde turns on his side and notices that Ralph's eyes are moist. "What's wrong?" Clyde asks.

"Nothing." Ralph tugs at Clyde's nightgown. "Where'd you get this?"

Clyde swats his hand away. "I bought it, silly. Now about our trip..."

"We can leave tomorrow morning," Ralph says.

Clyde squeals and throws his arms around Ralph, giving him a peck on the cheek. Ralph kisses Clyde on the forehead.

—◊◊◊—

Ralph and Clyde screech to a stop in Ralph's 300ZX in front of a car dealership at Hollywood and Vine displaying a collection of exotic and vintage automobiles. They exit Ralph's illegally parked car, and Ralph pulls Clyde along by the hand leading him straight to a silver Porsche Spyder 500 convertible with the words *Little Bastard #130* stencilled on the hood. He pulls his video camera out of his pack and walks around the car taping it, then he points the camera at Clyde.

"What do you think?" Ralph asks.

Clyde shields his face with his hand and glances sidelong at Ralph.

"What do you think?" Ralph repeats.

Clyde lets out a loud breath and drops his hand. "This is the one?"

"Not the *actual* one. It's a replica. But this is the place where he actually bought it."

Clyde walks around the car and Ralph follows him with the camera. "Kinda small, isn't it?" Clyde says.

"Size is important to you?"

Clyde curls his lip and runs a finger along the side of the Porsche. "It's nice, for a sports car." He opens the passenger door and slips inside. "What happened to the original?"

"Are you kidding me?" Ralph hands the camera to Clyde, who points it at Ralph the way he showed him earlier. Ralph hops into the driver's seat. "It was smashed to bits." He grins at the camera. "I think it's beautiful. One day I'm going to own one of these."

"I'm surprised you haven't stolen it."

The smile disappears from Ralph's face. He takes the camera from Clyde and switches it off.

A middle-aged saleswoman with a blonde crew cut, man's suit, and black leather orthopaedic shoes strolls up to them and clears her throat.

"Don't think it hasn't crossed my mind a few times," Ralph whispers.

"Back again?" the saleswoman says, holding her clipboard over her chest. She scans across Ralph and arches her eyebrow at Clyde.

Ralph switches the camera back on and points it at her.

Clyde holds out the palm of his hand at the woman. "Do you mind leaving us alone, sir? We're trying to get empowered."

—◊◊—

Ralph and Clyde drive into the entrance of the Pierce Brothers Memorial Park in Westwood and roar around the circular drive toward a complex of lonely buildings at the far end. A moment later they are standing in front of Marilyn Monroe's burial crypt with their heads bowed. Ralph reaches for the video camera as Clyde digs a couple of candles out of his purse and glowers at him.

"Will you put that thing away already?"

He waits while Ralph sheepishly stores the camera, then shoves one of the candles at Ralph, who fires it up with his fancy lighter. Taking Ralph by the hand, Clyde pulls him to his knees, where they remain with their heads bowed. After several minutes, Ralph glances at Clyde and sees that his eyes are shut tight, and his lips are moving.

"How do you feel?" Ralph asks.

"Shhh, don't speak." Clyde holds up his hand. "This is hallowed ground."

"Are you feeling empowered yet?" Ralph asks as they walk back to the car, his camera now out and trained on Clyde.

"Each time I come here it's like a true religious experience."

Clyde brushes the passenger door with his fingertips and looks back over his shoulder at the crypt, his face clouding over. Ralph moves in for a close-up and notices tears standing out in Clyde's eyes.

"Did it feel like you were visiting your own grave?"

Clyde whirls on Ralph. "Of course it did. What the hell kind of question is that?" He gets into the car and slams the door shut and holds his purse tight against his chest.

Ralph climbs into the driver's seat and touches Clyde's shoulder. "Steady there, Marilyn. I'm interested in what's going through your head, that's all."

"This is all a game to you, isn't it, Mr Fake James Dean?" Clyde says. "Well, it's not to me. This is my life." Clyde reaches over and switches off the camera. "And don't you have any respect for the dead?"

"Of course, I do," Ralph snaps, setting aside the camera. "What kind of a question is *that?*"

Clyde jumps out of the car and pitches his purse at Ralph's head full force. "I've never met anyone as selfish as you in my whole damned life," he screams. "Stealing people's shit wasn't good enough for you, was it? Now you're trying to steal someone's soul." Clyde runs down the drive toward the exit.

Ralph sprints past him and blocks his way, holding out his hands at Clyde.

"I'm sorry, OK?"

Clyde punches him in the chest and pushes past him.

"Will you calm down, please!" Ralph shouts. "I thought we were making a movie. Isn't that what we agreed? Sacred places and all that? Or am I crazy?"

Clyde halts and stares at the passing traffic outside the gates of the cemetery, his eyes red and swollen, his mascara bleeding down his cheeks. Ralph approaches and hands him his purse.

"I don't like it that way," Clyde says after a moment.

"What way?"

"The way you pull out your camera like that anywhere, anytime, no warning, and asking whatever comes to your head. That's pretty shitty if you ask me."

"It's a style of filming, that's all. Like a documentary. I didn't mean anything bad by it."

"Well, I don't like it. If you want to write a proper script and run it past me in advance so I agree with everything you're going to do, that's fine. The way the big boys do it. But I'm not going to agree to be your plaything."

"OK, fine. I agree. I'll write a proper script."

"And you'll put the camera away for now?"

"No more camera for now. I promise."

Ralph holds out his hand, and Clyde stares at it, then looks back up at Ralph, who flashes a sad smile at him.

"Friends again?" Ralph says.

They walk back to the car holding hands and sit inside, neither of them saying a word. The air is heavy with humidity rising from the heavily irrigated lawn of the memorial park. The faraway sound of traffic mixes with the sound of summer crickets and the occasional chirping of a bird. Clyde pulls up his legs on the seat and rests his head on Ralph's shoulder, who stares pensively at the headstones. They sit quietly that way for a while, then Ralph pitches forward and turns the key in the ignition. He circles out of the cemetery, makes a right onto Wilshire Boulevard, and drives for a couple of miles before turning left onto Santa Monica Boulevard and speeding toward Hollywood.

Clyde raises his head. "Where are we going, Jimmy?"

Ralph holds up his hand. "Give me a moment, please."

Clyde sits up and frowns at Ralph.

A few minutes later, Ralph turns into the drive of Holly-wood Cemetery and circles around the park to an inner gate. At a security kiosk, Ralph exchanges a few words with the guard, then drives forward, shepherding his car along the meandering drive among the graves and parks kerbside at the far end of the cemetery.

"What are we doing here?" Clyde asks.

Ralph hops out of the car and strolls across the damp grass, and Clyde follows close behind. Ralph stops in front of a grave and pulls a black velvet skullcap out of his back pocket. Placing it on his head, he closes his eyes for a few moments, then reaches into his pocket again and pulls out a small stone, which he places on the grave next to several other pebbles of various sizes. Clyde looks past Ralph, trying to make out the words on the headstone as Ralph traces them with his fingers. After a moment Ralph steps back and chants something in another language. When he finishes, Clyde moves forward and takes his hand.

"Who's buried here, Jimmy?"

"My mother."

"The lady in the wheelchair?"

Ralph lets go of Clyde's hand and stares at him.

"I peeked at your photo album, sorry."

Ralph looks back at the headstone. "I'd prefer it if you didn't touch my stuff without my permission."

"OK." Clyde brushes Ralph's hand with his fingers. "I'm sorry, Jimmy."

Ralph nods and walks back to the car, stuffing the skullcap into his back pocket and lighting a cigarette. Clyde catches up to him, and they walk the rest of the way holding hands.

"What happened to her, Jimmy?" Clyde asks once they're back inside.

"I was a bad son. I made her sick, and she died." Ralph turns the key in the ignition and the 300ZX roars to life. "I have that effect on people. So be careful with me."

Clyde's heart races at the wild look in Ralph's eye as he guns the engine, making the tyres squeal on the tarmac.

"Where to next, Marilyn?" Ralph shouts.

Clyde shrugs. "It's your turn now." He fastens his seat belt and grabs hold of the safety strap.

Ralph peels out of the cemetery and drives north on the Hollywood Freeway. He opens it up when they reach the Grapevine, climbing the hills at high speed, then screams over the Tejon Pass and assaults the perilous grade in the direction of the valley below, eyes wide, nostrils flaring, his knuckles white on the steering wheel and stick shift.

"Now I'm feeling empowered!" he shouts.

"Slow down, will you? I'm fucking shitting my panties here."

"No way, baby. We're travelling James Dean's Via Dolorosa now, just the way he did."

The wail of a siren breaks through the roar of the engine. Clyde spins around and sees a chippie speeding toward them with red lights flashing.

"Great." Clyde punches Ralph in the arm. "Now you're going to get a ticket."

Ralph pulls onto the shoulder, and the chippie swoops in behind.

"It's perfect," Ralph says. "Exactly as it happened forty years ago." He slips on a pair of Wayfarers and stares straight ahead.

The fresh-faced, ginger chippie steps to the driver's side, his hand dancing on his holster.

"What's your hurry?"

"He's travelling James Dean's Via Dolorosa, officer." Clyde pulls a compact out of his purse and freshens up his lipstick.

The chippie scratches his head.

"Please remove the sunglasses, sir. I'll need your driver's licence."

Ralph claws the Wayfarers off his face and tosses them aside, then hands his driver's licence to the chippie.

"I clocked you at ninety miles an hour, sir. You planning on getting yourself killed like him too?" The chippie writes a ticket.

Ralph laughs. "I want to go out with a bang, officer."

"Yeah?" He points his pen at Clyde. "How about her? Or him? Are you planning on going out with a bang too, sir?"

Clyde snaps shut the compact. "Lay off, will you? Just give him the damned ticket."

After the chippie speeds away, Ralph shepherds the car back onto the highway and drives the rest of the way down the Grapevine taking care to keep within the speed limit.

"It wasn't supposed to happen like that." He tunes the stereo to a classical music station. "He wasn't supposed to actually give me a ticket."

"Get over it already, Jimmy." Clyde closes his eyes. "I'm tired."

Ralph turns off the main highway and drives a few miles, bringing the car to a stop at a bend in the road. Clyde sits up and sees an open field where several vintage automobiles from the 1950s are parked. A group of around a dozen people hover over a plaque under a tree. Ralph and Clyde get out of the car and join them. As the group thins out, Clyde steps up to the plaque and sees that it identifies the spot where James Dean was killed.

Clyde takes Ralph's hand. "How did it happen?" he whispers.

"They're not exactly sure." Ralph leads him away from the crowd. "Some say he took that bend there at around ninety miles per hour, spun out of control, and hit that tree. But I think he came around the bend at more like forty miles an hour. When he reached this spot here, there was a tractor in the road. He swerved to avoid hitting it. That's how he lost control. The car flipped over into this field. He was killed instantly. The impact practically decapitated him."

Clyde's head snaps around. "How do you know all that?"

"I can feel it." Ralph looks back at the tree. "Just now. It's as if I was there, watching it as it happened. From *inside* his car." He lets go of Clyde's hand and dries it on his jeans. "That's evidence, isn't it?"

—⁓—

Ralph and Clyde pull up to a low-slung brick hospital building and hop out of the car.

"So this is it, eh?" Ralph looks at the patients and hospital staff flowing in and out of the building.

"This is where it all ended," Clyde says, "…and where it all began."

"Was it murder or suicide?"

"Suicide."

"August 5, 1962, just after midnight…" Ralph says. "Right?"

Clyde nods. "All things are recycled."

They step into the hospital and stroll past the receptionist toward the cafeteria.

"So, when you were pronounced dead," Ralph says as they stroll hand-in-hand toward the cafeteria, "your soul transmigrated—that's the term, isn't it?—into the body of…what was his name?"

Clyde pulls up short and frowns at Ralph.

"Well, he had to have a name, didn't he?"

"Oh, Jimmy…" Clyde reclines against one of the pasty blue walls, his eyes moist with emotion. "All of a sudden I feel sad."

Ralph squeezes his arm.

"What are you doing?" Clyde shakes his head.

"I won't hurt you, Marilyn, I promise."

"Yes, you will. You told me to be careful; you have victims." Clyde looks into Ralph's eyes. "Those people on your wall. Those two boys. Even your own mother."

Ralph pulls Clyde close, wrapping his arms around him and holding him tight. Clyde rests his head on Ralph's chest. The freshly laundered scent of his clothes reminds him of Kevin.

"I've never—" Clyde closes his eyes and takes a deep breath.

"It's OK, Marilyn. Don't worry about it."

"His name was Clyde," Clyde whispers.

"Clyde..."

"Please, don't."

"I just—"

"No, please... Let's be quiet for a while, Jimmy."

They hold each other as hospital staff and visitors move past them in waves. But Clyde doesn't notice them. He feels as if time has come to a standstill. He feels Ralph's breath on his head, steady and warm. At first. Then it becomes shallower. Clyde feels Ralph's body trembling and holds him tighter, feeling suddenly protective, but not wanting to look directly at him. After a few minutes, they disengage from each other. Clyde straightens his hair, and Ralph wipes his eyes on his sleeve.

"Sorry," Ralph says. "I don't know what came over me."

"It's all right, Jimmy." Clyde touches up his makeup.

"It hasn't been an easy day."

"No, but I think we accomplished what we set out to do." Clyde kisses Ralph on the cheek. "We should feel empowered, right?"

Ralph brings his fingers to his face. He feels the moist spot where Clyde's lips were a moment before. "What do you say to our wrapping up the day with a nice dinner?"

Clyde smiles. "That sounds nice, Jimmy." He shoulders his purse and takes Ralph's hand. Taking one last look at the hospital corridor as they reach the entrance, they step out into the waning sunlight.

—⚉—

A belly dancer undulates and twirls to the climax of *Alf Leyla wa Leyla* and the diners erupt into cheers. She bows with a dramatic flourish and withdraws from the stage as the orchestra and singers finish off the piece before taking a break. Recorded music takes over and plays softly over the clink of glasses and cutlery on ceramic and the murmur of conversation.

Clyde and Ralph finish off their second bottle of red wine, with Clyde having had the greater part.

"So, what do you think?" Ralph asks, shaking the bottle to dislodge the last few drops into Clyde's glass. "Do you feel empowered now?"

Clyde laughs and drains the glass. "Not really, no. I feel drunk."

Ralph waves a white-robed waiter with a red fez over to the table and speaks to him in a foreign language. The waiter clicks his slippered heels and slides away.

Clyde sets down the glass and stares at Ralph. "You speak Moroccan too?"

"It's Arabic, not Moroccan," Ralph says. "And, yes, I speak it fluently, along with Hebrew, French, and Spanish."

"Oooh, you're Arabian? Like Rudolph Valentino in *The Sheik*?"

The waiter returns with a new bottle and pours Clyde and Ralph another glass.

"I'm Israeli," Ralph says as the waiter moves away from the table. "My grandparents were from Syria. They spoke Arabic between themselves; I picked it up from them when I was growing up and also on the streets in Jerusalem."

"You're Israeli, really? But your English is perfect."

"I've been here a long time."

"I know," Clyde says. "I saw you before."

Ralph sets down the glass. "What do you mean?"

"I saw you in Doctor Menner's office when I was eleven. You were there with your father. The tall man in your picture album. You were dressed all in black, and you were wearing a round black hat. The kind they wear in England."

Ralph blinks at Clyde and shakes his head slightly.

"I remember you raised your eyebrows at me like Groucho Marx."

Ralph narrow his eyes and stares into the middle distance conjuring up a memory. "You were sitting on a sofa in the waiting room?"

"Yes, it was just for a second. You took a picture of me. And then you and your father walked out."

Ralph slaps the cushion next to him. "Yes, I remember now."

"What a strange coincidence, don't you think?" Clyde says. "It's, like, destiny."

Ralph slams back half a glass of wine in one gulp, then lights a cigarette and takes a long drag on it.

"What's wrong, Jimmy?"

"You were seeing that asshole?"

"Who, Doctor Menner?"

"Yeah."

"It was for my juvenile probation, for getting into a fight. The court sent me to see him. It's a long story. Why?"

"Did he ever put you under hypnosis?"

"Not back then. What's this about, Jimmy?"

Ralph pitches forward. "What do you mean, not back then?"

Clyde shakes his head.

"Tell me," Ralph says.

Clyde's eyes fill with tears, and he dabs at them with his napkin.

"OK, fine." Ralph leans back against the cushions. "We'll talk about *him* later."

"Thank you, Jimmy."

Ralph snaps his finger at the passing waiter and barks something at him in Arabic, then he turns back to Clyde. "Let's talk about *you*, shall we?"

"I'll tell you anything." Clyde takes a sip of wine, then puts the glass back on the table and pushes it away.

"Tell me about the person who was born at the same time Marilyn died. Tell me about Clyde. That cute kid who was sitting in the waiting room all those years ago."

Clyde stares open-mouthed at Ralph for a moment and shakes his head emphatically.

"Don't you trust me yet?"

"There's nothing to tell."

"Listen, I know that you're the reincarnation of Marilyn Monroe. I have no doubt about that. So get over it already. You have absolutely nothing to prove to me on that front."

"Well, then—"

"But today, *in this life*, you're not *just* Marilyn. Today you're Clyde layered on top of Marilyn. And in your next life you'll be Suzie, or whomever, layered on top of Clyde, layered on top of Marilyn. Like a *tel*."

"Like a fuck *what*? What are you babbling on about?"

"Think about it. It's only logical." Ralph rests his hand on Clyde's thigh. "You've had experiences Marilyn Monroe *never* had."

"Name one."

"Well…" Ralph moves his hand up Clyde's leg. "Your dick, for instance. Marilyn never had a dick."

Clyde stands and accidentally knocks over the bottle, sending wine spilling everywhere. "How dare you? How dare you speak to me like that?"

The waiter rushes forward to clean up the spill. Clyde rescues his purse and backs away from Ralph. The other patrons murmur among themselves at the scene Clyde is making.

"What gives you the right?" Clyde screams.

"Listen to me." Ralph reaches for Clyde, who slaps away his hand. "Will you calm down for a second and listen to me?" He nods toward the crowd and points at the cushion.

Clyde looks around at the other patrons and sees them gaping at him, then drops back onto his cushion and whisper-screams at Ralph, "What do you want from me, huh? Now that you've got me good and drunk, you want to strip me naked right here in front of the whole world. What do you want me to tell you? That I'm a second generation Japanese-American faggot from Pasadena, whose father is an alcoholic child abuser and whose mother runs a dress shop in the barrio? Is that what you want to hear? Are you satisfied now?"

Clyde's lips quiver, his eyes bloodshot and full of tears.

"I'm sorry. I didn't mean—"

"Real glamorous, isn't it?" Clyde wipes his face with a cloth napkin, leaving tracks of mascara on his face and smearing his lipstick.

"I'm sorry."

"You know…I just realised something." Clyde stares unfocussed across the restaurant. "I've never been happy. Not for one moment in my entire life. Can you imagine that?" He lowers his head to the table and quietly weeps.

Ralph places his hand on Clyde's back.

"God," Clyde says through his tears, "I'm so messed up."

"We're all messed up, in one way or another. Every one of us. Damaged goods."

Clyde sits up and draws a deep breath. "Sometimes I wonder if I'd be happier if I had it cut off."

"Had what cut off?"

"My dick. Maybe then it would be easier for people to believe me when I tell them who I really am."

—⟪—

Ralph and Clyde finish making love on Ralph's waterbed. They separate, and Clyde rests his head on Ralph's chest. The hypnotic sounds of Pink Floyd's *Dark Side of the Moon* play in the background.

"Fuck, that was good," Ralph says. He reaches into a drawer of his nightstand and pulls out a joint. "Where'd you learn to move like that?"

"This girl's been around the block a few times." Clyde traces an infinity sign in the hairs on Ralph's chest.

Ralph smirks, then takes a long hit on the joint and holds it in. He offers it to Clyde, who pulls a face and lays back on his pillow.

Ralph shrugs and lets out the smoke, blowing a half-dozen little rings. "We're both empowered now," he says.

"I only feel empowered on the inside." Clyde pokes at one of the rings with his finger.

Ralph laughs. "Well, I should *hope* so."

Clyde fake-smacks Ralph's stomach. "I don't mean that. I'm talking about my soul versus my body."

Ralph blows another of series rings. "What's that supposed to mean?"

"That I'm still unfinished on the outside in a cosmetic sort of way, if you get what I mean." He pulls the sheet up between his legs and hides his penis. "There's more work to do."

"Right." Ralph extinguishes the joint and places it in an ashtray on the nightstand. "You're going to discover the true you through self-mutilation."

"It's not self-mutilation, Jimmy." Clyde sits up. "I wouldn't be taking a knife to myself. That's the surgeon's job."

"Well, if my opinion matters at all"—Ralph peels back the sheet and uncovers Clyde's penis—"I think you're beautiful the way you are."

Clyde pushes his penis between his legs. "Wouldn't you prefer it if I was all woman?"

"Not at all. Actually, I was considering how we might make use of it next time." He winks at Clyde, who slaps him again, this time a bit harder. "But if that's what you want, I won't stop you."

He draws Clyde to his chest, and they kiss deeply.

—⁓—

Ralph sits at his desk writing in his notebook. Clyde watches from under the covers as he flips it shut, places it into the strongbox, and locks it away in the bottom drawer.

"Jimmy…?"

Ralph looks over his shoulder at Clyde, his eyes dull and expressionless. "You're still awake?"

"I've been watching you write for the past hour."

"I thought you'd gone to sleep."

Clyde wraps the sheet around himself and shuffles up to Ralph. "What are you writing?" His fingers dance on Ralph's bare shoulder.

"I'm working on the script. For our movie. Like you asked for."

"Why do you keep it locked in that box?"

Ralph pulls Clyde onto his lap. "Because my whole degree depends on it. I don't want it to get lost or damaged before it's finished."

"Can I read it?"

"Once I've finished the first draft. Any feedback at this stage will kill the inspiration."

"But if I don't like where you're going with it, isn't it better if you know that now?"

"If you don't like it, I can always change it or chuck it. They're only words. Let me worry about that. If any ideas come to your mind, let me know. Or you can write them down if I'm not around. I might be able to work them into the story. Deal?"

Clyde looks doubtfully at Ralph then gazes over his shoulder at the stairs leading to the ground floor and lets out a loud sigh.

"Now..." Ralph caresses Clyde's shoulder.

Clyde pulls back and cocks his head at Ralph. "Now what?"

"Is it OK if we talk about why you were seeing Doctor Menner? Sorry to ask; but it's sort of important to me."

Clyde passes his hands over his knees a few times and closes his eyes. "It hurts to talk about it, Jimmy." He brings his hand to his chest. "Right here. You have no idea. It should be ancient history, but it isn't."

Ralph hugs Clyde and kisses his neck. "You're safe with me, Marilyn."

Clyde nods.

"You trust me, right?"

"It's too soon for trust, Jimmy. But I'll do my best."

"That's all I ask. No pressures."

Clyde stares over Ralph's shoulder into a dark corner of the loft, conjuring up the past. "Clyde had a brother," he whispers. "His name was Hiro. He died before Clyde was born. He developed a psychotic disorder when he was young and died in a hospital in Norwalk. From an accident, they said."

"I'm sorry," Ralph says.

Clyde holds up his hand at the interruption. "When Clyde was born, his parents made him sleep in Hiro's bedroom. They wouldn't let him change anything in there."

Ralph reaches into his pencil drawer and fishes a fresh joint out of a plastic sandwich bag. Clyde watches as Ralph lights it up and takes a drag on it.

"I told you it was a long story."

Ralph releases the smoke. "Don't worry about me; I'm all ears." He offers the joint to Clyde, who crinkles his nose at it and shifts into another chair before continuing.

"There's a lot that happened to Clyde when he was young that he couldn't remember. He learned to block things in his mind, I guess. Bad stuff mainly. But one day the blockers came off and everything that happened before flooded his mind. That's the day he finally realised that his father had hurt him when he was little. I can't even repeat what he did. But it was bad. What's worse was that Clyde's father covered up by saying that I…by saying that something was wrong with Clyde…that he was carrying the insane spirit of his brother Hiro inside him."

Ralph shakes his head. "Sounds like a real *mensch*."

"Anyway," Clyde says, "fast forwarding to the part about Doctor Menner. Clyde got into trouble for cracking a classmate on the head with a rock."

Ralph coughs and splutters, then crushes out his joint in an ashtray. "Say what?"

"I know, I know, it sounds crazy," Clyde says. "But the point is the Juvenile Court judge sent Clyde to Doctor Menner for an assessment, which happened to take place on the same day you were there."

Ralph narrows his eyes for a moment as if seeing through Clyde. "There were other people in the waiting room with you..." he says, his voice barely audible.

"Those were Clyde's parents. They were meant to be part of the assessment. But Clyde went into the room alone first and took the opportunity to finally tell someone—*Doctor Menner*—what his father had done to him all those years before. That led to Clyde's father being arrested and put in prison."

"Thank God for that," Ralph says. "If anyone deserves to have his dick cut off it's that guy, if you don't mind my saying so."

Clyde nods. "He's out now. He's the reason I'm homeless. Prison made him meaner."

Ralph looks up at Clyde. "Hold that thought, OK? Back to Doctor Menner for a second. You said he didn't put you under hypnosis back then."

"Clyde only saw him that one time for the assessment, then the court sent him to a child psychologist closer to home for regular therapy."

Ralph touches Clyde's knee with his index finger, letting it linger there for a moment. "Can we try something, please? Just to make things a bit easier for me to follow this."

Clyde nods.

"Do you think you might substitute the pronoun 'I' for the name 'Clyde'? For this story only. Then we can go back to the other."

Clyde closes his eyes and sits still for a few seconds, causing Ralph to think he may have dozed off. But then he nods his head.

"So when *did* Menner put you under hypnosis."

"Recently, right before you and I met."

"You mean you're seeing him now?"

Clyde stands and stretches his legs, then drops face down on Ralph's waterbed and bobs around on the waves. "I got in trouble again, and the court sent me to Doctor Menner for therapy as part of my probation. One-on-one sessions and some group shit. He uses hypnosis during the one-on-ones."

"Does he still use a prism to induce hypnosis?"

Clyde sits up. "Sometimes it's a prism; sometimes he makes me focus on the tip of a felt pen."

"The bastard."

"Don't call him that. Doctor Menner's a nice man."

Ralph sneers and lights up the joint again. "Nice man my ass. He's a certifiable pervert. He used to feel me up when I was under hypnosis; it went on for weeks. I can't believe he's still out there getting away with it."

"Doctor Menner is not a pervert. He's never laid a finger on *me*."

"How would you know what he's doing if you're under hypnosis?"

"How would *you* know?"

"Because the hypnosis didn't work for me."

"You mean you were conscious the whole time?"

"Yep, that's right."

"So then you were *letting* him feel you up."

Ralph blinks. "I—"

"If it went on for weeks, and you were fully conscious, why didn't you stop him?"

"I *did* stop him. That time I saw you there; that's the day I stopped it." Ralph pulls out his strongbox and digs around in it, then hands Clyde a few faded photos from his sessions with Doctor Menner. "That's the proof."

Clyde shuffles through the photographs. "How did you get these?"

"I had a secret camera in my book bag."

Clyde's head jerks up, and he casts about the room.

"What are you doing?"

"Do you have a secret camera in here?"

"What? No!"

"Are you sure? Maybe you were taking pictures of us when we were having sex. It wouldn't surprise me, the way you videotape everything."

"Hey! I told you I was making a movie."

"Movie, shmoovie. There's something wrong with you, Jimmy." Clyde shoves the photographs back at Ralph. "Did you at least report him to the police?"

Ralph puts the photographs back into the strongbox and shakes his head, a dark expression clouding his face.

"Why not? And why were you seeing Doctor Menner anyway?"

"It was for a court-ordered assessment too, at first. For the time I got caught stealing the silver. When Menner reported back that I was suffering from some kind of OCD-related kleptomania, the judge ordered long-term therapy that was meant to continue until Menner reported improvement in the condition. Three years on, I wasn't getting any better, and there was no end in sight. So when I discovered what he was doing to me, I used the pictures to get him to release me from therapy."

"You mean you blackmailed him."

Ralph stands and steps back into the shadows. "Why are you taking that tone with me? I'm the victim here. I was only a kid; he was my therapist. There's no excuse for what he did."

"No, there's not. But there's also no excuse for what you did either. Each of you is guilty of your own crime. Can't you see that, an intelligent guy like you?"

Silence descends over the room, and Clyde pulls a blanket over his shoulders to shield himself from the cold radiating off the brick wall. He scoots back on the bed and reclines against the pillow and peers at Ralph, who is standing in the dark, unmoving.

After a moment, Ralph speaks, his voice hoarse with emotion, "Haven't *you* ever dreamt of revenge?" He steps forward into the soft glow coming through the skylight. It cuts across his face, lending a jagged appearance to his features. One of his eyes glows red. "Against the people who have hurt you? Your father, for instance."

Clyde creeps forward to the edge of the bed on his hands and knees. "We were talking about blackmail, not revenge."

"Answer me."

"Of course I've dreamt of revenge. Who hasn't? What's your point?"

"My blackmail, as you call it, was a form of delayed revenge. It helped me get what I needed, which was a release from the pre-textual therapy that wasn't working anyway, and at the same time, it held a threat over the head of the person who was abusing me. It was a righteous exercise of power against evil."

"But by not reporting him, you allowed him to continue abusing his patients. Patients like me. Did you ever think of that? No, you didn't. Because at the end of the day you're just a stuck-up, selfish prick who only thinks of himself. '*I'm a klepto*', boo hoo hoo; '*God doesn't listen to me*', boo hoo hoo; '*I have victims*', boo hoo fucking hoo!"

Ralph moves toward the bed, his eyes wide and bloodshot, his nostrils flaring, his forehead deeply furrowed. "Why are you attacking me? I've been nothing but understanding and gracious with you."

"You said we were friends."

"We are. Or at least I thought we were."

"Well then, guess what, Jimmy. Friends tell each other the truth."

Ralph arches an eyebrow. "Is that so?"

"Yes."

"Then shall I tell *you* the truth?"

"As long as you're not doing it to hurt me for calling you out, then be my guest."

Ralph stares open-mouthed at Clyde for a moment, then closes his eyes and shakes his head.

"I thought so," Clyde says, scooting back on the bed.

"Maybe you're right," Ralph whispers. "Maybe I *am* a selfish prick."

"There's no maybe about it, Jimmy. You are. The question is, what are you going to do about it?"

"That's the million-dollar question."

"Well, if you ask me, the first thing you have to do is admit you have a problem."

"And then what?"

"Then do stuff to help other people instead of only yourself, I guess. Jeez! Do I have to think of everything?"

"I took you in when you were homeless. Doesn't that count for something?"

"Not really, because that might have been mixed up with your wanting me to be in your dumb movie, and maybe some other stuff too, like what we just did."

Ralph's mouth pulls back into a half-smile. "It *was* good, wasn't it?"

"Best sex I've ever had, Jimmy. But not the point."

"OK, I got it. So then let me *really* help you, with no benefit to myself. Let me help you get that revenge you've always dreamt of."

"Nice try."

"What?"

"Helping me get revenge *would* be of benefit to you, Jimmy. You get off on revenge. It's like a drug for you. Think of something else."

"So I get off on revenge, whatever. Nobody does anything for purely selfless motives, Marilyn. That's a myth. Everyone does what they think is ultimately in their best interest. So come down off your high horse and either accept what I'm offering or not. If you want to get back at your father, say the word, and I'll help you. You can finally confront him from a position of power. Then you can help *me* do the same with Doctor Menner. Let's get closure with these two freaks so we can move on with our lives."

At the mention of the word closure, Clyde flashes on his telephone call with Yoshi earlier that day.

"How exactly do you propose to help me?"

Ralph shrugs. "I don't know enough about the situation to say yet. I'm sure we can come up with something."

Clyde screws up his face for a moment and looks back at Ralph.

"Cars…"

"Say what?"

"He's an auto mechanic. Has his own garage. He specialises in Japanese cars…"

"Right. And I have a Nissan."

"You could drop in on him to sort out some problem with your transmission…"

"And then…"

Clyde rises up on his knees. "Yes."

Ralph nods.

"Nobody gets hurt, right?" Clyde says.

"We'll scare the living shit out of both those bastards. But nobody gets hurt. I promise."

—᠓—

Yoshi Koba checks the door to the tool room to make sure the junior mechanics have locked it up properly, then drags himself to the office, grabs a beer out of the refrigerator, and pries off the cap with his teeth. He stares at the papers strewn over the top of his desk and swears under his breath, thinking again, as he does at the end of each workday, that he needs to replace the secretary who quit on him and his partner Sam Higashi the day he returned from prison.

Taking a long swig of beer, he looks out the window. The streetlights blink to life in the darkening evening as the rush hour traffic on this stretch of Fair Oaks thins out. Just as he is about to suck down another mouthful, his attention is drawn to a shiny, black Nissan 300ZX cruising past the shop at a reduced speed. The driver, a young Middle Eastern-looking man dressed in black, cranes his neck in the direction of the garage and squints at the building. Yoshi flips over the sign on the door to indicate the shop is closed, then he moves back to the fridge, drains the bottle, and grabs another one. A moment later a rapping on the door startles him.

"We're closed," he roars, not bothering to turn around.

Yoshi feels the blood rise to his face as the rapping continues. Slamming the bottle onto his desk, he strides to the door, throws it open, and finds himself facing the Middle Eastern man from earlier.

"Can't you read English?" Yoshi jerks his thumb at the sign. "It says we're closed."

"You specialise in Japanese cars, right?" The young man nods at his 300ZX idling behind him. "I need something checked."

Yoshi squints at the car and back at the young man. "But we're closed."

"But I have money." The young man smiles broadly. "Lots of it."

"Am I supposed to be impressed?"

The young man swivels around and switches off his car with a remote, then pushes past Yoshi into the office.

"Hey, what the fuck—" Yoshi follows the young man inside and finds him looking around the room.

"Nice place you've got here, Mister. A bit disorganised; could do with a bit of dusting. But overall not bad." He swings around on Yoshi. "How long have you been here?"

"Get out before I call the cops."

"You're the owner, right?"

"What's it to you?"

"I'm a potential customer with a problem who's willing to pay a lot of money to have it fixed—even more than what's customary, since you're obviously closed. So *if* you're the owner, I would think you'd be willing to stay a little longer to have a look-see and earn yourself some extra cash. I can come back tomorrow if it's not something you can repair quickly. The way I see it, it's a win-win. That is, unless you're discriminating against me for some reason."

The young man reaches into his pocket and pulls out a few hundred-dollar bills and fans them out. Yoshi steps forward and stares at the bills. The young man raises them and passes them under Yoshi's nose. A few minutes later, the young man's 300ZX roars into a repair bay.

"Maybe you'd better close the garage door so people don't think you're still open," the young man says as he steps out of the car. "And you might want to turn off the lights of your office while you're at it."

Yoshi sneers at the young man and pulls down the garage door, grumbling to himself. When he returns he finds the young man sitting on the hood of his car, his legs crossed Indian-style.

"The engine's making a funny sound. Tick, tick, tick. You know, usually when it's idling, like when I'm waiting at a traffic light. But sometimes it happens when I'm cruising around town. It's fine one minute, then tick, tick, tick for a few minutes more."

Yoshi runs his dirty fingernails through his unkempt grey and black hair and points at the hood.

"Climb down off of there. I'll need to take a look at the engine."

The young man hops off the hood and bows at the car with an exaggerated flourish. "She's all yours."

Yoshi pops open the hood and stares at the engine for a moment, then checks a few of the connections.

"Her name's Marilyn," the young man says.

Yoshi freezes mid-motion, then lifts his head and stares at the young man.

"The car," the young man says, flashing a wide grin. "I call her Marilyn."

Yoshi straightens up, his fingers turning white as his hand tightens on his wrench.

"She's my baby." The young man passes his hand over the roof of his car. "I'd be ever so grateful if you could fix her up."

"I think we're done here," Yoshi says.

The young man pulls a pistol out of his waistband and holds it idly at his side. "I don't think so."

Yoshi's eyes go wide at the sight of the firearm and his hand twitches on the wrench.

"I'd drop that if I were you." The young man lifts his head at the wrench, and Yoshi lets it fall to the floor with a loud clang.

"What do you want?"

The young man points the pistol at a chair. "Sit there, Yoshi."

"How do you know my name?"

The young man beams a broad smile and raises the gun at Yoshi's chest. "I know a lot of things. We'll talk about them in a moment. Right now, though, I need for you to shut the fuck up, *metumtam*, and sit in that chair."

Five minutes later Yoshi finds himself tied to the chair, bound arms and legs with a few lengths of rough twine and a canvas strap pulled tight across his mouth. The young man finds another chair and positions it in front of him, then takes the next few minutes to unload photographic equipment from his car and set it up—one camera on a tripod facing Yoshi and another facing the empty chair, and some open-faced lights to illuminate the area. Once it is all in place, the young man removes the canvas strap from Yoshi's mouth and stuffs it into his back pocket and switches on the harsh lights and the cameras.

"Who are you?" Yoshi croaks.

The young man drops into the chair opposite Yoshi. "Today, I'm Raphael the Avenging Angel. And this is your day of reckoning."

"I don't have any money, if that's what you want."

"If only it were that easy, Yoshi. But first, before I get to the fun stuff, I'm going to turn this show over to a very special guest." Ralph points his remote at his car and pops open the trunk, out of which climbs Clyde, dressed in jeans, a white chiffon blouse, and a pair of black pumps. He straightens his hair and struts over to where Yoshi is sitting with his mouth hanging open. Shielding his eyes against the lights with one hand, Clyde snaps his fingers at the cameras.

"Shut those things off."

"It's best if we record it all," Ralph says.

Clyde spins on his heels and glares at him. "I said shut it off. *All* of it."

Ralph holds up his hands and quickly moves to shut off the equipment.

"Leave me alone with him." Clyde points at the office door. "I'll let you know when we're ready for you."

Ralph looks at Yoshi for a moment and back at Clyde, then lights a cigarette before exiting the work area.

"Well, fuck me," Yoshi says once he and Clyde are alone. "Don't you look pretty."

Clyde sits opposite him and stares at him.

"What are you looking at?" Yoshi says.

"You tell me."

"I'm the man who raised you, you little shit. And this is how you repay me? By having your Arab boyfriend tie me to a chair and threaten me with a gun?"

"He's not an Arab. He's Israeli. And he's not my boyfriend."

"Israeli? That's ten times worse. A fucking Jew."

"Leave him alone. This is about you and me."

Yoshi arches an eyebrow. "And who exactly *are* you?" He tosses a quick glance at the office door, then narrows his eyes at Clyde and says in an exaggerated whisper, "You don't actually believe you're Marilyn Monroe, do you?"

Clyde puffs up his chest and touches his hand to it. "She's inside here. Where cruel people like you can't touch her."

Yoshi barks a bitter laugh. "You're a delusional freak."

"You're wrong. I'm a star."

Yoshi chuckles. "More like a black hole."

Clyde leans forward and hisses, "You'll see soon enough; you'll *all* see."

Yoshi cuts hate-filled eyes at Clyde. "Listen to me, Kimitake Koba, you're destined for obscurity or worse if you don't drop this ridiculous charade."

"Oh, so you're giving me advice now, are you?"

"Look at yourself. You're an embarrassment to us all, your mother included. If you keep carrying on like this, you'll end up in the kookoo house like your brother. And look at what happened to him. Is that what you want for yourself, you sick fuck?"

Clyde lunges forward and punches Yoshi in the face hard, bloodying his nose.

"Say it again, and I'll crack you another one, you goddamned bully."

Yoshi spits blood at Clyde. "You're a coward, hitting a guy when he's tied to a chair. Cut me loose. Let's make this a *fair* fight."

"Look at who's calling who a coward. The guy who took a knife to a two-year-old. What was fair about that, eh?" Clyde punches him again, this time in the mouth, splitting Yoshi's lip against his jagged front teeth. "What's fair about you guzzling whiskey and terrorising Momma and me each time you got drunk?" Clyde snatches a crowbar off the ground and raises it over his head. "Answer me!"

Ralph bursts out of the office and stays Clyde's hand as Yoshi squeezes his eyes shut waiting for the final blow. "Steady there, Marilyn," he says.

Clyde tosses aside the crowbar with a ringing clatter that echoes throughout the garage and grabs Yoshi by the lapel.

"Answer me, goddamn you! What did we do to deserve what you did to us? What did we fucking do?"

Yoshi pries open his eyes and glares at Clyde. Then he spits blood on the floor and says, "Bring me some water."

Ralph exits the room and returns a moment later with a Styrofoam cup brimming with cold water. He hands it to Clyde, who dashes it in Yoshi's face. "There's your water. Now answer me."

Yoshi shakes his head to dislodge the water streaming down his face and peers at Clyde out of one eye. "What did I do to deserve being put into a fucking relocation camp when I was just a kid and all the shit that went along with that? What did I do to deserve a wife who always felt she was better than me? What did I do to deserve a firstborn son who lost his mind? The answer is nothing! Shit happens to everyone. To some more than others. It's only stupid people who look for a reason. The truth is, there *is* no reason."

"There's no reason?" Clyde straightens and looks at Ralph, who is staring at Yoshi, his eyes wide and shot through with red. He looks back at Yoshi. "Then how about an explanation? Why did *you* treat me so badly?"

"Because she wanted to replace Hiro. Because I hated you. Because I wanted to die."

Clyde leaps to his feet. "Because you hated me?"

Yoshi closes his eyes. "Yes," he says through gritted teeth, "I hated you. You're no son of mine."

"That's a lie," Clyde screams.

Yoshi opens his eyes and glares at Clyde. "Your mother's a whore, and you're a whore's son."

"Stop it!" Clyde screams. "Stop saying that." He grabs the gun out of Ralph's hand and before Ralph can stop him, he pistol-whips Yoshi across the face. Then does it again. And again. Ralph grabs at Clyde, but Clyde shoves him away and kicks out at Yoshi's chest, sending the chair flying backwards crashing into the camera and knocking the lights on top of Yoshi.

Ralph tackles Clyde and wrestles him to the ground, then holds him there, his arms pinned to his sides, until Clyde stops struggling and the two of them are left gasping deep gulps of air. A deathly silence descends over the garage, the only sound their heavy breathing. After a moment they look over at the tangle of camera equipment and the upended chair where Yoshi was sitting. Ralph releases Clyde and crawls over to inspect the mess. Clyde sees him move aside the camera equipment and disappear behind the chair. After a moment, he straightens up, his face contorted in fear.

"He's dead."

Clyde lets out a muffled scream and scrambles forward. Yoshi is staring blankly, a puddle of blood spreading out from under his head where it bounced from the concrete onto the tripod leg of one of the lighting fixtures, impaled on a thick screw. "Oh, shit, oh, shit, oh, shit!" Clyde turns away and casts about the room as if looking for an escape.

"Why the hell did you have to go and do that?" Ralph says. "No one was supposed to get hurt. That's what *you* said."

"I know, I know, I know..." Clyde says, wringing his hands and looking down at Yoshi. "But when he started saying all those things, I lost it. Fuck! What are we going to do now, Jimmy?"

"What are *we* going to do?" Ralphs backs away from Clyde and points at Yoshi. "This is your mess, baby doll. I didn't agree to this shit."

Clyde pushes Ralph back against the wall. "Don't kid yourself, babe. You're the one who tied him up; you're the one with the gun. I'm sorry, but it's your shit too."

Ralph shakes himself free of Clyde. "The least you can do is cover his face." He hands Clyde a bandana and points it at Yoshi.

"Right, and then what?"

"Just—" Ralph raises his chin at Yoshi. Clyde drapes the bandana over Yoshi's face and straightens up.

"It's not true, you know," Clyde says.

"What isn't?"

"What he said about Momma and Clyde."

Ralph closes his eyes and shakes his head. "Whatever…"

"So what do we do now, Mr Genius?"

Ralph narrows his eyes at Clyde. "You should turn yourself in," he says after a moment. "The sooner, the better. Considering your history with him, you'll probably only get done for man-slaughter."

"What about you?"

"I don't have the same defence as you. They could get me for felony murder. It's best if I pack up my stuff and get the hell out of here."

"Why should I have to go to jail and you get to go free? That's not fair."

"It's fair that I get done for murder when you're the one who went and killed your own father without my having a say in it?"

Clyde turns away from Ralph and stares across the garage with tear-filled eyes. "I'm not turning myself in alone."

"Then we only have two choices. We can either take the body with us and get rid of it somewhere, or we can try and hide it here."

Clyde blinks away tears and wipes his face with the back of his arm. After a moment, he lifts his head and stares over Ralph's shoulder, narrowing his eyes at the back of the garage. Ralph turns to see what Clyde is looking at and looks back at Clyde.

"What is it?"

"Albacore…" Clyde whispers, lifting his arm and pointing at the tool room.

"Albacore?"

"He used to keep fish in a freezer in there."

Ralph jogs over to the tool room and jiggles the handle. "It's locked."

Clyde stoops down and pulls a jangle of keys out of Yoshi's pocket, then runs over to the tool room and tries a couple of them before finding the one that unlocks the door. He and Ralph step inside and push past the various tool carts to the back of the room, where they find the humming freezer. Clyde unlatches it and pushes aside several layers of packaged fish, unmistakably scarred with freezer burn. He turns to Ralph, holding one of the packages. "Nobody's opened this thing in years."

Ralph nods, and the two of them spend the next few minutes removing the fish from the freezer. Once it's completely empty, they locate a discarded tarp, wrap Yoshi's body in it, drop him into the freezer, and reload the frozen fish on top of him. Once they are sure the freezer looks as it did before, they stare at each other for a moment as if entering into a wordless agreement and set about finishing the job of cleaning up the garage before quietly backing Ralph's car out of the driveway at a few minutes past three in the morning and driving off.

—✦—

Ralph and Clyde hop onto Highway 2 and drive in silence toward the Angeles National Forest, both of them shell-shocked and neither knowing what to say. North of La Cañada, they leave civilisation behind and roar into the wilderness, bounded on both sides by massive pines and California oaks. As they reach the turnoff to the Switzer Falls trail, Clyde kicks out at the glove box and whirls on Raphael.

"Everything that happened back there...it's all your fault. I hope you know that."

Raphael glances at Clyde, then calmly pulls a cigarette out of his breast pocket and lights it with a trembling hand. "Of course, it is."

"I'm serious, Jimmy. None of that would have happened if you hadn't riled me up with all that revenge talk."

"I'm not arguing. That's the way it's always been with me. Everything always ends up my fault."

"Well, this time you *really* took the cake. You made me kill my father! That's the worst kind of sin in any religion. He didn't deserve that no matter how bad he was."

Ralph pulls his car into the dirt lot at the Switzer Falls trailhead and switches off the headlights, plunging them into the darkness of a moonless night. The soft glow of the Milky Way bears down on them from between the dense trees of the forest.

"Look, Marilyn," Ralph says after a moment, "I get that you want to put it all on me, which, between us, is fine if it makes you feel better. But as far as the law is concerned, you're as responsible for this as I am, if not more. I think you should get that into your pretty head."

Clyde kicks the glove box again and rolls down the window to gulp down some fresh air.

"And now that we've actually taken steps to hide the evidence," Ralph continues, "there's no way out for us. We're well past the point of no return. This is a game changer—for both of us."

"What do you mean, a game changer?" Clyde says, staring into the dark.

"I mean that no matter what we do from now on, both of us know what's in that freezer. And one day someone's going to find it. It could be ten years from now; it could be tomorrow. We can go about our business—together or separately, it doesn't matter—always wondering whether the trail will lead back to us; always wondering if whatever we've built will come crashing down on us."

Clyde turns to look at Ralph, straining to see his eyes in the darkened car. "It's like being cursed," he whispers.

Ralph lowers his forehead to the steering column and lets out a long sigh.

"What are we going to do, Jimmy?"

"I don't know."

After a few minutes of silence, Ralph steps out of the car and walks to the trailhead, leaving Clyde behind. He stares into the darkness trying to clear his mind. The cool, sage-scented breeze caresses his face, and he closes his eyes and draws it in once, twice, feeling the calming effect of the exercise. Up ahead he senses the rustle of rabbits or similar scampering in the brush. Nature is more benign here than in the Negev, he reflects. Little chance of being bitten by a viper. Danger here lurks *inside*, not out there.

A cold hand touches his arm, and he opens his eyes and looks back at the car. The windows are fogged up, but he can still make out the figure of Clyde pitched forward in the passenger seat.

An inexplicably warm current of air cuts through the early-morning freshness, coming from the direction of the trail. Ralph turns away from the car and hikes further into the woods to investigate. Up ahead in the distance beyond a bend in the trail, he sees a soft glow at ground level, orange, yellow, red—strong enough to illuminate the trees around it. Ralph instinctively reaches into his back pocket for a kippah, but finding none, he fishes out his bandana, ties it onto his head and moves forward, compelled by a force at his back.

The air gets progressively warmer as he nears the source of the glow, as if he is approaching an open oven. And there, dead ahead, he sees it, a fire in a clearing, an acacia bush ablaze. Ralph removes his shoes and socks and moves toward the bush, which, like its biblical counterpart, appears unconsumed by the flames.

"Is that you?" Ralph asks the bush.

His question is met by the crackling of the fire.

Ralph looks up at the sky, at a trail of aromatic smoke ascending to the heavens. Then he looks back at the bush.

"I'm sorry," he whispers. "I know I was supposed to be your special son. But instead, I've been a total fuck-up. My whole life—one disaster after another. I thought I'd be able to turn it around somehow at some point. But after tonight, I see that's never going to happen, is it?"

Ralph steps closer to the flames, feeling the searing heat on his face, smelling the singe and sizzle of his hair as he reaches out his arm toward the burning bush, yanking back his arm at the pain. He drops to one knee, feeling a crushing sensation in his chest, and he cries out, "Help me fix it!" He breaks down into loud choking sobs. "Show me the way, please. Give me a chance. Once last chance. I promise I'll return. I promise. I swear it. On my life, I swear it. I'll return."

"Jimmy?"

Ralph opens his eyes and finds Clyde standing over him in the darkness. He whips around and looks for the acacia bush, but the clearing is empty with no sign of either the bush or the fire that enveloped it. He lets out a groan and absently sifts a handful of dirt through his fingers.

"What happened to you?" Clyde asks.

Ralph staggers to his feet and glances around the clearing. "Let's just go home," he says after a moment, his voice weak, barely audible.

"And then what?"

"Nothing. We wait. If there's anything to be done, the answer will come."

"What about in the meantime?"

"We carry on like nothing's happened—for now."

Clyde looks off to one side for a moment and back at Ralph.

"I'm scared, Jimmy."

Ralph nods. "Me too."

Clyde tries to draw Ralph into a hug. But Ralph squirms out of the embrace and trudges back up the trail toward the car.

—�∭—

Sometime in the middle of the night, a distant wail jolts Clyde awake. He throws out his arm to reach for Ralph and find an empty bed, the sheets soaked through with sweat. As he struggles to establish his bearings, he notes the mournful baying of an electric guitar floating up from the ground floor, and he creeps downstairs to investigate. Just off the kitchen, he finds Ralph in his music room curled up on a leather lounge chair listening to Pink Floyd's *Comfortably Numb* at full volume. He is grasping the framed photograph of the soldier to his chest, his face turned away from the door.

"Jimmy?"

Clyde's voice is swallowed up by the music. Stepping into the room, he notices Ralph's mother's photograph strewn on the floor near the foot of the chair. As he bends down to pick it up, Ralph's head jerks up. He stares at Clyde bleary-eyed, a stream of drool draining onto his chest from the corner of his mouth.

Clyde drops the photograph onto Ralph's lap, then backs out of the room. He races upstairs and scrambles into the guest hutch, his heart pounding in his ears. Pulling the pillow over his head, he rigidly holds his position until he no longer hears the music and eventually loses consciousness, overtaken by dizzying exhaustion, his mind flooded with images of murder and gore and the last cursed words his father uttered on this miserable planet.

—⚏—

The next morning, after stealing out of the loft while Clyde was passed out in the hutch, Ralph hyperventilates in the car park of his former synagogue. He plays out the garage scene in his head over and again: Tying Yoshi up at gunpoint; Clyde kicking Yoshi in the chest; Yoshi's lifeless face staring up at him; loading Yoshi's body into the freezer. Raphael the Avenging Angel. What was he thinking? Anger and regret surge within him. Sweat streams down his face, and he is racked by shudders as he runs through alternate scenarios, seeking justification for what has happened, trying to figure out how to undo what's already done.

Clawing out a bottle from the glove box, he downs a Quaalude and waits for the drug to take effect, deliberately slowing down his breathing, trying to regain control. After a few minutes, he feels the familiar warm rush that takes the edge off. The tension in his muscles dissipates. Confidence replaces anxiety. Noting the engine is still running, he snaps it off and yanks the keys out of the ignition.

What Clyde said was true. He *had* encouraged Clyde to confront his father from a position of power, as a form of revenge. If it wasn't for that, Yoshi would still be alive. *But the old bastard deserved it*, Ralph reasons. Still, Clyde shouldn't have to go down for murder. He considers turning himself in and taking the blame for everything, explaining the whole thing as a dispute over a car repair gone wrong, something done in the heat of the moment. Whatever the explanation, it would be the right thing to do, to suffer the punishment.

The thought of punishment brings back the words Saba taught him from childhood: "Everything happens for a reason." *Perhaps this is the moment it all catches up with me. This is the moment I start to pay for all my crimes.*

"And *Adonai* said," Ralph recites out loud, "'the voice of your brother's blood cries out to me from the ground.'" *The blood of Ima, Tomer, Aunt Penina, and countless others. And now Yoshi. There's no turning back.*

He launches out of the car and strides into the building. He feels his way along the long, darkened corridor to the empty sanctuary and stands in the back gazing at the ark. Seeing a prayer shawl folded over the back of a chair, he feels an unexpected urge to pray and drapes it over his head. The blessing for donning the shawl takes control of his brain, and his lips mime the ancient words.

Then he makes his way to the *bima* and ascends the steps, his eyes fixating on the ark, imagining the Torah scrolls inside. The last time he set foot in a synagogue was for the joint funeral of Aunt Penina and Tomer. Others had dragged him there, had taken him from his hospital bed in utter sedation and positioned him in the front row, moaning and drooling and fighting the temptation to throw himself into the crater. And now here he was again.

"I'll give you one last chance," he whispers.

"Can I help you?" a familiar voice echoes off the hard walls of the sanctuary.

Ralph turns and sees Rabbi Mordechai standing in the back. He takes the prayer shawl off his head and drapes it over his shoulders.

"Hello, Rabbi."

Ralph descends the bima and meets the rabbi at the front row.

"It's me. Raphael."

The rabbi reaches out a hand tentatively and touches Ralph's arm. "Baruch Hashem."

Ralph looks down and squeezes his eyes shut. He feels the rabbi's hand on his shoulder. He shakes his head. He feels like crying. He swears to the highest heaven he'll kill himself right then and there if he does.

"Welcome back," Rabbi Mordechai says. "I was waiting for this day."

"I'm not back, Rabbi." Ralph looks the rabbi in the eye. "I came to say goodbye."

The rabbi frowns and looks around at the empty room. He takes Raphael's hand. "Come sit for a while."

The two of them sit in the front row and stare at each other for a few seconds.

"With respect, Rabbi..."

"Speak your mind, young man."

"Sending me back to Israel was a mistake. You see that now, don't you?"

"The story's not over yet."

"How can you say that? I lost myself completely; people got hurt. My life is complete rubbish. And my love for Torah, the *only* thing I ever truly loved, died there. In Israel."

"You were *not* responsible for what happened in Mitzpe Ramon. It was an accident."

"I get that! But, don't you see, if nobody was responsible, if it was all just a string of accidents, then where is He in all of this?" Ralph points a finger at the ark. "Where was He when an Egyptian shell hit Yossi's tank? Where was He when Aunt Penina and Tomer were burning?"

"He was right there with them in the midst of the flames, and His heart was breaking. Just as He's here right now in this room waiting for you to return."

Ralph stands and removes the prayer shawl.

"I don't understand any of it, Rabbi." He folds the shawl and hangs it on the back of a chair. "In any case, I don't think I can ever return. I'm too far gone."

"It's never too late, young man. Be patient with yourself."

"Goodbye, Rabbi." Ralph moves down the aisle.

"Your sister came to see me recently," Rabbi Mordechai says.

Ralph turns around. "What about it?"

"She's trying to track you down."

"Why?"

"It's not for me to say."

Ralph raises his shoulders. "Of course not."

"Go see him."

Ralph flashes a sad smile, then turns around and walks out of the sanctuary.

—⁂—

Ralph drives down Wilshire Boulevard toward downtown Los Angeles, determined to turn himself in to the police, but all the while hearing the rabbi's voice playing a loop in his head. *Go see him.* What did he mean by *him*? Hadn't he said it was Gabriella who was looking for him? Maybe he meant his father. Or perhaps the rabbi had confused his words. Ralph's heart rate increases, and dark spots dapple his vision in the glare of the late-morning sunlight.

As he reaches the intersection of Wilshire and Santa Monica, he wonders whether this might not be the sign he begged for last night, especially as he has just offered Hashem one last chance. Executing an illegal U-turn, he roars up Wilshire back to West-wood and up Beverly Glen to Holmby Hills.

Driving along the lanes of his old neighbourhood, Ralph feels a surge of emotion and the sting of tears and wipes at his eyes with the back of his sleeve. He turns onto his street and brings his car to a halt in front of the gates of his family home. The driveway is empty, as he would expect at this time of day, and he switches off the engine and waits. His eyes feel heavy in the drowsy heat, and he reclines his seat and nods off into a restless sleep.

The roar of a leaf blower jars him awake. Glancing at the digital clock, he is surprised to see that it is nearly three in the afternoon. He stares at the still-empty driveway, and, feeling the pangs of hunger, he climbs out of the car and approaches the gate, dodging the small army of gardeners who are tidying up the grass running along the outside wall.

Grasping the bars of the gate, he stares through them at the front door, throwing back his mind a decade and summoning up the feeling of this place as home, his father studying Talmud in the living room, his mother haunting the halls in her wheelchair. He thinks of his bedroom and wonders whether his father has kept it as it was, or whether he has turned it into a guest room or a study.

The twin forces of hunger and curiosity drive him to punch the access code into the security pad and push open the side gate. Moving up the drive to the front door, he enters the security code to unlock it. But the code doesn't work. After trying it a few times more without success, he rings the doorbell and raps repeatedly on the front door, hoping that the cook or one of the housekeep-ers might still be around.

As he is about to head around to the back of the house, a grinding metallic sound emanates from the other side of the door followed by the unlatching of the lock. The door swings open slowly, and Ralph gives it a little shove. Stepping inside, his breath catches at the sight of Yossi staring up at him from a wheelchair, dressed in a thin white tank top and tan-coloured army fatigues shortened to fit the stumps where his legs used to be.

The cousins stare at each other with widening eyes. In the ten years that have passed, Yossi's face has grown angular, framed by a poorly groomed beard, and his once-friendly eyes look harder, more like his mother's than ever before. His upper body is strong, the muscles standing out on his arms, biceps, and triceps. Ralph reaches out a hand, and Yossi responds by wheeling his chair around and moving down the hallway toward the living room.

"Yossi, wait." Ralph jogs after his cousin and intercepts him as he rolls down the ramp and brings his chair to a halt next to the sofa.

"I don't want to see you," Yossi says, his voice barely audible. He focuses his gaze at a random corner of the room.

Ralph lays his hand on Yossi's shoulder, but Yossi shakes it off.

"I didn't know you were here," Ralph says.

Yossi tosses a sidelong glance at him. "What difference would it have made if you had? No one has heard from you in ages."

"I'm here now."

Yossi wheels his chair around to face Ralph. "Please don't tell me you're here to apologise, because I'm not having any of that."

"I'm not."

Yossi lifts his chin at Ralph.

"I'm sorry about what happened, achi. But *none* of it was my fault. Not the fire, not the war, not your injuries—"

"You didn't know that at the time."

"No, but it still didn't make me responsible."

"And what about your disappearing act afterwards? Not your fault either?"

Ralph passes a hand through his damp hair and wipes it on his trousers. "Look at it from my side, Yossi. I was seventeen; still a kid. I felt like a murderer for what happened in Mitzpe, and also responsible for what happened to you. The guilt was horrendous; I couldn't deal with it. It's a miracle I didn't end up tossing myself off a cliff or worse. And by the time I found out *none* of it was my fault, the whole experience had already wounded me to the very core of my being. I'm *still* trying to make sense of it. So, I'm sorry if I wasn't around to deal with the aftermath. But I couldn't face up to it. I couldn't face *you*."

"So you *are* here to apologise."

Ralph drops into his father's chair and lowers his head into his hands. "I don't know why I'm here. The rabbi told me Gabriella was looking for me. He said I should come see her. I came here; I found you." He raises his head. "Fuck if I know."

Yossi shakes his head and pivots his chair away from Ralph, who stands and touches his shoulder. This time Yossi doesn't flinch. Ralph puts his other hand on Yossi's other shoulder and gently massages his neck and back, finding spots of tension that he kneads with his thumbs, eliciting groans from his cousin. After a few minutes, he steps forward and embraces Yossi from behind, bringing his cheek to rest against the side of Yossi's head. Yossi leans into the gesture, and Ralph kisses him on the top of his head.

"I'm here for a couple of weeks," Yossi says after a tentative moment of silence, "for a mental health conference for injured IDF soldiers co-sponsored by the Skirball Center. It starts on Monday."

"And after?"

"After, I'm returning to Israel. I'm living in Haifa now."

"Are you with someone?"

Yossi shakes his head.

"Stay."

Yossi wheels his chair away from Ralph.

"You can live with me, achi. I have a big place. I'll take care of you. We can start again. It'll be a new life for both of us."

Reaching the bottom of the ramp, Yossi glances back at Ralph for a moment. Ralph lunges forward to help him, but Yossi's hand shoots up halting him mid-stride. Then he struggles up the ramp, the muscles bulging on his arms with the effort. When he reaches the top, he wheels his chair around and looks down at Ralph.

"I'm glad we had a chance to talk, cousin."

"Yossi, I—"

"But this is as far as things are going to go with us."

"We could at least *try* to start over, couldn't we?"

"We *could*," Yossi says. "But I don't want to. I understand everything you've said, and I'll do my best to find a way to forgive you—for my sake. But you've been out of my life for over ten years, and I don't want you back again. You're bad news, cousin; trouble follows you wherever you go. I wish you only the best. But I need to protect myself. So, if you truly care for me, you'll do us both the favour of never contacting me again. Yes?"

Tears stream down Ralph's face as he watches the image of Yossi recede down the darkened hallway toward his old bedroom. He fights the urge to race after him, to beg his forgiveness, to try to convince him to change his mind. But Yossi's words continue to echo in his mind. *You're bad news; trouble follows you wherever you go; I have to protect myself.* They conflate with the image of Yoshi lying at the bottom of a freezer, buried under a pile of frozen fish.

Wiping his face with the back of his sleeve, he takes in a deep breath and strides out of the house.

—⁂—

Clyde wanders out of the kitchen in his nightgown and a pair of satin monogrammed slippers he dug out of Ralph's closet, balancing a bowl of Cap'n Crunch in his hand. He returns to the music room and sits in the lounge chair to eat. A quarter through the bowl, he sets it aside and walks around the room, looking at Ralph's collection of album covers, which cover an entire wall like a functional collage. Spotting a copy of *Goat's Head Soup* by The Rolling Stones, he slips the vinyl disc out of the cover, carefully places it on the turntable, and plays "Angie".

He climbs back into the lounge chair, draws his legs up, and munches down some more of the sickly sweet breakfast cereal, letting a sad, nostalgic feeling wash over him. The image of Kevin the day he left for England haunts him, as it does each time he hears this song. He had seen him again a couple of years later, all grown up and barely recognisable, having put on excess weight, his face pasty and bloated. He'd returned home to see his parents during half term, and Tomoko had driven an excited Clyde over to see him. Clyde recalls the cold, aloof look Kevin had tossed when he walked through the door. He remembers how Kevin's body had stiffened when he'd hugged him, how he'd excused himself and gone back upstairs to his room.

When Tomoko and Auntie Doreen had settled into a conversation, Clyde snuck upstairs and poked his head into Kevin's room, where he found him sitting on his bed reading a book. All the James Dean memorabilia was gone; the walls were bare; the room was as lifeless as a wigless mannequin stripped bare. Kevin had looked up from his book and, taking the cue, Clyde climbed the rest of the way into the bedroom and had stood across from him.

"You're not happy to be back?" Clyde asked. "Because I'm happy to see you."

Kevin shrugged and looked back at his book.

"I decorated my room the way you told me I should, Kev." Clyde had snapped his fingers in the air. "It's absolutely fabulous. You should come see it."

Kevin had clapped shut his book and dropped it onto the bed.

"Why are you acting like that?" Clyde asked.

"Like what?"

"All stuck up."

"I'm *not* happy to be back. I miss my friends. I wish I were back home—in England at my school."

Clyde could hear the hint of an English accent. It sounded fake to him.

"I thought you'd at least be happy to see me, you know, after what happened before you left. I still have the ring you gave me."

Kevin crossed the room and grabbed Clyde's arm.

"Nothing happened, OK? Wipe it all clean." Kevin pointed at the walls. "Like this room. All clean. A blank slate. James Dean doesn't live here anymore, get it? His spirit has returned to *Jigoku* to haunt someone else."

When the song finishes, Clyde snatches the record off the turntable and rakes his cereal spoon across the vinyl. He sticks out his tongue at the deep gash and returns the disc to its cover.

He dumps the half-eaten cereal into the sink and deposits the bowl into the dishwasher, then strolls across the room to the mirror and admires his reflection, primping and posing, giggling and blowing kisses at himself. After a few minutes, he manages to banish all thoughts of Kevin from his mind and shimmies away from the mirror.

When he gets to the foot of the stairs, Ralph's shrine catches his eye. There are four candles now, and all the photographs are back in their respective places. Clyde picks up the photograph of the boy on the table and stares at it. He turns the frame over in his hand, looking for some clue as to the boy's identity. Finding nothing, he reverently places it back on the table. Then he takes down the photograph of the soldier. There is a forlorn look in his dark eyes, and a carpet of hair visible above the top button of his crisp uniform. He touches his finger to the glass, which is stained with what look like watermarks, then touches his finger to his tongue and tastes salt.

He returns the photograph to the wall and goes back to Ralph's room and rummages through his closet and dresser drawers. He pops into the bathroom and inspects all the bottles in the medicine cabinet. He goes to Ralph's writing desk, pulls on the bottom drawer and finds it locked. Then he pulls open the pencil drawer and finds among the flotsam a couple of random letters addressed to Ralph from USC's School of Cinematic Arts. Stuffing one of them into his purse, he sits on the bed and switches on the TV. He flips to KTLA, his favourite channel for late-morning classic movies and giggles at a Palmolive dishwashing soap commercial as Madge the manicurist shocks yet another customer by announcing she's soaking her fingernails in dishwashing liquid.

Clyde slakes his thirst with a sip of water from Ralph's water glass as the commercial fades and the unseen host announces: "We now return to Al Pacino and Chris Sarandon in *Dog Day Afternoon*." Clyde stretches out on his stomach, rests his chin on his fists, and watches with great interest as the story unfolds.

—⟋⟍—

Ralph bursts through the door of his loft and races upstairs. He looks around at the empty bedroom, switches off the TV, and pokes his head into the bathroom. Seeing nothing, he races downstairs and searches the rest of the apartment.

In the music room, he finds that the stereo system is on, the turntable rotating. Switching it off, he returns to his bedroom and inspects it more closely, noticing the rumpled, still-warm sheets, the half-opened drawers, a couple of discarded, lipstick-smeared Kleenexes on the floor.

Whirling around he looks at his writing desk. He bends down to test the locked bottom drawer and sees an envelope from USC on the floor next to the wastepaper basket. He picks it up and stares at it for a few seconds, then looks inside his pencil drawer and searches for the other one. Finding nothing, he straightens up and looks back at the empty bed, feeling his heart leap into his chest.

"Fuck, fuck, fuck!" he says as he races out of the room.

—◦◦◦—

Ralph's 300ZX roars into the student parking lot, and he leaps out and sprints across the campus to the film school. As he nears the building, he sees Clyde standing on the steps dressed in a white chiffon blouse and a black satin knee-length skirt, his hair done up in classic Marilyn glamour waves. A crowd of students have gathered around him. Ralph rushes up to Clyde's side.

"Oh, Jimmy dear, there you are," Clyde says. He gives Ralph a peck on the cheek. "You look like shit."

"Yes, Jimmy, *here* you are," one of his classmates says with a smirk. "Your friend here's been asking about you. I was about to take him up to your advisor's office."

"Watch it, there," Clyde says. "I'm not a him." He turns around to show off his body, his eyes closed, a blissful smile on his face. "This girl's all woman."

Ralph's classmates erupt into peals of laughter and loud applause. Clyde flashes a toothy smile, then takes a bow.

"I think they recognise me," he says as Ralph shepherds him to one side.

"What are you doing here?" Ralph whispers to him.

"Surprise!" Clyde says, pulling the envelope from his purse. "I may be blonde, but I'm not dumb."

The crowd of students presses in around them, keen to listen in on their conversation.

"OK, guys," Ralph says, waving a hand at them, "the show's over." He grabs Clyde's arm and pulls him away from the crowd, and Clyde shakes himself free.

"Hey, what's the big idea?"

"Come with me, please." Ralph jerks his thumb in the direction of the parking lot.

"But I came here to see you in your element. I was hoping you might give me a tour or something. Also," he says, his face brightening, "I came up with an idea. And this seemed like the perfect place to pitch it to you. You know, for your project."

Ralph stares at Clyde for a moment and shakes his head. "Are you fucking out of your mind?" He steps forward and lowers his voice. "After what happened last night? You're, like, what? Over it? Ready to play?"

"You're the one who said we should carry on like nothing happened, remember. Well, this is *me* doing just that, Mister Genius. What are *you* doing?"

Ralph looks up at the sky and takes a deep breath, then walks away from Clyde. "Follow me. We can talk about this someplace else."

Clyde catches up with Ralph as he reaches the student parking lot, and they both jump into Ralph's 300ZX. Ralph tears out of the lot onto Exhibition Boulevard and hops the freeway toward Santa Monica, weaving in and out of traffic, clocking seventy–five miles per hour.

"Slow down, will you? We don't need the police stopping us."

Ralph takes a random off-ramp, pulls into a petrol station, and parks the car. Then he lowers his head to the steering wheel and sobs. Clyde stares at him for a moment, then reaches out a finger and pokes his arm.

"Hey, I'm sorry. I didn't mean to upset you. I just thought it would be a nice surprise to drop in on you at school."

Ralph lifts his head and glares at Clyde. "It doesn't have anything to do with you. Not everything does, you know."

Clyde crosses his arms. "You don't have to be an asshole about it, Jimmy. Tell me what's wrong. Or don't. It's up to you..."

Ralph holds up his hand. "I'm sorry. I'm upset, that's all. Family stuff."

Clyde reaches over and rubs Ralph's shoulder. "I'm all ears, Jimmy."

Ralph nods. "After the Doctor Menner thing, my parents sent me back home to Israel to live with some relatives in the desert. They thought it would be good for me; that it would straighten me out. There was an accident; some people died."

"The people in your shrine?"

Ralph nods and stares absently out the window at the passing cars.

"One of them," he says after a moment, "the young boy. He was my cousin. He and his mother died in a fire that everyone thought I caused. Turns out it was caused by a short in a neighbour's refrigerator of all things."

"What about the soldier?"

"That's Yossi, my cousin." Ralph closes his eyes for a moment. "He's still alive—lost his legs in the war."

"What war?"

Ralph studies Clyde's face. "One of those wars we have in Israel."

"Oh." Clyde crinkles his brow. "So how was that your fault?"

"I don't know," Ralph says. "It just was. Everything was my fault. Anyway, I suffered a nervous breakdown because of all that, and they put me in the hospital. It took me a while to recover. My mom died while I was in there, and I didn't find out about it until much later."

"I'm so sorry, Jimmy." Clyde strokes Ralph's arm. "My mother was put in one of those places too when I was a little girl. That's how I ended up in a bunch of foster homes. I wrote about it in my book *My Story*."

Ralph cuts his eyes at Clyde.

"Sorry, back to you."

"When I finally recovered, the doctors considered me unfit for active military service." He takes a long, drawn-out breath, then looks at Clyde out of the corner of his eye. "Especially since I'd started hearing his voice in my head."

"Whose voice?"

"James Dean's voice, of course."

Clyde narrows his eyes at Ralph. "Seriously?"

"Yes, seriously."

"Why didn't you say anything about that before?"

"I did! I told you I thought I might be the reincarnation of James Dean."

"Yes, and then I asked you what evidence you had. But you never mentioned you heard his voice."

"I must have."

"You didn't. Which means either that you're a major loony or that you're making it all up."

"Trust me, I'm not making it up. Anyway, since they wouldn't let me serve, I got a discharge and went to university in Tel Aviv instead and studied photography. After graduation, I came back here to earn an MFA in film. Then I met you and added accomplice to murder to my list of achievements."

"Gee, thanks. Is that it?"

"No. This morning I seriously thought about turning myself in to the police. But when I was on my way downtown, I swung by my father's place and found my cousin Yossi there. It's ten years since I last laid eyes on him. At first, he didn't even want to look at me. Finally, he told me he doesn't want to have anything to do with me. That killed me."

"You were going to turn yourself in without telling me, you motherfucker?"

"Hang on a sec. I was planning on taking the blame and putting it all down to a dispute gone wrong, which would have cleared you. But the whole Yossi thing upset me so much that I didn't have the stomach to go through with it. End of story."

"That's it?"

"Yep."

"That's what you were boo-hoo-hooing about?"

"Yes, goddamn it; that's what it's about."

"Well, I'll be a baboon's shiny red ass. You should write all that down. Because *that* would make a hell of a movie." Clyde grabs a bottle of mineral water resting on the front seat and takes a sip.

"My life's not a movie. It's private. I'm only telling you this because now we're in big shit together."

Clyde holds up both hands and shows Ralph crossed fingers. "Can't get any worse, right?"

Ralph shrugs.

"That's the spirit," Clyde says with a smirk. "So, let's break the impasse and push this baby to the limit." He points at Ralph's keys in the ignition. "Drive."

Ralph starts the engine, presses on the gas pedal and makes it roar. Then he peels out of the driveway and heads back to the freeway. "Where are we going?"

"Just drive, Jimmy. Now, it's my turn."

"Your turn for what?" Ralph says as he takes the on-ramp and heads west.

"I was watching TV and got an idea."

"Don't tell me, another field trip, right?"

"Did you ever see a movie called *Dog Day Afternoon*?"

Ralph shoots a glance at Clyde and looks back at the road. "Uh...Al Pacino tries to rob a bank. He gets caught. Yeah, what about it?"

"Why did he want to rob the bank, Jimmy?"

"I don't know. I guess because he wanted the money."

"No, that's not it. Think, Jimmy. Why did Al Pacino rob the bank? Why did he *need* the money?"

"Let's see..." Ralph glances in his rear-view mirror and makes an abrupt lane change, roaring into the fast lane on the extreme left.

"He...oh yeah, it's all coming back. He needed the money for...a sex change operation, right? Yeah, a sex change operation for his lover—"

Clyde nods his head slowly, a broad smile on his face, and Ralph's eyes go wide.

"That's your idea?"

"Uh huh ... "

"But he gets caught."

"But *you won't*. You're an *excellent* thief."

"That's a crazy idea. I've only ever stolen small stuff. Banks are way out of my league."

"Don't worry about it, Jimmy. I've got it all figured out."

"Oh, have you?"

"Yes, I have. We'll rob a bank in San Diego, then we'll cross the border into Tijuana and lie low for a while. Like Butch Cassidy and the Sundance Queen. We'll be the talk of the town. Then, with the money, and with your knowledge of Spanish, we'll find a doctor to perform the operation. And you can film it all for your project."

"And how are we supposed to rob a bank? What's your plan for that?"

"I don't know, Jimmy. That's your department. We'll wear masks or something."

"I told you that I like you the way you are. You don't have to get a sex change operation."

"But I *want* one, damn it. I need your help with this, Jimmy."

"OK, fine, you want a sex change operation. But we don't need to rob a bank. I can get the money for you."

"What kind of a thief are you? I thought you'd like the idea. I thought you'd jump at the challenge of robbing a bank. No more stealing ashtrays or pocketing tips off tables in restaurants. No more shoplifting. No more simple residential cat burglaries. That's all kid's stuff, Jimmy. You're a man now. It's time to leave your mark. Besides, we're *already* in a shit storm. Don't you think it's better if we do something unforgettable rather than hide for the rest of our lives, always looking over our shoulders, afraid of our own shadows, never knowing if and when we're going to be found out. We'll be taking back control."

"I thought you didn't approve of stealing."

"I don't. But this would only be temporary. We'd pay them back. You can arrange for that beforehand. This is about PR, Jimmy. *Think* about all the publicity we'd get. Everyone would finally know about us. Plus, to ensure nobody gets hurt, we wouldn't use real guns."

Ralph exits the freeway at Santa Monica and takes the Pacific Coast Highway north toward Malibu.

"Aren't you even tempted?"

"I want to think about it, Marilyn." Ralph turns into the parking lot of a seafood restaurant and parks the car. "It's a big step."

"We're both empowered now, Jimmy. I can feel it. It's time to manifest our destiny."

Ralph glances at the restaurant and back at Clyde.

"I said I want to think about it. Right now I really need to get some food in me and clear my head. Let's just *please* stop talking about robbing banks."

Clyde kisses Ralph on the cheek.

"I know you'll make the right decision."

The two of them stroll to the restaurant and take a table facing the Pacific. They order lunch and sit quietly looking out past the empty beach at the waves pounding the shore. When the food arrives, Ralph immediately attacks his plate of mahi-mahi with a ferocity that surprises Clyde, who picks at a sizzling skillet of shrimp fajitas. Clyde stabs a piece of shrimp with his fork and holds it out to Ralph.

"Want some?"

Ralph shakes his head. "I don't eat shellfish, thanks."

"Why not? It's yummy." Clyde puts the piece of shrimp in his mouth and chews it.

"I'm sure it is. But I'm fine with this, thanks."

"Is it because you're Jewish?"

"Something like that."

"I thought you weren't religious anymore."

"I'm not. But some things die hard."

Clyde nods and looks out at the ocean. He watches a lone seagull hovering above the churning water.

—✺—

Media input appears to jar the subject's sense of reality. For example, his insistence that I aid him in robbing a bank seems to have sprung entirely from a film he saw on television. His request puts the research for my project in a precarious position.

Ralph picks up his steno pad and rereads the notes for his film treatment. He glances over his shoulder at Clyde, who is snoring softly on the bed. Then he turns back to his pad and continues writing.

I fear that if I continue to refuse, he may become suspicious. Or worse, I may lose the subject altogether. At this point, I feel I have no other option but to act as if I will go through with the robbery. This may afford me more insight into his obsession with Monroe, which can only benefit the documentary.

As an aside, I have to admit that the idea of robbing a bank does hold some attraction for me.

—✺—

The next morning Clyde finds a note on Ralph's desk that reads:

I'll be back before noon. Get yourself ready. (Don't touch anything!)

Clyde squeals with delight and spends the next couple of hours showering, doing his hair, making up his face, picking out something to wear, having breakfast, picking up the apartment, and looking out the window at the car park every so often to see if Ralph has returned. Then he grabs his purse and sits on the sofa and waits, hopping up every now and again to pace the room.

When the wall clock shows noon, Clyde runs to the window and looks out at the car park but doesn't see anything. Pitching his purse across the room in frustration, he plods to the kitchen to rummage through the refrigerator.

An hour later Ralph explodes into the apartment with his video camera on record and finds Clyde sprawled on the sofa asleep, a lipstick-smeared, half-eaten banana in his hand.

"Ready?"

Clyde opens his eyes and sits up on the sofa tossing aside the banana.

"What took you so long?" He looks up at the wall clock, blinking away the stupor of a heavy nap. "Your note said before noon. It's already past one." He cuts his eyes at the camera, which Ralph has brought close to his face.

"I have a surprise. Go out the door and down the back stairs." He plants a lingering kiss on Clyde's cheek. "You look fantastic, by the way. Like a real star."

Clyde's face lights up, and he blows Ralph a kiss, then he sashays out the front door, and Ralph follows with the camera. When they reach the back stairs, Ralph rushes ahead and down the steps and tapes Clyde's descent to the ground floor.

"I've got you on close-up now, baby. Don't look at the camera. Just react naturally."

Clyde pauses in the stairwell. "What am I supposed to be thinking?"

Ralph pauses the camera. "What do you mean?"

"If I'm reacting naturally, there must be something on my mind, right? Like I've either come from doing something, or I'm about to do something."

"Obviously, you've been waiting for me. I've just arrived home and asked you to go outside for a surprise. This is *our* story, Marilyn. Just react naturally."

Clyde collects himself for a moment, then pastes a bland expression on his face. "OK, fine. This is me acting naturally— and a teensy bit annoyed if I'm honest."

"Got it. Sorry. I promise I'll make it up to you." Ralph points at the emergency exit. "Now... I'm going outside. You wait here. Count to thirty, then come out this door and look to your left. Got that?"

"Count to thirty, then come out?"

"And look left."

"OK, I look left. What's out there?"

"It'll ruin the surprise if I tell you."

Clyde frowns at Ralph. "Real actors are able to act surprised even when we know what we're about to see. Films are scripted, you know. They're not just impromptu free-for-alls. We've been over this already."

"This *is* scripted." Ralph touches his finger to his forehead. "In here. Trust me."

Clyde rolls his eyes. "Famous last words."

Moments later Clyde bursts out of the building into a small side car park. He shields his eyes with his purse against the brilliant summer afternoon sun. Looking left, he sees a tarp-covered automobile. Ralph encourages him forward with a sweep of his hand.

"What's this?" Clyde says, giving the back tyre a little kick.

Ralph hands Clyde the camera, then pulls off the tarp and reveals the silver Porsche Spyder convertible from the vintage car lot. He touches his finger to the words *Little Bastard*. "Now, we're fucking empowered," he says, smiling broadly into the camera. Clyde switches it off and throws his arms around Ralph.

—◆—

Ralph and Clyde speed down the Santa Ana Freeway toward San Diego weaving in and out of traffic with Queen's "Brighton Rock" blaring from the stereo system. Clyde closes his eyes and relishes the rush of wind through his hair. He wedges his hand between Ralph's thigh and the seat to feel the delicious weight of his body, and remains like that until they hit parking lot-dense traffic at San Juan Capistrano, which slows them way down until they break free of it at San Clemente with a roar of the engine.

"You should be recording this," Ralph says, nodding at the camera nestled at Clyde's feet.

"Can we please not?" Clyde says. "I'm enjoying everything as it is. Holding a camera will just get in the way."

"But what about the movie?"

"Jimmy, please. We *are* the movie. We're living it now. If everything goes according to plan, other people will write about us; they'll make movies about *us*, Jimmy. The way they do about other people, like Butch and the Kid, and Leopold and Loeb—"

"And Ahab and Jezebel."

"Who?"

"Never mind. Fine, no more camera."

Roaring past the engorged tits of the San Onofre nuclear facility, Ralph reaches under his seat, pulls out a green plastic bag, and drops it in Clyde's lap, never taking his eyes off the road, fighting to maintain control of the car on the curves, which come one after another. Clyde peeks inside the bag and pulls out two rubber masks, one of Marilyn Monroe and one of James Dean. At the bottom of the bag, he finds two black plastic toy guns and grins at Ralph just at the radar detector screeches.

Ralph reduces his speed and exits the freeway. He drives along the slip road running parallel to the freeway and pulls into the shade of an underpass. Just then, a CHP squad car races overhead, sirens blaring and red lights flashing, in pursuit of another vehicle.

"We'll stick to the highway from here on out." Ralph manoeuvres the Porsche back onto the slip road. "We're kind of conspicuous in this."

Clyde stuffs the masks back into the bag as Ralph takes the coastal highway and they speed along next to the ocean. He stretches out in the bucket seat and smiles, imagining their new life in Mexico, the two of them toast-of-the-town celebrities living a life of glamour, holding court in a mansion overlooking the Pacific, like Elizabeth Taylor and Richard Burton in Puerto Vallarta in the '60s, a cute Mexican houseboy serving them mojitos on the veranda.

Ralph puts his arm around Clyde and drives with one hand, and Clyde scoots close to him, resting his head on Ralph's shoulder. He lets his hand drop in Ralph's lap and rubs it against the growing bulge in his jeans. Checking his rear-view mirror to confirm that they are a safe distance from the car behind, Ralph switches the station from rock to classical and lifts himself a bit off his seat to help Clyde lower his jeans to his knees. Then he pulls off the road into a strawberry field and drives down a dirt track to the cliff's edge facing the Pacific, where they make love. Afterwards, they lay back and catch their breaths to the sounds of Handel's *Water Music* as the sun starts its late-afternoon descent into the ocean.

"You know, Jimmy, I wish we could stay like this forever; just snap our fingers and stop time."

Ralph stares at the expanse of the ocean and nods. "Me too. It's perfect."

Clyde draws up his knees and wraps his arms around them. "Can I ask you something, Jimmy? Something that might seem a weensy bit silly?"

"Sure."

"Do you love me? Wait, don't answer yet. I mean, I know we haven't known each other that long and all that. But we've already gone through a lot together. More than most people. And there's a lot more ahead. And I wouldn't do any of this with just anyone."

Ralph looks sidelong at Clyde.

"What I mean to say is that *I* love *you*." Clyde takes Ralph's hand and kisses it tenderly. "I was hoping you might love me too."

Ralph kisses Clyde's hand in return. "Of course, I love you. Very much. That's what this is all about, isn't it?"

"Thank you, Jimmy." Clyde pulls a handkerchief out of his purse and dabs at his moist eyes. "I feel happy. For the first time in my life, I feel really happy."

—⁓—

Ralph watches through the window of a San Diego hair salon as the stylist applies the finishing touches to Clyde's new Marilyn hairdo. Clyde whips off the pink apron and primps in front of a mirror, then blows a kiss at the stylist and walks with her to the cash register. Ralph steps inside and hands the stylist a credit card.

"She's quite a looker, this one," the stylist says to Ralph as she processes the payment. "You're a lucky guy."

Ralph reddens a bit and smiles at the stylist.

"I'm happy to give you my autograph." Clyde points at a notepad next to the till.

The stylist glances at the notebook and back up at Clyde, who snatches a random pen out of a bottle and scribbles the name *Marilyn Monroe* into it.

"Save this, dear," he says. "This is going to be worth a fortune very soon."

Ralph and Clyde drive down the road and park in front of a large costume shop. They hop out of the car and sweep into the shop. Clyde tries on a red, satin evening gown, which hangs off his shoulders, a pair of long white gloves, and some expensive-looking costume jewellery. A gasp escapes his mouth as he steps up to a full-size, three-panel mirror. The transformation is complete. He is Marilyn Monroe.

Ralph struts into the room wearing a red leather jacket over a crisp white T-shirt, a pair of tight, pegged Levis, and brown penny loafers, his blue-black hair combed back into a fifties-style pompadour—a Levantine version of James Dean in *Rebel Without a Cause*. He takes Clyde's hand and strikes a bad-boy pose.

"Oh, Jimmy," Clyde whispers, tears standing out in his eyes, "we're magnificent."

"Yes, we are." Ralph kisses Clyde on the mouth and settles up with the proprietor with a credit card. Then the two of them run out of the shop holding hands and hop back into the Porsche.

Ralphs discreetly snorts a couple of lines of cocaine before revving up the engine and tearing out of the parking lot entrance, tyres squealing, narrowly missing a white station wagon driven by a soccer mom.

"Be careful, Jimmy!" Clyde punches Ralph in the arm.

"Relax, baby; everything's under control."

Ralph gets back onto the freeway, and they drive in silence for about twenty minutes before exiting onto San Ysidro's main commercial drag and cruising past a small bank at the far end of a near-deserted strip mall. They crane their necks in the direction of the bank as they drive past, then glance at each other. Ralph nods sombrely at Clyde. Clyde smiles and hugs Ralph, who circles the block then creeps into the parking lot and parks at the side of the bank on the backside of the mall out of view of the main road. Then, reaching under his seat, Ralph pulls out the plastic bag, and he and Clyde don their masks.

"I'm shitting my panties, Jimmy."

"Me too."

"But we've come this far."

"We don't have to do this. Remember, I can *get* you the money for the sex change."

"We've been over this already, Jimmy. This is about us taking control. After today, everyone will be talking about us the way they're meant to. They'll finally know who we are." Clyde squeezes Ralph's hand. "This has never been about the money *or* the sex change."

Ralph stares at the bank out of the eyeholes of his mask, mentally rehearsing his exit strategy. Clyde will wait in the back of the bank covering the door; he'll hand the teller a note explaining everything, stalling until the police arrive. No threats, no demands for money. Just a crazy Jap in Marilyn drag and an innocent, well-meaning film student bamboozled into pretend-robbing a bank. All great fodder for his documentary exposé about a delusional fan. As long as Clyde doesn't blab about his father, everything should work out perfectly.

"OK, remember," Ralph says, "this is going to be a quick in and out like we planned. You cover the door; I'll talk to the teller. Then when it's all over you run out, bring the car around front, and I'll jump in. Then we'll drive straight across the border, which is literally right there, and head for the Rio district." He points at the US-Mexican border complex a couple of blocks away and tosses Clyde the keys. "It's almost closing time, so there shouldn't be anyone in there besides the employees."

"I got it, Jimmy. Let's get this over with already."

"And we abort at any sign of trouble."

The two of them push through the door of the empty bank and stroll casually in the direction of the teller windows at the other end of the small building. As they cross the floor, they spot a security guard in the corner sitting backwards in a chair sipping coffee from a Styrofoam cup. Clyde frowns and elbows Ralph in the ribs, then breaks rank and dashes forward. Ralph's heart leaps into his chest as he watches Clyde rush the windows waving his gun and screaming orders. The security guard's eyes spasm open, and he jumps out of his chair, tossing aside his coffee and pulling out his service revolver. Ralph runs up to him, holding out his gun, and the guard nervously lowers his weapon. Ralph takes it from him and babbles an explanation of what's happening—the delusional patient, the fake guns, the planned surrender—as Clyde calls forward each teller, one after the other, demanding that they empty their cash drawer into a plastic bag. But all that comes out of Ralph's mouth is an unintelligible babble of Hebrew, English, and Nadsat.

"Bring him over here," Clyde screams, now finished and holding the tellers in a huddle at gunpoint.

Ralph escorts the security guard to where the tellers are standing, and Clyde grabs him by the arm and pushes him into the group.

"What the fuck are you doing?" Ralph whispers to Clyde. "This wasn't our plan."

"Neither was he." Clyde points his pistol at the security guard. "You stay here."

Clyde grabs the security guard's revolver out of Ralph's hand and orders the supervising teller at gunpoint to show him the vault. When they disappear from the room, Ralph tries to reassure the hostages that nothing is going to happen to them, but the wild looks in their eyes tell him they don't understand a word he is saying. Perspiration streams down his face inside the hot rubber mask and mixes with his tears. For the first time in years, he chants a prayer, begging God for mercy and forgiveness, vowing to return everything he has stolen and to dedicate the rest of his life to the service of others. If only... But all he hears in his head is *kipur*—the Hebrew word for atonement—and he accepts his fate.

Clyde returns with the supervising teller, his bag brimming with cash, and breathily orders her to rejoin her colleagues. Then he blows a kiss at the group, curtsies, and quickly exits the bank, pirouetting as he goes, cash flying everywhere. A few moments later, the roar of the Porsche's engine is followed by a sound of a car horn. Ralph backs away from the crowd and bows dramatically, then dashes out of the building. The security guard immediately disengages from the group and signals one of the tellers to sound the alarm, then chases after Ralph, grabbing a spare sidearm out of his desk as he goes.

Ralph sprints toward the Porsche Spyder as it pulls away from the kerb. The security guard bursts out of the bank as Ralph leaps toward the automobile. He drops into a squat and fires off a couple of shots at Ralph, who tumbles over the side of the car into the passenger seat just as the Porsche tears out of the lot, leaving the guard huffing and puffing in a cloud of smoke and dust.

Ralph screams out in pain; Clyde rips off his mask.

"What happened? What's wrong?"

"He shot me, you imbecile. Oh, God, oh, God." Ralph reaches around, and his face contorts from the pain. He pulls back a blood-soaked hand.

"Oh, my God," Clyde screams. "What should I do? What should I do? Should I take you to a hospital?"

"No, no...just keep driving. We're almost there."

"Are you sure, Jimmy?"

"Yes, I'm fucking sure. Just go."

The Porsche roars toward the crossing point. As it reaches the customs and immigration kiosk, the Mexican border guard suspiciously eyes them. Clyde tosses him a hundred-dollar bill, which the guard nonchalantly stuffs into his pocket before waving them through.

They cross into Mexico and mount the overpass that leads to the various districts of the sprawling border city. They follow the signs that indicate the Distrito Rio and exit onto a major boulevard with a series of large traffic circles, one after another, honouring the heroes of Mexican history with gargantuan bronze statues, just as dusk descends and the lights of the city blink on. As they round the traffic circles, Ralph wordlessly points the way, his face pale and tense.

They turn off the main boulevard and rumble down a dark side street pitted with potholes and littered with discarded tyres. The stench of burning rubbish wafts over the neighbourhood. Ralph points out a large, nondescript brick building at the end of the street with a blinking sign on the roof that says Hotel Don Quixote. Clyde pulls up to the kerb, just off the driveway leading to the registration office, and shuts off the engine. He leans over Ralph and passes a hand over his sweating forehead. Ralph waves him off weakly.

Clyde runs to the reception office. He pulls open the door and looks inside but doesn't see anyone.

"Hello? *Buenos dias?*"

He steps into the office and, as he reaches the desk, he catches the sound of laboured breathing in the background.

"Hello?"

Noticing a call bell hiding behind a dying fern, he snatches it up and bangs on it repeatedly.

"Buenos dias, hello," he yells.

A moment later a pillow-creased, middle-aged woman with a greasy mane of black-and-grey hair peers around the corner from a back room and squints at Clyde.

"*Sí?*"

"I need a room."

The woman moves into the office, buttoning her blouse, and pulls out a guest register. She puts on a cracked pair of half-glasses and arches a pencil-thin eyebrow at Clyde, who is still dressed in full Marilyn drag. A bare-chested teenager pokes his head around the corner from the back room for a moment, then hides again. The woman senses the teenager's presence and glances over her shoulder in his direction. Keen to return to her young man, and not caring if it shows, she turns back to Clyde.

"*En que te puedo ayudar, eh … señorita.*"

"I need a room, *please.*" Clyde drums his fingers on the counter nervously.

The woman looks up and down at Clyde for a moment and shakes her head.

"*Lo siento. No tenemos habitaciones. Adios.*"

She turns to leave, and Clyde slaps down a hundred-dollar bill on the front desk. The woman eyes the money, then looks back up at Clyde and shrugs. He frowns and slaps down another one, then another.

A moment later, Clyde dashes out of the office, a room key dangling from his hand. He runs to the car and checks on Ralph, who smiles at him weakly. Then he drives up to the nearest stairwell, grabs Ralph's trench coat out of the trunk, and drapes it over him before helping him up the stairs to their room on the second floor.

The hotel clerk peers out at Clyde and Ralph from behind a tattered curtain. The teenager stands behind her in his boxer shorts looking over her bare shoulder at the pair as they ascend the stairs. At one point, Ralph stumbles, and Clyde helps him up. The woman turns and looks quizzically at the teenager. He shakes his head and grabs her by the waist, pulling her away from the window. Then he kisses her passionately on the mouth, and they fall on the bed entwined.

Clyde helps Ralph into the darkened room and lowers him on to the hastily made bed. He finds the light switch, flips it on and moves to Ralph's side. Ralph's eyes are open, but glazed over. He removes Ralph's jacket and T-shirt and turns him over. His back is oozing blood, and the mattress underneath is already quite stained.

"Shit," Clyde hisses.

Grabbing an empty ice bucket from the desk, he runs to the bathroom and fills the bucket with scalding hot water, staring intensely at the stream gushing out of the faucet. Suddenly he hears a breathy whisper.

"Psst, hey there."

Clyde looks up at the steamed-up mirror and sees Marilyn staring back at him. She smiles and blows a kiss and beckons for him to join her. Clyde frowns at the mirror and looks back down at the overflowing bucket, then turns off the faucet.

He carries the bucket back into the room together with a few towels and sits at Ralph's side. Dipping a hand towel into the hot water, he gently cleanses Ralph's wound.

"Ahh, fuck!" Ralph reaches around and grasps at Clyde's hand. Clyde grabs his wrist. "I've got to clean it before I can tend it."

"It hurts!"

"I've got to try and stop the bleeding; then I'm going to find a doctor."

Clyde continues washing Ralph's wound.

"No doctors," Ralph snaps. "I don't want us to get caught."

Clyde looks closely at the wound. "Jesus…you're oozing blood out of two places. The bullet probably went in here and went out there." He grabs Ralph's hand, places a dry towel into it. "Hold this against your side while I make a tourniquet."

Clyde tears off his dress and pulls his hair back into a tight ponytail. Then he opens the closet and pulls out a folding bed. He unlatches it and removes the fitted sheet. Casting about the room, Clyde spots a small wooden desk. He drags it away from the wall and tries to fray the sheet by rubbing it back and forth against a rough edge while Ralph watches.

"Where'd you learn to do this stuff?" Ralph croaks.

"In the Boy Scouts. Keep still."

"In the Boy Scouts?" Ralph laughs, then winces in reaction to the stabbing pain it provokes. "Marilyn Monroe was in the Boy Scouts?"

The sheet frays in Clyde's hand.

"Shut the fuck up."

Clyde rips the sheet into long strips. Then he pulls Ralph's hand away from the wound and confirms that the oozing has abated before wrapping his torso in strips of cloth. When he finishes, he helps Ralph onto his stomach, then goes into the bathroom and refills the bucket and a couple of plastic cups with cold water. He returns to Ralph's side and places the water on the nightstand within easy reach, then examines the wraps.

He frowns at a thimble-sized spot of blood in the middle of the wrapping.

"It's too tight," Ralph says.

"The bleeding hasn't stopped completely. But it's under control for now."

"I'm hungry."

"That's a good sign." Clyde sits on the bed next to Ralph and strokes his hair.

"I'm in pain, but I'm hungry. Go find something for us to eat."

"I'm not going to leave you."

"You've got to stash the car anyway if it hasn't been stolen already."

"God damn it. I'd forgotten about the car."

"There's supposed to be a body shop around the corner according to the map. Give whomever's there a couple hundred to store it for a few days. Promise more for when you pick it up. Don't forget to bring up our stuff before you go, including my strongbox."

"What if they're closed? It's already night-time."

Ralph stays quiet for a few seconds. "If it's closed, ditch the thing anywhere. Then go bring us something to eat."

"But I barely know any Spanish. Besides, I hate Mexican food."

"Then look for some Japanese food. But I'm warning you, I don't know how to use chopsticks—" Ralph is taken with a sudden fit of painful coughing.

Clyde stands and looks down at Ralph, his face tense with fear. After a moment, Ralph recovers and breathes more easily.

"I'm OK, really. I'll be all right, I promise. I'm feeling better."

Clyde rechecks the wraps and is relieved to see the blood spot has not grown. He returns an hour later, his arms laden with brown paper sacks and finds Ralph sitting up in bed mesmerised by the blue flicker of the TV, which is tuned to a San Diego English-language station. He rushes to his side and covers his face in kisses. Ralph snaps out of it and smiles weakly as he watches Clyde pull white takeaway containers from the paper sacks.

"Look what I found." Clyde opens one of the containers and shows Ralph some steaming yaki-soba. "I couldn't believe it. Japanese Mexicans. And just two blocks from here." He sets aside the container and pops open another one that is full of rice.

"Did you speak to them in Japanese?"

"Hell, no. I just pointed. This one's vegetarian. I made sure, you know, because of the Jewish thing."

He feeds Ralph yaki-soba with a pair of chopsticks. After the first few bites, Ralph looks away and grimaces.

"No more. It's too greasy."

Clyde pulls Ralph's head back around by the chin.

Ralph pulls a face at the food dangling from the chopsticks. "What did you do with the car?"

"The body shop was closed, so I ended up parking it around back in a field. But forget that for now. I want you to eat something if you can. You need to build back your strength."

Ralph nods at the TV as the pre-broadcast graphics of the eleven o'clock news play out on screen. "Turn it up, please."

Clyde points the remote at the TV and ratchets up the volume as the programme cuts away to the anchorman, who launches into the top story.

Good evening. Marilyn Monroe and James Dean rob a San Ysidro bank this afternoon.

"Will you listen to that," Ralph says, wiping the grease from his lips with a paper napkin.

Clyde sets aside the food container and sits up.

That's right, folks. Two suspects, one disguised as Marilyn Monroe and the other as James Dean, held up the border branch of Jacaranda Bank late this afternoon just before closing time.

The broadcast cuts away to a grainy CCTV video of the actual robbery as it transpired. It shows Clyde ordering the tellers into a huddle.

411

"Oh, my God." Clyde jumps to his feet and points at the TV. "Look, Jimmy. I'm a star! I'm really a star!"

Ralph's hand shoots up at Clyde. "Calm down. I can't hear."

The video cuts to another shot showing Ralph escorting the security guard into the teller's cage.

"Look, Jimmy, it's you. This is fucking fantabulous!"

Ralph shoots Clyde a sidelong glance, which silences Clyde, then he looks back at the TV as it cuts to the anchorman.

It's believed one of the suspects was injured while fleeing the scene when a security guard fired live rounds at him. The automobile in which the two fled, an unidentified silver sports car, was last seen speeding toward the US-Mexico border. Anyone with information leading to the capture of the two suspects, both of whom are considered armed and dangerous, is requested to call the following number.

"Turn it off, please."

Clyde frowns and switches off the TV. "What is it?"

Ralph scoots down the bed and rests his head on the pillow. "Lie down next to me."

Clyde gets back into bed and passes a hand through Ralph's damp hair. Ralph gazes at him for a few moments.

"We have a long road ahead of us, you and me. You know that, right?"

Clyde nods.

"I need you to promise me something." Ralph closes his eyes. When he opens them a moment later, they are burning with emotion. "I want you to promise you'll never hate me, even if I turn out not to be the guy you think I am."

"I could never hate you, Jimmy."

"Don't put me on a pedestal. I did that once, and it ruined me."

"With who?"

Ralph points at the ceiling.

Clyde sits up. "God?"

"I believed in him more deeply than anyone I knew. More than my father; even more than our rabbi. I did everything right, followed every commandment by the book. But he never helped me when I needed it, not even when I begged him. He made my mother hate me, killed my cousin, and took away the only person I ever loved."

"The soldier?"

Ralph nods. "My cousin, Yossi. It kills me to think of him now, helpless in his wheelchair refusing to speak to me."

"I see. Thus, 'there is no God'."

Ralph glares at Clyde.

"Listen, Jimmy, my religious Aunt Doreen once told me about some rich man in the Bible who did everything right—and I mean everything—no being a bad son, no stealing, no stuffing dead bodies in freezers. You know, a totally perfect person. And still, your God killed everyone he loved and took away everything he had. And then, to make matters worse, he made him, like, completely sick, covered in boils from head to foot."

"That was Job. He was being tested."

"Yeah, right. I'm sure it didn't feel that way to him."

"Maybe not." Raphael looks at his hands for a moment then looks back at Clyde. "*Hen yikteleini, lo ayahel.*"[1]

"What's that?"

"It's what Job said to his friends when they told him to curse God and die. It means, *Though he slay me, still will I trust him.* He never lost his faith regardless of what God did to him."

"If you ask me, Jimmy, it's not God that's the problem. It's your *idea* of God that's wrong. You and my Auntie Doreen think of God as a person up there who watches everything we do and who's supposed to reward or punish us depending on whether we follow certain rules—like some kind of nice daddy. But God's not like that at all! In *my* mind, God is the indifferent life force that flows through everything and recycles everything. I'm afraid *your* God is an illusion, Jimmy."

הֵן יִקְטְלֵנִי, לֹא (לוֹ) אֲיַחֵל[1]

Ralph nods and looks around the hotel room, then he looks sidelong at Clyde. "You know about illusions, don't you, Clyde?"

Clyde looks down and plays nervously with the edge of the sheet.

"Are you an illusion, Jimmy?"

"The name's Raphael."

"That's a nice name. Raphael then... are you? An illusion?"

Raphael looks straight at Clyde, his expression softening. He takes his hand and kisses it. "Less and less."

Later that night Raphael wakes up screaming. Clyde flips on the table lamp.

"What is it? What's wrong?"

"It hurts... God, it's burning."

Raphael flails in bed, the sheets underneath him are stained with blood, and his wraps are soaked through.

"You're bleeding again! I'm getting you to a hospital. I don't care what you say."

Clyde grabs the phone and dials.

"No—"

"I'm not fucking losing you, goddammit."

Raphael stops flailing and is wracked with shivering. Clyde slams down the receiver.

"It's dead. I'll be right back."

Clyde leaps out of bed, pulls on a pair of cut-off jeans and some tennis shoes, and bolts out the door. He rushes down the stairwell and pounds on the office door.

"Help! Help, please!"

He rings the night bell and tries the door handle, but the door is bolted shut.

"Open up, somebody. We need a doctor!"

Clyde's screams echo back. He pounds on the door a few more times, then gives it a good kick before moving to the street. He runs down the darkened road in the direction of some music and turns left into a wide, garishly illuminated bar-lined boulevard jammed with drunks, hookers, and street toughs jostling past each other on a rubbish-strewn pavement. Ear-splitting dance music screams out of strip joints, beer halls, and the hotel lobbies that serve as fronts for whorehouses. A river of junky cars flows past incessantly honking and spewing clouds of exhaust into the humid air already heavy with the stench of burning rubbish. Clyde stares at the scene in bewilderment. Spotting a pay phone a block away, he fights his way to it through the crowd.

A rotund drunk sitting against a smashed-in parking meter hungrily tracks Clyde's approach. He staggers to his feet, spits in his hand, and rakes his motor-oil-stained fingers through his unkempt black hair. Then he smoothens out his drool spattered T-shirt and lurches forward just as Clyde reaches the pay phone.

Clyde lifts the receiver, but the phone is dead. He screams in frustration and slams the receiver repeatedly against the metal case until it breaks in his hand just as the drunk approaches from behind and grabs a generous portion of Clyde's ass. Clyde whirls around furiously and shoves the drunk against a parked car. His dentures fly out of his mouth as his head hits the windscreen, and he crumples unconscious to the ground. Clyde storms away down the cracked pavement.

The altercation catches the attention of three hard-faced, black-clad bouncers standing outside a strip club, a flat-nosed one in his twenties, the other two in their mid-forties, one short and round with a shaggy moustache, the other tall and hobbled by a clubfoot and bad knees. They exchange a conspiratorial look, then step into the crowd and shadow Clyde from a distance.

Clyde moves from person to person, gesturing wildly, trying as best as he can to ask for a doctor. The people ignore him, laugh at him, shove him aside. Up ahead, another block away, Clyde sees a sharp-looking police officer leaning against a railing in front of a large church and breaks in his direction. He pushes through the crowd, which is thickest at this point, in the direction of the church. The three bouncers pick up their pace behind him, elbowing their way through the crowd. They reach Clyde the moment he breaks free of the crowd at the intersection. The younger of the three clamps his hand over Clyde's mouth, and the other two help drag Clyde, kicking and scratching, back into the crowd. The police officer glances with mild curiosity in the direction of the kidnap scene, but, seeing nothing, yawns and checks his wristwatch.

—〰—

Ralph sits up in bed in the midst of a coughing fit and covers his mouth with the edge of a sheet. During a brief respite, he glances into the sheet, and his breath catches at the sight of the spattering of fresh blood that stains it. He grimaces and wipes his mouth.

He moves painfully off the bed and struggles over to his strongbox, which sits on the desk. He digs through the pockets of his jeans, which are draped over a splintered wooden chair, and pulls out a set of keys. Opening the box, he pulls out his notebooks and lovingly passes a hand over them. He opens up one of them to a page marked by a clipped article from the *Los Angeles Herald-Examiner* and quickly rescans the article, which reports the attempted burglary of Marilyn Monroe and Joe DiMaggio's honeymoon home in Beverly Hills, and which is illustrated by a colour photo of the modest-looking house, a black-and-white picture of Marilyn and DiMaggio in a booth at the Brown Derby, and a grainy image of Clyde in the courtroom sitting next to his public defender.

Setting it aside, he sifts through some newspaper clippings and old photographs. He picks out a colour glossy of Yossi, still young and healthy, standing proudly in his military uniform holding his machine gun at a forty-five-degree angle across his chest. He stares at the photo for a few fleeting moments, focusing on Yossi's beautiful eyes, at the thick black eyebrows that frame them, and presses his lips to it, holding them there for a few seconds. Then he places the photo on the nightstand against the lamp so that it faces the bed, and returns to the desk.

He reaches deep into the box and pulls out a blue velvet bag embroidered with Hebrew writing, a black felt kippah, and a prayer book. He pulls a set of tefillin out of the bag and arranges them on the table, the head tefillin on his left and the arm tefillin on his right. He stares at the black boxes and leather straps for a moment, slipping on the kippah, then he closes his eyes and rocks gently.

"Hen yikteleini, lo ayahel. Hen yikteleini, lo ayahel. Hen yikteleini, lo ayahel."

Tears course down his face as he chants the ancient words from the book of Job again and again and again until he is cut short by a fit of coughing. He reaches for a glass of water and takes a few calming sips. When the coughing subsides, he grabs up the ritual items and takes them to bed.

Sitting with his back against the wall, he looks at the photo of Yossi and cries again.

"Hen yikteleini, lo ayahel…"

He stares at the tefillin in his lap, passes his fingers over the leather straps, then raises the arm tefillin to his lips and kisses it. Putting his arm through the loop, he places the black box on his bicep below the halfway point between his shoulder and his elbow, directly across from his heart, the way his father taught him when he was a young boy. He utters the blessing while tightening the strap around his arm, then wraps it twice around his biceps, seven times around his forearm, and once around his palm, leaving a length of leather to be tied around his hand later.

Raising the head tefillin, he recites the blessing and places it on his head, centring the black box above his forehead directly over the point between his eyes. Then he stares at the remainder of the strap hanging from his fingers.

A car horn outside breaks his concentration. He looks around the room and sees the shambles, the ripped and bloody sheets, the overturned ice bucket, the mess of papers on the desk. Then he catches sight of himself in the closet mirror, a pitiful sight in his blood-spattered underpants, unshaven, black circles under his eyes, a black box on his head, and his arm bound in a black leather strap.

And then he starts to laugh.

—〰—

The bouncers drag Clyde toward a strip joint with loud '70s disco music pouring out of the doorway. They haul him inside and carry him through the smoke-filled auditorium where an over-weight stripper on the stage coaxes a burro to mount her in time to the music under the flash of strobe lights. The patrons whoop it up and fall over themselves laughing, barely noticing the three thugs dragging a young man across the floor.

The bouncers shove Clyde through a door in the back of the club and drag him down a stairwell illuminated only by a bare red light bulb. The bouncers struggle to hold Clyde as he bucks and bites. One of his legs breaks free, and he kicks at the light bulb, breaking it off at the base and startling the thugs as the stairwell is suddenly plunged into darkness. Clyde spins free as their grip loosens, which sends all four of them tumbling down the stairs.

Clyde crash lands on top of the young one as they hit the con-crete floor of a foul-smelling red lit cellar, then scrambles away as the young tough swings at him and screams obscenities in Spanish. He reaches the other side of the room just as the other two tumble out of the stairwell, both smashing into the young tough. Clyde tries to run around them to reach the stairway. But the two older bouncers leap to their feet and slam him back against a brick wall, stunning him for a moment. The young one tosses them a few lengths of twine from across the room, which they use to spread-eagle Clyde, tying his wrists to two metal hooks embedded in the brick for the purpose. Then they roughly pull off Clyde's shorts and panties, exposing his cock. Clyde karate-kicks the short, fat one in the balls and he crumples to the ground.

"*Es una luchadora,*" says the taller one, "*Eso sí me gusta en una mujer.*"

He hammers Clyde in the face with a closed fist, bloodying his nose. Clyde spits at him. The thug wipes off the spittle with one sweep of his dirt-caked hand and flashes a mouthful of gold.

"*Amarrale las piernas,*" he says, spitting on the ground.

The younger one rushes forward and winds twine around Clyde's ankles.

"What are you doing, you cocksuckers?" Clyde screams.

The younger one pulls a stiletto out of his back pocket; the blade shoots out, glinting in the dim red light.

"*Callate la boca, pendejo, o te hago pedazos.*"

"*Cortale los huevos, Sixto!*" the short one says, clapping his hands.

The other two thugs break into hysterical laughter at the suggestion.

Sixto caresses Clyde's testicles with the blade.

"*Primero me la voy a cojer, Taco. Después le cortamos lo malo que le sobra.*"

He retracts the blade, slides it back into his pocket, then unhooks one of Clyde's arms. "*Agarre, carnal.*" He holds out the rope to his short comrade Taco, who yanks it tight.

Sixto grabs Clyde by the chin and shoves his head upward.

"Wait, wait!" Clyde screams. "Money…you want money?"

"*Que dice la perra, Pedro?*" Sixto asks the tall one over his shoulder.

"Money… *dinero* … I'm worth mucho dinero!"

"*Dice que tiene dinero,*" Pedro says.

Sixto yanks Clyde's hair.

"*Donde esta el dinero?*"

"Ahhh! Let go of my hair, you big ox! I'm a fugitive. *Fugitiva.* There's a big reward for whoever turns me in."

"*Ahora que dice?*" Sixto asks.

"A reward…ahhh, ouch! Clyde screams. "*Una recompensa…*"

"*Dice que su padre es rico…y que pagará un rescate.*"

"*Que mierda,*" Sixto says, unbuttoning his trousers and stepping back. "*Inclínala sobre la mesa.*"

Pedro unhooks Clyde's other hand and pulls the rope tight.

"Wait!" Clyde screams as they drag him across the room to a table and bend him over it. "Wait just a fucking second!"

Sixto approaches him from behind with his trousers around his ankles, holding his cock in one hand and a tub of lard in the other.

"*Desatale las piernas y extiéndelas.*" Sixto shakes his cock at Clyde's ass. "*Necesito acceso abierto.*"

"*Dice que esperes, carnal,*" Pedro says, reaching down to free Clyde's ankles from the twine.

"*Espere para que?*" Sixto asks, putting the tub of lard on the table and dipping a finger into it. "*Quieres que me ponga un gorrito primero, cariño?*"

Clyde looks over his shoulder and catches his breath at the sight of Sixto greasing up his fully erect cock with the lard. His heart pounds and his mind works quickly trying to figure out how to survive this assault.

"That's a really nice, big cock you've got there," he says as Sixto grabs for his ass, forcing a smile. "Why don't you let me suck it first?"

"*Te la quiere mamar, carnal,*" Pedro says. "*Dice que tiene hambre.*"

"*Es cierto?*" Sixto grabs Clyde's hair. "*Te gusta mi vergota, perra?*"

Clyde grits his teeth and nods his head. "Oh yeah…let me swallow that juicy cock of yours. I'll get it nice and wet, then you can ram it up my tight ass."

"*No sé lo que está diciendo, pero me parece bien,*" Sixto says. "*Bajamela.*"

Pedro and Taco pull Clyde away from the table and on to his knees. Sixto pulls out his stiletto and flicks it open. He grabs Clyde by the hair and draws his face level with his crotch.

"*Empieza a mamar, maricón.*"

Clyde lunges forward and sucks Sixto's cock.

"*Ay sí...*" Sixto closes his eyes, a twisted grin spasming his mouth. "*Mmmm, es cierto que chupa bien. Que ricura.*"

The other two watch enthusiastically. Taco unbuttons his trousers with his free hand.

"*Apurate, carnal. Ahora es mi turno.*"

Sixto thrusts deep in and out of Clyde's mouth.

Taco holds out his end of the rope to Sixto. "*Vamos, carnal, aguantala tu un poco.*"

"*Callate, buey,*" Sixto snaps. "*Me estás haciendo perder la concentración.*"

Noticing the friction developing between the thugs, Clyde comes up for air.

"Let me use my hand. It'll feel a lot better."

"*Que dice?*" Sixto asks.

"*Dice que es mi turno.*" Taco shoves the rope at Sixto.

Clyde shakes his head and nods at Sixto.

"No, I want *him.*" He smiles salaciously at Sixto. "I like you, big boy. *Me gustas.* Let me use my hand. My *mano.*" Taking advantage of the slack on the rope on Taco's side, Clyde makes a stroking gesture with his hand and licks his lips at Sixto.

"*Te quiere chaquetear, mano,*" the tall one says.

Sixto waves his stiletto at Taco. "*Ándale! Sueltale el brazo.*"

Taco releases the rope and masturbates. "*Está bien, pero apurate. No me quiero venir esperando mi turno.*"

Clyde simultaneously sucks and strokes Sixto with his hand. Sixto moans loudly as he gets very close to orgasm.

"*Vengate ya, maldito,*" Taco yells. "*Es mi turno.*"

"*No, ahora me toca a mi,*" Pedro says. "*Me lo merezco, ya que me ha tocado traducir toda esta mierda.*"

Clyde's eyes roll up into his head as he braces himself and bites down on Sixto's cock with all his strength, severing it at the base. Sixto lets out a deafening screech. Pedro and Taco recoil in horror as Clyde rears up, wielding the severed cock in his hand, and the rope slips out of Pedro's hand.

Clyde leaps up and pitches the severed cock at Taco's face. Then he rushes forward, grabs him by the hair, and smashes his head into the brick wall. Taco falls to the ground in a heap. Pedro lunges at Clyde, who sidesteps him and wraps a piece of rope around his neck, tying it as tight as he can until Pedro passes out.

Sixto runs around the small cellar howling, looking for something with which to stop the profuse bleeding. Spotting the switchblade on the ground, Clyde snatches it up and cuts off the ropes. Then, rescuing his shorts and panties from a corner, he pulls them on and bolts up the stairs.

Clyde pushes his way through the crowded strip club, wild-eyed and taking in deep draughts of the smoke-choked air. On the stage he sees a massive black woman sodomising a seventy-something with a dildo, and the sight makes him feel like retching. He breaks free of the crowd at the door and tumbles out of the club, then he crosses the pavement to the street and vomits into the gutter.

Straightening up at the sound of angry voices approaching from the distance, he staggers away from the boulevard in a state of total disorientation and spends the next thirty minutes stumbling aimlessly up one side street and down another. Finally, hobbling into a short cul-de-sac, he drops to his knees in a state of total exhaustion, his vision a blur. After a moment of rest, his head clears sufficiently for him to see that he is across the street from a two-story building with the words *Clinica Medica Familiar* stencilled in gold letters on the front window.

Clyde struggles to his feet and moves to the building. He knocks on the front door, feebly at first, then more forcefully as his adrenaline kicks in one last time. The faint sound of a TV reaches him from a distance. He resurveys the building from the middle of the road. A soft blue light flickers in the upstairs window. Approaching the building once again, he locates a side staircase then ascends it to a second-story landing and bangs on a door there insistently.

"Help me, please... help me..." he calls, then collapses.

When he returns to his senses, he finds himself on an examination table in a dingy cream-coloured room, dressed in a hospital gown. Painfully raising himself on one elbow, he catches sight of himself in a mirror. His right eye is swollen shut, but the cuts and scratches on his face are washed and dressed. He tenderly touches his eye and grits his teeth against the pain that radiates into his face from the pressure, then falls back onto the table. A moment later he hears a noise emanating from outside the room and calls out.

A dark, squatty man in his early forties, wearing a white lab coat pulled over red plaid pyjamas, appears in the doorway drying his hands with a dishtowel. He regards Clyde with a concerned yet cautious look on his face.

"What is this place?" Clyde feels the room tilting on its axis. "Who are you?"

"You collapsed on my doorstep," the man says in perfect prep school English. "I treated your wounds."

"You're a doctor." Clyde struggles to sit up. "You speak English, and you're a doctor."

The doctor crosses the room and eases Clyde back onto the examination table. "Remain still, please. You may have suffered a concussion."

"No, you don't understand." Clyde tries to sit up again against the firm pressure of the doctor's hands. "I'm not the one who needs a doctor."

"You're hurt—"

"I have a friend," Clyde whimpers. "He's injured badly, he's losing blood."

The doctor raises an eyebrow at Clyde.

"Please, we have to hurry."

Clyde grabs the doctor by the wrist and looks him in the eye.

"I have money."

—⁓—

Clyde bursts through the hotel room door followed by the doctor and sees Ralph's body dangling from a radiator pipe on the ceiling, at the end of a black leather strap wrapped around his neck—his skin blue, his eyes wide and bulging, his tongue hanging out of his mouth. The chair lies on its side, half in the bedroom, half in the bathroom.

Clyde screams and crosses the room. He upends the chair and climbs it to unhook Ralph's body, sobbing hysterically. The doctor moves forward to intervene, but Clyde slaps him away. He lowers Ralph's body to the bed and desperately claws away the leather straps from Ralph's neck. Then he hugs Ralph's body tight and repeatedly kisses his face between loud choking sobs. The doctor touches Clyde's shoulder.

"Get out!"

"Please, let me help," the doctor says.

Clyde arches his back and whips around, baring foaming teeth at the doctor.

"I said get out!" He leaps from the bed and shoves the doctor toward the open door. "Get the fuck out of here!"

The doctor falls to the floor and crawls the rest of the way out of the room. Clyde slams the door shut behind him, then starts back to the bed when he sees Ralph's strongbox on the floor, its contents spilt out across the room. He moves to it, almost afraid to touch it, and picks up the papers and photographs and various notebooks with trembling hands. Then he lifts the strongbox onto the table and lovingly places the items inside. He spots a manila folder under the desk out of which have slipped a few newspaper clippings. Stooping to pick them up, a headline catches his eye:

Transvestite Arrested for Trespass at Former Monroe/DiMaggio Honeymoon House

Clyde stares at the headline for a moment, his heart pounding in his head, not comprehending, and not wanting to comprehend. He picks out another clipping and gasps as he sees a photograph of himself at his arraignment. Then he snatches up the rest and cries out as he realises that all the articles are about him. He turns and looks at Ralph's corpse in horror. The corpse stares back, wide-eyed and silent.

Clyde turns back to the strongbox and pulls out the notebooks, much less reverently, and skims through them, one after another after another, through the various versions of Ralph's treatment for his documentary about *Clyde Koba, a demented Monroe-obsessed fan*, shaking his head with increasing vehemence.

"No…no…no!"

Shoving the strongbox away, he lets out a loud animal-like wail and falls to his knees. He drops his head to the floor, wraps his hands around his neck, and moans loudly. In his head, he hears Marilyn's voice beckoning.

Psst, hey there! she coos soothingly.

Clyde clamps his hands over his ears and shakes his head. But Marilyn's voice only grows louder. Clyde shakes his head more and more violently.

Hey there. Don't let them get you down.

Clyde looks up and finds Marilyn staring back at him from the closet mirror. He leaps up, grabs the strongbox, and flings it with all his strength at the mirror, shattering it to pieces.

—✵—

The Porsche barrels south down the scenic coastal highway that runs along the edge of the cliffs between Tijuana and Ensenada.

Tears flow freely down Clyde's face as he attacks hairpin turn after hairpin turn, barely keeping the tyres on the road. Several police helicopters fly swiftly in his direction.

As the road levels off, Clyde sees a collection of squad cars blocking the road a half-mile ahead. He can make out scores of Mexican federales standing behind the cars with their rifles drawn and pointed in his direction. Clyde sets his jaw and guns the engine. Seeing the Spyder roaring straight for them at full speed, the federales scramble into the hills and take position among the rocks. The helicopters swoop in overhead and land behind the roadblock.

Clyde blinks at the scene laid out before him as he races toward his doom, and flashes on his life, on Momma, Hiro, Kevin, Auntie Doreen, even his bastard of a father now lying at the bottom of a freezer under a pile of frozen fish. They hurt him; they made him strong; he was a victim; he was a manifestor. He had the power to do anything. Even now, on the doorstep of oblivion, at the receiving end of a hundred high-powered rifles, he could still take control. In his past life, he had chosen suicide, like that fake idiot Raphael. "Not this time," he says out loud, as he reduces his speed. "I'm not going to go kamikaze for the sake of an illusion."

He brings the Porsche to a complete stop a few feet from the roadblock and raises his arms over his head.

The federales look at each other and breath deep sighs of relief. They clamber out of the rocks and from around the road-block and approach the Porsche with rifles drawn. Clyde's face is inscrutable, almost catatonic. A tall twenty-something federale breaks from the others and opens the driver's side door. He takes Clyde out by the arm and escorts him to a waiting squad car. Clyde doesn't react. He just stares ahead blankly.

—ɯ—

Kimitake
1982–1983

—ɯ—

—〰—

US-Mexico Border Complex, San Ysidro, California

26 December 1982; 1 a.m.

A retinue of heavily armed US marshals mills about in the semi-darkness of the transfer facility awaiting the Prisoner. A loud clang of metal-on-metal echoes through the room, and a bank of glaring spotlights snaps on. The marshals group together and stand at attention as a cortege of Mexican federales escorts the Prisoner into the room. He is shackled and dressed in a tattered orange jumpsuit, head lowered, non-reactive. His yellow-blonde hair hangs in his face; his black roots are showing.

One of the federales goose-steps forward and presents the US commander with a document. The commander quickly scans and signs it, handing it back to the federale. Another marshal pats down the Prisoner and notes that he raises his eyes at the reflective glass on the opposite wall; upon seeing himself, his head instantly snaps down, and he squeezes shut his almond-shaped eyes.

The marshals whisk the Prisoner out of the featureless concrete building by the arms, one on either side of him, toward three identical black squad cars idling in the distance. He squints painfully in the harsh glare of a searchlight positioned on the top of an adjacent building and pointing at him. The marshals shove him into the back of one of the squad cars and slam the door shut. A moment later, the squad cars speed north up Highway 5 caravan-style, sirens blaring.

—⁂—

U.S. District Court, Los Angeles, California

10 January 1983; 10 a.m.

The Prisoner sits rigidly at the counsel table next to his government lawyer, his hair slicked back into a short ponytail, long streaks of black infusing his dyed blonde hair. He is dressed in a dark blue suit that is one size too large for him, an oddly creased white dress shirt straight out of the packet, and a clip-on red necktie. He stares straight ahead, expressionless and unblinking, as the trial unfolds around him in stop motion. Sounds reach him as if filtered through molasses.

The gallery is sparsely populated. The Prisoner's mother sits alone in the middle of the second row, wearing a canary yellow sundress. She wears no makeup, and her grey roots are showing. She leans forward, anxiously straining to catch the Prisoner's attention. Sitting at the end of the row behind her is the Prisoner's psychiatrist, one Doctor Seth Menner. He observes the trial through half-closed eyes, every so often scribbling in a notepad and then looking back up at the long string of witnesses that gives testimony in front of an angry-looking judge and an impassive jury over the course of the day: a car saleswoman, the owner of a fancy dress shop, a bank teller, a security guard.

The prosecutor plays a video of a bank robbery on a screen set up at the front of the courtroom. At a critical point, she snaps her fingers and instructs the video operator to stop the tape and enlarge the frame. The image of a person wearing an evening gown and a rubber mask comes into focus. The prosecutor uses a long pointer to indicate what looks like a gun trained on a group of people standing in front of the masked person. She then picks up a bag off the floor and pulls a rubber mask and toy gun out of it and offers the items into evidence over the half-hearted objections of the Prisoner's defence lawyer.

The afternoon sun streams through the west-facing window of the courtroom as the jury files back in for the last time, and the foreman hands a verdict form to the bailiff, who carries it to the judge. The Prisoner's lawyer stands and pulls up the Prisoner by the arm as the judge reads out the verdict of guilty. The crack of the gavel resonates through the courtroom. The Prisoner's mother collapses, striking her head on the edge of the bench. The court attendants rush to help her as she convulses on the tiles. The bailiff leads the Prisoner out of the room.

—ɯɯ—

Metropolitan Correctional Center, Los Angeles, California

Prison Processing Center

07 March 1983; 8 p.m.

The Prisoner stands naked in a long queue of naked male inmates. Two marshals move down the queue and perform a full body cavity search on each one of them. The Prisoner watches nervously out of the corner of his eye as the marshals dig into the rectum of the inmate next to him, who is bent over and holding his ankles.

—ɯɯ—

The Prisoner sits in a barber's chair with his eyes tightly shut as the barber buzzes off all his hair with six passes of an electric razor, leaving behind only a blue-black shadow on his scalp. He swings the Prisoner's chair around to face a large mirror. The Prisoner keeps his eyes squeezed shut.

—⟋∿⟍—

Metropolitan Correctional Center, Los Angeles, California

Parking Structure

08 March 1983; 7:30 a.m.

The Prisoner and six other inmates move sluggishly toward a waiting van escorted by two armed marshals. They are hand-cuffed and shackled. Two transport marshals watch them as they climb into the back of the van and arrange themselves on the bench seats, facing each other, three on one side, four on the other. The transport marshals slam shut the doors of the van and chain them closed.

The inmates quietly regard each other as the van heads south on the Santa Ana Freeway on its way out of the city. The day is heavily overcast. Downtown Los Angeles looms in the background, barely visible through the barred and blackened window on the back door. One of the inmates, a thin man in his middle thirties with watery green eyes, flashes a crooked smile at the Prisoner, who returns the smile with a scowl. The inmate shrugs and turns to a stocky Middle Eastern man in his late forties sitting to his right who is staring at the floor.

"What are you in for?" asks the thin inmate.

The Middle Eastern inmate is startled out of his introspection. He regards his neighbour with a sideways glance.

"Are we allowed to say?"

"I don't see why not. I'm Bleeker, by the way."

The Middle Eastern inmate turns his head away. "Wire fraud," he mumbles and looks back at Bleeker. "Not that it's any of your business."

Two of the other inmates chime in that they also got done for wire fraud.

"How much time did they give you?" Bleeker asks.

"Three years, eight months. How about you?"

"Computer theft. They gave me six years."

"Jesus!" a tall inmate sitting to the left of the Prisoner says from across the van. He keeps his head low to avoid banging it against the roof whenever they hit a bump in the road. "Six years for stealing computers?"

"Not for stealing computers, buddy," Bleeker says. "I used a computer to transfer money out of people's bank accounts into an account in Switzerland."

"Oh, we got a genius here," the tall inmate says. "How much money we talking about?"

"A couple hundred thousand."

"That's not bad." The tall inmate thrusts out his long legs, positioning them between the legs of the two inmates across from him and rests his head against the front of the van. "They gave my ass fifteen years for transporting three hundred kilos of mushrooms over the border."

The Prisoner looks at the tall inmate and arches an eyebrow.

"I didn't know there was such a big market for mushrooms," says a Hispanic inmate sitting to the right of the Prisoner.

"Not yet there isn't," the tall one says. "You might say me and some other businessmen were starting up a little joint venture."

The Hispanic lets out a sarcastic chuckle. "What's wrong with this picture, eh? Mr Genius there gets six years for stealing hundreds of thousands of other folks' money, while a respectable businessman like yourself gets fucked for fifteen years."

"Or *doesn't* get fucked," a pimply faced inmate barely out of his teens sitting across from the tall inmate says with a nervous giggle.

The inmates laugh at the joke.

"I wouldn't be so sure about that," Bleeker says.

The laughter quickly dies down, and the inmates eye each other suspiciously as the van skirts the foothills of the San Bernardino Mountains, speeding in the direction of the Coachella Valley. Patches of snow are visible on the hillside out of the window.

A professorial-looking inmate in his thirties wearing a pair of black horn-rimmed glasses and sitting to Bleeker's left clears his throat and raises his hand. The others turn their heads and stare at him.

"You don't need to hold up your hand, precious," Bleeker says. "This isn't exactly grammar school."

"We should introduce ourselves properly."

The others look at each other and nod.

"You go first, darling." Bleeker winks at his neighbour.

The professorial-looking inmate flashes a shy smile, exposing a mouthful of braces. "Okay, my name's Dick."

The others laugh a bit.

"Is that your first name or your last?" Bleeker asks.

"Last."

"What's your first name? Little?"

Dick reddens as Bleeker's comment draws even more laughter from the others.

"I'm just yanking your chain, man," Bleeker says, wiping his eyes with his sleeve. "Anyway, as I said, I'm Bleeker." He turns to the Middle Eastern inmate on his right. "It's your turn."

"I'm Mehmet."

"What's that?" Bleeker says. "Arabic?"

"It's Turkish. I'm originally from Istanbul."

Mehmet points at the pimply faced inmate. "It's your turn."

"I'm Rugger."

"I'm Mushman," the tall one says. He turns to the Prisoner.

"How about you, China Boy? You've been awfully quiet. What's your name?"

The Prisoner closes his eyes; Mushman shrugs at the others.

"I'm Lopez," the Hispanic to the Prisoner's right says.

"Well, okay," Dick says, "I'm here for tax evasion; I got five years. So, let's see, we've got three wire frauds, one theft by computer, one drug trafficker, one tax evader..."

"How about you there, Mr Sociable?" Bleeker asks. "What are you in for?"

The Prisoner opens his eyes. "Armed robbery and felony murder."

His response draws an exchange of confused looks and intense murmuring from his comrades.

"Those aren't federal offences," Bleeker says.

The Prisoner flashes a menacing look at Bleeker. The others grow very quiet.

"Maybe he got on the wrong bus," Lopez says.

The van speeds through a yellow sand desert dotted with Joshua trees. A high wind forcefully lashes grit against the windows.

Six hours later the van drives through the gates of the United States Penitentiary in Tucson, Arizona, and stops in front of the Quonset hut that serves as a temporary intake centre. The transport marshals hop out, unchain the rear doors, and pull out the inmates one by one. Two reception marshals meet them at the back of the van. The inmates stretch their legs and regard their surroundings and the barren, open desert in the distance. They shield their eyes against the driving wind.

"Welcome to paradise," Dick says.

"This way, scumbags," one of the reception marshals says.

Over the next couple of hours, they are processed into the penitentiary. Once dressed in their new red jumpsuits, the reception marshals usher them into a featureless auditorium where the prison warden reads from an orientation script in a barely audible monotone. He informs them they will soon be assigned a job that best matches their professions and skills, and then launches into a litany of prison rules and regulations. As he drones on and on, the Prisoner stares out a large window at a vast yard bordered by numerous unpainted concrete blockhouses connected by concrete sidewalks that meander throughout the yard. Assorted unaccompanied inmates in identical red jumpsuits cross the yard heading to their various blockhouses.

"Please note the band on your wrist," the warden is saying when the Prisoner mentally rejoins the orientation. "On it, you will find a unique identification number."

The inmates examine their wristbands.

"This is the number your relatives will use to locate you. It is the number they will use to address mail to you. Memorise this number. It's your name now. You will also find a number that corresponds to your assigned blockhouse and the cell to which you've been assigned."

One of the reception marshals hands each of the inmates a sheet of paper with tiny writing on both sides.

"You are now being handed a copy of the rules of this institution, on the back of which is a listing of all the penitentiary offices and facilities."

Two junior marshals escort the Prisoner to Block House K. They lead him down a long corridor to Cell 35. The Prisoner steps into the large cell and sees three bunk beds, four blue metal writing desks, one chrome latrine, and four inmates all gawping at him—two on their bunks, one at a desk, and a noticeably obese one sitting on the latrine with his jumpsuit pulled down around his ankles.

"Which one of these bunks is three-up?" the Prisoner asks.

One of the inmates, a bear of a black man stretched out on a bunk, points at the one above his. The Prisoner moves to his bunk and climbs into it. The inmates exchange glances with each other, then look back at the Prisoner.

"What is this?" asks the Prisoner, "a convention of predators?"

The man on the latrine lifts his hand at him. "Hi, I'm Smythe," he says with an English working-class accent. "What are you in for?"

"Shut up, fat ass," the Prisoner snaps. "Don't talk to me while you're taking a shit."

The inmates stand up as one, and an awkward silence descends over the cell broken only by the faraway echoes of footfalls on the hard concrete outside.

"Obviously, our little yellow boy here doesn't know how to make friends," the Bear in the bunk below says after a moment.

The Prisoner hops off his bunk and grabs the Bear by the throat.

"I ain't nobody's little yellow boy. And I ain't here to make friends."

The Bear breaks free of the Prisoner's grip and jumps out of his bunk, towering head and shoulders over the Prisoner, who drops back into a defensive karate stance, palms open. The Bear swings a fist; the Prisoner grabs his arm and yanks it, throwing the Bear off balance and sending him careening toward the latrine. Smythe leaps off the latrine just as the Bear falls onto it. The Prisoner pounces on the Bear and proceeds to beat the shit out of him, finishing by pushing the Bear's head into the latrine. He then straightens up and looks around the cell. The other inmates drift back into the corners of the cell, eyes wide, mouths open.

"What are you guys still staring at?" The Prisoner stands feet wide apart, arms akimbo.

The inmates quickly look away and go back to their business. The Bear lies groaning on the floor.

Later, in the yard, the Prisoner sits cross-legged on the ground alone, his back against the wall of his blockhouse, looking bored. Some of the other inmates perform callisthenics in groups. Others mill about gossiping or sharing cigarettes among themselves, glancing every once in a while at the Prisoner and murmuring among themselves.

The Prisoner reaches into his pocket and pulls out the sheet of paper the warden distributed at orientation. He unfolds it and reads through the list of rules and regulations, then he turns it over and browses the other side. Spotting something of interest, he sits up and brings the sheet closer to his face. After a moment, he rocks onto his feet and sprints past the other inmates, who break off what they are doing and follow him with their eyes as he moves down the sidewalk to the Administration Building.

One of the guards inside the Administration Building points out a brown wooden door in the middle of the hall. The Prisoner thanks him and jogs down the corridor. Slowly pulling open the door, he peers inside and sees a well-stocked library with a few reading tables tucked in the corners, and a circulation desk in the middle. He steps inside and looks around, moving up and down the aisles between the stacks, noticing mainly law books.

"Hello?" he calls. His voice echoes back from the windowless concrete walls.

Circling back from the stacks, he spots a bulletin board on the back of the door where he finds a notice that says:

Inmates may help themselves. Books are to be used ONLY in the library and are not to be removed. DO NOT RESHELVE THE BOOKS.

–The Administration

The Prisoner moves back to the stacks and spends a few minutes methodically browsing the books. He stops at the psychology section and selects a book that interests him and takes it to one of the reading tables.

At breakfast, the Prisoner sits at a crowded table in the mess hall wholly absorbed in a book. Every now and again he stabs at something on his plate and brings it to his mouth.

Bleeker walks past carrying a tray of porridge and coffee and notices the Prisoner. He returns and squeezes in between two other inmates directly opposite the Prisoner just as a metallic-sounding voice of ambiguous gender blares from the loudspeaker:

Attention: Inmates from Blockhouses A through E: Chow is over.

"Excuse me, guys." Bleeker spreads his arms and legs to guarantee himself plenty of space at the table.

"Sure thing, Bleek," says a jittery bespectacled inmate to his right. "I was just leaving." He picks up his half-empty tray and scampers away.

"How are things going in Records?" asks a Slavic-looking inmate with jutting cheekbones sitting to Bleeker's left. He wears his jumpsuit unbuttoned to his sternum to show off his hairy blonde chest.

Bleeker tears off a piece of cold toast with his teeth. "It's a cush job," he says with his mouth full. "What've they got *you* doing?"

"Kitchen duty." The Slav pushes away his tray. "I should'a studied computers like you."

Bleeker shrugs and flashes a mouthful of mush. Looking across the table at the Prisoner, he extends his arm. "Hi, I'm Bleeker."

The Prisoner lifts his eyes from his book and looks blandly at Bleeker.

"We've met."

The Slav tosses Bleeker a glance, then leans across the table.

"Bleek's a good one to know, Kid. Works in Records. He's in tight with the warden."

The Prisoner looks back at his book and continues reading.

The Slav blinks at the Prisoner, then looks back at Bleeker and shakes his head.

"So… anyway, Bleek, what's the word about the league?"

"Don't know yet. Could go either way." Bleeker stares at the Prisoner between sips of coffee.

"What's the deal with that anyway?"

"Who knows? Maybe they're afraid we'll enjoy ourselves too much." Bleeker sets down his cup loudly on his tray. "Hey, Koba, you play baseball?"

The Prisoner's head jerks up from his book.

"Who told you my name?"

Bleeker's mouth pulls back into a half-smile. "I work in Records, remember?"

Attention: Inmates from Blockhouses F through J: Chow is over.

The Slav grabs his tray and gets up from the table.

"Gotta run. See ya, Bleek."

Bleeker raises a hand as the Slav moves away and drops off his tray on his way out the door. A new batch of inmates files into the nearly empty dining hall.

"You didn't answer my question," Bleeker says after a moment.

Koba slaps down his book, making his tray jump.

"What do you want to know? Whether I play baseball?"

"That's what I asked." Bleeker's voice is serene. He raises his eyebrows expectantly. "Why are you so hostile anyway?"

"Why are you so friendly?"

"Because I like to make friends … Marilyn."

The colour drains from Koba's face. He looks around quickly and back at Bleeker. "How do you know about that?"

"I work in Records, remember. But, don't worry, sweetheart. Your secret's safe with me. As long as we stay friends." He touches his finger to his eye.

Koba recovers himself and lifts his book. "Yeah, well, from now on I'll pick my own friends, thank you. You can tell whomever you want. I don't care."

"Okay…" Bleeker narrows his eyes at Koba. "Now, about baseball—"

"I give up." Koba closes the book and pushes it to one side. "All right, *yes*, I used to play baseball when I was a kid."

"Little League?"

Koba nods.

"What position?"

"Pitcher. Seven years."

Bleeker sits up and grins. "A regular Hideo Nomo, right? Would you be interested in playing on our team, once the league gets approved?"

"No, thanks. I don't play anymore."

"Why not?"

"I just don't. That part of my life is dead now. Baseball died with it."

Bleeker rakes his fingers through his hair.

"Uh huh…well, there's always the penitentiary's Christmas Chorale. That is, if you're keen on singing. I think they're doing Handel's Messiah this year."

Attention: Inmates from Blockhouses K through O: Chow is over.

"That's you," Bleeker says, flashing a smile.

Koba nods, then picks up his tray and moves away from the table.

Smythe and the Bear stroll past Bleeker carrying their trays on their way to the door.

"Hey, Bleek, what's the chink boy in for?" the Bear says into Bleeker's ear. Smythe strains to hear the answer.

"Armed robbery and felony murder."

"You see, Elijah," Smythe says to the Bear. "What did I tell you?"

"No shit?" Elijah says to Bleeker.

"What's he doing in our cell?" Smythe asks. "That's what I want to know."

"Why?" Bleeker asks.

"He's one *mean* mother," Elijah says.

—⚏—

Koba mans one of four stations of an old-fashioned PBX switchboard in a cooped-up windowless room, along with three other inmate operators. Between calls, he reads from Freud's *The Interpretation of Dreams*. His hair has grown back in, cut short in the front and sides and down to his collar, and he sports a few days' growth of beard.

Just as he starts a new chapter, the door to the room creaks open and a prison runner sweeps inside and hands him a pale blue visitor's slip. Koba sees the name *Tomoko Koba* on the slip of paper and returns it to the runner with a curt shake of his head.

—ɯ—

Koba sits on his bunk reading a long letter from his mother while his cellmates play poker around the writing desks, which they have pushed together in the middle of the cell to make a makeshift table. All of them lift their heads at the sound of approaching footsteps that stops outside their cell. A moment later, the sally port grinds open, and a thin, narrow-shouldered, fuzz-faced inmate about Koba's age with tight brown curls and thick, black horn-rimmed glasses appears in the doorway. Koba peers out at him from behind his letter.

"All right, freak, you'll sleep on *two-down*," the reception marshal behind him says as he shoves him inside.

The young inmate stumbles forward. He looks back at the marshal and pushes up his glasses, which have slipped down his nose.

"Have fun with this one, guys." The marshal shuts the sally port and walks away whistling "Walking on Sunshine" by Katrina and the Waves.

Elijah narrows his eyes at their new cellmate, leaps to his feet, and runs to the sally port.

"Hey, Screw, wait up."

Within seconds, the marshal's face reappears through the bars of the sally port. Elijah jerks a thumb at the young man.

"What gives with this guy?"

The new inmate glances over his shoulder at Elijah, then moves forward timidly. Smythe points at bunk *two-down* and the shy young man shuffles toward it as the *susurre* of whispered conversation between Elijah and the marshal fills the cell.

"He's a what?" Elijah says.

"Like I said… Enjoy yourself, Klein," the marshal calls out to the new inmate before moving away.

As the echo of the marshal's footsteps fade into the distance, Elijah steps up to the group ranged around the poker table. "Guess what we've got there, boys." He sniffs at Klein who is climbing into his bunk.

"A Jew?"

"A *maricón*?"

Klein pulls up his legs and hugs them tight, staring at the others with wide eyes that look enormous through his thick glasses.

Elijah swaggers over to Klein's bunk and points imperiously at him.

"Not only is this a Jew *and* a fairy…" Elijah pauses dramatically for effect. Koba sets aside the letter and sits up on his bunk. "… this sad excuse for a piece of excrement is also a convicted child molester." Elijah punctuates his pronouncement by banging his fist against Klein's bunk, causing it to shake violently.

The other inmates react with visible disgust, slamming down their cards and pushing away from the table.

"Bloody hell," Smythe says. "What in God's name is he doing here? Child molestation is *not* a federal offence."

"According to my reliable and official source," Elijah says, pointing at the sally port, "it *is* when it happens on a transcontinental flight."

"I think I'm going to be sick."

"You're disgusting."

Smythe spits in Klein's direction. Elijah sinks to his knees and peers into Klein's bunk, hungrily eyeing the trembling young man.

"Yes, he is indeed a freak, an abomination in the sight of the Lord God Almighty. And we, my friends, shall be the instruments of His justice." He swings around and looks at the others. "The question is, what shall we do with him? That is, what shall we do *to* him, and in what order?" He looks back at Klein and reaches out to touch his knee.

Klein jerks his leg away from Elijah. "Leave me alone, please. It isn't true."

Elijah leaps forward and grabs Klein's ear, and Koba drops out of his bunk and swoops in behind Elijah.

"Let go of him."

Elijah glares at Koba over his shoulder, still holding on to Klein's ear.

"Haven't you heard a single word I've said? Don't you know what this piece of garbage is?"

"I said, let go of him." Koba drops back into an attack pose, his arms raised and spring-loaded. "*Now*, motherfucker."

Elijah hesitates a moment, then frowns and releases Klein.

"Man, you don't know what you're doing. You ain't gonna get you any poontang for a long-ass time, not with what you've done. Might as well bang some scum as long as you got it." He points at Klein. "Just look at this bitch, all trembling in the corner. She's gonna be good for a whole lotta action."

Koba shoves Elijah away from Klein's bunk.

"Listen, all of you, I will kill anyone who so much as breathes on this guy."

Klein breaks down and sobs loudly.

"I thought he wasn't here to make friends," one of the inmates says.

"I reckon he wants the fairy all for himself," Smythe says. "I heard from Bleeker that he's not exactly the straightest plank on the floor."

Koba walks over to Smythe; the rest of the inmates scoot away and give him plenty of room.

"Smythe," Koba says, "You're a pig."

Smythe looks at the floor. Sweat trickles down his forehead and down the sides of his pustule-covered face. Koba lunges forward and swipes an open hand within inches of Smythe's nose. Smythe screams and falls backwards off his chair, then scrambles away into a corner. Koba looks at the others.

"Would anyone else like to discuss this? One at a time, or all at once, it doesn't matter to me."

The others shake their heads or look away.

Koba returns to Klein's bunk and stares at him deadpan. Klein has pulled himself together and is wiping his face with the edge of his sheet. After a moment, Koba sits on the edge of the bunk and extends his hand.

"Are you all right?"

Klein looks at Koba's hand for a beat, then shakes it. "I've been better."

Koba casts a quick backwards glance at the others, who have returned to their card game, occasionally exchanging angry looks among themselves. He looks back at Klein and flashes a sad smile.

"Thanks for that, by the way. I'm Albert... Albert Klein."

"Nice to meet you. I'm—" Koba hesitates and looks down just as the overhead lights flash and the loudspeaker crackles to life.

Lights out! This is lights out! The amplified voice echoes off the walls of the blockhouse.

"We can talk later," Koba says. He pats Klein's leg just as the lights switch off and they are left in semi-darkness. He looks up as the others climb into their respective bunks then looks back at Klein. "Get some rest."

—⚘—

Tomoko sits alone in the darkness of her living room, dressed in a powder blue nightgown and watching an old 8mm movie of a young boy playing baseball projected on a blank wall. Tears stream down her face as the boy hits a line drive and the shaky camera follows along the sideline as he sprints toward first base. The shortstop scoops up the ball and shoots it to the first baseman. The young boy slides into first as the ball hits the tip of the first baseman's glove and bounces into the sideline. The young boy leaps to his feet and races to second base. The camera swings around to show the crowd in the bleachers going crazy.

Tomoko catches sight of herself in the bleachers looking young and attractive, the only person sitting impassively, a serene smile gracing her perfectly made-up face. The image sets her crying again, and she reaches for a box of tissues on the coffee table. Settling back to watch the rest of the movie, she senses someone approach from behind. A moment later, she feels a large hand come to rest on her shoulder.

—∽—

Koba approaches Klein in the mess hall and places his hand on his shoulder. Klein looks up and smiles at Koba, then scoots to one side to make room for him at the half-empty table.

"Where'd they take you this morning?" Koba dips a piece of buttered toast in his coffee.

"They assigned me to early-morning garbage detail."

Koba pantomimes putting a gun to his head and pulling the trigger and munches on his toast.

"I agree." Klein takes a sip of coffee. "Thanks again for what you did last night."

Koba shakes his head. "Any trouble they give you just let me know."

"Thanks—" Klein looks up as a large group of inmates parades past the table, his cup poised in mid-air. Once they pass, he exhales loudly. "I'm sorry, I didn't catch your name."

Koba smiles tightly and shakes his head again.

"Oh, I'm sorry. I didn't mean—" Klein raises his eyebrows at Koba. "Did I say something wrong?"

"No." Koba looks around at the bustling mess hall as a new shift of inmates files in. "It's just been so long."

"So long? What do you mean? Oh, I'm sorry, I'm prying. I do that sometimes. Never mind."

Koba looks down at the table and closes his eyes for a moment, then grits his teeth and squeezes out the word: "Kimitake." He lets out a long breath, then opens moist eyes and looks directly at Klein. "My name's Kimitake Koba."

Klein opens his eyes wide. "Oh, I understand…" He leans toward Koba and whispers, "I'm not so crazy about my name either."

The other inmates look in their direction as Koba's laughter rings through the mess hall.

Later that morning, Koba opens the door to the library and ushers Klein inside, closing the door behind them. Klein steps up to the circulation desk and looks around, a broad smile breaking out on his face.

"Welcome to my sanctuary," Koba says.

"Where's the librarian?" Klein whispers.

"That's just it," Koba says loudly, his voice echoing off the walls. "There is no librarian." He walks up to a stack, pulls out a book and hands it to Klein. "This one's by Karl Jung. In English, of course."

Klein holds up his palm and wanders around the stacks.

"Look, they have a whole section on religion." He pulls a book from the shelf and turns it over in his hand."

"I know. They have books here on everything."

Klein takes the book to one of the tables and sits down. Koba disappears behind the circulation desk, then emerges a moment later with a spiral notebook and a pen. He joins Klein at the table and starts to write.

"What's that?"

Koba looks up at him. "Huh?"

Klein points at the notebook.

"Oh." Koba passes his fingers over the page. "I'm writing my memoirs. Why?"

Klein shrugs. "I don't know… just curious."

Koba nods and returns to writing in his notebook.

"I'd be interested in reading it."

Koba looks up at him for a moment, then flips through the notebook and slides it across to Klein. "You can read this bit." He circles a passage with his finger. Klein picks up the notebook and reads:

You know me as Clyde, the son of Tomoko and Yoshiro Koba. But my actual birth name is Kimitake, after Momma's favourite brother, a failed kamikaze pilot who ran out of fuel somewhere over the Pacific and nose-dived his Zero-model combat plane into the ocean before he could reach Pearl Harbor. Clyde is the so-called "American name" my father stuck me with early on so that people wouldn't look down on me for being Japanese. The irony is that no parent in his right mind in the 1960s would have dared saddle his kid with the name Clyde, at least not in Los Angeles. Thanks to my father's stupid decision, kids everywhere taunted me to no end. I soon came to hate the sound of my name, American or not. To make matters worse, Momma couldn't pronounce the name Clyde and called me Ku-rai-do instead. It was the best she could do, English being her second language.

Klein hands back the notebook to Koba and nods.

"I've never shared that with anyone."

"Thanks, I'm honoured."

Koba closes the notebook.

"So, why me?" asks Klein.

"I don't know. It felt right at the moment." Koba looks directly at Klein. "Don't make me regret it, please."

"No, don't worry. You can trust me."

"We'll see. Trust doesn't come easily for me." He places his notebook to one side, then grabs the Jung book and opens it up to a marked page.

"It's not true, you know," Klein says.

Koba looks up from the book. "What's not true?"

"That I'm a child molester."

Koba places the book face down on the table.

"I don't care if you are."

"But I'm *not*. I mean, technically I am. But—"

"You're a technical child molester?"

Klein claws off his glasses. "A joke? I'm about to bare my soul to you, and you make a joke?"

Koba squeezes his arm. "I'm sorry. Why don't you just tell me what happened?"

Klein shakes his head and puts his glasses back on. "I was on a flight from New York to LA, going to a religious conference."

"A religious conference?"

"No jokes, remember?"

"I wasn't going to make a joke! Jeez…"

"Anyway, I was sitting next to this person who seemed to be coming on to me."

"Was this person male or female?"

"That's not important. What matters is that I thought they were over eighteen. I swear, they looked like they were at least twenty."

Koba looks down and fiddles with his wristband.

"I followed the person to the lavatory. We had sex. Safe sex. I didn't force them or anything. Everything was mutual."

Koba looks up at Klein, a hurt look clouding his face.

"The feds were waiting for me at LAX when we landed."

"Albert, are you afraid of me?"

"Afraid of you? God, no. Where did that come from?"

"Why won't you tell me whether it was a male or a female?"

"Because it doesn't matter."

"It does matter. If you want me to trust *you*, you have to trust *me*."

"But, I'm… No! You'll get the wrong idea."

"If I was going to get the wrong idea, I would've gotten it already. Believe me."

"All right, okay, yes, it was a male. But I'm not gay."

Koba looks down for a beat, then puts his hand on Klein's shoulder. A look of utter panic comes over Klein as the blood drains from his face.

"I'm not," Klein says.

"How do you know?"

"I don't know, but I'm not. I *can't* be." He slaps the table. "It's wrong."

"If you say so."

"It is! The Bible says it's wrong. My religion says it's wrong."

"But you're attracted to guys?"

"Look, Kim, I was raised in a very sheltered, religious environment. I wasn't allowed to be around girls, at least not by myself."

"And all your friends were boys, right?

"Exactly."

"Boys who were also raised in sheltered, religious homes ..."

"Yes, right. So all this is a phase I'll grow out of eventually."

"Uh huh ... And how many of those other boys have turned out to be gay?"

"Not one. They're all married now."

"I figured as much."

"What are you saying? That you think I'm—"

"What I think is that you're going to have to accept yourself no matter how hard it is for you. Otherwise, you're going to spend however long you have on this planet going through major grief. Believe me, I know."

"That's easy for you to say. You're not gay."

Koba stares meaningfully into Klein's eyes.

"*Are* you?"

"Albert ..."

"What?"

Koba pushes his notebook across the table to Klein.

"Have I got a story to tell you."

—⟋⟋⟍—

Koba and Klein sit with their backs against the wall of their blockhouse. A group of inmates walks past them carrying baseball equipment. Bleeker stops in front of them holding a catcher's glove.

"Hey, guys."

"Yeah?" Koba looks up at Bleeker, shading his eyes from the noonday sun with his hand.

"Hi, Bleek," Klein says.

Bleeker ignores him and speaks to Koba. "The warden approved our team request. They're going to let us play."

"I can see that." Koba smiles at him. "Congratulations."

"Come on, then."

"No thanks, we'll pass."

"Come on, damn it," Bleeker says, returning the smile. "Recapture your childhood."

Koba waves him off. "Nah, that's all gone. As you Christians say, 'I've put away childish things.'"

Bleeker shrugs. "I'm no Christian."

"We're waiting for chorale rehearsal to start. Thanks anyway."

Bleeker nods at Koba and sprints after the other inmates, who are busy marking off the bases.

Thirty minutes later, Koba and Klein stroll into the reception centre, which is doubling as a rehearsal hall. They walk toward the platforms set up at the far end of the room where a dozen other inmates are jostling for position while the accompanist warms up on the piano with an ascending series of major scales. Just as Koba finds his place on the top platform in the baritone section, a runner bursts into the room and calls out his name.

"Visitor," the runner says, waving a slip of blue paper.

Klein exchanges a glance with Koba, who pats him on the shoulder. He steps off the platform and follows the runner out of the room and across the vast yard in the direction of the visitor centre. They wind their way through a maze of long, featureless corridors and sally ports that clang shut behind them. They eventually emerge into a large antechamber lined with low wooden benches ranged along the walls and coloured lines painted on the floor. A polarised glass panel takes up the upper half of the far wall. Koba can just make out the movement of persons behind the glass.

Runner, take a seat! comes a voice out of the loudspeaker.

The runner hands Koba the slip of paper and sits on the stool reserved for him. Moments later, a visitation marshal steps out of the control room and approaches Koba. He holds out his hand, and Koba hands him the slip of paper, which the marshal reads and compares with the number on Koba's wristband.

"All right." The marshal folds the slip and stuffs it into his shirt pocket. He snaps his fingers at Koba. "Off with those."

Koba drops his jumpsuit to the floor while the marshal pulls on a pair of latex gloves. He spends the next several minutes conducting a thorough body cavity search of Koba. Once he's satisfied that Koba's clean, he steps away from him and nods curtly, pulling off the gloves.

"Pull those up. Your visitor's in room three. Follow the blue line."

Koba buttons up his jumpsuit and watches the marshal return to the control booth, then winks at the runner and follows the blue line around the corner to a door labelled Room 3, where he waits outside for a few seconds. A loud buzzer echoes through the hallway and the heavy metal door makes a loud clicking sound. Koba leans on it and pushes into the room. Tomoko is sitting alone at a table, dressed in a white summer dress, a delicate blue cardigan embroidered with little red cherries, and a necklace of natural pearls with a matching set of earrings. She sits up and looks at her son with loving, tear-filled eyes as he leans heavily against the door to close it and takes a seat across from her.

"Hello, Momma." Koba slides his hand across the table at her.

Tomoko hesitates a moment, then places both her hands on his. Koba tries not to react, but his face trembles slightly at the contact, the weight of his mother's hands, the coolness of her skin, a sense of love transmitted.

"Your father's disappeared," she says after a few quiet moments. "Months ago."

Koba looks down and nods.

"I know… I got your letters."

Neither of them says anything in the silence that lingers.

"How's that for you, Momma?" Koba says finally, his voice barely a whisper.

Tomoko shrugs and looks to one side. "I'm getting used to it, I suppose. Sam Higashi's taken over active management of the garage and sends me Yoshi's share of the profits. So thank God for that."

Koba glances up at the ceiling for a moment, then looks back at his mother and nods.

"Why didn't you answer my letters?" Tomoko asks.

"Because I'm bad," Koba says quietly.

"Don't say that."

Koba looks up at her. "Why not?"

Tomoko squeezes his hands. "You were always a *good* son."

"A good son… and a bad daughter."

Tomoko looks into Koba's eyes, and he turns his head away. She squeezes his hand again, this time more forcefully.

"A good son, and a *wonderful* daughter."

Koba smiles a bit and looks back at his mother. His eyes are moist with emotion.

A half hour later, Koba re-enters the waiting area and sees that the runner's stool is empty.

Take a seat on the bench until the runner gets back! calls the voice from the loudspeaker.

Koba nods vaguely at the darkened glass window, sits on the wooden bench, and lets out a loud sigh. After a few moments, he lifts his gaze at a mirror on the opposite wall. The instinct to avert his eyes kicks in, developed over months of conscious avoiding of his reflection to keep from seeing *her*. This time, however, he forces himself to gaze directly into the mirror. But Marilyn is gone. Instead, he finds himself staring at his own handsome reflection for the first time in a decade. He stands and moves to the mirror, his eyes wide with wonder, and reaches out his hand.

Hey, you! Sit the fuck down!

Koba smiles at his reflection and returns to his place on the bench. _____

After a few minutes, the runner returns and escorts Koba back to the auditorium where the choir is powering through the last series of Hallelujahs from Handel's *Hallelujah Chorus*. Koba jogs to the platform and takes his place next to Klein in the baritone section. Klein takes his hand, and together they belt out the final *Hallelujah*.

Glossary

Abba	Father (Heb.)
Achi	My brother (Heb.)
Adafina	Sabbath Stew (Ladino)
Ades	Great Synagogue Ades of the Glorious Aleppo Community, located in Jerusalem's Nachlaot neighbourhood
Adonai	Lord (Heb.)
"Al Bostah"	Song title: "The Bus" (Arab.)
Aieki	Semen (Jap.)
Amidah	Central prayer of the Jewish liturgy
Arvit	Evening prayer (Heb.)
Baklava	A rich, sweet dessert pastry made of layers of filo filled with chopped nuts and held together with honey (Turk.)
Balagan	Fiasco (Heb. From Russ.)
Bar Mitzvah	Jewish coming of age ceremony; lit. Son of the Commandment (Heb.)
Baruch Hashem	Thank God; lit. Blessed be the name (Heb.)
Ben-zona	Son of a whore (Heb.)

Bima	The raised platform in a synagogue from which the Torah is read and services led (Heb.)
Buzuq	A long-necked fretted lute (Arab.)
Caravanserai	A roadside inn (Pers.)
Chag	Festival (Heb.)
Challah; Challot	A special bread in Jewish cuisine, usually braided and typically eaten on the Sabbath and other major Jewish holidays (Heb.)
Chaver	Friend (Heb.)
Chinchin	Child's word for Penis (Jap.)
Chippie	California Highway Patrol (CHP) motorcycle officer (Slang)
Cholo; Cholos	Member(s) of a Mexican street gang (Span.)
Esnoga	Synagogue (Ladino)
Ful	A dish of cooked fava beans (Heb. From Arab.)
Gever	Man (Heb. Slang)
Gulliver	Head (Nadsat from Russ.)
Hakujin	A white person (Jap.)
Hashem	God; lit. The Name (Heb.)
Havdalah	A Jewish religious ceremony marking the end of the Sabbath; lit. Separation (Heb.)
Hazzan	Cantor; prayer leader (Heb.)
Homes	Friend; from "Homeboy" (Mex.-Am. Slang)
Ima	Mum; Mom (Heb.)
Jigoku	Hell (Jap.)
Karma	Universal principal of cause and effect (Sansk.)
Kiddush	Literally, "sanctification"; is a blessing recited over wine or grape juice to sanctify the Shabbat and Jewish holidays (Heb.)
Kintama	Testicles (Jap.)
Kippah	Skullcap (Heb.)

Kol Nidre	Prayer sung by Jews at the opening of the Day of Atonement service on the eve of Yom Kippur; lit. "All Vows" (Aram.)
Kotel	The Western Wall, or Wailing Wall; remains of Herod's Temple (Heb.)
Levanta	Lifting of the Torah Scroll (Ladino)
Madei Aleph	Off-duty uniform (Heb.)
Makhtesh	Erosion crater typical of the Negev in Israel and the Sinai in Egypt (Heb.)
Mamzer	Bastard (Heb.)
Mene mene tekel upharsin	From the Bible: The words that appeared on the wall during Belshazzar's Feast, interpreted by the prophet Daniel to mean that God had doomed the kingdom of Belshazzar; lit. numbered, numbered, weighed, divided (Aram.)
Mensch	A person of integrity (Yid.)
Meshuga	Crazy (Heb.)
Metumtam	Moron (Heb.)
Mezuzah	A parchment inscribed with biblical texts and attached in a case to the doorposts of a Jewish home as a sign of faith (Heb.)
Mi casa es su casa	My home is your home (Span.)
Mikveh	A bath used for ritual immersion in Judaism to achieve ritual purity (Heb.)
Mijwiz	A double-pipe, single-reed woodwind instrument (Arab.)
Mincha	Afternoon prayer service (Heb.)
Minyan	A quorum of ten adult males required for traditional Jewish public worship (Heb.)
Mitzvah; Mitzvot	Commandment (Heb.)
Motek	Sweetie (Heb.)
Nadsat	A fictional argot used by the teenagers in Anthony Burgess's novel *A Clockwork Orange*

Namu Myōhō Renge Kyō	Central mantra of Nichiren Buddhism
Nargileh	Water pipe (Turk.)
Neko	Cat (Jap.)
Omeko	Vagina (Jap.)
Otanjoubi Omedetou	A popular birthday song (Jap.)
Oud	A Middle Eastern lute or mandolin (Arab.)
Ptitsa	Chick (Nadsat)
Riqq	A Middle Eastern tambourine (Heb.)
Rosh Hashanah	The Jewish New Year; lit. Head of the Year (Heb.)
Saba	Grandfather (Heb.)
Sababa	Cool (Arab.)
Sarong	A garment consisting of a long piece of cloth worn wrapped around the body and tucked at the waist, traditionally worn by men in Southeast Asia (Mal.)
Savta	Grandmother (Heb.)
Shacharit	Morning prayers (Heb.)
Shabbat	The Sabbath (Heb.)
Sheli	Belonging to me; mine (Heb.)
Shema	Prayer that serves as a centrepiece of the morning and evening Jewish prayer services. It is traditional for Jews to say the Shema as their last words, and for parents to teach their children to say it before they go to sleep at night. (Heb.)
Sherut	Shared taxi (Heb.)
Shofar	Ram's horn (Heb.)
Shtiebels	Place used for communal Jewish prayer; lit. *little room* (Yid.)
Shuk	Marketplace (Arab.)
Tallit	Prayer shawl (Heb.)

Tallit Katan	Small prayer shawl worn under the clothing (Heb.)
Talmud	Primary source of Jewish religious law and theology. (Heb.)
Tefillin	A set of small black leather boxes with leather straps containing scrolls of parchment inscribed with biblical verses. They are worn by observant adult Jews during weekday morning prayers. (Heb.)
Tel	In archaeology, an artificial mound formed from the accumulated refuse of people living on the same site for hundreds or thousands of years. (Heb.)
Torah	The first five books of the Bible (Heb.)
Yad	A ritual pointer in the shape of a hand used for reading a Torah scroll (Heb.)
Yalla	Let's go (Arab.)
Yarbles	Testicles (Nadsat)
Yeshiva; Yeshivot	An Orthodox Jewish college or seminary (Heb.)
Yom Kippur	The most solemn religious fast of the liturgical calendar; lit. Day of Atonement (Heb.)
Za'atar	A Middle Eastern condiment made from dried hyssop leaves, mixed with sesame seeds, dried sumac, and often salt as well as other spices. (Arab.)